W9-BTI-620

KISSING THE HIGHLANDER

The sudden twinkle in James's eyes let her know he'd noticed it. His amusement calmed her nerves and softened the fierceness on his handsome face. Keeping herself raised on one elbow, Davina slowly reclined beside him. Bracing her hand against his chest, she leaned close and pressed her lips to his cheek. It was rough with stubble, but she found it to be a pleasant sensation.

Her mouth shifted, lingering over his lips. She could feel the warmth of his breath, smell the sweetness of the wine he had drunk at dinner. The embers of desire began to glow inside her as she anticipated the feel of his lips and tongue tangling with hers.

"Are ye going to tease me or kiss me, lass?"

"Kiss," she murmured.

She flicked her tongue lightly along the rim of his lips, tempting them both, then embraced him utterly, devouring him with all the pent-up ardor that had been locked inside her for years. . . .

Books by Adrienne Basso

HIS WICKED EMBRACE

HIS NOBLE PROMISE

TO WED A VISCOUNT

TO PROTECT AN HEIRESS

TO TEMPT A ROGUE

THE WEDDING DECEPTION

THE CHRISTMAS HEIRESS

HIGHLAND VAMPIRE

HOW TO ENJOY A SCANDAL

NATURE OF THE BEAST

THE CHRISTMAS COUNTESS

HOW TO SEDUCE A SINNER

A LITTLE BIT SINFUL

'TIS THE SEASON TO BE SINFUL

INTIMATE BETRAYAL

NOTORIOUS DECEPTION

SWEET SENSATIONS

A NIGHT TO REMEMBER

HOW TO BE A SCOTTISH MISTRESS

BRIDE OF A SCOTTISH WARRIOR

THE HIGHLANDER WHO LOVED ME

Published by Kensington Publishing Corporation

The
HIGHLANDER
Who LOVED ME

ADRIENNE BASSO

ZEBRA BOOKS
KENSINGTON PUBLISHING CORP.
http://www.kensingtonbooks.com

ZEBRA BOOKS are published by

Kensington Publishing Corp.
119 West 40th Street
New York, NY 10018

Copyright © 2016 by Adrienne Basso

All rights reserved. No part of this book may be reproduced in any
form or by any means without the prior written consent of the
Publisher, excepting brief quotes used in reviews.

To the extent that the image or images on the cover of this book
depict a person or persons, such person or persons are merely
models, and are not intended to portray any character or characters
featured in the book.

If you purchased this book without a cover you should be aware
that this book is stolen property. It was reported as "unsold and destroyed" to the Publisher and neither the Author nor the Publisher
has received any payment for this "stripped book."

All Kensington titles, imprints, and distributed lines are available
at special quantity discounts for bulk purchases for sales promotion,
premiums, fund-raising, educational, or institutional use.

Special book excerpts or customized printings can also be created
to fit specific needs. For details, write or phone the office of the
Kensington Sales Manager: Attn.: Sales Department. Kensington
Publishing Corp., 119 West 40th Street, New York, NY 10018.
Phone: 1-800-221-2647.

Zebra and the Z logo Reg. U.S. Pat. & TM Off.

First Printing: January 2016
ISBN-13: 978-1-4201-3767-5
ISBN-10: 1-4201-3767-0

eISBN-13: 978-1-4201-3768-2
eISBN-10: 1-4201-3768-9

10 9 8 7 6 5 4 3 2

Printed in the United States of America

*To Mary Jo & Mike Walsh,
the best next-door neighbors, EVER.
We will miss you both so much!*

Chapter One

Dunfermline Abbey, Summer, 1329

"I can scarcely believe he's dead," the young knight whispered, his voice low and respectful.

"Aye. 'Tis a sad day in the Highlands as well as the Lowlands to be burying such a great king," Sir James McKenna answered as he pushed his way into the crowded church.

A burst of unease passed through James as he searched, and failed, to find an empty seat. All his life he had heard tales of his king, the heroic Robert the Bruce. Firsthand accounts from his father and uncle who had fought beside their king as Robert broke the iron fist of English rule and united the clans of Scotland.

The tragic defeat at Methven, the victory at Loudoun Hill, the triumph at the Battle of Bannockburn. All were fine examples of the king's courage, cunning, and audacity. But today the warriors of Scotland were not here to celebrate the king's victories or remorse over his defeats—today they were gathered to bury their leader.

James craned his neck, trying to get a better view of the solemn ceremony. As his eyes scanned the pews, he spied the back of his father's head, and beside him, the dark-hued hair of his older brother, Malcolm. As befitting an important chieftain, Laird McKenna was seated in the front of the chapel, his eldest son and heir, Malcolm, beside him. And, as usual, James was left to fend for himself at the back of the church, with the lesser nobles and other second and third sons.

Still, his McKenna height gave James the advantage of a clear sight line in the abbey. He felt the wave of sorrow washing over those in attendance as the king was interred beneath the high altar, his remains placed beside his queen, Elizabeth. Then one by one, the warriors filed past, paying their final respects, bidding their final farewells.

The somber mood lifted as the mourners gathered in the courtyard, but the talk quickly turned to politics. Though the king had been ill for over a year, the clan chiefs were restless and uncertain of the succession. The king's only son and heir, David, was a mere lad of five years old. The Earl of Moray had been appointed as the boy's guardian and would rule until David was old enough to rule on his own.

Some were reassured by this decision; others were not. Scots were independent thinkers by nature and many clans had solid claims to the throne. All were wary now, wondering if anyone would make a bid for the crown and upset the hard-fought peace among them.

Never one to be overly interested in politics, James had mixed feelings on the matter. A war might give him the chance to better his position in life, mayhap even gain a keep of his own. That was if he fought for the winning side in the conflict—and somehow survived it. A risky business at best.

"I'm glad to see ye made it, James," a deep male voice cried out. "It would have been a slight on my honor not to have my two oldest sons attending such an historic event."

James pivoted around at the sound of that familiar voice and gave his father a rueful grin. "I'm certain that no one took notice of me cramped in the back of the chapel."

"Ye stand a head taller than most of these warriors," another male voice chimed in. "And the McKenna plaid is neigh impossible to miss."

"Uncle Ewan!" James broke into a wide smile as he embraced his uncle-by-marriage. James had been fostered at Ewan's castle as a young lad and had many fond memories of that time. He was also very aware that he owed a goodly portion of his prowess with a sword and his leadership skills to his uncle. "How do things fare at Tiree Keep?"

Ewan shrugged. "All is much the same as when ye were with us. Young Cameron begged to come along on this journey, but yer aunt wouldn't hear of it."

James smiled in understanding. His aunt Grace was fiercely protective of her children. James had always found her to be a reasonable, sweet-tempered woman, but she also possessed a stubborn, hardheaded determination that characterized those who carried McKenna blood.

"My sister coddles her sons," Brian McKenna declared. "I cannae believe that ye allow it, Ewan."

Unoffended by his brother-in-law's remarks, Ewan merely shrugged. "I prefer peace in my home. Yer sister rarely disagrees with me, but when she does, I've learned 'tis to my advantage to do as she asks."

Brian McKenna scoffed and James lowered his chin, hiding his smile. His father could bluster all he wanted, but he indulged his wife's whims far more than most other husbands, for Aileen Sinclair McKenna would have it no other way. His mother was a formidable woman and over their years together, his father had developed the good sense to realize it.

The conversation ceased as a group of chieftains approached. James blended respectfully into the background, while his older brother, Malcolm, moved forward, placing himself at their father's side. The pang of resentment stabbed sharply at James, then quickly faded. His brother was being groomed to one day lead the clan; 'twas fitting that he be a part of this discussion.

James recognized many, but not all, of the men who gathered together. Some were stoic, others looked unsettled, and a few were openly defiant. James could hear his father's voice raised above the others as they spoke of the future of Scottish independence and the treachery of the English.

Brian McKenna seemed unfazed by the uneasy talk that swirled around him, but James knew his father was concealing his true feelings. He had been a loyal king's man for too many years to simply stand idle while others questioned the boy king's right to rule.

Sir James Douglas approached the group and joined in the discussion. He was a broad-shouldered man who carried himself with a distinct air of self-importance, yet he did not appear to have the same influence over the others as Brian McKenna. James noticed several of the men shifting on their feet while the Douglas spoke. Once he was finished, most walked away.

James angled his face toward the cloudy sky, then

looked to his father, wondering if he wanted to start their journey home now or linger and try to ensure that some of the other clan chiefs would support the boy king.

"Malcolm rides with the Douglas clan," Brian McKenna said as he came to stand beside his son. "I'd like ye to accompany the Armstrongs as they ride home to their lands, James, and stay as long as they have need of ye."

James turned in surprise. "'Tis fitting that Malcolm rides with the Douglas clan, since his betrothed is a Douglas lass. But why must I to go with the Armstrong clan?"

"Ye're always pestering me about the dull routine at McKenna Castle. Well, lad, here's yer chance to have an adventure."

His father gave him a tight, even smile, but James was not fooled by this sudden jovial manner. There was something more to this request than a simple show of friendship. James felt certain of it.

Brian McKenna was used to being obeyed without question, but the expression on his son's face somehow prompted further explanation.

"Alliances are more important now than ever," his father confided. "Did ye happen to notice the chain around Sir James Douglas's neck and the silver casket dangling at the end of it?"

"Aye."

"'Tis the king's embalmed heart that's locked inside."

James winced. "I heard one of the other knights speak of it, but I thought it only a rumor."

"Nay, 'tis the truth. The loyalty of the Douglas clan to the boy king and the monarchy willnae be questioned by such a show of devotion."

James glanced over his shoulder to see if anyone was near, then lowered his voice. "Is that devotion genuine?"

"I think the Douglas clan will happily support the king fer as long as it benefits them," the McKenna replied bluntly.

"What of the Armstrongs? Are they not loyal to the crown?"

"Laird Armstrong is cautious. 'Tis understandable, yet we cannae allow any breech in the clan alliance. At the first hint of weakness, the English will pounce and our hard-fought independence will be at great risk." The McKenna cleared his throat and sniffed. "I want Laird Armstrong to know I value him as an ally and will offer my support to him if he ever has need of it. Sending ye home with him is a clear sign of my good faith."

James forced his face into calm, so as not to betray his excitement at being charged with such an important task. "If ye believe my presence will help, I'll gladly do as ye ask."

The McKenna nodded approvingly, then rewarded his son with a genuine smile.

James felt his chest swell. As always, even the smallest crumb of approval from his proud, distant father produced this sort of reaction. But it wasn't just pride in himself he felt; 'twas also a newfound respect for the man who had raised him.

The McKennas were a powerful, wealthy clan. James had always believed that was due to his father's strong leadership and unmatched skill with a sword, but he now realized his father's cunning and political acumen played an important part in the clan's success—and survival.

"I guess this is farewell for a while, brother. Father said ye are to go with the Armstrongs."

James looked over at his brother, Malcolm. He had

been blessed with the best features of their parents—their father's height and broad, muscular build and their mother's expressive blue eyes and winsome smile. He carried himself with the confidence and swagger of a man comfortable in his own skin. James felt a twinge of envy, yet remained hopeful he, too, would one day feel the same.

"And ye will be riding with the Douglas clan," James replied.

Malcolm grinned, then playfully punched James in the upper arm. "Dinnae make a pest of yerself, little brother."

James grumbled under his breath, then threw a sly glance at Malcolm. "Ye'd best heed yer own advice. I'm not the one with a betrothed making cow eyes at me all the time."

Malcolm's eyes strayed to the area where the Douglas clan was gathered. A burst of female giggles could be heard clear across the yard. "She's a comely lass, my Margaret."

"And a bold one, too. I'd wager that she'd not protest too much if ye've a mind to anticipate yer wedding night." James jostled his brother's shoulder teasingly, but Malcolm did not smile.

"Hmm, I fear ye may be right. I believe I have more care fer Margaret's honor than she does."

James's brow shot up. His sexual experience was limited to a few willing McKenna widows and while he found the dalliances satisfactory, he always wanted more. The idea of turning away a lovely, willing lass seemed to be the height of foolishness.

"Do ye not find her attractive?" James asked.

"She's pretty enough, but much too eager to please."

James scratched his head. What could possibly be

wrong with that? "I should think ye'd want an amenable lass as yer wife."

"Och, the innocent words of an untried youth." Malcolm clapped his brother on the back. "The thrill of the chase makes the capture of the prize all the more enticing."

"Ye want Margaret to resist ye?"

Malcolm smiled ruefully. "I'll follow Father's lead and out of respect willnae take any other women to my bed once I'm married. But I fear life can become rather dull and boring with such a docile, obedient wife."

"Yer brain is addled, Malcolm."

"And ye, little brother, are thinking with yer cock." Malcolm leaned over, his expression serious. "There's more to a woman than the pleasure she can bring ye in bed. Ye'll do well to remember that when ye choose a bride of yer own."

With a nod of farewell, his brother walked off, leaving James to ponder his final remarks and wonder what sort of female he would want for a wife. Pretty and eager to please seemed a fine combination to James. How characteristic that Malcolm did not appreciate the good fortune that so easily found its way to him.

Only two years apart in age, they had been inseparable as lads, but their close friendship had eased through the years while the competition between them had risen. Malcolm was the heir, his father's favorite and James hadn't openly regretted it, but at times he could not help but be envious of it.

Laird Armstrong's sharp tone drew everyone's attention as he called for his men to make ready to leave. After a quick good-bye to his father and uncle, James obediently hurried toward his horse. The ground was wet. Fat, heavy drops had fallen as the king's funeral service began, slowing to a trickle when it ended. James glanced skyward, mindful of the gray clouds forming on the horizon. 'Twould be a miracle if they remained dry before they either reached a dwelling to shelter them or made camp for the night.

James mounted his horse with ease, turning the animal into position. As he did, he caught a glimpse of the three women riding in the contingent, each carefully placed in the center of the column for maximum protection. The older female was obviously Lady Armstrong and the two younger women had to be her daughters, though their coloring was as different as night and day.

One daughter was a small brown wren and the other a glowing blond swan. They were both slender and well formed, but his eyes were immediately drawn to the golden splendor of the young woman sitting so tall and straight on her horse. Her face was heart-shaped, her cheekbones high and well defined, her mouth wide, with soft generous lips. She was a rare beauty who had the power to capture the attention of every male orbiting in her sphere.

Well aware of the attention she was receiving, the blonde tossed her head, causing her blond braid to shimmer, even on this cloudy day. Then she smiled, at no one in particular, a calculating affectation that lacked warmth and honesty.

His interest immediately began to cool. James recognized that knowing look—a woman flaunting her beauty, spinning a web in which to trap any male who was foolish enough to be drawn to her.

He pressed his knees against his horse's flanks and the animal obediently turned. They splashed along the muddy grass as James took his place near the head of the column. The Armstrong men gave him a courteous nod, but kept to themselves. James understood. He was an outsider. He would be tolerated but not accepted unless he proved himself.

A light drizzle began as they made their way out of the churchyard. James hunched over his mount and plodded onward, easily keeping pace. They rode at a fast clip on the flatter ground, then made a slow and careful climb along the rocky face of a steep hill. Once they reached the other side, the signal was given to make camp.

Deciding to see to the needs of his horse before his own, James followed the sound of water through a small patch of forest. Finding the source, he let the animal drink its fill. As he turned to leave, he noticed a woman walking purposefully toward the stream, a wooden bucket in each hand.

Recognizing her cloak, he realized it was one of the laird's daughters. The hood was drawn over her head, but he suspected it was not the blonde goddess, but rather the little brown wren. His suspicions were confirmed when she knelt by the water's edge. She slowly dragged one of the buckets through the stream. Her hood slipped back and he saw the dark hue of her hair.

"Ye should have asked one of the men to fetch the water fer ye," he said, stepping forward.

She let out a small shriek of surprise and dropped the buckets. One caught on the current and floated downstream. James bent down and plucked it from the water, then moved forward and scooped up the other. He filled them, then set each on the ground, just within her reach. Yet she made no move to retrieve them, instead staying crouched at the water's edge.

"Ye startled me," she declared, wrinkling her brow as she studied him cautiously.

"I beg yer pardon," he replied, squirming slightly

under her accusing gaze. "I dinnae expect to find a lady hauling water like a servant. One of the men should have seen to yer needs."

Her eyes widened and she dipped her chin. James thought he saw the hint of a smile, but could not be certain.

"The men are busy setting up camp and attending to other matters," she replied. "I dinnae want to be a bother. Besides, my aunt prefers that I make myself useful. She and my cousin will need fresh water to wash the dirt from their hands and face and since we brought no maids with us, I was charged with the task."

"Cousin? The other young woman is not yer sister?" he asked.

"Goodness no," she replied with a quick shake of her head. "Joan is my cousin. Our fathers were brothers, mine being the younger of the two."

"Was?"

"Aye. He died five years ago; my mother, too." Her voice trembled slightly at the words and a trace of sadness gathered in her eyes.

"Yet the wound is still fresh," he said sympathetically.

"There are times that I feel the loss more keenly than others. I suppose attending the king's funeral was a stark reminder of the finality of death and in turn I've felt the pain of the loss anew." She curled her bottom lip between her teeth. "Ye must forgive me fer being so emotional. My cousin Joan often reminds me how annoying that can be and says that five years is more than enough time to heal the wounds of loss."

He disliked hearing the defeat in her voice. How could her kin be so cold and unfeeling to her pain?

"A true heart suffers more than a false one," he said kindly.

She lifted her chin a notch and James felt a rush of

admiration. She was so determined to appear strong. His eyes met hers, and suddenly he could not pull away. The warmth and emotion shining forth from those sweet brown orbs seemed to reach inside his chest and wrap tightly around his heart.

God's bones, she was pretty. She did not have the mesmerizing golden beauty of her cousin, but her features were delicate and refined and wholly pleasing. An oval face with a generous mouth and smooth skin the color of fresh cream.

Her dark hair was neatly tied in a braid that cascaded down her back, ending in the middle of her shapely backside. It glistened in the dull light that filtered through the branches and leaves. There was a clean, fresh fragrance emanating from it that drew him closer. With effort, he suppressed the urge to reach out and touch it, knowing it was both rude and inappropriate.

Instead, he squatted down to his haunches, commanding her attention with his eyes. They were a glimmering shade of golden brown, fringed by long lashes and framed by finely arched brows, but it was the open honesty reflected in their depth that pleased him more than he could say.

"We have shared a confidence and yet I dinnae know yer name, milady," he said gently.

"I am Davina."

"James."

"Aye, I know."

He stood, then reached out his hand to help her gain her feet. She frowned in puzzlement, then blushingly placed her bare hand in his. James could feel the delicate bones of her fingers as he drew her upward. For a wicked instant he thought to pull her off balance, so she would need to steady herself against his body, but he resisted such an unchivalrous notion.

"I salute yer strength and courage in the face of yer grief," he said quietly.

She shook her head. "There are so many in this world that know the anguish of real suffering. I can hardly place myself among their numbers, fer I have been provided shelter, food, and protection. I know I am viewed as a burden by my relatives, but they have not shirked their duties and fer that I am truly grateful. Rarely a day passes that I do not miss my parents, and yet I know that I am a fortunate woman."

Her words were honestly spoken, yet there was a touch of yearning in her voice, edged with sadness. He had been blessed with loving parents, raised within the security of a proud, noble clan. She had been taken in by relations because they felt it was their Christian duty and obviously keenly felt that obligation. Yet she had not succumbed to self-pity, but instead had risen above it.

"I will provide ye escort back to camp," he said commandingly.

Her eyes startled and she lowered her chin. "I dinnae wish to impose, Sir James."

"'Tis my duty."

"Duty?" Her lips pursed in confusion.

"Aye. To aid a beautiful lady in distress. I beg ye not to deny me the chance to act the noble knight."

"We are but a short distance from camp," she protested even as he hoisted her onto his mount.

She instinctively pressed her knees against the horse's flanks to keep from falling and James admired the shapely outline of her legs as the skirt of her simple gown tightened around them.

"A fair maiden should ride whenever possible," he said before executing a low bow. "Especially one as lovely as ye."

He was flirting and saw the moment she realized it.

Her eyes rounded with surprise, but to his delight, he saw an impish glint enter them. His instincts had proven correct—she was gentle and refined, yet hardly a prudish female. A bubble of amusement rose to his lips and he smiled.

Davina dipped her chin, then smiled back.

He lifted the filled buckets and looped the rope handles over the saddle pommel. Then James placed his foot in the stirrup and vaulted behind Davina. She gave a startled cry, but held her seat. Unused to the extra weight, the horse neighed and tossed his head, but James soon had the animal under control.

He allowed the horse to begin ambling toward camp before casually placing the reins in his right hand and encircling Davina's small waist with his left arm.

"Relax," he said softly, as he drew her slowly against his chest.

She stiffened for a moment, then he heard her release a soft, sweet sigh. A surge of passion pulsed through his veins. Holding his breath, James waited to see what she would do next. Then, to his utter delight, she followed his command and pressed—nay nuzzled—herself into his embrace.

James closed his eyes in heavenly delight as he breathed in her enticing scent. Aye, traveling to the Armstrong castle might prove to be a far more delightful task than he had the right to expect.

A few days later Davina admitted the daylight hours in the saddle no longer made her tired and sore, while the nights sleeping in a crowded tent no longer left her restless and weary. And the explanation for that change was very simple—James McKenna.

The young knight had proven to be a delightful distraction, regaling her with amusing tales and insightful observations. She enjoyed his company tremendously and looked forward to their time together with an eagerness that surprised and excited her.

"I saw ye talking with Sir James again this morning before we broke camp," Joan snipped as she pulled her mount alongside Davina's. "What can he possibly have to say to ye?"

Davina dipped her chin shyly, ignoring the trace of spite spilling over her cousin's casual remark. Joan was a beautiful young woman, used to receiving the lion's share of attention whenever men were present. Though not openly rude—for Davina was convinced her gallant knight incapable of such pettiness—'twas obvious to all, and especially Joan, that Sir James preferred Davina's company to that of her cousin.

"Sir James had drawn a map in the dirt," Davina replied. "He was merely showing me how much farther we needed to travel before reaching home."

Joan's eyes narrowed. "Ye were cackling like a hen laying an egg. How can a map in the dirt be so funny?"

"James has a gift. He can make anything fun and amusing."

"What a perfectly useless accomplishment," Joan sneered. "I suppose I shouldn't be shocked that ye would be drawn to that sort of man, but I had hoped ye would have more sense."

That sort of man? Davina struggled to hold back another *hen cackle*. Handsome, well spoken, with a sparkle in his eye and a dimple in his chin. Aye, she did like that sort of man. Any lass would be daft not to be intrigued by him.

But it was not just his square jaw, heart-melting

smile, and handsome face that called to Davina. As an
heiress to a small estate, she had on occasion received
a small bit of male interest when Joan was otherwise
occupied, especially now that she was a marriageable
lass of seventeen. But there was something very different about James McKenna.

He had a confidence that she found reassuring
rather than arrogant, a gentleness that belied his warrior's frame and training, a sense of humor that was the
most heightened when it was pointed squarely at himself. Though Joan would deny it with her final breath,
Davina could well understand her cousin's jealousy and
was even able to summon up the charity to forgive it.

"James is a kind, polite man," Davina said. "I find
him interesting and enjoy being in his company."

"Ye are spending far too much time with him," Joan
insisted. "Others are starting to talk of it."

"Nay!"

"'Tis true. I'm only speaking of it to save ye from
making any more of a fool out of yerself with this silly
infatuation."

Davina's lips tightened. "I'm not acting like a fool."

Joan shrugged. "Ye do know he is only showing interest in ye because he's heard that yer family keep is
part of yer dowry?"

Nay! The second protest sprang to her lips, but
Davina remained silent, not wanting her cousin to see
how much the words had wounded. For an instant her
joy dimmed and the demons of self-doubt crept inside
her heart. Was Joan right? Did James have an ulterior
motive for showering her with so much attention?

"I cannae believe that a small holding like Torridon
Keep would hold much appeal to a McKenna," Davina
said, with far more conviction than she felt.

"He's a second son," Joan replied with a malicious tilt of her chin. "They crave land like a man gasping fer air."

The self-doubt intensified for a moment as Davina considered the possibility and then forcefully cast it aside. She glanced at her cousin, taking in the mulish set to Joan's lips. 'Twas jealousy, pure and simple, that caused such spiteful words to fall from her cousin's lips. It had to be.

Though she claimed to have no interest in him, Joan was irked because James was bestowing his favors upon Davina, not her. Davina knew her cousin possessed the ability to act callously, even cruelly when she was displeased.

Almost as if sensing he was the topic of their conversation, James glanced over his shoulder and looked at her. The moment their eyes met, Davina felt her breath catch and her stomach tighten. A shiver ran through her, but she wasn't cold—nay she was flushed with a warm glow that radiated from deep inside her being.

'Twas a response that defied logic.

And it could not have pleased her more.

The following day, they passed onto Armstrong land. No one said anything, but James could tell by the relaxed shoulders of the soldiers and their frequent smiles that they were nearing home. He felt a sudden pang of regret, realizing his time with the sweet Davina would soon come to an end.

Then again, his father had not demanded that he return home quickly. If Laird Armstrong was amenable, he could stay awhile. Perhaps until late summer. Or fall.

He glanced at Davina, who rode beside him. She

favored him with a shy smile, then licked her lips. James felt his belly clench with desire. He had not yet worked up the nerve to steal a kiss—yet another reason he needed to stay.

"Armstrong Castle is just beyond that hill," she said, pointing toward the horizon. "We should arrive by nightfall."

"Why do ye not smile when ye say that, lass? Are ye not weary of traveling?"

She tilted her head to one side as though considering his words. "A comfortable bed and a roof over my head will be most welcome. But life will seem very dull after this adventure. And what of ye, are ye anxious to return home?"

James shrugged. "I've spent many years at the McKenna castle. It feels good to escape for a bit."

"I've heard tell that the McKenna castle is vast and formidable."

"Aye, it looms over the valley below."

"In a friendly manner?" she asked, a teasing lilt in her voice.

James boomed with laughter. "Nay, 'tis menacing. Or so our enemies say. But 'tis a comfort to our clan. They know those strong walls, and the men within them, will protect and defend them."

"It sounds like a fierce place."

"It can be," James answered, thinking of the high walls, battlements, four watchtowers, and large moat. "But my mother has worked hard over the years to soften the starkness. There are always fires burning in the great hall to keep out the dampness and she has replaced many of the weapons decorating the walls with finely woven tapestries. There is even stained glass in the windows of her solar."

"Truly?"

James grinned. Aye, it was spectacular. Though he grumbled about the cost, Brian McKenna never denied his wife any luxury she desired.

"The colored sunlight dancing on the floor is a sight to behold," James revealed. "It always entranced my brothers and sister when we were children. Mother always told us 'twas the fairies bringing the magic into the chamber."

"'Tis difficult to imagine such a thing," she murmured.

His lips twisted into a smile. "Well, then, ye'll just have to see it fer yerself one day, Davina."

Her smile brightened. "Aye, mayhap I shall."

Chapter Two

Davina nodded to the guards as she hastened through the open gate, leaving the high walls of the castle behind her. Smiling, she hugged her woolen shawl tightly across her shoulders to ward off the chill of the fall air, then fairly skipped through the valley. The afternoon sunshine bolstered her spirits, but it was the secrecy of her errand that brought true joy to her heart.

Her delight remained an hour later when she reached her destination. Shading her eyes with the back of her hand, Davina gazed at the summit of the craggy hill. The tall, male figure perched at the top was easy to recognize.

James. My James.

He waved and Davina's heartbeat quickened, as it always did when he gazed at her. She closed her eyes, took a deep breath, and savored the moment. The one thing she had prayed for, had longed for these past five years, had finally come to pass. For the first time since her parents had died, she had someone of her own.

Someone who held her and comforted her and laughed with her. Someone who listened to her thoughts and feelings, admired her wit, encouraged her to speak her mind and share her dreams. Someone who valued her as a person—who regarded her as a woman.

She lifted her skirts and sprinted up the hill. Arms resting comfortably on his hips, James waited for her. Breathless when she reached him, Davina stretched up on her toes and quickly kissed his freshly shaven cheek.

"Och, now, Davina, is that any way to kiss a man?"

Teasing laughter bubbled to her lips. "Cease yer bellyaching. Ye are the man who taught me how to kiss, James McKenna, therefore ye've no right to complain."

She gave him a saucy wink, then spun around and raced to the trees. Playfully, he gave chase, catching her quickly and easily. Laughing, he drew her close and they swayed together on the uneven ground.

"I dinnae teach ye that sort of kissing, Davina Armstrong," he said. "Give me a proper kiss."

Davina flushed with heat. James's kisses were the most magical, wonderful things she had ever experienced. The more she had, the more she craved. Challenged by his teasing, she slowly twined her arms around his neck and leaned into him, molding her body against his solid strength. Hungrily, she again went up on her toes, then pressed her lips ever so softly against his.

He remained still, his arms at his sides, allowing her to do the kissing. She pressed her mouth more firmly to his and let her hands travel over his shoulders to his back. After a moment she felt his hands slide down to her hips and rest there. Davina squirmed with pleasure at his warm touch, wantonly slipping her tongue along his bottom lip.

James groaned, a sound that ignited her own growing desire. His tongue poked out and tangled with

hers. Fire ignited between them. Davina gasped and
arched in pleasure, eager to show him the passion he
stirred within her.

She shifted slightly, tasting the salt of his skin as her
lips traveled to the exposed area of his throat, then up
to the hollow behind his ear. She could feel his warm
breath as he nuzzled the top of her head. It gave her a
puzzling sense of comfort and she relished the feeling.

I must truly be besotted to feel such things. Her hands
moved down to his chest and she raised her eyes to his.
The passion and tenderness she beheld brought a rush
of emotions.

He lowered his head and she leaned into him, eager
for another kiss. He obliged her with several, but then
drew back.

"Dinnae stop, James," she wailed. "Not now."

He heaved a heavy sigh, but kept his distance.

Disappointment surged through her.

"Ye make my body sing and my heart soar, but ye are
a lady born and bred and I shall treat ye with the honor
and respect ye deserve."

His gallant words did little to calm the trembling
passion Davina felt, though she was humbled by his
chivalry. And distracted enough that she allowed him
to take her by the arm and stroll across the hilltop. By
the time they reached the other side, her passion had
calmed enough to be under control.

Though a twinge of disappointment remained.
Their relationship had grown and flourished these past
months, blooming like the crops in the fields. She wanted
nothing more than to give herself to him, to belong to
him body and soul.

James professed to want the same and while Davina
believed him, a small part of her wondered how he
always managed to control himself, to stop himself

before they consummated their desires. Though she had little experience with men, she did know that most would greedily and swiftly take what she was so eager to give.

Yet James had not.

These worrisome thoughts swirled in her head as they walked, clouding out the beauty of their surroundings. James lifted a branch and Davina ducked under it. She strolled ahead, halting at the edge of a grove of trees. Gazing down, her eyes followed the looping river as it meandered through the valley and then emptied into the loch.

'Twas a beautiful, tranquil scene. A blush rose to her cheeks with the month-old memory of the morning she had spied James swimming in those clear, blue waters—wearing not a stitch of clothing. Concealing herself behind a tree trunk, she had boldly watched him traverse the entire width, swimming with long, powerful strokes, before rising from the water like a pagan god of old.

Beads of water had rolled from his broad shoulders down his lean, hard, muscular arms and legs, sliced over a taut stomach, and finally trickled through a whorl of springy hair at the juncture between his legs. Her breath caught and held, for cradled there was the most fascinating piece of male anatomy she had ever seen.

The image of that proud display of manhood had raised her maidenly curiosity to a fevered pitch. Lacking the courage—and confidence—she dared not approach James, but instead retreated into the anonymous safety of the woods. Yet the memory of what she had seen had kept her awake for more nights than she could count.

At the sound of a snapping branch, Davina pulled

herself back into the present. Feeling an odd sense of guilt, she turned her attention back to James.

He took a step toward her, extending his arm. "Davina, give me yer hand."

She smiled and set her hand in his and his warm, strong fingers closed around it. Eyes locked with hers, he went down on one knee and then bowed his head respectfully over their clasped hands.

Merciful heavens! Davina's heart began pounding in an erratic rhythm. Could this truly be happening?

"Davina Armstrong," he said, "my dear, sweet, lass. The affection I held fer ye has grown into a deep love. Will ye make me the happiest man in all the Highlands and do me the great honor of becoming my wife?"

For an instant she couldn't think straight. The emotions and intensity of the moment were almost too much to bear. She squeaked. A short, nervous yelp. James lifted his head. Their eyes met again, and Davina experienced a burst of joy so pure, so profound it brought a rush of warm tears to her eyes.

She tried to calm her heart, to capture this nearly perfect moment in time, when everything in her world was filled with hope and bright with promise.

"Aye, James, I'll marry ye. Gladly."

He leapt to his feet. She threw her arms around him, pressing herself so tightly against him it felt as though the heat of his body entered her own.

"Ye must promise me one thing," he said solemnly. "Ye are not to be too biddable a wife."

"What?" Davina lifted her head to gaze at him, deciding that he had to be teasing her.

James combed his fingers through his hair and gave her an embarrassed grin. "Pay it no mind. 'Tis something my brother Malcolm once said to me, but I realize it has nothing to do with ye. With us."

Not caring that she didn't understand, Davina nuzzled into James, savoring this incredible moment. James was holding her heart, along with her body, and it made her feel like the luckiest woman alive.

Her mind raced with plans for their future. How quickly could the wedding be arranged? It need not be a grand celebration, though the McKennas would expect something befitting a son of the laird, even if James was not the heir. Her uncle would not be pleased to spend a great deal of coin on her wedding, especially with his own daughter still unwed.

Yet he could not appear miserly and he would be pleased with the alliance. The McKennas were wealthy, respected, even feared. This would bode well for the Armstrong clan.

"Now then, lads, what do we have here?" a booming male voice inquired.

Davina whirled her head so quickly it smacked James on the chin. Ignoring the pain, she felt her eyes widen as she beheld a group of men climbing up the hill toward them. Five, nay six, all heavily muscled and armed with both swords and dirks. They wore no clan colors; their clothes were worn and stained, their eyes bright with the haunted look of outlaws. She recognized none of them.

Quick as a flash, James drew his sword and pushed Davina behind him. She stumbled on watery legs, yet managed to stand. Frantically, her eyes darted to the horizon, her heart sinking when she realized how far they were from the keep. From help.

"What business do ye have here?" James challenged.

"We want a taste of that fine morsel ye've got, laddie," said the man standing in the lead. His lips parted in a perverted grin, revealing several rotting teeth.

"This woman is a lady," James snarled. "My lady."

His reply brought a chorus of hoots and jeers from the men.

"Did yer mother not teach ye to share yer possessions, lad?"

"Nay. But my father taught me how to defend what was mine," James declared as he positioned his sword to strike.

Davina swallowed back the fear that was closing her throat and willed her heart to slow its thunderous pace. James was studying the men with a watchful expression on his face. It gave her a momentary confidence, until she took the full measure of the six men he faced.

They might be ill dressed and dirty, but they did not look undernourished. To a man they were broad of shoulder, each with a predatory gleam in his eye. If they attacked, James would be outnumbered and outmatched. She did not doubt that he would fight to the death, but that valor would end in tragedy for both of them.

Davina's throat tightened again. They had to get out of there. She put a hand on James's back to steady herself and felt him draw himself to his full height.

"Ye cannae fight them all," she whispered.

"I can. I will." His voice was strong and reassuring, but Davina knew it was an impossibility.

No longer able to restrain herself, she spoke. "Ye are on Armstrong land. If ye have business with the laird, then ride to the castle. If not, then ye best be gone before ye are discovered. My uncle does not take kindly to trespassers."

"I see no Armstrong soldiers, lass," the tallest man sneered, his hand going to his sword in a threatening gesture. "Only a single knight and a frightened female, who doesn't know when to stay quiet."

He let loose a merciless bark of laughter, but it was

the gloating expression on his face that brought a shiver of fear to Davina's heart. Struggling to ignore the desperation she felt, she faced the brigand with a cold stare.

"Ye would be wise to heed my advice," she declared steadily.

Her words were met with more whoops and hollers from the men. As they were joking among themselves, James suddenly let out a bloodcurdling yell and charged them at a full run. The sound nearly scared the wits out of Davina.

She watched in horrified awe as James cut the leader down with a single, deep sword strike across the belly, then punched a second man in the face.

Davina heard the outlaw scream and clutch his nose. A stream of blood shot through his fingers before he swayed and crumbled to the ground. Swords drawn, two others charged James, but he managed to hold his position and deflect the blows.

"Run, Davina!"

Reacting to the sharpness of James's voice, she followed his command, but one of the outlaws was fast upon her. Davina got no farther than a few steps before a strong arm snaked around her waist and hauled her to the ground.

Lancing pain shot through her body and she hit the dirt hard. She tried rolling away, toward the safety of the trees, but a beefy hand grasped her shoulder and turned her on her back. Davina opened her mouth to scream, and her attacker raised his fist and struck her.

Stunned, she stilled momentarily. Pressing the advantage, the man straddled her waist. Her legs kicked wildly as she struggled against the brute who tried to pin himself on top of her, but she could not escape.

She fought him with both her arms and legs, flailing, using every ounce of her strength.

He grunted, then clamped his hand over her mouth, cutting off her air. She tried to gasp for breath, but the filthy hand tightened its grip.

Davina batted at his chest and hands to no avail. Above her she could hear the clash of swords, the grunts and straining of the combatants. Fear and desperation combined and robbed her of the ability to do anything else but pray. *Please, oh, please, dear God, dinnae let James fall.*

Somehow she managed to turn her head. She heard a loud cry and saw James's opponent clutch his sword arm. Blood spurted through the fingers pressed against the wound. The man let out a loud curse before collapsing on the ground. Another brigand jumped into the fray. He was the largest of the group and it soon became apparent his skill with the sword was superior to the others.

He struck relentlessly, pushing James back. Somehow, James managed to stay on his feet, but Davina could see he was tiring with each parry, blowing out a loud breath with each swing of his sword.

James lifted his leg, planting it in the center of his attacker's chest, and sent him flying through the air. The man landed on his back. Bellowing with outrage, he scrambled to his feet and picked up his sword. Davina could see the murderous intent in his eyes as he advanced on the unarmed James, but just as he drew near, James pulled a thin-bladed dirk from his boot and plugged it into his attacker's chest.

Davina felt her own heart explode with hope at the sight.

James is winning! Seeing that stiffened her resolve to somehow escape. Gathering her wits, she planned her next move. Her blood throbbed wildly as she reared up again, swallowing back the revulsion that filled her when she caught sight of the brute on top of her. She renewed her struggles, straining away from her captor, but his grip was unyielding.

The hope she had so recently found quickly abandoned her as she saw her captor once again raise his arm. She shifted her body, trying to avoid his fist a second time, but an explosive pain in her head let her know she had failed.

Her ears rang, her brain scrambled, and the very last thing she heard before being plunged into darkness was James's cry of distress, followed by a chorus of crude male laughter.

James awoke with a start, wincing as a stabbing pain sliced through his throbbing skull. He turned his head only to find himself struggling to overcome an attack of light-headedness. Blackness whirled around him, forcing him to shut his eyes and press his head against the pillow.

Deep breaths, deep breaths.

Gradually, the fog surrounding him eased, replaced by an onslaught of agony so sharp it stole the breath from his body. Every inch of him, from his scalp to his toes, ached and throbbed with a fiery pain. Dizzy and sweating, James pulled himself into a sitting position, only to immediately slump back down.

Bloody hell, what's wrong with me?

He did not want to open his eyes, but finally, slowly, he did. Thoughts churning, he lifted the blanket covering his naked body. James glanced down and cringed, his blurry eyes taking in the sight of bloody bandages swathing his arm, chest, belly, and legs. He blew out another puzzled breath, but then suddenly his throat seized as faint memories of the attack filled his aching head.

"Davina," he whispered.

Tears filled the corners of his eyes. He eased himself upright, the ropes beneath the mattress squealing in protest when he moved. The sound tore through his head, but he fought through the pain.

Leaning gingerly against the headboard, James searched his scattered memory for details. They had met on the hilltop, in their secret place. Davina had smiled and teased and kissed him with her usual passion and excitement. His heart had been near bursting with emotion when he asked her to be his wife and when she had agreed—och, his joy had been boundless.

But then . . . then . . . they had been set upon by brigands. A foul group of outlaws intent on causing them harm. He had fought fiercely, had killed several of them, but there were too many to defeat. He remembered striking his final opponent in the heart with his dirk, but after that there was only blackness.

What happened to Davina? Had she escaped? Been kidnapped? Been killed?

Ignoring the pulsing pain racking his body, James again whispered his beloved's name, then began shouting, "Davina! Davina!"

The bedchamber door flew open. The silhouette of a burly man loomed in the doorway. "Are ye awake?"

"Aye," James croaked. He felt appallingly weak and confused.

"I'll get the laird."

The man left before James could question him. Frustrated, James forced himself to remain calm. Finally, Laird Armstrong entered the chamber, two men at his side. James recognized one of them as the captain of the guard. The other was unknown to him.

"I see ye've decided to join the living again," Laird Armstrong said, his booming voice rattling James's aching head.

Ignoring the expression of discontent clouding the laird's features, James asked, "Where is Davina?"

"She's confined to her bed." The laird's eyes grew dark. "She's in a terrible, disgraceful state. Bruised and beaten. She shudders with nightmares, cries out in terror. My men found ye both miles from the castle, struck down and bleeding. What happened?"

Davina lives! James's heart beat with elation, followed swiftly by sadness. Alive, aye, yet badly injured.

"We were attacked," James replied.

"By who?"

"Brigands. Outlaws."

"My men saw no one. There was no looting in the village, no crops destroyed, no cattle stolen." The laird lifted his brow. "What can ye tell us of them?"

James took a deep breath, shuddering at the searing pain it caused in his chest. "There were six men. None wore plaids or carried shields with clan markings. They surprised us."

"I can only imagine what ye were doing in such a private, secluded place with my niece that caused ye to be so distracted," Laird Armstrong growled.

James grit his teeth and jerked his head in denial. He would not stand for Davina's honor to be questioned, even by her own kin. "I love Davina. I would never do anything to compromise her honor or virtue."

Laird Armstrong snorted in disbelief. "Six men

approach and ye heard nothing? I thought the McKenna trained his men better."

He did. Guilt, swift and sudden, stabbed through James. He lowered his chin in shame. "The men were on foot, not horseback. They had the advantage of surprise when they ambushed us."

The laird's eyes sparked with sudden anger. "We've not had any trouble with brigands on our lands fer years."

"Not while Robert the Bruce was king," the captain of the guard added.

James nearly shouted in frustration. He had no care for the political implications of the attack. His main concern was finding the criminals and punishing them for hurting Davina.

"It could have been a group of English scum," the other man suggested.

"We're too far north for the English to be troubling us," the laird insisted.

"Nay, they were Scots. I could tell by their swords; to a man they carried Claymores." James's voice felt choked and tight. "I killed two of them and wounded two others. After that . . ." he said, his voice trailing off in confusion.

"We found no bodies," the captain of the guard challenged.

James drew in a ragged breath, fighting the need to argue. "They must have taken the dead and wounded away."

"Two men took four others away?" the laird asked incredulously.

James shook his head and stared across the chamber. He had no answers to give, no explanations that made sense. "What did Davina tell ye?"

The laird shot him a sidelong look. "She cannae speak of the incident without becoming hysterical."

James cursed. "The last thing I remember was an explosion of pain inside my head."

The captain of the guard nodded. "Ye've got a fine, swelling bruise on the back of yer skull. Ye must have been struck from behind."

James lifted his arm and ran his fingers over the growing lump behind his right ear. At the touch, he felt a ferocious, nearly blinding pain so strong that it turned his stomach. He bowed his head and fought the sickness, not wanting to disgrace himself further in front of these men.

They were still scrutinizing him, some openly, some covertly, but all with grave suspicion. James saw the looks that passed between them. They spoke among themselves, their voices deliberately low, so he could not hear the conversation. 'Twas a stark reminder that he was not a member of the clan, but rather an outsider. No matter that he was a McKenna, the son of a powerful and respected chieftain. He had lost their trust when he failed to protect Davina.

God, he needed to see her. But he feared he could not leave this bed without aid and he was too proud to show further weakness in front of these warriors.

The discussion continued, with frequent glances in his direction. The chamber was soon brimming with tension, yet James found that he didn't really care. He rubbed a hand over his brow, trying to ease the pounding in his forehead. His eyelids grew heavy and slowly closed. He struggled to reopen them, succeeding, but within seconds they closed a second time.

He had the sensation of someone drawing closer to his bed, speaking to him, but the words made no sense.

There were waves of pain crashing through his head. But even worse, over and over the image of Davina falling prey to those brigands flashed before his eyes.

And then suddenly, mercifully, there was only darkness. And silence.

Chapter Three

When James next awoke it was pitch dark. Disoriented in the inky blackness that surrounded him, he pulled at his clouded mind, trying to orient himself. He let out an angry huff as his memory returned, along with the shame of failure.

Davina! James's breath caught. The need to see her consumed him. Grunting loudly, he pulled himself into a sitting position. Stars spun before his eyes at the tortured pain that seared every part of his body and he nearly fell back. 'Twas only by sheer force of will he remained upright.

James waited a few moments, his breath coming in deep bellows, before reaching for the tunic that lay at the foot of the bed. It took three attempts before he was able to pull it over his head and four more before he was able to put his good arm through the left sleeve. He let the other arm dangle; the thick bandage on his shoulder prevented him from putting his arm through the other sleeve.

Exhausted from the effort, James waited again, then pushed to a standing position. He felt himself start to sway, pitching toward the floor. He thrust his good arm forward. Thankfully, the bed was near enough to cushion the fall. He sprawled facedown on the mattress, his pulse thumping rapidly. Disgusted, James closed his eyes, yet refused to allow weakness to claim him.

He lay there for a long time, with only the sound of his deep, even breaths for company. Feeling himself starting to drift off to sleep, James slammed his fist against the wooden headboard, letting the rage inside him wash away his weariness. As the rage grew, it fed his need and bolstered his strength. Clenching his fists, James pushed himself upright. Awkwardly, he pulled his brais over his bandaged legs, then thrust his feet into a pair of leather half boots. Searching in the darkness, he found his dirk and slipped that inside his footwear.

On unsteady feet, James made his way through a darkened hallway. He saw no servants scurrying about, no men-at-arms or members of the household strolling the corridors, making him realize that the hour must be late and all in the castle were sleeping.

His first week in residence, James had learned which bedchamber Davina occupied. Since there were but a few private chambers in the castle, it was simple to find it now, even in his weakened condition. He was momentarily annoyed to see there was no guard placed at her door, then chided himself for such foolishness.

The danger was now past. She was safe within the walls of the Armstrong holding. James lifted his hand to knock, hesitated, then fearing he might be denied entrance, he turned the latch and slowly pushed at the door. It groaned open.

The bedchamber was shrouded in darkness, with only a single candle illuminating the room. James stepped inside. The cool breeze fluttering through the room hit him square in the face, jolting his senses.

Limping painfully, he approached the bed that was positioned at the far side of the chamber.

The elderly maid sitting at Davina's bedside jumped at the sound of his uneven footsteps. She leapt guilty out of her chair, then pressed the back of her hand to her mouth to stifle her scream.

"Jesus, Mary, and Joseph, ye scared the life out of me, sir. 'Tis the middle of the night. I expected no one at this hour."

"Beg pardon. I've come to see Davina."

"She's sleeping, poor lamb."

"I'll not disturb her." Not waiting for permission, James carefully approached. There were dark shadows dancing about the room near the bed, but if he squinted, he could detect the shape of her body beneath the blanket. "Bring the candle."

The maid hesitated. He glowered at her, a near perfect imitation of his father. The maid seemed startled, but followed his order with no further protest.

Yet when James gazed down at his dearest Davina, he almost wished the older woman had defied him. Everything inside him tightened with a sickening anger when he saw the condition of his beloved.

She lay on her back, with a blanket covering her to the waist, her limp arms resting at her sides. Her face was ashen, the delicate skin bruised and swollen on one side. Scratches and cuts marred her cheeks, looking angry against the paleness of her flesh. A deep purple bruise, edged in red, ringed her neck, indicating that one of the brigands had tried to choke the life from her.

Thank God he had not succeeded.

"Why is she so still?" he croaked.

"'Tis the medicine. They gave her a potion to help

her sleep. She was near hysterical this evening when they examined her."

"Was she . . . did they . . ." James's voice trailed off. The words were impossible to imagine, let alone say.

"Violate her?" The maid shook her head in sympathy. "It seems likely, though the midwife was unable to complete her examination. The poor lass screamed and thrashed, pushing the midwife and the healer away whenever they touched her."

"Merciful God!" James bowed his head, hardly believing the pain inside him could get any stronger—yet it did. His mouth filled with the acid taste of coppery blood as he bit the inside of his cheek.

He sat carefully on the edge of the bed and took Davina's hand into his own. 'Twas cold as ice. He noted her fingernails were torn and jagged, with bits of dried blood beneath them. She had fought fiercely to save herself. For that he was profoundly thankful.

Yet failure and shame gnawed at his gut, the pain so deep it rooted him to the spot. This was his fault. He should have saved her, protected her. He could feel his throat closing tightly with emotion as his mind and heart filled with despair.

Suddenly, Davina stiffened and gasped. Her eyes opened and shifted wildly about while deep, anguished moans spilled from her quivering, bruised lips. His blood ran cold, the sound tearing through him like a knife.

"Hush," he rasped, trying to soothe away the raw pain that seemed to be radiated from every pore of her bruised, battered body. "Be still, my love."

She turned her head toward him. James's hand reached out to cup her chin, trying to offer some comfort. At his touch, her eyes widened in horror. James felt his heart sink to his knees when he realized she had just recognized him.

Her trembling started as a small shudder, but quickly grew. Davina began whimpering, a pitiful, almost inhuman cry of pain. He tried moving closer, needing to soothe away her panic, but she held out her arm to push him away. He gazed into her eyes and clearly saw the fear and distress.

It broke his heart.

The maid pushed to the bed. "Ye'd best take yer leave," she commanded. "Ye're frightening her."

The truth of those words was nearly unbearable. It made him feel as low as the men who had beaten and abused her. Shaking, James stood and backed away from the bed. "I'll return tomorrow. Hopefully, Davina will be more herself."

The maid cast him a doubtful, worried look, but James refused to be deterred. He would return in the morning.

Limping slowly, he made his way back to his small chamber and fell into his bed, too exhausted to even groan in pain. Eventually, James slept, waking to a dull and gray morning, thick with clouds.

The gloom fit his mood. An ominous foreshadowing of what was to come. His body ached even more this morning, the pain dull and deep in his bones. There were more people about the hallways as he made the long, agonizing walk to her bedchamber. None spoke to him; many averted their eyes.

When he presented himself at Davina's bedchamber door, he was told that she refused to see him. Lacking the strength to argue with the determined maid, James retreated, but stubbornly returned the next day. Where he was again given the same message—Davina wanted to be left alone.

Disheartened, James respected her wishes. He returned to his small chamber and rested, allowing his body to heal. He ate the food he was brought, allowed the healer to change his dressings, drank the foul-tasting medical potions he was given.

He had no visitors except for the servants who brought his meals and the healer who tended his wounds. Against her instructions, he gingerly walked the confines of his small bedchamber to regain his strength, determined to hasten his recovery. He was polite, congenial to all he saw. But inwardly, he brooded.

For the next seven days, every morning and every evening, he made the long, slow, painful walk to Davina's chamber, each time receiving the same response from the stoic maid. But on the eighth day it was not the maid who stood watch at his beloved's chamber door. Instead he found himself face to face with Davina's cousin Joan.

"Lady Joan."

He inclined his head in a respectful bow, then simply stared. She was a strikingly beautiful woman, with expressive blue eyes, golden hair, and refined features. Yet he knew her loveliness was only skin-deep.

"Good morning, Sir James," Lady Joan replied. "I see that yer wounds are healing. Hopefully, ye will soon be fully recovered."

James flexed the hand of his sprained arm. His body was slowly improving, yet his mind would have no relief until he spoke with Davina. But Joan stood in his way.

Not particularly caring that it seemed rude, he attempted to push past her, but she placed a restraining arm on his shoulder.

"Davina has asked me to speak with ye. My cousin

wishes to be left in peace and begs that ye stop insisting on seeing her. She finds it most unsettling."

'Twas impossible to miss the gleam of satisfaction in Joan's eyes as she delivered the message. It immediately made James suspicious. "I dinnae believe that Davina would say such a thing."

Joan lifted one eyebrow. "Refusing to accept the truth willnae change it," she replied haughtily.

"I'll accept it if, and only if, I hear those words fall from Davina's lips," James answered. "Until then, I will continue to press my suit."

"What a rude, selfish reply! Yet I would expect nothing less from the likes of ye." She favored him with a mocking scowl that set his blood to boiling.

"Dinnae speak to me of selfishness, Lady Joan. I've been here long enough to see the truth of what lies beneath yer pretty face. Ye are jealous of Davina and the love I have fer her and will stop at nothing to keep us apart."

"That's a lie," Joan hissed. "I care nothing fer Davina's childish devotion to ye. What does it matter to me? My father is besieged by men who desire me as their bride. Men who are great warriors and noble, wealthy leaders of their clans, not inconsequential second sons."

"The laird will have to provide a very substantial dowry in order to entice any man to have a viper like ye fer a wife," James countered.

Joan's eyes narrowed with anger, but James was through talking. Gritting his teeth, he shook off Joan's hand, opened the chamber door, and stepped inside.

Davina was alone in the room. She was sitting in bed, resting against a pile of pillows. Her lips tightened when she spied him, then with knotted fists she pulled the blankets up to her chin, covering her body completely.

His gut heaved at her obvious fear of him, yet he walked forward until he was standing nearer to the bed.

"Did ye not get my message?" she whispered, sinking beneath the covers.

"Joan said ye dinnae wish to see me, but I knew I cannae trust her word." He took a few steps closer, needing to see her face. Her eye was still swollen, her face pale, but the bruises had started to fade. "Ye are my betrothed, Davina. 'Tis only right that we spend time together."

"Oh, James." She brought her hand up to her mouth and shook her head. "I feared that yer nobility would force ye to honor yer proposal, but I shall not hold ye to it. I release ye from the pledge to wed me."

"Nay!" He touched her cheek with his knuckle and she began to tremble. "We shall be married. It need not happen soon—we both need time to heal."

She turned an uneasy gaze toward him. "I know in time my body shall mend, but the memories and fear of the attack will always remain. 'Tis unfair to saddle ye with such a broken woman fer a wife."

He shook his head vehemently. "I dinnae feel that way."

"But I do!" She shouted the words, but the effort drained her strength. Davina slumped against the pillows and he saw a tear slide down her cheek. "Why must ye torture me with visions of what can never happen? I can never be yer wife, James. I can never be any man's wife."

"I love ye, Davina." He curled his fingers gently over hers, but she wrenched her hand away. "We shall face this together, overcome it together."

Beneath her covers he saw her shiver. "The memories willnae leave me."

"Davina, they will eventually fade, if only—"

"Dear Lord have mercy! Are ye not listening to me? 'Tis best this way, James."

"Ye cannae mean it, Davina."

"Aye, I do." Sorrow and shame crowded into her eyes and he felt his heart shattering into a thousand pieces.

"Ye must give it time, lass. Ye'll feel differently in a few weeks."

"Nay. Time only makes the memories of the attack more vivid and hateful. 'Tis why I beg the healer to dose me with potions that make me sleep, that help me forget." She made a sound deep in the back of her throat that was part frustration and shame. "Please, James, as soon as ye are able, take yer leave of Armstrong Castle. Return home and forget about me."

"Never!"

Her eyes focused on him. "If ye ever had any true feelings fer me, ye will accept this and do as I ask. Leave and never return."

James was stunned. He grimaced, tortured emotions of anger taking control of him, spreading like a fever through his entire body. He lifted his arm, needing to smash something, but Davina's sudden cry stopped him cold. Somehow mastering his crushing pain, James slowly lowered his arm.

There was silence in the chamber. Davina turned her head and pressed her face into the pillow. He could hear the soft sobs that she tried to muffle and his heart broke anew.

Scowling, he left the chamber.

Thankfully, the corridor was empty. Never in his life had he felt so completely alone. He steeled himself to courage as he stood there, knowing that somehow he must find the strength to do as Davina asked.

'Twas such a part of his nature to fight for what he wanted in life, but in this case James knew he was defeated. It was his fault that Davina was so frightened, so scarred, so broken. He had failed her. He had no right to expect her to still love him, though he knew his heart would forever belong to her.

Even if she no longer wanted that heart.

Sleep was impossible to achieve, but James forced himself to stay in his bed for the remainder of the day and through the long night. He arose as dawn was breaking, carefully dressed, and then packed his belongings. Having too much pride to sneak off like a thief in the night, he waited in the great hall until the household gathered to break their fast.

He bid the laird and Lady Armstrong a polite farewell. The latter made an impassioned plea for him to remain until he was fully healed, but James could not abide staying within these walls another day. He also declined the laird's lackluster offer of an escort, his stubborn McKenna pride refusing to acknowledge the need for assistance of any kind.

He saddled his horse himself. After securing a dirk in each of his boots, James hoisted himself into the saddle. A sharp pain raced up his arm and his legs quivered, but he managed to settle himself.

Moisture collected on his upper lip and brow, but he ignored the pain. Head held high, a brokenhearted James rode through the gates of Armstrong Castle, over the drawbridge, and through the village.

Though sorely tempted, he never once looked back.

The brigand arrived at the private glen well before the appointed meeting time. He kept his head lowered, to avoid the biting wind, though his ears were attune to the surrounding sounds. Dismounting gingerly from his horse, he placed his sore, bruised hand on his sword hilt and strode into the dense forest. A light, misty rain had started falling, but the trees still retained enough of their leaves to provide an adequate cover from the worst of it.

Damp, aching, and miserable, he waited. A sudden noise warned him of a presence. The brigand spun around, then turned and peered ahead through the underbrush. He saw no one.

Suddenly, a bolt of lightning cracked and sizzled about his head, illuminating the area in unnatural brightness. The wind picked up to a violent fury, spraying moisture in his face, the droplets of water clinging to his scraggly beard.

A flock of birds scattered wildly in the sky. A second thunder crack brought another flash of intense light and, startled, he cried out, for a cloaked figure stood not ten feet away.

"I dinnae hear ye approach," he blustered.

"Aye,'tis what I intended," the figure answered. "Where is Drummond?"

"Dead. His wounds festered. He told me where to meet ye before the fever turned him into a babbling half-wit." The brigand sniffed and wiped his nose with the back of his sleeve. "Did ye bring the payment?"

"I did."

He raised his arm and caught the leather purse that was tossed his way. Frowning, he weighed the pouch in his left hand. "It feels light."

"'Tis the price that was agreed upon."

"But the task was more complicated. We should be paid more to compensate fer the injuries and deaths."

The figure sighed with annoyance. "Ye are lucky to get what I give ye. I never instructed Drummond to be so brutal to them. I wanted Sir James driven away and the relationship between them ended. That's all."

The brigand felt his jaw twist and set. "We did what ye hired us to do. I saw McKenna ride out two days ago."

"Aye, and no thanks to ye," the figure accused. "He could barely sit upon his horse."

"Ye dinnae tell us that McKenna was such a wild one!" the brigand blustered. "Ye said it would be easy to surprise them, to frighten him off. But he fought like a man possessed, killing two of our men outright and badly wounding two others. Drummond has already gone to meet his maker and 'tis doubtful if Eudard will survive."

The cloaked figure regarded him with a penetrating stare. "Then ye've no cause to complain about the wages ye have earned. I have paid the price and now there are fewer to share it, leaving more fer each of ye."

Ever practical, the brigand had no rebuke for that chilling, heartless logic. The gray, murky air swirled about them, the wind screeching and moaning. He thought to make one final plea—nay a veiled threat— for more coin, when a bolt of lightning flashed, striking a tall tree. It burst into flames, burning in an angry glow despite the misty rain.

Startled, he turned to watch the eerie sight, feeling the heat of the flames on his flesh. A mist, cool and dense, rose from the ground, mingling with the smoke from the fire. It looked like the bowels of hell, a place of evil and fear. Unsettled, the brigand turned back around, only to discover the cloaked figure was gone, vanishing into the fog, like an unworldly apparition.

Crossing himself, the brigand recited a quiet prayer, then limped slowly back to his horse.

Chapter Four

Five years later

From the privacy of her tower bedchamber, Davina gazed out the small window at the stark, barren landscape below. Another winter was fast approaching and the earth was preparing to lie dormant. The days would be short, the nights long, leaving far too much time for thinking.

How could it be that time hung so heavy, yet the seasons moved with lightning speed? The darkening horizon blurred and she realized that tears were stinging her eyes. She wiped them away. She was grieving again, lamenting the sorrow of the past, the loss of what she had once held so fleetingly within her grasp that was now gone forever.

James.

He was no longer in Scotland, but instead on Crusade, fighting in the Holy Land. Yet it would not have mattered if he resided but a few miles away, for it was far more than physical distance that separated them.

His face haunted her dreams, the memory of their

love whittled away at her soul. Once she had believed they would marry and fill their home with children. But a cruel, unforeseen act of violence had denied her that happiness.

Disgusted with her weakness, Davina angrily turned away. Her days were so often a struggle against her natural inclination to run and hide from the world and she fought that as best she could. Victories were rare, however. Oh, she managed with the members of her family, with the household servants she knew, even with one or two of the older Armstrong warriors that took their meals at the table nearest hers in the great hall.

But she struggled mightily with unknown men, became shy and tongue-tied around women when first making their acquaintance. Hoping to spare her this distress, her family had encouraged her to withdraw, to protect herself from this pain by keeping away from the cause of it.

Directly after the attack, this simple solution had been a balm to her bruised mind, but as the days turned into weeks, then months and finally years, the loneliness of living such a sheltered existence began to eat away at Davina, enveloping her like a shroud. And the cowardliness of this isolated life began to shame her.

I must not allow the fear to paralyze me—I must not, she told herself. But she also needed to learn how to stop the brooding. It did her no good, thrusting her further into the darkness of her mind.

The weak evening light spilling into her chamber dispelled some of Davina's gloom and strengthened her resolve to find a way to move beyond the circumstances that surrounded her. It had taken her far too long to come to the realization that she could not change the horror that had ravaged her past, but neither did she have to remain a prisoner to it.

The healing had in fact begun three years ago when she received a letter from Lady Aileen McKenna, James's mother. Davina's skill at reading and writing were rudimentary, but she was able to decipher the brief message, which inquired about her health and ended with prayers and good wishes. Oddly, it had brought such a calming sense of comfort that Davina felt compelled to reply.

The next message from Lady Aileen spoke of her worry for her son, James, who had gone with Sir James Douglas on Crusade. It ended with an invitation to visit McKenna Castle. The idea of traveling such a distance to stay with strangers was terrifying, so of course Davina promptly declined.

Thankfully, Lady Aileen took no offense and continued to correspond. Davina continued to answer. The invitations to visit also persisted, though they were not in every letter. And then somehow, Davina still was uncertain exactly why, when she answered a missive a few weeks ago, she felt emboldened to accept Lady Aileen's invitation to come to McKenna Castle and celebrate the Christmas holiday.

Well, bold or desperate, Davina was honestly unsure which emotion was strongest.

It was only several days after she had said yes that the reality of her actions took hold in her mind. And as she grappled with the events she had set in motion, she continued to do as she always did—keep her own counsel.

But now several weeks had passed and it was beyond time she told her aunt and uncle of this impending journey. Pressing her hand against the knot forming in her stomach, Davina walked with long, purposeful strides to the great hall in search of them. She located the pair easily, gathered with several of the local tradesmen in front of the blazing fireplace.

Hanging back in the shadows, Davina waited until the men had concluded their business and departed before approaching. Closing her eyes for a brief moment, she took a deep breath, blurted out her news, and then braced herself for their shocked reaction.

"Ye plan on going where?" her uncle asked incredulously.

"To McKenna Castle, to celebrate Christmas," Davina repeated. "Lady Aileen has invited me."

At her announcement, everything went silent. Not a sound could be heard, except for the crackling and hissing of the fire burning in the large fireplace at the center of the great hall.

"Why, I've never heard of anything more preposterous," Aunt Isobel sputtered. "Ye haven't ventured beyond the walls of this castle fer five years. How can ye possibly make such a long journey? And if somehow ye were able to get there, how will ye possibly manage in an unknown place, among strangers? Among strange men. Ye need to have the safety of these strong walls around ye and the solace of yer family about ye, to chase away yer gloomy thoughts and fears."

"That's why Lady Aileen suggested I visit for the holiday, when there will be the added merriment of celebration."

"Ye told that good lady about yer affliction?" her aunt asked. "Have ye no pride left?"

Davina felt her cheeks begin to heat with shame. "I wrote nothing specific. I merely mentioned that at times I suffer from melancholy. She confessed to the same and suggested that perhaps we could offer each other comfort."

In truth, Davina had merely hinted at her suffering,

but Lady Aileen had been quick to address it, offering sympathy and support.

"What of her son?" Aunt Isobel asked, whispering in Davina's ear. "Will James McKenna be at the castle, celebrating with his family?"

The genuine worry lurking in her aunt's eyes brought on a rush of emotions, bringing to life Davina's memory of herself sobbing in her aunt's arms the fateful morning when James was preparing to leave Armstrong Castle.

"I heard tell that Sir James wishes to marry ye, Davina," her aunt had said. "Uncle Fergus will speak with him, if ye agree to the match?"

"I cannae," had been Davina's muffled reply.

Aunt Isobel had clucked her tongue in sympathy, but refused to remain silent. "Circumstances force me to be blunt, Davina. Sir James might be yer only chance at having a husband, and one day, God willing, children of yer own. There willnae be many men offering fer yer hand after what happened."

"'Tis best. I fear I cannae be a proper wife."

"Those feelings shall pass," Aunt Isobel had insisted.

Davina's head had shaken violently. "Nay! The very idea of being intimate with a man repulses me. Even with a man that I love."

"Hush, ye'll make yerself ill with all this weeping." Aunt Isobel had gently stroked her hair, bringing on a fresh bout of tears, for the kindness was both unexpected and desperately needed. "We shall not force ye to do anything that brings such fear and sorrow to yer wounded soul."

Nay, they had not forced her. In fact, they had done their best to protect her and keep her safe. Perhaps that was why she now felt an odd sense of guilt, as if her desire to break free of her fears was somehow a betrayal of their years of care.

"Just this morning we received a message that Joan intends to come home with her husband and baby fer the holiday," Uncle Fergus said. "She'll be sorely disappointed when she arrives and discovers that ye aren't here."

Davina shrugged, meeting her uncle's eyes with bland innocence. Four years of marriage to the Fraser laird had not mellowed Joan's self-serving, spoiled ways. It was always decidedly unpleasant for Davina when Joan and her family came to visit. Little did her uncle realize that avoiding her overbearing cousin was an enticement to leave, not stay.

"I can spare only a few men fer an escort," Uncle Fergus muttered.

"By the Saints!" Aunt Isobel screeched. "The journey to McKenna Castle will take days. Davina willnae step foot outside our walls unless she has a full complement of our best warriors at her side. I'll not have her traveling on unsafe roads with only a few men to protect her. Especially at this time of year. Food is scarce when the weather is cold. Who knows what sort of thieves and brigands lurk on the roads, eager to prey on unsuspecting travelers?"

"Exactly!" Uncle Fergus scowled. "Another reason why 'tis a daft idea. I forbid ye to go, Davina. Ye shall stay here with yer family, where ye will be safe and protected."

Uncle Fergus and Aunt Isobel turned expectantly toward her. Davina swallowed hard, knowing they were waiting for her to agree. "Lady Aileen is sending an escort."

"What?" Aunt Isobel's jaw lowered.

"How many men?" Uncle Fergus asked.

"Never mind the men," Aunt Isobel interjected. "Is she also sending a maid? We have none to spare and ye cannae be left alone in the company of a group of McKenna soldiers fer so many days and *nights*."

Unable to answer, Davina lifted her hands in a helpless gesture and shrugged. Her aunt clucked her tongue in disapproval. Her uncle snorted in derision and the two began listing myriad hazards that she could encounter, one more distressing than the next.

The more they talked, the faster Davina's panic started to rise. Biting her lip, she looked from one dismayed face to another. *Are they right? Am I mad to consider such a journey?*

The idea of going to McKenna Castle had been so bold, so freeing, but now it was feeling like a bad, impulsive decision.

Agitated, Davina started pacing in front of the fireplace. The fears inside her began to emerge, starting first as a small trembling, then progressing to a shortness of breath.

Engulfed in the shame of her failure to conquer these fears, Davina opened her mouth, ready to acquiesce to their demands that she abandon the notion of visiting Lady Aileen. But before she could speak, a lad ran into the great hall, his voice heavy with excitement.

"Riders approach! Angus sent me to tell ye he spied them from the battlements."

"Can ye see their colors?" Uncle Fergus asked anxiously.

"Aye. 'Tis the McKenna banner they carry."

"What the devil?" Uncle Fergus scratched the stubble on his chin. "How could they have gotten here so quickly?"

All eyes turned toward Davina. She felt her heart slam against her ribs, but somehow managed a weak smile. Apparently, there would be no time to reconsider the rashness of her actions in accepting Lady Aileen's invitation.

Her McKenna escort had just arrived.

As his horse thundered through the open gates of Armstrong Castle, all Sir Malcolm McKenna could think of was his sore arse. He had pushed himself, and his men, hard on this journey, riding long hours both day and into the night and his muscles were finally rebelling against the abuse.

The cold, damp weather hadn't helped much either. It seeped into the bones and pulled at the muscles, bathing them in stiffness. Yet his personal discomfort had no effect on his decision to make this journey in as short a time as possible.

This ridiculous journey, he amended in his head.

Determined to ignore the soreness, Malcolm gave no hint of his pain as he dismounted from his panting, sweating horse. Tossing the reins to a waiting servant, he stood in the nearly deserted bailey, hands on his hips, stretching out the cramps in his legs.

With a wry grin he noticed that several of his warriors were also moving a bit slower than usual, yet none dared to complain. Tonight they would sleep indoors, near a warm hearth, after filling their bellies with good food and drink.

Malcolm's eyes turned expectantly toward the heavy, oak door of the great hall, waiting for the laird and his lady to appear and bid him welcome. Yet the door remained tightly shut. Puzzled, Malcolm looked to the lad who held his horse, but the youngster refused to meet his gaze and instead stared at the ground.

Ballocks!

Malcolm had succumbed to his mother's pleas to ride out to this godforsaken keep and escort Lady Davina Armstrong to McKenna Castle because he could no longer bear to see the painful flashes of loss that lingered in her eyes. His father had agreed it was an ill-advised journey, but Lady Aileen was convinced that Davina Armstrong could shed light on his brother James's behavior.

Malcolm and his father were not as certain. James had left Scotland to fight for a noble cause. It was that simple. Yet his mother refused to believe her son would leave without first telling his family and then bidding them a proper farewell. And she was certain that Davina Armstrong was the key to unlocking that mystery.

They had learned of James's whereabouts from a traveling priest, the hastily scrawled letter he was entrusted to deliver arriving months after James had departed from Scotland's shore. Since then, there had been little news. There had been no word of Christian victories against the infidel.

In truth, most of the Highlanders who had gone on Crusade had returned. Yet James had remained.

Or so the family believed.

The sky rumbled with thunder and Malcolm felt the first fat, cold raindrop land upon his head. 'Twas the final insult. He was not about to become drenched in a downpour while standing like a beggar in the Armstrong bailey. Nor would he allow his men to be treated so rudely.

Nostrils flaring, he strode uninvited to the closed door

of the great hall and flung it open. If the Armstrongs refused to show good manners, then why should he?

His sudden appearance startled the few occupants of the great hall. A maid shrieked and scurried behind a trestle table, another dropped the basket of bread she held. He saw two men reach for their swords, but they stopped before drawing them when the order to stand down was shouted by a tall, brawny fellow who Malcolm assumed was the captain of the guard.

Malcolm's lips twitched into a grimace as he slowly moved his hand away from the hilt of his own sword. This was hardly the welcome of an expected guest.

What the devil is going on?

Malcolm glanced over his shoulder to verify that his men stood behind him. Then keeping his expression blank, he cautiously advanced toward the trio standing near the fireplace. He recognized the laird and his wife and assumed the woman at their side was the infamous Lady Davina.

Laird Armstrong was short, stocky, and red-faced, his eyes forming into beady slits as he scrutinized Malcolm. Lady Armstrong was a bit more circumspect than her husband, though he felt the intensity of her wary gaze just as keenly. She, too, was round in shape, with a beak-nosed face and a suspicious demeanor.

No matter. He was not here to impress either of them. He was here at his mother's request, to escort Lady Davina safely to their home.

"Laird Armstrong. Lady Isobel. I am Sir Malcolm McKenna." He bowed respectfully before turning his eyes sharply toward the young woman who stood beside them. "Lady Davina?"

"Sir Malcolm." She dipped a hasty curtsy. "Welcome to Armstrong Castle."

The words sounded stiff and rehearsed, but he was

distracted from the message by the sweet, lyrical sound of her voice. One might describe it as angelic, but for the husky edge that instantly stirred a man's senses. Intrigued, Malcolm's eyes swept over her, taking her measure.

She was not a raving beauty—he had certainly seen prettier women. And females with a more buxom, enticing figure. Yet there was much to admire. Her features were refined, her skin flawless, her liquid brown eyes soulful. Most would call her attractive, yet there was something about her, something undefinable, that had the power to draw his attention, almost against his will.

Laird Armstrong cleared his throat. "Forgive our poor greeting, Sir Malcolm. We were only just made aware of Davina's plans and were startled by yer arrival."

Reluctantly, Malcolm tore his gaze away from the mysterious Davina. "I had wondered if there was a problem. But I assure ye that all is in order. My mother eagerly awaits Lady Davina's arrival."

"Well, sir, we have several things that must be settled before we allow ye to take our Davina away," Lady Isobel bristled.

"Aye," Laird Armstrong seconded.

Malcolm glared at the pair in puzzled annoyance. *Take Davina away?* He was not some marauder who had come to steal their treasurer. He was here to provide an escort. Nothing more.

"I shall make every accommodation to ensure that Lady Davina travels in comfort and safety," Malcolm said with a winning smile. "Or else I shall have to answer to my good lady mother. I confess I'd rather face an army of English curs than defend myself against her wrath."

Malcolm's attempt to lighten the mood failed utterly. Lady Isobel made a disapproving sound in the back of her throat, while a shadow crossed over her husband's face. Malcolm glanced at Lady Davina. Her head was bowed in supplication, as though she dared not look at him.

His confusion, along with his irritation, increased. For some reason the Armstrongs were not at all pleased with this arrangement, and for the life of him, Malcolm could not fathom why.

Taking a deep breath, he dug his heels into the wooden floor planks. His jest about pleasing his mother had been more than just an attempt at humor, for it held several grains of truth. Aye, his mother would indeed be sorely disappointed in him if he failed at this task.

McKenna men did not fail their women. His father had taught him that important lesson. Even if he had to resort to kidnapping the lass, he would be returning to McKenna Castle with his mother's holiday guest in tow.

As he conversed—or rather sparred—with her aunt and uncle, Davina's downcast eyes remained glued to Malcolm McKenna. Her hidden gaze traveled the length of him, hungry to see a resemblance between Malcolm and his brother, but there was little of James to be found in the elder McKenna. Malcolm was taller, his hair darker in color, his eyes blue and intense.

His hair was windswept and wild, falling to the top of his shoulders. His features were uncommonly handsome, bold and striking. Square jaw, straight nose, broad brow. Fine lines creased the corners of his eyes, and a shadow of a beard shaded his cheeks.

His fur-trimmed surcoat and brais were mud-stained from travel, the leather boots that hugged his muscled calves dusty. Yet their quality and cost was unmistakable.

He was everything a lass could want. Strong, handsome, beguiling. Yet all Davina could think about was turning on her heel, running to her chamber, and bolting the door behind her.

Never in her wildest dreams had she considered that Lady Aileen would send her eldest son, heir of the clan, as her escort. She had expected a much older, seasoned retainer would be sent to lead her escort. Not a young, virile warrior of wealth and privilege.

It was a circumstance that both assured and terrified her in equal measure.

Davina's heart had not ceased its erratic beating from the moment Sir Malcolm strode so boldly into the great hall as if it were his own, confidence and strength in each step. He carried an air of danger and a swagger of command that bespoke a man used to being in charge.

Accustomed to being obeyed.

His voice boomed—deep and low—when he spoke. The sound of it sent a shiver racing down her spine. The uneasiness she always felt whenever she was near a man came to life in her stomach and it took every ounce of courage she possessed to stand her ground.

Fidgeting nervously, Davina swept an errant strand of hair away from her face. Aunt Isobel gave her a sharp look, but the older woman's gaze softened when she saw how badly her niece was trembling.

"Davina, go and tell Cook to prepare refreshments

fer our guests," Aunt Isobel commanded. "I'm sure Sir Malcolm and his men could do with a bit of food and drink to tide them over until the evening meal is served.".

"Ye are most kind, Lady Isobel," Sir Malcolm replied. "My men and I are grateful fer yer hospitality."

Davina could not help but admire the smooth tone Sir Malcolm used to deliver his subtle jab at the less than gracious reception he had received, as it made it impossible for her aunt to take offense.

After delivering the message to the cook, Davina took a few moments to collect her composure before returning to the great hall. As she entered, she saw that Aunt Isobel, Uncle Fergus, and Sir Malcolm were gathering at the high table.

Turning at her arrival, Sir Malcolm gave her a confident smile and politely offered his hand to assist her to her chair. Gulping back a protest, Davina glanced down worriedly at his extended, ungloved hands. They were large and well formed, with powerful fingers that boasted calluses and even a small scar on the top of one of his forefingers.

Determined to leap over this new hurdle, Davina sternly reminded herself that if she was ever going to conquer her fear of men, she had to find the courage to act normally when in their company. Sir Malcolm was simply being chivalrous—nothing more.

Yet as she watched his strong, masculine hand draw nearer to hers, Davina let out a small cry and pulled back, preventing any contact. Immediately ashamed of her skittish response, she risked a glance at Sir Malcolm, fearing that she had insulted him. But his face was devoid of any expression. 'Twas almost as though he was unaware of her actions, but of course, that was impossible.

Davina breathed a small sigh of relief, grateful he chose to ignore her odd behavior rather than comment upon it. Other men were not nearly as gracious, displaying open disdain whenever she revealed her nervous demeanor.

Hastily, she took her seat, then laced her fingers together to still their trembling. As two young pages brought platters of cold meat, bread, and cheese, along with pitchers of ale and wine, Davina deliberately slowed her breathing, hoping to release some of her pent-up anxiety.

She was dimly aware of the conversation between her aunt and uncle and Sir Malcolm swirling around her, but was too preoccupied to give it too much attention. That is, until her aunt cut to the matter at hand.

"I fear that Davina shall not be able to go with ye, Sir Malcolm, as she cannae travel without a maid," Aunt Isobel suddenly declared.

Sir Malcolm abruptly ceased chewing a piece of coarse, brown bread and squinted at Aunt Isobel in understandable confusion. Davina was certain he believed this to be a woman's problem and none of his concern. Truth be told, he was right.

"Naturally, accommodations shall be made for Lady Davina to bring her servant," he replied graciously, wiping his fingers on the piece of cloth that hung like a swag from the edge of the table. "She may bring two women with her, if she desires."

"There is not even one maid, let alone two, that can be spared," Uncle Fergus grumbled.

"Aye, we've holiday preparations of our own to see to," Aunt Isobel huffed. "All hands are needed here."

The confusion on Sir Malcolm's face deepened.

Davina felt a jolt of pity for him, as he seemed at a total loss in how to solve this dilemma, or more importantly, why he was being presented with it at all.

"There are plenty of servants at McKenna Castle," he said. "I'm certain my mother can arrange fer one of them to attend to Lady Davina's needs while she is with us."

"She is an unmarried lass," Uncle Fergus stated emphatically. "A delicate, frail female. She cannae travel as the only woman in the company of so many men. 'Tis unthinkable!"

If her uncle believed Sir Malcolm would be thoroughly chastised by such a remark, he was in for a rude awakening. The handsome knight favored them with a haughty lift of his brow. "Lady Davina need not bring a servant. Any respectable female in yer clan can serve as her companion. My mother often travels in the same manner when she visits her relations."

Uncle Fergus sputtered at the simple solution, yet could find no fault with it. Aunt Isobel looked as though she had taken a large sip of sour wine, but she too had no protest to offer.

"I shall ask Colleen," Davina said slowly, speaking for the first time. "I believe that she would enjoy the change of scenery. She has been grieving mightily since her husband died this past spring."

"A widow. Perfect." Sir Malcolm favored Davina with a relieved smile and she felt a blush stinging her cheeks. "'Tis settled. We leave tomorrow, at first light. Now, if ye will excuse me, my men and I need to see to the care of our horses."

The chair scraped noisily against the floor as Sir Malcolm stood. Uncle Fergus also rose.

"We will have a small chamber where ye may rest fer

the night," Uncle Fergus said. "The barracks are full, but yer men may sleep in the great hall."

'Twas a rather beggarly offer of hospitality, but Sir Malcolm accepted it with a smile. Still, Davina could not help but wonder what he was truly thinking.

"I'll see ye at the evening meal, Lady Davina." He bowed, then turned and walked away.

She rubbed her forehead. Gracious! He seemed to take all the air from the chamber with him.

"Merciful heavens, Davina, ye cannae mean to leave the security of these walls with the likes of him," Aunt Isobel exclaimed, sending her a hard look. "Who knows what could happen?"

The outrage in her aunt's voice gave Davina pause, yet she did not yield. Her hand moved down to her throat and she pressed her fingers sharply against the pulsing veins.

"The McKennas are honorable men. I shall be perfectly safe," Davina declared breathlessly, knowing if she could survive a journey with Sir Malcolm McKenna leading her escort, she would be well prepared to deal with any man.

Chapter Five

Davina did not attend the evening meal. Though she had assured her aunt that she was eager to make this journey, she was not quite prepared to again be in such close proximity with Sir Malcolm. Besides, she had little time to make her preparations, since he wished to leave at first light, and there was much to do to get ready.

Fortunately, Colleen was pleased to accompany Davina and the widow proved to be a big help organizing the clothes and other items that would be needed for the journey and the time they spent at McKenna Castle.

Trunk packed, Davina ate a light meal in her chamber, checked everything one final time, then crawled into bed. Yet she was far too restless to sleep. Eyes wide open, she stared at the ceiling, trying to ignore the doubts and fears that plagued her mind.

Tossing fitfully, she finally drifted into a light sleep a few hours before dawn. But her scant slumber was filled with a vivid, disturbing dream.

A tall, broad-shouldered warrior stood before her, teasing her for a kiss. Though his face was handsome and his manner pleasant, the idea of a kiss made her nervous—very nervous.

With a hesitant smile, she politely refused. In the blink of an eye his pleasant manner vanished. He captured her in his arms, refusing to release her. Not when she demanded. Not when she begged. Not when she began to weep.

Holding her tightly, the warrior laughed as she struggled to pull away. He kissed her neck, then bit her behind the ear. Shame and fear engulfed her as he started pawing her like an animal, lewdly fondling her breast.

Tears of frustration squeezed from her eyes. She tried to scream, but no sound came out. A beefy hand twisted in her hair as the warrior pulled her to the ground, flipping her on her back. He swiftly straddled her, his hips pressing against hers.

Hysteria bubbled to the surface. His features morphed into a grotesque blur as she felt him reaching for the hem of her gown, yanking it up . . .

Davina awoke with a cry, gurgling and gasping for breath. *Merciful God!* It had been many months since she had been tormented by such terrifying dreams. No doubt the notion of leaving the safety of Armstrong Castle had brought them roaring back to life.

She closed her eyes and took several small, steadying breaths. She could feel the moisture gathering behind her lids, yet Davina refused to allow the sobs to come, knowing if anyone heard them, they would tell her aunt and uncle, proving that she was not strong enough to make this journey.

Her breathing still ragged, Davina slowly got to her feet. She walked across her small chamber—nearly tripping over her packed belongings—settled herself into a chair, and bowed her head. *Are Aunt Isobel and Uncle Fergus right? Will leaving home cause the fear that lurks so close to the surface to consume me?*

Wincing, Davina lifted her head and glanced at the small wooden box tucked into a stone shelf in the corner of the chamber. Inside the box was a bottle of the medicine she took whenever her nerves became overset. 'Twas a brew the clan healer had created especially for her. Encouraged by her aunt, she had taken it several times a day after the attack, welcoming its mind-numbing effects, drinking bottle after bottle for months on end.

Gradually, however, Davina realized she was becoming far too dependent upon it. At first, 'twas impossible for her to abandon it completely, for her fears were so vivid and strong, yet she managed to discipline herself to use it only when her need was most dire. The hard-fought results were gratifying and she was proud of the fact that not a drop of the potent brew had crossed her lips for many, many months.

Feeling agitated, Davina walked to her small window and pulled back the leather cover. The cold air hit her square in the face, but the bracing wind was not enough to clear her head. Hastily, she moved away, glancing again at the box. *I need it or else I'll never find the courage to leave in a few hours.*

Lips pursed, she allowed her feet to carry her across the chamber. Staring hard, she waited a long moment before lifting the lid and removing the bottle.

Only one wee sip.

The medicine tasted bitter on her tongue and the urge to take a large swallow was strong, but Davina resisted. With a determined shudder, she pressed the cork tightly back into the neck and was rewarded with a feeling of control. Yet instead of returning the bottle to its proper place, Davina slipped it carefully into her small trunk.

* * *

The first day of her journey to McKenna Castle passed quickly, with little incident. Uncle Fergus and Aunt Isobel were silent and stoic as Davina bid them farewell. Though Davina hated to see the hint of hurt upon their faces, she pointedly ignored their disapproval and acted as if all was fine.

Davina's knuckles were white beneath her leather gloves as she approached the gates of the castle. *Five years. Five years since I have been on the other side.*

Gritting her teeth, Davina pressed her knees against her horse's flanks, encouraging the mount to increase its speed. An icy quiver of unease prickled up the nape of her neck and she felt every eye in the bailey staring at her, but Davina kept her gaze forward and her back straight.

"Well done, milady," Colleen whispered.

Davina turned to the older woman riding beside her and gave her a small smile. The breath she had been holding released in a rush. *I've done it!*

The urge to shout the news with triumph overcame her, but Davina tempered her response. 'Twas only the first of many challenges she would need to conquer. Still, it felt rewarding to have success and the boost to her courage was much appreciated.

Quietly, Davina savored her victory, thankful also that Sir Malcolm was busy ordering his men into formation and therefore unaware of the swirling tension surrounding the significance of her passing through the gates of Armstrong Castle.

The weather was cold, but free of snow. Davina wore her warmest gown and heavy woolen cloak, yet the occasional gust of wind tore through her with a chill that reached her bones. Sir Malcolm rode at the head of the column, leading his men, though every now and then he would turn to look over his shoulder at her.

Each time his gaze met hers, her heart would nervously trip over itself, yet she managed to bestow a pleasant smile upon him, hoping to convey that all was well. She appeared to succeed, for Sir Malcolm would then nod his head and return his attention to the road. After a few hours they made a brief stop to water the horses and eat a bit of crusty bread and cheese, washed down with wine. Sir Malcolm approached as Davina pulled her aching body back atop her mount.

"We must travel until nearly dark in order to reach Montgomery Abbey, where we will take shelter fer the night," he explained. "Will that pose any difficulty fer ye and yer companion?"

"Nay, we shall be fine," Davina muttered, averting her gaze so he could not see the doubt in her eyes.

It had been many years since she had ridden for so long and her cold, stiff muscles were already protesting. But she refused to complain, refused to slow their progress.

'Twas only after hearing Colleen groan as she settled herself upon her own horse that Davina felt a pang of worry.

"Och, how thoughtless of me, Colleen, fer not asking how ye fared before answering Sir Malcolm. Shall I call him back?"

Colleen shook her head. "Nay, milady. I might be older, but I am used to riding in the cold weather. Far more than ye."

The truth of those words rankled, but Davina lifted her chin. "I fear ye are right, but 'tis past time I became used to it again."

Her determined words, and many fortifying deep

breaths, gave Davina strength to endure the bone-jarring afternoon. Taking her at her word, Sir Malcolm paid her no heed, turning his attention to other matters. For that, Davina was grateful, for she was uncertain she could adequately hide the extent of her physical discomfort if he scrutinized her too closely.

After what felt like an eternity, salvation arrived. Bathed in the glow of the setting sun, Davina caught a glimpse of the spires of the abbey, admitting they were the most welcoming sight that she had seen in a very long time. Spirits buoyed, she stretched the soreness from her back and shoulders and urged her mount onward.

The abbot stood in the yard, ready to greet them, and Davina realized that Sir Malcolm must have sent one of his men ahead to make certain all would be ready. 'Twas a small thing, yet showed surprising consideration.

James would have done the same. The truth of that notion brought a wistful smile to her lips.

Sir Malcolm leaped gracefully down from his horse, then turned to assist Davina. A bolt of alarm sank into her gut. She started shivering, mostly from the cold, but also at the notion of Sir Malcolm placing his hands upon her.

She attempted to scramble off the horse on her own. Sir Malcolm noticed her trembling and, assuming it was due to the cold, insisted they get inside at once. Without waiting for a reply, he reached up and encircled her waist. She jumped, but his grip was firm and never faltered.

She swayed slightly when he set her on her feet, her heart drumming so loudly she was certain he heard it. She raised her arms, struggling with the intense urge to bat his hands away. Fortunately, he released her before it was necessary.

Still, she could feel his eyes upon her, staring at her, and she could only imagine what he was thinking. Hoping to distract him from her odd reaction, she gave him a quick smile of thanks, but inside she felt wooden. The physical contact had left her with a feeling of panic so severe it nearly robbed her of breath.

Perhaps this was a colossal mistake. Leaving the shelter and familiarity of her home was too much for her delicate nerves. No doubt she would make a fool of herself many times over before they even arrived at McKenna Castle. And the good Lord only knew what else she would do there before the visit ended.

As they walked into the section of the abbey reserved for overnight travelers, Davina considered feigning an illness and requesting that she be brought home in the morning.

Yet as quickly as the thought appeared, Davina dismissed it, clenching her fingers into tight fists, angry with herself for having such cowardly thoughts. Nay, she would not flee. She would see this through and fight for her independence.

But not this evening.

"We are grateful fer yer kind hospitality," Davina said as the abbot showed her the simple chamber that she and Colleen would share. "We shall partake of our meal in here and then go directly to sleep."

The abbot looked momentarily stunned, but recovered quickly. "We are not a restricted order. Women are welcome to join us in the hall for the evening meal."

Davina felt herself blushing and she turned her head away. Sir Malcolm's eyes were practically boring a hole into her, making her even more determined to avoid him.

"Thank ye, but I fear we are too tired to be good company. I bid ye all good night," she said hastily, before fleeing to the safety of her chamber, Colleen following obediently behind her.

Davina awoke the next morning groaning at the soreness and stiffness of her body. Hunched over like an old woman, she hobbled to the washbasin. Colleen clucked her tongue like a mother hen as she helped Davina dress.

"Ye are in no condition to ride again today, milady."

"I'll be fine once I loosen my muscles," Davina replied with a grimace. Perhaps if she told herself that enough times, she would believe it.

"I doubt Sir Malcolm would agree," Colleen countered.

Aye, he most likely would not agree, but Davina was not about to say anything. The sooner they arrived at McKenna Castle, the sooner she would be away from his constant scrutiny.

"Ye shall say nothing to Sir Malcolm," Davina insisted, in a stern voice that she hoped brooked no argument.

Colleen merely clucked her tongue a second time and shook her head. But she loyally kept silent when they gathered to depart.

Tucking a windblown strand of hair back behind her ear, Davina settled her aching muscles atop her mount and said a silent prayer that she would be able to stay there without being in total agony. The path curved sharply as they left the abbey courtyard and Davina was grateful it required a slower pace. Yet all too soon they reached an open stretch of road.

After two hours of hard riding, they finally slowed.

Breathless and aching, Davina nudged her mount forward across a small stream. The wind rustled the few leaves that clung to the trees that crowded the path. Forced to ride in single file, as the trees grew thicker, Davina cautiously watched her horse's footing, since large tree roots and stumps lined the road.

Soft light filtered through the canopy of branches over their heads. If her muscles had not been aching so fiercely, Davina knew she would have enjoyed this rare taste of freedom. She sighed, then stilled as she felt an odd tingling sensation down the back of her neck. She turned to gaze through the sparse winter foliage, thinking she saw a movement of something.

She opened her mouth to ask Colleen if she had seen anything when a tree crashed in front of them and a battle cry mingled with the thundering sound of approaching horses suddenly filled the air. Time seemed to hang suspended as Davina watched a contingent of men break through the woods from both sides of the narrow road. Swords raised, they attacked with precision and force.

Riding in the lead, Sir Malcolm turned, his face contorting into a surprised frown and then his voice rang out loud and clear, "'Tis an ambush! McKenna to me!"

Though taken by surprise, the McKenna retainers quickly organized. They somehow formed a protective ring around Davina and Colleen in the small space and bravely faced this unknown enemy. The air soon filled with the ringing of clashing steel, the shouts of men, the screams of horses.

Their attackers wore no clan colors, yet they fought with training and skill. As the battle raged, they drew close enough that Davina could see the cold, bloodthirsty expressions on their faces. Her heart missed several beats and started to pound erratically. She swayed as a wave of nausea overtook her, nearly causing her to fall from her mount. But Colleen's scream of fright as a McKenna warrior fell pulled Davina from her fear.

She grasped the reins of the widow's horse and tugged insistently, hoping to lead them both farther into the center of the circle. A part of her wished she could shut her eyes to the sights around her, but Davina feared being caught unawares. If somehow their side lost, she would not go blindly to her death—she would look upon the face of the man who dared to plunge a dirk into her heart.

Despair ravaged through her as the memories of another time, another attack, clouded her thoughts. But today it was different. Though outnumbered, the odds were not as lopsided. Though she almost dared not to believe it, Davina could see that the tide was turning.

The McKenna retainers had beaten back several of the attackers, while sustaining only a few injuries of their own. Her breath began to slow and then suddenly a deep-throated scream from one of the men startled her horse. The animal reared. Davina clung tightly to the reins, but her balance was compromised.

She hit the ground hard, pain shooting through her entire body. Terrified, she curled into a ball, trying to protect herself from being stomped by the horses' hooves. A dozen thoughts and fears flitted through her mind, but she had little time to think. All she could do was keep her body as small and still as possible— and pray.

A hazy blur surrounded her as the ringing in her ears put her in a confused fog. Gradually, the sounds of battle eased. After what felt like an eternity, a shadow fell across her. Nearly hysterical with fear, Davina nevertheless managed to keep her eyes open as she lifted her head.

A frowning Sir Malcolm gazed down at her, concern lining his face. He gently cupped her cheek to look into her eyes. "Are ye hurt, Lady Davina?"

"I dinnae think so," she whispered through trembling lips.

With infinite care, Sir Malcolm slowly ran his hands over her body, searching for injuries. Davina's mind was still so filled with shock and fear she didn't even flinch at the intimate gesture.

"Ye appear fine." Gently, he helped her to her feet. Davina leaned heavily on him, averting her eyes from the prone bodies that lay unmoving upon the ground. "Colleen? Where is Colleen?"

"I'm safe, milady."

The sound of the other woman's voice brought a rush of relief to her heart. Davina stumbled forward and the two women embraced, clinging tightly to each other. Try as she might, Davina was unable to cease her shivering. Odd how blue the sky was, with nary a cloud to be seen, yet in her mind's eye all she could see was darkness, all she could feel was terror.

"How fare the men?" she heard Sir Malcolm ask.

"Young Edgar has a gash on his arm and a nasty cut over his eye that willnae stop bleeding. And Harold's shoulder has been cut clear through to the bone," one of the retainers replied.

Sir Malcolm cursed beneath his breath, the sound drawing Davina away from her own fears. "Colleen and I will tend to them," she announced.

Her hands shook slightly as she pulled a clean linen from under gown and the small vial of medicine from the trunk strapped to the back of her horse. She and Colleen made their way over to the men, who had been propped up against a tree trunk.

Davina's belly heaved at the sight of so much blood

and mangled flesh, but she swallowed it down. These men had become injured while trying to protect her; the least she could do was see to their comfort.

Fresh water was brought so the wounds could be cleansed. Davina's healing skills were limited, but thankfully Colleen had experience with stitching deep wounds. She assisted the widow with the gory task and following her instructions carefully bound the wounds with strips of cloth she had torn from her gown.

"No need to ruin such a fine garment on my account, milady," young Edgar said, shy gratitude in his voice.

Davina smiled at the lad, judging him to be no more than fifteen or sixteen years old. "I am honored to make such a small sacrifice in light of all that ye and yer brave comrades have done to protect me and Colleen," Davina answered.

"Och, ye had me worried fer a minute, lad," Sir Malcolm interrupted. "I thought yer injuries severe, but if ye have the strength to flirt with a pretty lass, then I know ye'll be fine."

The lad blushed and lowered his chin, but Davina could see the taut lines of pain pulling at his mouth. Hoping she was judging the dose accurately, she bade Edgar to drink the medicine she held to his lips, knowing its numbing effects. After giving Harold an even larger dose—as he was nearly twice the size of Edgar— she returned what was left of her torn shift and the medicine to her trunk.

Sir Malcolm followed her to her horse. "I'll not feel safe until I've put ye behind the walls of McKenna Castle," he explained. "Unless ye'd rather return home?"

His question surprised her. She was used to being told what to do for so long, it felt strange to have her opinion considered. "I'd like to continue to McKenna Castle, unless ye advise against it."

Briefly, he looked pleased, then he grew solemn. "There is a less traveled, more direct route to get there, through the jagged mountain range. The terrain is difficult to negotiate, with steep cliffs and rugged ledges. Do ye think ye'll be able to cross it?"

"I'm not afraid of heights," Davina answered, almost embarrassed to admit that was one of the few things that didn't cause her fits. "What about the wounded? Will they be able to manage such an arduous journey?"

"We will make certain to rest as often as they need and watch them closely to see if they take a fever. Beyond that, 'tis in God's hands."

Davina nodded and prepared to mount her horse. Sir Malcolm turned away, but not before she caught the worried look in his eyes he tried to conceal.

Sir Malcolm kept his word. Though the pace was harsh, he stopped frequently to rest the horses and check on his wounded men. They made camp each evening just as darkness was setting and rode out at first light. Davina and Colleen tended the men's wounds as best they could, pleased that no fever had claimed them, relieved the wounds had not opened.

The final day of their journey, the weather turned bitterly cold. Teetering on exhaustion, Davina's spirits were lifted when one of the men announced they had crossed over to McKenna land. The pounding sound of the horse's hooves mingled with the relieved sighs of the men, jubilant at returning home.

It took several hours before they climbed the final ridge and at last the castle came into view. For a moment,

Davina was speechless. McKenna Castle was truly a sight to behold.

The square towers and turrets were massive in size. Elegant in design, they spiraled toward the heavens, with pennants snapping in the wind above them. There were walkways connecting the numerous towers and armed guards patrolling the parapets. The pale gray stone curtain wall that protected the castle was the tallest Davina had ever seen, surrounding the entire structure, making it a nearly impenetrable fortress.

At the base of the wall stood a large village, the cottages and shops a labyrinth of winding paths. Though the hour was late and dusk was fast approaching, the clan came out of their homes to greet them. They waved and shouted words of welcome, cheering raucously as they rode past.

Sir Malcolm smiled and waved back, calling to several men and women by name. There was little doubt that he was the McKenna heir, destined to one day lead and protect these people. 'Twas also clear that he had already earned their loyalty and affection.

They passed through the large gate and into the bailey, which was a hive of activity. Servants scrambled forward to take charge of the horses, while maidens greeted their men and boisterous soldiers called out to their comrades.

For a moment, Davina wondered about Sir Malcolm's wife, but then remembered that Lady Aileen had written that her older son was a widower, having lost his young wife to a harsh illness two years ago.

As Davina contemplated how she was going to dismount from her horse without her tired legs collapsing beneath her, she spied an older couple standing at the entrance to the great hall. Clearly they were awaiting their arrival, welcoming smiles upon their faces.

"My parents," Sir Malcolm whispered, though Davina had already surmised their identity.

Sir Malcolm had the same commanding demeanor as his father, his body tall and full of strength. The protective way he hovered over the lady at his side made it obvious that she was Sir Malcolm's mother. James's mother.

Davina's heart began to race and her hands felt cold and sweaty beneath her gloves. She was so distracted by her nerves at meeting Laird and Lady McKenna that she barely took notice of Sir Malcolm when he grasped her around the waist and hauled her off her horse.

Feet unsteady, muscles tingling, Davina held on to him and allowed herself to be led to his parents. Still clinging to Sir Malcolm's arm for support, she dipped into a low curtsy.

When she rose, Lady Aileen took her hand and squeezed it affectionately, then embraced her like a long-lost relative. "I'm so happy that ye are finally here."

Davina felt her emotions rise to the surface. Unable to find her voice through her constricting throat, she smiled broadly and answered by returning the hug.

Her smile faded, though, under Laird McKenna's appraising scrutiny. His sharp eyes took in every aspect of her appearance, eventually forming an opinion that Davina feared was not nearly as favorable as his wife's. The tight grin he finally bestowed upon her did little more than bare his teeth. Then he turned to his son. "I see that young Edgar and Harold are wrapped in bandages. What happened?"

"Nothing we could not manage," Sir Malcolm answered, bending down to kiss his mother on the cheek.

"Come inside out of the cold," Lady Aileen admonished, ushering everyone through the thick oak door.

The pleasant scent of beeswax mingled with the aromas of freshly baked bread and roasting meats assaulted Davina's nose. Her belly rumbled and she realized she had eaten very little for the past few days.

"I'm afraid there's barely enough time fer ye to wash away the travel dust before the evening meal is served," Lady Aileen said. "But I can have a warm bath prepared fer ye to enjoy in yer chamber later tonight."

"A bath sounds like pure heaven," Davina replied.

"Good. Megan will show ye to yer chamber, but please hurry back. The McKenna men dinnae like to be kept from their food."

Her chamber was lovely. A woven rug covered the stone floor, a pair of colorful tapestries hung on the walls. A welcoming fire blazed in the hearth and the fragrant dried herbs and flowers sprinkled in the bed linens perfumed the room. 'Twas too dark to admire the view, but Davina suspected it would be as spectacular as everything else.

Davina washed her hands and face in the warm water that was provided and quickly changed into a fresh gown of green wool with embroidered trim. The round neckline showcased her long neck and the tight fit along her waist and hips gave her an illusion of height and elegance. Colleen braided her hair, then placed a gauzy veil over her head, securing it with a gold circlet.

"Ye look lovely, milady," Colleen said approvingly.

The compliment gave Davina's confidence a much-needed boost. It lasted only until she reached the great hall, where she found a large, boisterous crowd gathering in the cavernous space, talking, shouting, and laughing.

Davina felt a pang of trepidation slide through her as she moved forward. So many unknown faces made her stomach tighten with nerves. It only worsened when she was noticed. Davina saw several men nudge each other before looking her way and one woman whispered something in another woman's ear.

Her discomfort under their pointed stares grew as she wound her way around the many trestle tables toward the dais. Her eyes searched fruitlessly for a familiar face and she felt herself flushing when she was unable to find one.

Davina was considering returning to her chamber and waiting there until summoned, when a young child dressed in a pale blue gown came running toward her at full speed. Yelping with astonishment, Davina tried to step out of the lass's way, but the child adjusted her course, skidding to a stop only inches in front of her.

Davina glanced down at the little girl, wondering who she was and why she was in such a hurry. She was just about to ask the child when her gaze caught Sir Malcolm and Lady Aileen approaching.

"Och, Papa, have ye brought me a new mother?" the little girl asked, peering at Davina with hopeful eyes. Then before anyone could reply, the child threw her arms around Davina's waist and loudly proclaimed, "She is just perfect. I love her already. Thank ye, Papa!"

Chapter Six

The sweet sound of his four-year-old daughter's voice thundered in Malcolm's ears. She was clinging to Lady Davina like a climbing vine, her small arms tightly locked around the older woman's waist. Malcolm fixed his gaze on Lady Davina. Her eyebrows were arched in surprise, but they slowly lowered as the child snuggled into her.

"Let go of Lady Davina at once, Lileas," his mother admonished. "That is not the way a proper young lady greets a guest."

"Nay!" Lileas shouted, visibly tightening her grasp.

"Come now, Poppet, show yer good manners and do as yer grandmother commands," Malcolm cajoled. "Or else Lady Davina will think ye've been raised by wolves."

"She willnae!" Lileas insisted.

"Aye, she will and she'd be right," Malcolm proclaimed, his patience ebbing.

The eyes of his parents weighed heavy as they watched him. Though he deferred to them in most things, out of respect and regard, he disagreed when it came to the raising of his daughter. They felt he indulged Lileas, and her whims, far too often, to compensate for the time he spent away from her on clan business. Witnessing her unruly behavior now, he worried they were right.

Without another word, Malcolm reached down and scooped his daughter up his arms. He braced himself for the squawking that was sure to follow, but the little girl stayed silent. Yet his smile of relief soon faded when he saw that Lileas continued to cling to Lady Davina's skirts even as he held her aloft.

"Och, Malcolm, put her down before she tears Lady Davina's gown," his mother cried.

"Papa promised me," Lileas proclaimed with a dramatic sigh. "I dinnae want to be a motherless child anymore."

"Ye're going to be a lass with a sore backside if ye dinnae do as ye are told," Malcolm countered.

That threat caught his daughter's attention. Finger by finger, Lileas slowly released her grip on the delicate fabric of Lady Davina's skirt. When her hand was free, Malcolm set her on her feet, giving her a single swat on her behind.

"Apologize," he demanded, folding his arms across his chest and glaring down at his child.

Lileas's lower lip trembled and her eyes filled with tears. "I'm sorry, Papa. Please dinnae be mad at me anymore."

Malcolm felt his heart nearly crush with guilt. The lass looked so small and helpless and utterly chastised. He immediately regretted his scolding tone and physical punishment, though it had been but a light tap.

A few months ago, Lileas had come to the realization that the clan children she played with all had something she lacked—a mother. Malcolm believed she had accepted the answer that her mother was in heaven and she seemed content when he had blithely assured her that one day he would find her a new mother.

He had not anticipated her expectation that the promise would be filled immediately. Nor the depth of her need. Malcolm's guilt grew. If he were a better, more loving and attentive father, perhaps Lileas's need for a mother might not be so great.

"Lileas, make a proper curtsy to Lady Davina," the McKenna instructed.

Her brow furrowed with concentration, Lileas obeyed her grandfather, gracefully bending her knee. Malcolm stared at his daughter, pride spearing his heart. She looked like an angel.

"Are ye my new mama?"

Malcolm barely hid his groan. At least Lady Davina no longer seemed startled by the question. Fie, she'd heard it enough in the past five minutes to be used to it.

Lady Davina knelt and looked Lileas directly in the eye. "I willnae be yer mother, but I should like very much to be yer friend."

Lileas chewed her bottom lip as she considered the offer. "I like having friends."

"As do I. If yer father allows it, perhaps ye can show me around the castle tomorrow?"

Both females turned hopeful eyes toward him. He ran a hand through his hair, manfully resisting the cowardly urge to turn to his mother and let her decide. "Lileas will make an excellent guide."

That answer earned him a smile from all three females. Malcolm held his hand out to his daughter. She took it eagerly, skipping beside him as they made their way to the high table. He settled her on the special chair to his left, which was built with high, sturdy legs so the little girl could reach the table, then assisted Lady Davina, who was seated to his right.

His mother was on Lady Davina's other side, allowing him to focus most of his attention on his daughter since his mother was busy speaking with her guest.

Lileas happily filled his ear with news of the puppies that had been born a few days ago, the antics of her faithful dog, Prince, the fluffy gray castle cat she had finally been able to catch and pet for a few minutes before it squirmed away, and the pretty smell of the lavender satchels she had helped her grandmother make this morning.

Always a good eater, the child grew quiet as she concentrated on the food Malcolm had set on her trencher. He had chosen the most tender pieces of meats, cutting them into small bits, so they could be easily chewed and swallowed, and selected her favorite vegetables, though Lileas always ate them all. Ignoring his own hunger, Malcolm watched the child as she ate, marveling anew at how this beautiful, perfect, innocent creature had sprung from his loins.

From the moment of her birth, the love he had failed to feel for Lileas's mother had manifested itself in emotions so deep and strong for their child that Malcolm almost felt unmanned by it. The fierce, nearly obsessive desire he carried to protect Lileas and see her happy seemed to grow each day, never more so than when he had been away from her for a time.

Assured that his daughter had all that she needed, Malcolm relaxed slightly and turned his attention to his meal. The roasted venison was moist and succulent; the stew of vegetables and boar meat dripping in a rich, tasty sauce.

The sound of Lady Davina's rich, velvet voice invaded

his thoughts, causing Malcolm to pick up his head like a hound on the scent of its prey. Now, there was a puzzling female. She jumped like a hare at the sound of a deep male voice and yet she had retained her composure during that surprise skirmish in the woods.

She had further risen in his respect and admiration when she had volunteered to aid the men who had been wounded during the attack and had managed to do so without becoming overly emotional. 'Twas a reaction he had not predicted nor anticipated.

He understood well the feeling of fear; any warrior with wits experienced it when faced with battle. 'Twas only training that made that emotion fade into the background while instinct to survive took over.

He imagined it would be much harder for a lass, as she did not possess the means to defend herself, but instead must rely on those around her to keep her safe.

Malcolm began staring at Lady Davina. He knew it was rude, yet a part of him thought if he peered at her long enough, he might come to some understanding of her.

She must have felt his gaze upon her, for she turned to him, her eyes light with curiosity. He smiled. Her eyes widened. She tried, but only managed a very brief grin in return. 'Twas all the opening he needed.

"I must apologize fer Lileas's somewhat . . . uhm . . . exuberant greeting," Malcolm said. "I hope that ye dinnae find offense at her outburst."

"Nay. 'Tis rather flattering really, to think she would want me fer her new mother." Lady Davina speared a morsel of meat with her eating knife. "I understand the loneliness of growing up without a mother, though I was lucky to have mine until the age of twelve. 'Tis obvious that Lileas is well loved and cared fer, but that doesn't make it any easier."

Malcolm pondered her words, watching her as she took a drink of her wine. The drink left her lips looking plump and rosy. *Ripe for a kiss?*

"Perhaps 'tis time fer me to think about finding a bride," he said casually. "Ye aren't wed, are ye?"

She appeared stunned for a moment. Nervously, she took another sip of her wine, tipping it back until her goblet was empty. He reached over and refilled it. She took another long gulp. "I'm sure there are many fine, accomplished ladies who would gladly accept yer proposal, Sir Malcolm."

"Malcolm."

"Pardon."

"As ye are a guest in our home, 'tis acceptable fer ye to address me by my name. Will ye do me the honor of granting me the same privilege?"

Her cheeks flamed. "Of course. It seems foolish to be so formal. Yer mother has already insisted that I call her Aileen."

A teasing muscle twitched in his jaw. "So, Davina, what advice can ye give me regarding a wife?"

She brushed her hand over her brow, momentarily stopping to pinch the bridge of her nose. He thought he also heard her utter a short prayer—*dearest Lord, give me strength*—but could not be completely certain.

"As an unmarried woman, I am hardly the one to consult on such matters."

"Why are ye unmarried? If I might be so bold to ask?"

To his surprise, instead of blushing and turning away, she gave him a hard stare. "Ye may ask all that ye like, Si . . . Malcolm. But I dinnae have to answer."

"Papa." Lileas tugged on his sleeve. "I finished all my meat. May I have more?"

"Here, take this. I've already cut it into small pieces." Davina offered the meat from her trencher.

"Thank ye." Malcolm considered Davina as he placed the food in front of his daughter.

The burden of parenting would most definitely be lighter if he had a wife. And there would be more bairns. Companions for Lileas and an heir for the clan. He could feel a curious smile flitting across his face as he opened the part of his body he usually kept shut to unrelated females—his heart.

Malcolm thought himself hardened, even jaded toward the fairer sex. His marriage to Margaret Douglas had ended when a mysterious fever had taken her life and while he mourned the loss of a mother for his young daughter, he did not miss the responsibility of a wife.

Margaret had been clinging and demanding, quick to cry and quicker to complain. He would not go so far as to say she had ruined his taste for women—a willing widow or a softhearted harlot were always welcomed in his bed. But life with Margaret had convinced Malcolm that marriage was not something he was eager to embrace again.

Yet there was no denying that Lileas needed—nay, she deserved—a mother to fuss and care for her.

Why not consider Lady Davina? Lileas was already taken with her. Clan alliances were strong—the threat from the English weaker than it had been in years. He need not make such a strategic match this time. He had already done his duty by marrying Margaret Douglas and Lileas's birth assured the blood tie between them.

Aye, Davina deserved strong consideration. Besides, he had promised his daughter a new mother. And a McKenna always honored his word.

* * *

A trencher piled high with roasted meat and winter vegetables was set in front of Davina. She took a sip of the mulled wine, then another, finding it to be heady and strong. It warmed her body from the inside out, a pleasant sensation.

The tension that had been building since she had left the familiar gates of Armstrong Castle eased a bit, replaced by a sense of peace. Astonishingly, instead of being panicked, she felt a sense of safety surrounded by such a large crowd of people.

The laughter flowed as freely as the wine and ale. There were many smiles among the servants as well as those folks sitting at the tables and partaking of the meal. 'Twas all so different from the meals at her home, where everyone always seemed to be on their guard.

'Twas also a pleasant change not to be stared at with anxious eyes. Part of the reason she seldom took her meals with her family was the discomforting scrutiny she was usually afforded by her aunt and uncle. Of course, that was preferable to the looks of curiosity and pity the other clan members and servants bestowed upon her.

A few of the men started banging their tankards on the table, demanding more ale. They were soon joined by a group sitting at the table next to them. A harried bevy of servants rushed forward and Davina saw a brutal-looking warrior pull one of the serving wenches onto his lap and kiss her soundly on the lips.

Davina cringed, fearing the girl was being held against her will, then realized the lass was laughing the hardest. Still smiling, the girl pushed herself off the man's lap, reached for the pitcher and the man's tankard. Davina felt the suffocating tightness in her chest start to ease.

"My husband allows no abuse in his hall," Lady Aileen said smoothly. "All are treated with respect."

Davina smiled and stole a peek over Lady Aileen's shoulder to her husband. Laird McKenna did not strike her as an enlightened man; affording his female servants the freedom to reject any advances hardly suited his character. Or so it seemed.

Feeling his eyes upon her, Laird McKenna turned his head. He favored her with a brief grin, then turned to the priest who sat beside him. Davina guiltily lowered her chin, realizing she should not be so quick to judge.

There was more food and dancing as the night wore on. The troubadour sang several songs, then told a fine tale of a mystical maiden and brave warrior, earning a shining coin from Laird McKenna for his efforts. He was followed by a talented group of jugglers who leaped and jumped about as they tossed a variety of objects in the air.

They finished to loud whistles and shouts of approval from the crowd. Clapping along, Davina turned to Lileas, eager to see the child's reaction. But it was Malcolm's brawny form that captured her attention.

He was sprawled in his chair, staring at her with eyes that were heavy with interest. Normally, such scrutiny would have her squirming in her seat, but for some reason it didn't bother Davina. It was probably the wine making her less guarded. Or perhaps seeing how caring and devoted he was to his daughter aided in easing her fears. Whatever the reason, it gave Davina hope and encouragement.

"I'm very pleased that ye are here." Malcolm caught

her hand and ran his thumb slowly, intimately over her palm.

Davina gasped, her relaxed mood instantly vanishing. His touch was warm and hypnotic. Her first instinct was to snatch her hand away, run to her chamber, and bolt the door behind her. But she conquered her fear.

"'Tis most kind of yer lady mother to invite me," Davina muttered. His hypnotic caress brought on a vulnerable feeling that was not entirely unpleasant, for it was gentle and calm.

He brought her hand to his mouth. *Mercy!* That was too much. Davina twisted her arm and jerked away before his lips could connect with her exposed flesh.

His brow lifted in surprise. Davina held her breath, bracing for the possibility of a violent reaction, but instead Malcolm smiled. She saw the firelight from the flicker torches that lined the hall reflected warmly in his eyes and calmed.

"Ye must cease trying to seduce me, milady," he teased.

"Me! Seduce ye?" she protested breathlessly. "Have yer wits gone missing, Malcolm?"

He laughed, the sound deep and wicked and utterly delightful. Davina sputtered with indignation, but then found herself grinning back at him.

"I cannae help myself. Ye make it too tempting and far too easy to tease ye, lass," he replied.

Davina felt her cheeks blush, but she was not offended. "Have ye no shame, milord? Ye flirt with me while yer daughter sits beside ye. 'Tis unseemly."

"Nay, 'tis perfectly innocent. Therefore, there's no reason to hide it, especially when it pleases ye so greatly."

Davina cast her eyes downward. Aye, 'twas true.

When she managed to lose her fear, she was able to enjoy this harmless bit of flattery.

Her heart fairly leapt at the enormity of this discovery. *I can do it!*

This joyful revelation was overshadowed when she caught sight of a tall figure silhouetted in the glare of torchlight at the end of the great hall. He was garbed in a shirt of black mail, a broad sword at his side and two lethal-looking kirks thrust into the leather belt on his hips.

His sudden, daunting appearance startled the musicians so completely they ceased playing. The distinct sound of swords being drawn permeated the air, yet the man's hands remained rigidly by his side. Davina assumed this defenseless stance was the only reason he had not been challenged by one of the McKenna soldiers.

Well, that, and the fact that he looked prepared to cut down the first man who dared to move against him.

The man's face was cast in the shadows, hiding it from view, but when he reached the center of the hall, the blazing wall torches illuminated his features.

Jolted by the sight, Davina froze. She felt her blood run ice cold, then fiery hot. She stared at the stranger for what felt like an eternity before her mind accepted the impossibility of what her eyes were seeing.

James!

Davina's hand flew up to cover her mouth and stifle the startled cry that rose to her lips.

There was no mistaking that lean, square jaw and wide, sensual mouth. Davina lost her fragile grip on her goblet. It landed on the table with a dull thud, the deep red contents spilling across and then down the sides. The steady drip of the liquid on the stone floor broke through the stillness, shattering the unnatural silence.

"James!" Lady Aileen's scream of joy cascaded throughout the great hall. She dashed from her chair and weaved her way through the maze of tables, fairly leaping into her son's arms when she reached him.

Their mutual laughter could be heard throughout the great hall. It broke any lingering tension among the clan and the celebratory mood once again returned. The lively music and merriment resumed, yet it moved around Davina, for all she could feel was the breath that had become trapped in her lungs.

The image of the young man she had loved so completely had never faded from her mind, or her heart. Yet the man who stood so arrogantly holding Lady Aileen close to his chest was barely recognizable. He was much taller than she remembered, his shoulders broader, his muscles larger and more defined. There was an angry scar slashed through his left eyebrow and another, smaller one on his square jaw.

But it was his eyes that had changed the most. No longer teasing and kind, they were raw and unnerving, giving him the wild, primitive, dangerous look of a man who did whatever he wanted and damn the consequences.

A stab of regret pierced Davina's heart at the memory of the honorable young knight she had known and loved.

She steeled her expression as James drew near the dais, certain her heart was beating so fast and loud it could be heard clear on the opposite side of the chamber. A pain shot through her jaw and she realized it was because she was gritting her teeth so tightly.

His expression grew puzzled, then turned to one of stern disapproval as his gaze traveled critically over her. Davina felt her heart beating even faster now, but somehow she found the strength to lift her chin and stare straight at him.

For a brief moment they stared at each other without voice or movement, then James blinked several times and shook his head, as though confirming in his mind what his eyes were seeing.

"Davina?"

His voice was harsh with surprised anger. It cut through her shock with swift pain. She fought the strong urge to flee, ignoring an inner voice that commanded she turn and run, for truth be told, there was nowhere to hide.

He moved closer and she felt the heat of his smoldering eyes scorch her. The wine she had drunk earlier swirled through her head and she began to panic, knowing she had no control over this situation.

Another step forward sent the blood rushing from Davina's head and she suffered an all-consuming wave of light-headedness. She closed her eyes, struggling for calm. It did not come.

Instead, a numbness trickled down into her limbs and a loud buzzing sounded in her ears. From a great distance she heard young Lileas's cry of alarm and then suddenly, blissfully, all went dark as Davina fell over into a dead faint.

Chapter Seven

James watched Davina topple from her chair. He instinctively moved forward, but was too far away to afford much assistance. Not that it was needed. His brother, Malcolm, caught her easily in his arms and held her protectively against his chest.

The child seated beside Malcolm—a young lass—started shrieking, her worry for Davina obvious. Momentarily taken aback by all he was witnessing, James swallowed hard, concealing his puzzled anger.

What in the name of all that was holy was going on? Why was Davina at McKenna Castle and why was his brother acting so proprietary toward her? James had seen the smiling banter between them when he first entered the great hall; had noticed the affectionate way his brother took Davina's hand and raised it to his lips.

Where was his brother's wife, Margaret Douglas? And why the hell had no one taken that screeching brat away? Were they waiting until everyone turned deaf?

'Twas hardly the homecoming that James had anticipated. If the past few minutes were any indication of what was to come, he needed to turn around, get on his horse, and ride for the hills.

"Lord, what a commotion! Be quiet, Lileas!" His mother held tightly to his arm, steering him away from the drama and bringing him forward until he was standing in front of his father.

It took a moment before he realized he no longer had to lift his neck to meet his father's eye—they were the same height. With interest, James took note of the streaks of gray at the McKenna's temples, and the lines that had deepened on his face. His father had aged, yet he still carried himself with the proud strength of a noble warrior.

"Christ's bones, son, away five years with barely a word and when ye entered the hall, all hell breaks loose."

"Aye, 'tis good to see that nothing has changed while I've been away, Father."

The McKenna's eyes narrowed. Then he slapped James on the shoulder and pulled him into a bear hug. James was momentarily speechless. Growing up he had never doubted his father's love—but open signs of affection had ended when the McKenna sons had reached manhood.

James quickly recovered his wits, then found himself returning the embrace. He felt his body seize with emotion as he held his father close. When times were darkest and dangerous battles raged he had often wondered if he would ever see Scotland—and his family—again. And now, through God's mercy, he was here. 'Twas a victory to savor.

Before he pulled away, his father whispered in James's ear. "I'm very happy ye've finally come home, son, make no mistake. But ye've caused yer mother endless nights of worry and grief, and fer that ye'll answer to me."

Ah, now that was more like what he had expected. James stiffened, but nodded in agreement. He had been inconsiderate of his family, especially his mother. Of course he needed to be held accountable.

"Little brother! At last ye've returned."

James turned away from his father to face his brother. Malcolm had put Davina back on her feet. She stood behind him, clutching the table with one hand, her arm around the lass, who thankfully was finally quiet.

"Malcolm." James nodded.

Something flickered in Malcolm's eyes before a welcoming smile dropped into place. James immediately went on guard, wondering what his brother was trying to conceal.

Gilroy, the captain of the McKenna guard, appeared, a large grin on his face. His shout of welcome home was followed by a loud cheer from the guard. His mother's maid came forward next, followed by his former nursemaid. With tears in their eyes, each hugged him.

All seemed genuinely happy to see him, though his nursemaid took the opportunity to scold him for being away for so long. He suffered through it all good-naturedly, but then, heaving out a breath of annoyance, James turned to face the greeting he had been avoiding.

He could not erase from his mind the sight of Davina's pale face when she recognized him, her startled look of pure torture. It cut him sharper than a blade. Despite all his efforts to control it, his heart lurched when he looked over Malcolm's shoulder and for a second time met Davina's stunned gaze.

He narrowed his eyes sharply, then briefly wondered if she'd faint again.

"Davina Armstrong. 'Tis a most unusual surprise to find ye here."

"Not an unpleasant one, I hope," she replied softly, staring at him with luminous brown eyes.

He shrugged, though secretly he felt annoyed by her remark. This was *his* home, *his* family. He had traveled a world away to forget this woman, yet here she stood.

How was that possible?

"Yer mother invited me for the holiday," Davina continued, as though she could read the question uppermost in his mind.

Her perception startled him with the memory of how close they had once been. Close enough to at times even know what the other was thinking. But that was a very long time ago.

Damnation, I need a drink!

She had taught him well that love led to pure misery. Not always, a voice in his head nagged. It had been glorious in the beginning.

Tearing himself away from her hypnotic eyes, he looked down at her long, elegant fingers clutching her wine goblet. He remembered with agonizing clarity the feel of those fingers in his hair, caressing his cheek, entwined in his hand.

He failed to contain the sigh of appreciation that escaped his lips. The urge to claim her still ran strong. Almost as strong as the wild desire he felt to caress her until her brown eyes filled with pleasure and need.

He felt himself moving forward, reaching for her hand, and snapped back. A warning to resist any senti-mental weakness stirred within him. She had rejected him utterly, completely, and finally. He was not about to give her the chance to do it again.

A heartless lass is easy to resist. Yet even as he thought the words, James knew he was being unfair. Davina had not always been heartless. She had been pure and open and loving. 'Twas his fault she had turned cold, for he failed to protect her.

"I'm Lileas McKenna," the child at her side said. "Who are ye?"

"This is yer uncle James," Malcolm answered.

The lass tilted her head to one side and considered him solemnly. "The one that grandmother lights candles fer in chapel and prays will come home?"

"Aye, and my prayers have at long last been answered," his mother replied. She appeared again at his side, clutching James's arm tightly, as though she feared he would disappear. Guilt speared him for the worry he had caused her.

Aileen pulled her son onto the dais. Everyone shifted chairs to make room for him and somehow James ended up sitting between his mother and Davina.

He felt Davina stiffen, then she became fascinated by the contents of her trencher, looking through the various bits as though she had never before seen food.

"Where are Katherine and Graham?" James asked, hoping a glimpse of his other siblings would distract him from the emotions he was feeling being so near Davina.

"Graham is training with clan Morgan. He'll be with them until spring. Katherine has made a pilgrimage to the Shrine of the Blessed Mother in Inverness," his mother replied. "She'll be returning in a week or so to celebrate Christmas."

"And Margaret?" he asked, wondering about Malcolm's wife.

The smile on his mother's face melted away. "Gone, a year this past summer. 'Twas a powerful fever that took her from us."

James's brows drew tightly together. "I'm sorry fer yer loss, Malcolm."

His brother looked momentarily regretful, but then his gaze suddenly shifted to Davina. "It was a sad blow, but it's been hardest on my poor Lileas, growing up without a mother. 'Tis a lack I hope to rectify soon."

James speared a large chunk of venison and shoved it in his mouth to avoid saying something he'd regret. He glanced over at Davina and saw the hint of discomfort, along with a dash of confusion on her face.

"It has been a rather long day." Davina abruptly stood. "If ye will excuse me, I should like to retire."

His mother nodded and Davina turned. Somehow the hem of her gown became tangled and she stumbled. James reached for her, but Malcolm was there first. He gave James a quelling look and placed his arm protectively around Davina's shoulders.

She allowed it, but only until she found her footing. She lowered herself to a graceful curtsy, then scurried away as though she were being chased by demons. James refused to watch her retreat, refused to be concerned over how her shoulders dropped and her eyes clouded with emotion.

The table became eerily quiet once she was gone. Odd, how Davina seemed to take the very air with her. Craving a distraction, James signaled for more wine. As he raised the goblet to his lips, he felt the heavy weight of a measured stare. Snapping his neck around, he met the excited eyes of his niece. She had moved to sit in Davina's seat and was now openly gawking at him.

"Shouldn't ye also be going off to bed?" he growled.

The lass shrunk back at his gruff tone, but quickly

recovered, lifting her shoulders and puffing out her small chest. "I'm not sleepy," she replied forcefully. "Why do ye have two dirks in yer belt? Papa and Grandpapa and Gilroy only have one. Do ye really need to have two? And why are ye dressed all in black? Nurse says black is the devil's color. Are ye the devil?"

James lifted his goblet higher, hiding his smile. Seeing his amusement would only encourage her and the child was already too bold by half. "If ye keep asking me rude questions, ye might be very sorry to hear the answers."

Lileas's mouth turned down in thoughtful silence. 'Twas far too cryptic a response for a young child to understand, but achieved the desired effect of silencing her.

But the quiet didn't last. She tugged insistently on his sleeve and then in a cheerful voice announced, "Lady Davina is the most beautiful lady I ever saw. I like her smile. She's going to be my new mama."

James choked on his wine.

"Goodness, are ye still spouting that bit of nonsense?" the McKenna shouted.

"Aye, when my Lileas gets something into her pretty little head, there's no getting it out," Malcolm replied fondly.

Reaching over, his brother began to tickle the lass and she shrieked with laughter. "Ye promised me, Papa," Lileas huffed, between giggles. "I want a mama."

"And ye shall have one, Poppet," Malcolm answered, swinging the child up in his arms. "But fer now, 'tis off to bed with ye."

Malcolm brought the lass to his mother and father, and they each kissed her fondly on the forehead. James could sense his brother pausing beside his chair, but he refused to look up until he heard Malcolm turn away.

He watched his brother's retreating back. Lileas's arms were wrapped tightly around her father's neck, her chin resting on his shoulder as she stared out at the dais.

James unintentionally caught her eye. Her face scrunched together and then she stuck her tongue out at him. He nearly mimicked the gesture before catching himself.

"Gracious, that child is a handful," his mother remarked cheerfully. "Perhaps it would be a good idea fer Malcolm to remarry."

"Aye, 'tis time fer him to seriously consider it," his father added. "I need grandsons to carry on the McKenna legacy."

There was a murmur of agreement from those near enough to hear the laird's remarks. James refilled his goblet and took a long drink. *God help me. 'Tis going to be a very long evening.*

Emotions scattered, Davina somehow managed to negotiate the dimly lit hallways and find her chamber. Thankfully, someone had left a candle burning, though the chamber was filled with dark shadows. Heart racing, nerves drawn tight as a bow string, she scurried to her small trunk and started pawing through it, crying out in relief when her fingers closed around the medicine bottle.

Her fingers shook, clumsy with nerves, as she struggled to remove the cork. So intent was her concentration, she didn't hear the chamber door open.

"Gracious, milady, whatever are ye doing?"

Davina bit back her startled scream and slowly got to her feet. "Help me, please," she implored, holding out the bottle.

Colleen shrank away, her face twisted with disapproval. "That's not the answer. In truth, I believe it makes things far worse."

"What?"

"Ye heard me. Forgive me fer speaking so boldly, but it needs to be said. That medicine is nothing but a crutch and one that has imprisoned ye. Just as yer aunt and uncle have done all these years."

An indignant shiver raced up Davina's spine. "They love me!"

"Aye, they do. But their coddling has not helped ye. It's made ye a prisoner in both yer mind and body."

"No longer! I'm here, away from Armstrong Castle."

"That ye are, and I cannae be prouder of how far ye have come in conquering yer demons. But rendering yerself senseless with that medicine willnae aid ye in regaining yer strength and independence."

Davina pulled her bottom lip between her teeth, worrying it back and forth as a niggling thought played over and over in her mind. Colleen had voiced one of Davina's greatest worries. She knew the benefits of the medicine had long since faded—'twas the very reason she had resisted using it for the past year.

"Take it," Davina said impulsively.

Colleen's eyes widened and Davina faltered. Yet before she could change her mind, Colleen snatched the bottle away. "What shall I do with it?"

Davina took several deep breaths until she felt calmer. "Empty the contents in the privy."

Colleen's wide smile of approval eased the bolt of panic Davina felt as the widow hurried to follow the instructions. Needing a distraction, Davina began to prepare for bed. With all the excitement of James's unexpected arrival, she doubted the servants—or Lady Aileen—would remember that she had been promised a bath.

No matter. Davina would manage. She poured water from the pitcher into a basin and washed her face and hands, not minding that it was cold.

She removed her veil and circlet and started unbraiding her hair. Colleen returned just as she finished, and the widow helped her change out of her gown and into her nightclothes.

Davina folded her hands, ready to begin her nightly prayers, but her mind froze. What could she ask of God? Relieve her of this nightmare situation? Return her to a time when the love she shared with James was young and innocent?

Knowing the impossibility of those wishes, Davina recited her usual litany of prayers and ended by asking God to bless all the McKennas and Armstrongs. She then climbed into the narrow bed and hastily pulled the furs and blankets up to her chin.

The straw mattress was firm beneath her back, but it felt luxurious after spending so many nights sleeping on the hard ground.

"Do ye have enough warm covers?" Davina asked, as Colleen settled herself on the pallet near the wall.

"Aye, 'tis a welcome feeling of warmth to snuggle beneath them. And ye?"

"I'm fine. Good night, Colleen. And thank ye fer all that ye have done."

The widow muttered a soft reply. Colleen's gentle snores soon filled the chamber. 'Twas a comfort knowing she was not alone, but the noise was distracting, making it even harder to sleep.

Davina took several deep, long breaths, shut her

eyes tight, and commanded herself to sleep. But her mind refused to quiet, playing over and over the sight of James walking into the great hall.

Muttering with frustration, Davina threw off the covers and rose from the bed. The chamber felt closed and airless. She paced its confines slowly, carefully, mindful of the sleeping Colleen. Yet it didn't help. Pale moonlight spilled from the very narrow window, drawing her toward the fresh air, but there was little breeze blowing.

Turning back to her bed, Davina yanked off a wool blanket and draped it over her shoulders. Her chamber was at the end of the short corridor. She had noticed an archway just beyond it and assumed the staircase led to the battlements—where she would find the much-needed fresh air.

Moving quietly, she left the chamber and located the staircase. Holding the blanket around her shoulders with one hand, she placed the other on the rope banister to guide her up the narrow, slippery stairs. Knowing there would be guards posted on the wall, she did not venture onto it, but instead stayed on the top step.

The cold breeze hit her full force and Davina welcomed its bracing crispness. She could feel the moisture hanging in the air and idly wondered if it would be rain or snow that fell. She tipped her head to the sky and breathed deeply, clearing her head and focusing on the best way to handle her current predicament.

She would have to leave, of course. 'Twould be impossible to stay beneath the same roof as James, as well as unfair to both of them. However, explaining her decision to Lady Aileen would prove difficult, as she could not tell that good woman why she must go without revealing her past relationship with James.

It was obvious that he had never spoken of it with his

family, and while it pained her, Davina knew she had to respect that decision. Which left her with few logical reasons for a hasty departure.

'Tis a problem to ponder with a clear head, not with wits dulled from emotion and lack of sleep.

Davina took one final breath of cold air into her lungs, then carefully turned and negotiated her way down the staircase. When she reached the bottom she paused, allowing her eyes to adjust to the darkness.

A bolt of unease swept over her at the unexpected sound of footsteps approaching. She narrowed her gaze, peering ahead, her heart dropping into her stomach at the sight of a man. He took a step toward her and Davina felt her heart thudding into her throat.

"Jesus, Davina, I thought ye were a ghost."

"James." Davina wiped her sweaty palms on her nightgown. "Ye startled me."

A shiver raced up her spine at the look he gave her. The voice inside her head was shouting for her to get away. But her feet refused to obey.

His eyes hardened. "I thought ye had gone to bed."

Davina braced herself. She was shaking at his nearness, yet refused to let him see how intimidating she found him. "I felt the need fer some air."

"Ye plan on climbing up to the battlements dressed in yer nightclothes?"

Unless ye offer to carry me. The thought struck, but wasn't spoken. She no longer had the right to joke and tease with him.

"No one saw me. I stood at the top of the stairs in the shadows fer a few minutes."

"The guards should be disciplined at their lack of attention, though I suppose ye are small enough to easily remain unseen."

She thought she could see a flash of humor lurking

in his eyes, but it was too dark to tell. "I wasn't there very long," she replied, not wanting to cause trouble.

"Come, I'll escort ye to yer chamber." James's fingers closed around her upper arm.

Davina's body tingled, the contact between them unsettling. "'Tis but a few steps away," she protested. "I can see the door from here."

She made to push past him. James immediately released her arm, but stepped in front of her.

"I dinnae believe my eyes when I entered the great hall and saw ye sitting so regally beside my brother, looking as though ye belonged there," he said.

"I . . . uhm . . ." Davina's mouth went dry. She swallowed and tried again. "Yer mother invited me to share the Christmas holiday."

"So I've been told. Yet somehow that doesn't ring true." He leered down at her. "Why are ye really here, Davina? What cruel twist of fate has brought ye within my grasp, allowing ye yet another chance to torment me?"

Davina felt no surprise at the flash of anger in his eyes. After the way things had ended between them, she fully expected him to lash out at her. 'Twas no more than she deserved. Yet the sight wounded her all the same.

Trying to conceal her dismay, she answered him truthfully. "I had no idea that ye would be here, James. If I had known, I can assure ye, I never would have come."

He made a dismissive gesture with his hand. "Are ye going to marry my brother?"

The note of jealousy in his tone brought on a rush of melancholy. Avoiding James's eyes, Davina deliberately gazed over his shoulder into the darkness. "Nay. I cannae marry Malcolm. I cannae marry any man."

James growled. Grasping her chin, he forced her to look into his eyes. "God's truth?"

"God's truth," she answered.

As quickly as it came, the anger seemed to suddenly drain out of him. "Christ's bones, Davina, ye still have the power to unman me with a single look."

"James." She whispered his name, then extended her hand to him. "I dinnae want to anger ye or stir up any bitter memories. If ye believe nothing else, ye must believe that is the truth."

He gazed down at her hand for a long moment, then looked away without touching it. Without touching her. Davina felt a fist close around her heart.

"Our memories shall remain where they belong," he declared. "Buried in the past."

"I'm not yer enemy, James."

"Truly?" He cocked his head. "I'm not so certain."

Lightning cracked and flashed through the open archway window, the white light illuminating James's features. Davina felt herself pull back. He was as handsome as the devil, but the harsh line of his jaw and the hardness in his eyes frightened her. His hard gaze held her captive for a long moment.

Listening to his voice in the darkness, she could momentarily fool herself into believing all would be right between them, but seeing him in the bright, shocking light clearly brought the reality into focus.

He was not the lad she had loved; he was a hardened, bitter warrior. And she was no longer the lass she had been. Hearing the pain in his voice made her knees feel weak. She had not been the only one to suffer these past few years. Knowing she was the cause of James's pain made her guilt surge.

Another crack of deafening thunder hit, quickly

followed by a bolt of lightning. Davina felt as though it struck her body, straining every nerve and muscle.

"I'll leave in the morning," she promised, knowing it was the least she owed him.

"Aye,'tis what I expected. After all, that's what ye do best."

"Best?"

"Aye. Run away," he said softly.

Davina felt herself stiffen defensively. But curiosity won over pride. "I thought that would please ye. Do ye not want me to leave?"

He cleared his throat. "I have little care fer yer comings and goings. It makes no difference to me if ye stay or go."

With those parting words, James turned on his heel and left.

Shaken, Davina struggled to gather her wits. A loud cough from above alerted her to the changing of the watch. Fearful of being found lurking in the hall, she hurried back to her chamber. Once safely inside, she pressed her back firmly against the solid wood, willing her heart to slow and her breathing to return to a normal rhythm.

She climbed silently back into bed. She forced her eyes to close, but sleep would not come. She turned to prayer, for strength and guidance, and then offered a prayer of hope that tomorrow would be a better day.

For surely 'twas impossible for it be worse than today.

Chapter Eight

Despite a near sleepless night, James came awake as the first rays of morning light entered his chamber. Remaining still for a moment, he rolled his head toward the door and took in his surroundings. A table with two chairs around it, three windows lined with heavy glass, a thick carpet in a pattern of blue adorning the floor, a cozy fire burning in the hearth.

'Twas only one place in the world he knew that boasted such luxury.

McKenna Castle. Home.

He was surprised at the rush of pleasure he felt at the realization. Five years ago the idea of returning here had been unthinkable. The shame too great, the guilt too strong.

He had struggled mightily under the weight of dishonor that plagued him for being unable to defend Davina. It had taken years, yet gradually James realized he would carry that burden no matter where he laid his head each night. And thus, tired of the battles, blood, and death that had been his companions for far too long, he had come home.

To what felt like a more intense inferno.

James grit his teeth, rotated the tightness out of his shoulders, and got out of bed. A sudden rush of dizziness told him he had drunk far too much last night, and he fought to remain on his feet.

Staggering, he made his way to the door and flung it open. The leather hinges squealed, the irritating sound reverberating through his aching head. Annoyance spiked anew at the sight of a young page sulking in the hall. Clearly, the lad had been assigned to wait upon him, a lowly task that somehow did not appeal.

James dragged a hand over his face, then pressed his fingers against his temples. "Fetch hot water fer washing, a pitcher of ale, and something fer me to break my fast," he barked.

Terror replaced the sulking expression on the lad's face. Eyes wide, he took off at a run. Cursing beneath his breath, James watched the lad scamper away. His throat was parched and his belly growling for food. He only hoped it would not take an unreasonable amount of time for the lad to gain the courage to return.

James shut the door and returned to sit on the edge of his bed. The piney scent of rosemary, mixed with a dash of lavender, wafting from the sheets called to him. 'Twould be so easy to turn and rest his aching head against the downy soft pillow, but James refused to succumb to the lure.

It would take more than his mother's sweet-smelling linens to break his discipline. Training and conditioning were always his first order of business and that would not change just because he was home.

Besides, a morning of tough physical activity would keep him away from Davina. The events of last night had made him clearly see that he needed to banish Davina from his thoughts, for he could not stomach the notion of reawakening his feelings toward her.

That would only lead to disillusionment and shattered dreams.

Yet it would be no easy task when he would see her each day.

The door reopened and the lad stepped inside, his skinny arms straining under the weight of all he carried. James moved forward to help, but then pulled back. The boy seemed to lack confidence. Successfully accomplishing this duty on his own would build character.

The youngster nervously drew his bottom lip back and forth between his teeth as he carefully set down the tray of food. Next came the pitcher of ale, then a none-too-clean-looking tankard. The final item was the bowl of water for washing, which the lad balanced precariously on the inside of his left arm.

"Put the water on the table near the window," James commanded.

The lad jumped, barely muffling a yelp of distress. Eyes wide, he hurried to the table and hastily set down the bowl. It wobbled unevenly, spilling a good half of the contents.

James's jaw tightened in exasperation as he watched the precious hot water drip onto the floor. Though he prided himself on being an intimidating warrior, the lad's obvious fear was making him clumsy.

"What's yer name?" James asked.

The lad's chin trembled. "Co . . . Colin, sir."

"And what day is it, young Colin?"

Confusion darkened the lad's face. "'Tis Tuesday, sir."

"Aye." James absently rubbed his fingers over the thin scar under his jaw, remembering the feel of the knife blade as it was pressed against his throat. Remembering, too, the look of surprise on the enemy's face when he had slipped a blade between the man's ribs and twisted. "Well, I dinnae eat pages fer breakfast on Tuesdays."

"No, sir."

"I reserve that delight fer Fridays. Best ye remember it."

The hoped-for smile never emerged. Instead, Colin seemed even more uneasy, his eyes growing as round as a lost kitten. Taking pity of the lad, James dismissed him with a curt wave of the hand.

"I can go?" Colin asked hopefully.

James nodded. The lad gave a ragged shudder and ran from the chamber, even as James was sure he spied a spark of gratitude in the lad's eyes.

James felt his lip curl as a familiar guilt mingled with the anger brewing inside his gut. *The lad's grateful I gave him permission to leave me. First, Davina and now Colin. Seems I've mastered the art of frightening women and children. God's teeth, what's next?*

James splashed his face and upper body with the now lukewarm water, then used the rest to wash the tankard. His stomach rebelled at the idea of food, but he ate the oatcakes and hard cheese anyway, washing it down with the ale.

He took his time getting dressed, wanting to ensure that the great hall would be empty. He was in no mood to make small talk with anyone, especially his family.

As he picked up his sword, he wondered again if he had made the right decision to leave the Holy Land. The life of a Crusader was fraught with danger, but it was in many ways a simple, uncomplicated existence. You practiced, you fought, you cleansed your wounds, buried the dead, ate a hearty meal, slept, awoke, and began again.

It was a methodical, isolating life that James had come to accept. He had grown accustomed to the physical discomfort of his body and learned to ignore the suffering that plagued his spirit.

The sun struggled to emerge from behind a large, billowing gray cloud as James walked purposefully through the bailey. He felt his blood stir as he glanced at the horizon and beheld the rugged hills soaring into the distant mists. They had been shrouded in darkness when he arrived last night. Seeing them now in all their regal splendor reminded him that there was no place on earth more beautiful than the Highlands.

Even the air smelled different, he mused, as he inhaled deeply. Filled with tangy pine and a crisp dampness, it lifted the spirits even as it seeped into the bones.

Lord, how I've missed it!

The bailey was alive with activity at this hour of the morning. Women with baskets of clean, wet laundry on their backs hurried to hang the items out to dry before the temperatures dropped low enough to freeze the garments. The fragrant smoke of fresh baked breads and savory treats streamed out from the kitchen, contrasting mightily with the scents emanating from the stables and barns.

The practice yard was crowded with men, though the usual sounds of metal clanking against metal were missing as most were engaged in conversation rather than training. When James approached, an eerie hush filled the practice yard. He spied Malcolm sparring with a young man whose chin barely sported any whiskers and suddenly knew how to banish his conflicted mood.

His brother turned, then greeted him with a broad, toothy smile. "Och, ye've finally left the warmth and comfort of yer chamber. We were wondering if ye were going to spend the entire day abed."

"Not all day," James replied. "Just a good part of the morning."

"I thought the men of God's army trained and fought tirelessly," Malcolm teased.

"They do. 'Tis a harsh life, far more difficult than the easy one the Highlanders lead." James eyed his brother, wondering how quickly he could get a rise of temper from him.

"I see that ye still enjoy training with the youngest, untried recruits. 'Tis hardly difficult to display skill and agility when one is partnered against an inexperienced youth."

The taunt had its desired effect, for it was the sort of comment James knew his brother would be unable to resist.

"Teaching our men to fight is but one of my pleasures," Malcolm replied tersely. "Care to join us?"

"I might." James assumed a disinterested stance. "If ye can find me someone worthy to spar against."

"Sir Malcolm is our best swordsman," one of the lads proclaimed, as a murmur of agreement spread through the crowd.

"Is he?" James glanced over his shoulder at his father and the McKenna nodded. "Then I suppose he is the one I shall train."

Any hint of humor faded from Malcolm's expression. "I'd be pleased to face ye."

"Yer mother willnae like it," the McKenna stated bluntly, coming to stand between his sons.

James lifted his eyes to the sky, noting the position of the sun. "Does she not usually attend Mass at this hour of the morning?"

His father looked at him, the corners of his mouth lifting slightly. "She does."

"Then we best hurry."

Several of the men shouted and clapped their hands in excited anticipation and James could hear friendly wagers being made. He was not surprised that very few favored him to win, for it was not the McKenna way to bet against the clan heir. Yet as James donned his helmet he was determined that those few who had bet that he would be victorious would be rewarded.

And all would see clearly that he, too, was a worthy son of the laird.

James grinned as he heard the satisfying hissing sound of his brother's sword being drawn from its scabbard. Muscles taut and ready, James used the element of surprise to gain the advantage. Instead of raising the usual battle cry, he charged, silently, the steel of his blade whistling through the air.

He caught Malcolm square in the gut with the flat of his sword, knocking the breath from his lungs. Malcolm released a loud grunt. Though off balance, he managed a clean sword swing, aimed directly at James's head.

James ducked and spun around so quickly his brother barely had time to blink. Yet the blade had come close enough that James swore he could feel the breeze on his face. James feinted left, then swiftly swung his sword right. Malcolm was prepared, bringing his weapon up to block the strike.

Steel struck steel in sharp clangs. Again. And again. There were cheers from the crowd at the sound. Each man moved agilely, their power and strength nearly equal. James could feel the sweat pouring down his back as he and Malcolm crossed swords up and down the yard. His brother had the advantage of height, yet James knew he was quicker.

Curses fell from Malcolm's mouth as time and again he came close, yet failed to gain an advantage. James felt the blood pounding through his veins. His battle-hardened senses were humming as he drove forward, striking again and again. Malcolm successfully deflected each blow, but he could see his brother was tiring.

Then suddenly, Malcolm caught James's blade on an upward stroke. James planted his feet firmly, but could not stay upright. He crashed to the ground in a jarring bounce. For an instant his sight blurred, but he recovered just in time to see Malcolm's blade slicing through the air toward him in a clean arc.

Howling, James raised his sword to meet the blow. It came down hard, much harder than he expected. Pain shot up James's arm and he swore he could feel the vibration in the soles of his feet. Tucking his chin to his chest, he rolled to his side and leaped to his feet. Ducking low, he threw a fist into Malcolm's stomach.

"Did ye ever see a man move so fast?" the McKenna asked in an approving tone.

Malcolm doubled over. Staggering clumsily on his feet, he lifted his chin, his eyes stirring with grudging admiration. "Ye are far more skilled at swordplay than I remember, little brother."

Appreciation for Malcolm's none-too-subtle attempt to distract him flashed in James's eyes, yet his concentration never wavered. Nor did his determination to win.

Marshalling his strength, James circled left, hoping to pull Malcolm off his feet with the next strike. But as he raised his sword, his mother's angry voice filled his ears.

"Why are James and Malcolm fighting?" she cried.

"The lads are just having a bit of fun," the McKenna explained.

"By hacking each other to bits?" Aileen retorted in annoyance.

"Not hacking, just sparring," the McKenna answered.

"Malcolm is bleeding."

"'Tis only a small scratch."

"That can fester." Aileen tapped her foot impatiently. "They wear no armor, only helmets."

"'Tis training, not a battle."

"End it. Now."

"'Twould be madness to come between them," the McKenna protested. "I could get sliced to ribbons."

Aileen let out a grunt and grabbed her husband's arm. "Now, Brian."

The McKenna threw his hands up in the air, then bellowed at the top of his voice. "Malcolm! James! Enough! Ye've both proved yer skill and heart. Stop yer swordplay!"

At the sound of his father's voice, Malcolm turned his head. Seizing the advantage, James rushed him, knocking them both to the ground. They wrestled in the dirt. James wrapped his legs around Malcolm's hips, holding him in place, but the advantage was soon lost as Malcolm lashed out, bucking upward.

"Brian!" Aileen screeched.

"I did as ye asked," the McKenna countered. "They have dropped their swords."

Malcolm threw off the hold, flinging James onto his back. Instinctively, James reached for the dirk that protruded from Malcolm's belt, brandishing it recklessly at his brother's throat.

Startled, Malcolm's body tensed with humiliation at having his own weapon held against him. The knife blade flickered in the dull sunlight and he reached to gain control of it, but James evaded the maneuver.

"There! It ends in a draw," Aileen shouted.

A draw? Clearly, I'm the victor. James narrowed his eyes and gazed up at his brother. Malcolm's face revealed his surprise and equal displeasure at their mother's verdict. It was obvious he had no intention of stopping. There was still plenty of fight left in him.

Swiftly, James weighed his options. He had the upper hand now, but that could easily change. His brother was fit and skilled and angry. Realizing it served no purpose to jab at Malcolm's already bruised pride, James dropped the dirk and raised his hands in surrender. "Ye fight with skill and honor, brother, but these past five years I fought each day to stay alive. When yer life depends on the quality of yer sword, ye fast learn a variety of tricks."

"Trickery? A true Highlander fights with honor." Malcolm scowled as he got to his feet. He held out his hand to James. After a moment's hesitation, James accepted the gesture.

"Nay, lads, a true Highlander fights to win!" The McKenna came forward and draped his left arm around Malcolm's shoulders and the right across James's. "Ye did me proud. Both of ye."

"But they stopped before a true winner was named," one of the men protested.

"It was a draw," Aileen insisted.

"Nay, Malcolm was clearly bested by his brother," a deep voice shouted. "James can claim victory."

"Och, yer eyes must have been closed during the scrimmage," another chimed. "'Twas obvious that Malcolm would carry the day."

Aileen quieted the grumblings with a single stony stare of reproach. James dragged his arm across his dripping brow and watched in amazement as his mother brought the squabbling men to heel.

The McKenna turned to his wife and raised his beefy hand. A jolt of concern bolted through James. He moved forward protectively, only to watch his father tenderly caress her cheek. The natural, genuine display of love and affection struck James harder than any blow, for it reminded him of what he had once yearned to have.

And was now forever lost.

James grit his teeth against the pain that could still unexpectedly seize him. He blinked, then blinked again, fighting it back. Years on the battlefield had taught him never to betray a weakness of any kind. And he was determined to heed that lesson well.

The exhilaration of the swordplay passed slowly from him, leaving James once again restless. Striding across the practice field, he headed toward the stables, hoping a long ride in the brisk air would clear his head.

"James!" the McKenna boomed out. "Wait fer me in my private solar. We have much to discuss."

Though used to obeying orders, James's temper heated. He preferred solitude right now, not company. But one look at the expression of impatience on his father's face told James he had little choice in the matter. Resigned, he turned away from the stables.

His mood improved once he was inside, traversing the hallway on the way to the McKenna's solar. Winking at a serving lass who scurried past him, James snatched a full tankard of ale off the tray she carried. He gulped it as he walked, the cold brew pleasingly quenching his parched throat and helping to even out his temper.

The chamber was empty when he arrived, but within

minutes the door opened. Rising respectfully to his feet, James was startled to see his brother standing in the doorway. Malcolm favored him with an unenthusiastic glare and took up a position near the long, thin, window.

"Father commanded my presence," James explained, hoping his tone conveyed how little he wanted to be there.

Malcolm shrugged as if it didn't matter, but James could see his jaw moving back and forth in agitation. There was, however, no chance for further comments. The door opened and his parents entered. The sight of his mother startled James for an instant, and then a small grin emerged.

Lady Aileen wielded nearly as much power as her husband, especially when it came to family business. Naturally, she would want to be a part of any private conversations that involved her son.

James placed his tankard on a nearby table and politely offered his mother a seat. Aileen patted him affectionately on the arm before settling herself regally in the cushioned chair. As he looked down, James caught sight of a few gray hairs nestled among his mother's auburn tresses. The obvious sign of her aging caused him a pang of distress.

The McKenna narrowed his gaze and turned his full attention toward James. "Yer mother and I were sorely distressed to have ye leave us so suddenly."

"I sent word," James replied, knowing that was hardly an adequate defense.

The McKenna grunted with exasperation. "Ye wrote that you were following James Douglas on Crusade. What happened?"

A twinge of unease swept through James. Part of the reason he had avoided returning these past few years was knowing this day of reckoning would come. Yet how much of the truth was he prepared to reveal?

"As I'm sure that you know, Sir James was killed in Moorish Granada," he began. "We found his body and the casket containing the Bruce's embalmed heart upon the battlefield. Sir William Keith brought them both back to Scotland."

His father's accusing eyes met his. "Yet ye dinnae return."

"Nay, there were many who decided to stay and continue the fight."

"We've heard no reports of great victories," Malcolm interjected.

"Alas, we dinnae achieve our goal to reach the heart of the Holy Land. 'Twould have been glorious, indeed, to set foot in the Church of the Holy Sepulchre, and stand upon the very spot where Jesus rose from the dead."

Aileen released a hearty sigh and hastily crossed herself.

"I dinnae realize ye possessed such religious fever," Malcolm said dryly.

"Each of us show our devotion in our own way," James replied breezily.

"Tell us more about yer time across the sea," his mother pleaded.

James's brow furrowed. But he knew he owed them some explanation, so for the next thirty minutes he calmly answered their questions, though he deliberately glossed over the details of the more intense fighting. There was no need for his mother to hear how his head had nearly been severed from his body during the siege of Teba when he lost his footing on the blood-soaked ground. Or how he had single-handedly killed six men and wounded five others in a skirmish on Olvera Castle.

"Well, that is enough of my adventures," James said when he ran out of acceptable tales. "Tell me the news of the McKenna clan."

"Well, while ye have been off fighting fer the glory of the Church, we've had our own difficulties to face," Malcolm said.

"Is there much unrest in the land?" James asked.

"Enough." His father shrugged. "Some of the clan chiefs hunger fer power and prey on the weaker clans. Without a strong king on the throne to stop them, they grow ever bolder. 'Tis why alliances are now more important than ever."

"Aye, nothing has changed. It's not uncommon fer yer friend to turn into yer foe without any warning," Malcolm grunted. "We Highlanders must always be vigilant."

Aileen pursed her lips. "When I broke my fast this morning, I heard some of the men saying that ye were attacked on yer way home from Armstrong Castle, Malcolm. Why did ye not tell me?"

His mother crossed her arms and glared at Malcolm. His brother favored her with a winning smile, which miraculously seemed to soften her anger. "There's naught to tell. We fought off the knaves, incurring only a few superficial wounds. Neither Lady Davina nor her companion was harmed."

"Another easy victory fer the mighty McKenna warriors," James remarked, scowling inwardly at the thought of his brother doing what he had failed to accomplish—protecting Davina.

"The McKenna men fought bravely, but I'm not so

vain as to believe these ruffians ran when they saw our strength," Malcolm said.

"Perhaps once they drew near, they realized ye had nothing of great value," the McKenna suggested.

"Then why would they attack in the first place?" Malcolm shook his head. "Nay, this was not an ordinary raid. The men wore no plaids, carried no banners. We had a sizable contingent of retainers. We had no carts laden with goods that would attract a band of ambitious thieves. They were after something else. I'm sure of it."

"Something else?" Aileen idly rubbed her fingertips over the skirt of her woolen gown. "Or *someone* else?"

James was so startled by his mother's revelation that he promptly broke his vow to remain silent and uninvolved. "Do ye believe they were after Davina?"

Aileen shrugged her shoulders and raised her hands. "She is an heiress."

"Of a small, insignificant keep," James added.

"Have ye seen it?" Malcolm asked.

"Nay. But Davina spoke of it often, as it was her childhood home. Her father was a second son; the land belonged to his mother and she bequeathed it to him when she died. 'Tis a small place, on rough terrain, best fer raising sheep. I cannae believe that any would bother to fight to possess it."

"Well, someone sees its value," Malcolm speculated.

"Kidnapping an heiress and making her yer wife is one of the easier ways fer a man to obtain property," Aileen commented dryly.

"Ye mean *cowardly*," Malcolm interjected.

James found himself nodding in agreement.

The McKenna stroked his chin thoughtfully. "This will continue to be a problem fer the lass until she weds.

The best way to protect her now, and in the future, is to make certain that she has a strong husband. A good Highlander, skilled with his sword, loyal to the crown, would be the ideal match." He paused, looking first at Malcolm and then at James. "Are either of you interested in taking on the responsibility?"

Chapter Nine

Startled, James took a step forward. Annoyance crawled over his face at his father's poor humor, which quickly turned to irritation when he realized that his father was serious. Impossible! Yet a second, harder look proved that the McKenna didn't alter his expression or his firm stance, indicating he expected an answer from his sons.

James managed to keep his expression blank, yet wondered if his family could hear the grating of his teeth.

"Will ye not merely be taking on whatever troubles ye imagine come with the lass by bringing her into the clan?" James questioned.

"'Tis possible." The McKenna's attention focused on James. "But we could also be gaining fer the clan whatever these men seek."

James went still. He had had years to wonder if there was more behind the ambush on the hill that had ended his relationship with Davina and caused him to leave Scotland. But he had never been able to devise a reasonable cause. "The Highlands are a refuge fer all sorts of unsavory men. 'Tis no surprise that some of them would prey on travelers."

"Even an outlaw knows better than to attack a McKenna," Malcolm boasted.

James snorted in annoyance. "Ye have no proof that it was Lady Davina these men were after."

"But I've a feeling about it. A strong feeling," the McKenna answered stubbornly.

'Twas only through sheer will that James was able to resist rolling his eyes. His father's *feelings* were legendary and unfortunately over the years had proven to be correct just enough times to give them credence.

"We still have no right to pick a husband fer the lass," James insisted, trying a different tack. "'Tis a duty reserved fer her family."

"Aye." Intrigue radiated from the McKenna's eyes. "'Tis also a duty that has been sorely neglected. And it's clearly put the lass at risk."

"She wouldn't be at risk if she were where she belonged," James muttered. "Safely ensconced within the walls of Armstrong Castle."

"We can claim a distant relation to the Armstrongs from my father's mother," Aileen offered. "Her sister married into the clan."

"When? Sixty, seventy years ago?" James rubbed his temples. "That scarcely gives us the right to arrange a marriage fer her. Which brings me to another question—why is she even here?"

"I invited her to celebrate Christmas with us," his mother said. "I've wanted to meet her fer quite a while. We began a regular correspondence a few years ago, each seeking solace in our friendship. Though her letters never made direct mention of it, I could not shake the feeling that she's been a prisoner inside the walls of her family home fer years. 'Tis also another reason why I wanted her to come here, so I could see fer myself if it was true."

"Is it?" James asked impatiently.

He could see his mother's back stiffen. "Well, she has only just arrived. I've not yet had the opportunity to find out."

"'Tis true that her aunt and uncle acted oddly when she told them she intended to journey here," Malcolm volunteered. "But they dinnae prevent her from leaving."

"Perhaps they wanted her to leave so she could be taken in the woods," the McKenna said. "Those men might have been acting under the orders of her relatives."

"That seems a most far-fetched notion," James scoffed. "Especially since she resides under their roof. She is already under their control."

"I agree that something strange is going on," Aileen said. "Yer father is right to be concerned about the lass. The only way to secure her safety is to make certain she has a husband to protect her."

"I'll say it again, 'tis no business of ours," James insisted, searching for support from his brother. Malcolm could not possibly be in favor of this mad plan. But his brother met James's desperate gaze with curious interest.

Malcolm glanced at their mother. "I agree it could be the best solution."

James narrowed his eyes and took a deep breath before blurting out, "God's blood, ye cannae force her to marry!"

"Who said anything about forcing the wee lass?" The McKenna stared innocently back at his son. "Yer mother would have my head served on a platter if I demanded such a thing."

Aileen's head bobbed in agreement. "Though most think differently, I find it barbaric fer a man to take a bride against her will. I would never allow it. Nay, Davina will be given a choice of husband."

"And what of our choice?" James asked.

"I'll be giving ye the same power. Ye are free to decide if Lady Davina would be a suitable bride," the McKenna answered. "If ye both decide against it, I'm sure we can find another member of the clan who is worthy of the honor."

"Truth be told, 'tis something I'm already considering," Malcolm said casually. "She's a different sort, but a fine lady nevertheless. And Lileas likes her."

"Aye, but does she like Lileas?" The McKenna laughed and Aileen joined him.

James sucked in a loud breath. He started to walk away, then turned and stared at Malcolm, frustrated when he realized he could not read the emotion on his brother's face. Was Malcolm jesting? Or was he serious about taking Davina as his bride?

The impact of such an event struck James hard. Wounds he believed had healed slowly began to open and fester. He knew the trauma that Davina had suffered; he knew her reasons for not wanting to marry.

But that had happened years ago. Perhaps she was now ready to put the past behind her and consider becoming a wife. To Malcolm? James gave his brother a hard look. He was the heir, the one with more to offer. Yet beyond the material, women found him charming, clever, and fascinating.

Would Davina feel the same? The very idea rankled, taunting James. Frustration and anger rose inside him. Was it merely fate or bad luck that always seemed to place Malcolm in the more advantageous position?

"So, will there be a contest between us, James, to see

who can win the lovely Davina?" Malcolm smiled affably, but underneath was a steel glint of determination. No matter what the competition, his brother despised losing.

"Nay. 'Tis a game I have no stomach to play," James replied airily, hiding his tightly clenched hands behind his back. "If ye want her, and win her, then she is yers."

Even as he spoke the words, James knew he was deluding himself. Witnessing his brother claim Davina for his wife would be torture, a blow from which he might never recover.

And yet, he refused to say anything more on the matter.

"The McKenna wants to see ye," the maid said as she waylaid Davina in the hall. "I'm to take ye to his private solar."

A sense of unease stole over Davina. She swallowed back her nerves as all manner of thoughts entered her mind. Why did the laird want to see her privately? Had James said something to his father about her? Would she be asked to leave?

"Is something amiss?" Davina asked.

The servant hitched her shoulders, indicating her lack of knowledge. "'Tis the laird's business and none of my concern."

Yet despite her show of indifference, Davina could see the woman was bursting with curiosity. Castle life could become rather tedious, especially in the winter months when many were confined indoors. A juicy bit of gossip was something to savor and share, and the individual relating the news was often filled with self-importance. No doubt the maid was as eager to learn the cause of the summons as Davina.

Davina's mind continued to spin as she followed the maid. All too soon they stood in front of the closed door. The servant cast a sympathetic glance her way before respectfully withdrawing. Davina wiped her damp palms on the skirt of her gown, shook off her nervous thoughts, then timidly knocked.

A booming voice bade her to enter. Taking a deep breath, she pushed open the heavy oak door, coming up short when she saw that the laird was not alone in the chamber.

Malcolm stood near a narrow window, while James was at the opposite side. Malcolm smiled in welcome; James scowled. Ignoring them both—and the tension in the room—Davina turned her attention to the laird. She dropped a formal curtsy, then took the seat the McKenna indicated beside Lady Aileen. The older woman reached over and patted her hand reassuringly.

Davina's momentary relief quickly faded as all eyes turned toward her. She felt a sudden chill run up her spine. Folding her hands demurely in her lap, she struggled to overcome her foreboding.

"We were discussing yer journey here and the unpleasantness that occurred in the woods," the McKenna said abruptly. "I want to know what ye think of the matter."

Davina's tongue touched her lips. People rarely sought her opinion and never so directly. Apparently the laird did not feel the need to make small talk before easing into the business he wished to address.

"Our traveling party was attacked without warning or provocation. Sir Malcolm and his men fought bravely to keep me and my companion, Colleen, safe," she replied. "I am grateful and relieved that none were seriously injured and that nothing of value was stolen."

"Well said, lass." The McKenna nodded approvingly.

"But now that we have had some time to think upon the incident, we need to understand why the men attacked."

"They were thieves, were they not?"

"Most likely." The laird's sharp eyes narrowed upon her. "But we believe the treasure they sought to steal was ye."

"Me? That's impossible."

"Men will do almost anything to secure the hand of an heiress," the McKenna insisted. "'Tis the best, logical explanation."

"Hardly the only one," Davina muttered. "Besides, if a man had an honorable offer of marriage, he need only approach my uncle."

Where he would be soundly rejected. At my request.

The laird cocked his head. "Perhaps this man did and yer uncle turned him away. We all know a Highlander doesn't like to be denied."

"Aye, ye would not be the first Scottish bride kidnapped by an eager groom." Malcolm cleared his throat loudly. "I've heard tell that some lasses think it's romantic."

"Hogwash!" Lady Aileen reached over and slapped her son on the arm. "No woman would find being taken by force romantic."

A spot of color flushed Malcolm's cheeks. "I dinnae say I agreed with it. I was merely stating the fact."

Davina could feel her shoulders tense. If the laird only knew the truth about her, he would realize the absurdity of this conversation. Yet pride held her tongue from revealing her full circumstances. "There have been no offers of marriage. My uncle would have told me."

The McKenna frowned. "He might not have troubled ye with an offer that he felt was unworthy. That could prompt a man who was turned away to take matters into his own hands."

Davina's mind churned. It was true that her uncle would have neglected telling her of a marriage proposal that he rejected. But what man would be daft enough to suggest it? All the local clans knew she was a recluse and surely thought her an oddity.

Nay, the idea is absurd.

Davina stared at her knotted hands. "I am a woman of little consequence. I can assure ye that no man would waste his time trying to kidnap me."

"Yer modesty is admirable, though misplaced." The McKenna smiled. "But ye cannae deny that ye need protection and I've found a solution that will be sure to please ye. What do ye say to a Christmas wedding?"

"Fer me?" Davina squeaked.

"Aye. Either of my sons would make ye a fine husband."

Davina bolted upright in her seat. She suddenly found it difficult to breathe.

"Och, Brian, ye've made a fine mess of things," Aileen shouted at her husband. "The poor lass has gone as white as a linen shift."

"She's surprised, that's all, and filled with maidenly nerves," the McKenna insisted. "Once she has a moment to think upon it, I'm sure she'll be delighted at my suggestion."

A stunned silence tied Davina's tongue in knots. The very idea of marriage was unthinkable given her unease around men, though to be honest, she had made considerable progress in overcoming those feelings since arriving at McKenna Castle.

But marriage? 'Twas impossible!

She took a few calming breaths before formulating

her reply. "I am touched by yer concern fer me. Truly. However, I have no intentions of getting married."

"Ever?"

Davina pulled her mouth into a thin line and nodded. "I'll never wed."

The McKenna scratched his head. "Why not?"

Inadvertently, Davina's eyes flew to James, worried about what he might have told his family about their past relationship. But his expression was shuttered, giving her no clues.

With difficulty, she managed to find her tongue again. "My reasons fer remaining unwed are my own and have naught to do with ye, milord."

For an instant Davina fretted that her words had insulted him, but instead of appearing angry, the laird smiled at her. "I knew there was a bit of fire and boldness inside ye, lass. 'Tis good to see it fer myself."

Davina felt a smile form on her lips. "Though it makes no sense, I feel glad to have pleased ye."

"Then ye can please me even more by agreeing to marry one of my sons."

"Ye are wrong to think I was nearly kidnapped." She hesitated, then spoke from the heart. "But, if that were true, am I to be rescued from one man only to be given to another?"

"We willnae *give* ye to any man," Lady Aileen insisted. "The choice will be yers."

The McKenna nodded his head enthusiastically. "Malcolm and James will court ye, properly and respectfully."

James cleared his throat loudly. "I've already said that my brother alone will have the privilege of courting Lady Davina. 'Twill make her choice much easier."

Too surprised to hide her dismay, she allowed a small gasp to escape her lips. James would not court her?

Her cheeks reddened. "My uncle wouldn't approve," Davina said.

"He willnae object to an alliance with the McKenna clan," the laird said. "Especially when he sees how happy ye are at the match."

Davina could feel the edges of panic starting to invade. The McKenna was like a hungry dog refusing to give up a bone. She looked to Aileen for support, but the older woman smiled with approval. Malcolm was also smiling pleasantly and James, well, there was a flicker in his eyes that was impossible to read.

"I cannae marry without my uncle's approval."

"I'll deal with yer uncle when the time comes," the McKenna insisted. "All ye have to do is make a decision."

"And if I refuse?" she dared to ask.

Though he didn't move a muscle, Davina could feel the laird tense. "We have nearly sixty eligible men in the clan who would be honored to have ye as their wife. If ye refuse my sons, there are others to woo ye. Mark my words. Before the last of the Christmas greenery is taken down from the great hall, ye'll be a McKenna bride."

The brigand swore as the icy wind howled, cutting through the worn wool cloak he wore. 'Twas ripped in spots, patched in others, but it was his best garment, taken last year from a corpse after a knife fight. He was not anxious to report another failure, yet the two hours he'd been kept waiting were starting to anger him.

A rustling noise drew his attention, and the brigand moved, turning toward the sound. His breath caught in surprise when a familiar hooded, cloaked figure presented itself in front of him. The brigand shivered again, wondering at the seemingly mystical powers that were always swirling around his mysterious employer.

"Where is Lady Davina?"

The brigand hung his head. "We dinnae get her."

The cloaked figure scowled and looked at him in disgust. "Why not?"

The brigand cleared his dry throat. "There were too many experienced fighters guarding her."

A withering silence answered him. He could see the fabric of the cloak trembling in anger. Nervously, he continued. "Several of my men were hurt, two badly."

The gloved hand flashed in front of him. "And why would any of that be my concern? Ye were hired to steal her away and leave her somewhere near, so she could be easily found by her kin."

He swallowed. "Ye dinnae tell me that the McKennas would be riding as escort, led by Malcolm McKenna himself, nor that there would be so many men protecting her."

"And ye dinnae tell me that ye were a buffoon! Ye took my coin and said that ye'd have no trouble doing as I bid because ye were such a skilled fighter."

The insult stung, all the more because it held some truth. Frustrated, the brigand wrenched a nearby branch so hard it snapped off the tree. "The odds were uneven."

"Ye should have planned better."

"I could have been better prepared if I had more coin," the brigand retorted, his voice rising. "Ye paid me a pittance of what ye promised."

"And I'll not pay ye any more until the job is finished. Properly, as I asked," the figure answered, scowling darkly.

The brigand cringed, fists at the ready. But beating the person who had promised him payment was foolish. He had two bairns to feed, plus his widowed sister's three hungry children. Honest work was hard to find and would not provide him with the necessary coin to keep them all from starving.

Silently fuming, the brigand schemed, then tried to negotiate. "Lady Davina will be safely tucked away behind the walls of McKenna Castle. 'Tis a fortress not even an army can breach."

"A lackwit as well as a mediocre fighter," the figure taunted. "It appears that I must find a far more clever man to do this job."

"Wait!" the brigand cried. "I dinnae say it couldn't be done. Only that it would be harder."

"Beyond yer skill?"

"Nay! But I'll need more men and more money."

The figure's hand curled into a fist. "More?"

The brigand stiffened. "It willnae be easy to entice men to challenge the McKennas. But the promise of gold will make a difference."

"'Tis yer fault she reached the castle in the first place," the figure scoffed. "Why should yer failure cost me?"

The brigand narrowed his eyes. "We both know that given the circumstances, no other man could have taken her alive. Ye might not think me the best choice, but ye'll have to search high and low to find someone willing to try and snatch her from the McKennas."

The figure hesitated, raising the brigand's hopes. He heard the soft jangle of coins and felt a rush of relief when a small leather pouch appeared. He eagerly reached for it, cursing loudly when it was pulled away.

"This is yer last chance," the figure warned. "If ye fail, ye'll not be seeing me again."

The brigand licked his lips. "I want double that amount if I get her out alive."

"Nay!"

The brigand puffed out his chest in a bold show of bravado, but inside he was twisting with nerves. "The risk is far greater. Double the original price is more than fair."

The figure started to protest, then quieted and slowly held out the pouch. "Ye will earn double if Lady Davina is taken from the castle and left on Armstrong land."

The brigand swiped the pouch before it vanished again, feeling its weight. 'Twas far lighter than he had hoped. His men would grumble at the small share, but it was better than walking away with nothing.

Taking a calculated risk, the brigand dared to strike one last bargain. "If we are caught, the McKennas will fight hard to save the lady."

"I believe we have already established that fact," the figure snapped.

"If the lady is injured, will ye still pay me?"

The figure nodded, a scant shift of the chin. "Aye, if she's injured I'll pay ye the price we just agreed. Nothing more." The figure turned, tensed, then turned back. "But if she dies, I'll pay ye double."

Shocked, the brigand sucked in a breath. Killing Lady Davina would indeed make his job easier, but his stomach roiled at slaying an innocent young woman. Yet if that was what needed to be done in order to be paid, he had few choices.

The brigand watched the cloaked figure walk away, pondering this latest twist. He knew that they could be emotional, irrational, and unpredictable, but until he heard those instructions spoken so coldly, he never realized the full truth.

A woman could be as cruel and ruthless as a man.

Chapter Ten

"There ye are! I was worried that ye'd be packing yer trunks and planning yer escape," Lady Aileen cried.

Davina's head whirled. She had been sitting in the chapel contemplating her choices—which were very few—praying for divine guidance. None had been forthcoming.

"I would never be so rude as to slip away without saying good-bye," Davina said formally.

"I know." Lady Aileen sat beside her and gently patted her knee, as if aught were amiss. "We might have only met yesterday, but thanks to our years of correspondence, I feel as though I know ye well. I hoped that ye'd felt the same about me."

The words struck Davina like a blow. "I did feel the same. Until this morning."

Lady Aileen nodded. "Trust, once lost, is hard to reclaim. But I have not betrayed ye, Davina."

"Then why did ye not object when the laird said he would see me married to a McKenna?"

Lady Aileen peered over her shoulder. Only after she had examined every corner of the chapel and determined they were alone did she speak. "Brian

McKenna is a good man, with many fine qualities. He's also as stubborn as a summer day is long. I've been married to him for enough years to know that there's no use in wasting yer breath when he has his mind set on something. And fer some peculiar reason that I cannae claim to fully understand, he has his mind set on ye marrying a McKenna."

Hopelessness washed over Davina. "I cannae do it."

"Och, child, I never said that ye would. Forgive my boastful words, but ye'll find no better husband in all of the Highlands than my sons." Lady Aileen peered at her with interest. "The McKenna is wise in the way of warfare. He would never underestimate a threat and he believes there is one against ye. That's why he insists ye take a husband."

"I dinnae question the laird's sincerity. But he is wrong in this instance and I fear his mistake will cost me dearly." Davina pulled in a long breath. "I absolutely cannae marry," she added passionately.

"So ye've said."

"And I shall keep saying it until someone truly hears it!"

"Yer vehemence is rather puzzling. Marriage is a natural state fer a woman, especially one of noble birth. If ye had a religious calling, then ye'd be in a convent. Part of the reason ye came here was so that we could offer each other comfort in our melancholy, but that wouldn't prevent ye from marrying." Lady Aileen's elegant brow arched. "Do ye already have a husband?"

"Nay! Of course not!" Davina deepened her voice to emphasize the seriousness of her statements. "But there are reasons. Good reasons. Solid reasons."

Lady Aileen cleared her throat. "Will ye tell me?"

Davina opened her mouth, but Lady Aileen held

up her hand to stop her. "Besides needing yer uncle's approval."

Despite her resolve not to, shame warmed Davina's cheeks. She squirmed under Lady Aileen's shrewd gaze, for the older woman's eyes missed no detail, however small and insignificant. Davina stared at the floor, struggling to find the words, then met Aileen's gaze. Her voice was taut with emotion over the embarrassing words she must speak.

"A man expects his bride to be pure. I fear that I might not be a virgin," Davina admitted, with as much dignity as she could muster.

"Might? Ye dinnae know?"

"I . . . well . . ." *Heavens above, I sound like a half-wit!* Davina wrung the fabric of her gown between her hands, took a deep calming breath, and let the words tumble out. "I'm uncertain. A few years ago, I was brutally attacked, possibly violated, but I cannae remember. When I finally healed, the midwife examined me, but she said she cannae always tell if a lass is still a maid. She couldn't tell with me."

Lady Aileen's eyes filled with sympathy. "'Tis a sad tale and I am sorry fer what ye have suffered. But if ye marry a Highlander over the age of sixteen, I daresay he willnae be chaste."

Davina scoffed. "We both know there is a vast difference between what is expected of a groom and a bride. She must be pure, unsullied, untouched."

"Hmmm. Well, that might be true, but not all women go to their bridal beds virgins and most grooms dinnae even realize it. There are ways to, uhm, shall we say *disguise* the truth."

A strange flicker of guilt struck Davina's heart. She did know of these things and was ashamed to admit that she had thought about it, yet knew, in good conscience, she could never follow through with it. That is, if there even were a chance for her to marry. "I couldn't start a marriage on such a lie."

Lady Aileen's gaze never shifted. "So, ye would not try to deceive him, to pretend an innocence, to smear blood on the bed linens that wasn't yer own?"

"Nay! I'd have to tell him the whole truth before we took our vows."

"Even though he'd then have the right to walk away from ye?"

"Aye." Davina nodded vigorously.

"Well, given yer circumstances, if he walked away, then he wouldn't be worth keeping, would he?" Lady Aileen concluded with a triumphant grin.

The logic of the argument left Davina speechless for a moment. If only it were so simple. "There are other reasons," she ventured lamely.

Lady Aileen sent another pitying look in Davina's direction. "Apparently."

"I cannae speak of them."

"Then I'll badger ye no longer to share yer secrets."

"Thank ye, Lady Aileen," Davina said softly.

"I thought ye were going call me Aileen," the older woman scolded in a teasing voice.

"Aileen." Davina corrected herself with another blush. "I'm so relieved that ye understand and support my position."

"I do, but ye must trust me, Davina. The McKenna has his mind set on Malcolm and James courting ye. He'll be neigh on impossible to live with if he doesn't get his way." Aileen's eyes came alive with devilish mischief. "Therefore, ye must allow my sons the chance to earn yer affections and try to win yer hand. 'Tis the only way to appease the McKenna."

Davina's shoulders tensed. "But I willnae—"

"Aye, aye, ye willnae marry," Aileen interrupted, waving her hand expressively. "I understand. Ye willnae be forced, no matter how loud the McKenna bellows. Despite outward appearances, at his core, my husband is a reasonable man. If I counsel caution in this matter, he will listen."

"But will ye? Counsel caution?"

Aileen's eyes snapped with sincerity. "I make ye that solemn vow, here and now in this most holy chapel."

Aileen's promise sent Davina's mind in a whirl. She would have preferred to have the matter firmly settled and avoid the discomfort of being courted, but according to Aileen that was impossible.

"I cannae help but feel that I am willfully deceiving yer husband and Malcolm and that makes me most uncomfortable," Davina admitted.

"There is no deception in allowing yerself to be courted, even if yer mind is set against marriage," Aileen insisted. "And who knows, ye might very well change it. People wed fer many reasons: fer alliances, fer property, fer companionship, and a lucky few marry fer love. But in the end, a marriage is what the pair make of it."

"What about ye?" Davina asked.

Aileen smiled. "I thought my Brian was handsome, fierce, and far too full of himself. But I saw deep affection in his eyes whenever he gazed at me and I knew that if he ever fell in love with me, he'd be passionate, faithful, and loyal. 'Twas enough fer me to take the gamble."

"Were ye in love with him?"

"He made my pulse quicken whenever he was near and his kisses curled my toes. But I dinnae start to truly love him until he left to fight with the Bruce, a few months after we wed. When he rode through those gates, he took my heart with him.

"Some couples start out in love and lose it, others find love through the years together and come to cherish it. For some love is a great passion, for others 'tis comfort and security. Sometimes it matters, sometimes not. There are those who feel betrayed by love and others who are relieved to be spared the complications. Ye have yer reasons fer refusing to take a husband, but I urge ye to put them aside and ask yerself what ye would want from a marriage."

"To be left alone," Davina answered ruefully.

Aileen burst out laughing. "Well, ye certainly are stubborn enough to be a wife. I ask only that ye keep yer mind and heart open to the idea of becoming my daughter-in-law."

Bells of warning sounded in Davina's head. She believed Aileen would keep her vow and not force a wedding. But it was also clear that Aileen held out hope that Davina would change her mind and indeed marry a McKenna.

If she was going to follow Aileen's advice, Davina realized she needed to be cautious.

"Would ye care to join me in a game of chess, Davina?"

Davina looked up from the embroidery in her lap. Malcolm's smile flashed with so much glimmering charm, she blinked. "I have little skill at the game. I fear ye would find me a most unsatisfactory opponent."

"Yer modesty does ye credit." He smiled again, pulled a small table between them, and began setting up the board and pieces. "I'm sure ye will lead me on a merry chase."

"Sir?"

"Around the board," he clarified.

Davina nodded, her mouth dry. She had spent the morning in the woman's solar, but in the afternoon had chosen to work on her sewing beside the warmth of one of the large fireplaces in the great hall. It had been quiet and peaceful when she arrived; she assumed it would remain that way until preparations for the evening meal began.

Apparently she was mistaken.

Her stomach quailed at the idea of Malcolm paying court to her, but she had promised Aileen and was not about to go back on her word. Reluctantly, she put down her sewing and turned her attention to the board. The pieces were beautifully carved, with fine detail. Under different circumstances, Davina realized she would have enjoyed the opportunity to play with them.

They started the game in silence. Davina had not lied when she said she was not very experienced at the game, but Malcolm was quick to offer advice. He would hum, quirk his brow, or clear his throat each time she began a move. Rather than annoying, Davina found the silent advice helpful, for it caused her to rethink each move carefully before she made it.

"I'd forgotten how much this game is like warfare," she commented, as Malcolm captured her bishop. "As a knight, ye have the advantage."

"'Tis also a game of strategy and wits, which gives ye more than an equal chance at victory."

Och, he is good. Flattering her looks was too obvious a ploy, but commenting on her intelligence certainly got her attention.

They reached for her queen at the same time and his fingertips brushed across her hand. A teasing smile curved his lips, causing a pair of dimples to appear in his cheeks. Davina swiftly lowered her gaze. *I willnae be charmed by him!*

"Lady Davina, ye are still here!" Lileas cried out excitedly from across the great hall, then she broke into a run.

A long-haired hound trotted beside her, so large it towered over the child. For a moment Davina feared the animal would knock her to the ground, but despite its formidable size, it seemed inherently gentle, allowing Lileas to lead the way.

"This is Prince," Lileas explained. "He's my dog."

Hearing his name, Prince immediately began wagging his tail, swishing it across the stone floor. He had thick fur of varying shades of white and gray and expressive brown eyes.

"He is a very fine animal, indeed," Davina remarked. "Hello, Prince."

She closed her fist and held out her hand, appreciating the dog's friendly manner. It sniffed her knuckles, then lowered its head to sniff at her skirt. Apparently deciding that he liked what he smelled, Prince promptly sat beside her, leaned heavily against her leg, and placed his head in her lap.

Lileas burst into giggles. "He likes ye!"

"He's usually slow to take to strangers, but he's made his opinion clear. I always said that Prince was a highly intelligent dog," Malcolm added, humor in his tone.

"I'm sure he just smells the remains of the noon meal on my fingers," Davina insisted, though she was secretly pleased at the dog's affection. 'Twas a welcome relief knowing the animal wanted nothing more from her than a friendly pet.

Davina obligingly rubbed the dog behind his ears.

He snuggled closer and began making a rumbling noise deep in his belly, reminding her of a purring cat.

"Do ye have a dog?" Lileas asked.

"Nay, not a special fellow like Prince. At Armstrong Castle, the hunting dogs are kept in the kennels, though when the weather is bitterly cold they are allowed in the great hall. But they must stay in the corner and not bother anyone."

Lileas scrunched her nose. "That's mean. I would cry and cry if Prince couldn't sleep in my bed."

"Goodness, that great beastie sleeps with ye? Ye must have a very big bed." Davina laughed.

"Grandma says Prince smells, so Papa gives him a bath. But he doesn't like it and tries to run away."

Davina smiled, imagining a damp Malcolm chasing after the energetic dog. "Who doesn't like the bath—Prince or Papa?"

"Both!" Malcolm interjected. "My mother nearly fainted the first time she found Prince in Lileas's bed, but Lileas believes the dog protects her, so I persuaded my mother to allow it."

"Ah, there appears to be much that Lileas is allowed," Davina remarked.

"Aye, she's a spoiled little hellion and it's all my fault," Malcolm replied cheerfully.

"Prince is just like Guinefort. He's a saint dog." Lileas threw her arms around Prince's middle and hugged him tightly.

Davina wrinkled her brow. "I've heard the tale of Guinefort. He was the noble dog who guarded his master's child, killing a snake that tried to bite the babe as it lay sleeping in its cradle."

"Aye," Malcolm said. "Though when the nurse who had left the child alone returned, all she saw was the dog's bloodied mouth and head. She feared the dog had killed the child and screamed long and loud. The child's mother heard the screams, rushed in, saw the bloody dog, thought the same, and she too began screaming.

"When the master came, he also believed the dog had killed the child, so he drew his sword and slayed Guinefort. 'Twas only after he approached the cradle and found the child unharmed did he realize his tragic mistake. And when he discovered the snake torn to pieces by the dog's bites, he knew that Guinefort had in fact saved the babe."

"Guinefort went right to heaven, didn't he, Papa," Lileas stated confidently.

"He did, sweetheart."

"I'm glad." Lileas hugged the dog again.

Davina gave Prince a final pet on the head, then put her hand in her lap. The dog immediately began nudging her fingers with his cold, wet nose, demanding more attention. Davina smiled and complied, scratching him roughly behind the ears.

"If ye keep that up much longer, I fear that beast will never leave ye alone," Malcolm warned.

"Prince is the one male in this castle whose attention I dinnae mind," Davina answered truthfully.

Malcolm cleared his throat. Davina's shoulders tightened as she realized how rude her comment had been, but she did not retract it. Better that Malcolm realized sooner rather than later that she did not solicit his attention.

"Dinnae be so quick to turn me away," he said quietly. "Give it a chance, Davina. Perhaps in time yer heart will soften toward me."

His words were heartfelt, making her reply harder. But say it she must. "I'm enjoying myself this afternoon, 'tis true, and fer that I thank ye. But I must be honest and tell ye that I willnae marry ye. I willnae marry any man, despite yer father's determination."

The resigned look she hoped to see on Malcolm's face was not forthcoming. Instead, he flashed a charming, confident grin. "Then I shall be equally honest. I've overcome many obstacles thrown in my path. Winning yer hand is a challenge that I shall surely thrive upon."

"What game are ye playing?" Lileas asked, pushing herself into her father's lap. "Can I have a turn?"

"Aye, sweetheart. Ye can be on my side." His voice dropped to a whisper, but was loud enough to hear. "Together we will win against Lady Davina."

He was so utterly charming, Davina found it difficult to be annoyed. Her gaze shifted and she realized she was being watched. Expecting to see Aileen's approving smile, she lifted her head and instead caught James's hardened stare.

The moment their eyes met, he frowned and turned away. Davina forced her attention back to the game, surprised at how much his obvious indifference stung.

Despite his desire not to, James watched and brooded. Seeing Davina so cozy and relaxed playing chess with Malcolm was doing ridiculous things to James's mood. The expression on his brother's face was easy to read—he was being charming and seductive and 'twas obvious that Davina was enjoying the attention. The prospect of her marrying his brother suddenly loomed as a true possibility and it troubled James more than he wanted to admit.

Davina cast a shy smile at Malcolm. James clenched his fists and drew a fortifying breath. It took considerable effort to restrain himself from approaching his brother, pulling him to his feet, and punching him square in the jaw.

Though James struggled to avoid it, Davina had been reluctantly in his thoughts ever since his arrival. Thanks to his father's mad schemes, he was now subjected to the ungainly sight of his brother paying court to her. That she might actually succumb to Malcolm's charms was too repugnant to be considered.

If returning to the Crusades were not an impossibility, James knew he would be on the next boat. Life as a Crusader gave him a purpose, a reason to get up each morning. It also kept his mind too occupied to think overmuch on the past, to dwell on his failures.

He had matured, learned impressive fighting skills and techniques. A man with his abilities could earn a decent living in tournaments, but he would have to wait until spring if that was what he chose. In the meantime, he would simply have to grit his teeth and hope that Davina returned to her home soon after the holiday.

"Has she changed a great deal?" his mother asked.

James flinched. So great was his concentration on Davina, that he had not even heard his mother approach. He gingerly shifted on his feet, but refused to look directly at Aileen, knowing her perceptive gaze missed little.

"I assume ye are referring to Lady Davina?" he drawled.

"Who else? Years ago ye spent many months with the Armstrongs. Surely ye saw much of her."

His vision blurred at the edges as he recalled the young lass he had loved so completely. Resentment shot through him over the happiness that had been stolen from them, but seeing no other choice, he buried it.

"Laird Armstrong's daughter, Joan, was the great beauty of the family. A practiced flirt, who basked in male attention. All eyes were usually drawn to her. I dinnae remember much about Davina."

James could feel the heat of embarrassment burn on the back of his neck. He was a poor liar and felt even more guilt for holding back the truth from his mother. She had loved and supported him all his life; this was hardly the way to repay her.

Aileen gave him a hard look. "Were ye there when Davina was attacked?"

His breath seized and he turned his head sharply. "What do ye know about that day?"

"Nothing. I only know that it happened and it's part of the reason she doesn't want to marry."

He swallowed convulsively. He had dreaded this moment, but knew it could no longer be avoided. "'Twas my fault. I should have saved her."

He heard his mother's soft gasp. "Was that the reason ye left Scotland?"

"Aye."

Aileen sniffled. "I always knew there had to be something that made ye go. Why did ye not come to us first?"

"The shame was too great."

"Ye could never shame us, James." He watched the glimmer of tears in his mother's eyes slowly turn to love. The sight humbled him. She gave him a long, assessing look, then asked, "And now?"

"I'm learning to live with it," he confessed, hoping that would at last settle the matter.

"If ye dinnae wish to speak of it, I'll not pry further, though 'tis clear there is more to tell. Ye try to hide it, but I've seen the way ye look at Davina."

His embarrassment deepened. "Ye are being fanciful, Mother."

"Am I? Those who dinnae know ye well would easily miss it, but there are times that ye gaze at her as if she is yer last hope of happiness. Is she, James?"

James sucked in a deep breath. He looked down and saw the resolution marking the lines of his mother's face. "I might have believed that at one time," he admitted. "But no longer."

Her face softened, her eyes filled with sympathy. "What happened between the two of ye?"

"More than can be repaired," he answered flatly, the memory of disappointment nibbling at his heart.

A speculative light glowed in his mother's eyes. "Then build a bridge across the abyss."

"'Tis too late."

Aileen loosed a scoffing breath. "Nay. Until the vows are spoken, it's not too late. Do ye wish her to wed Malcolm?"

"She willnae."

"How can ye be so certain? Yer brother has a way with women and he seems intent on charming her."

James felt his nostrils flare. "She willnae marry him," he repeated, with far more confidence than he felt.

"Well, if she does, I want her to have no lingering feelings fer ye."

"I'll not court her, Mother." Amazingly, his voice sounded almost calm.

Aileen sighed. "Ye're as stubborn as yer father. I'll not demand something that is too painful fer ye to give. But I'll not let ye hide from her either. We are starting to put up the Christmas greenery and as always need more than what was gathered. I want ye to go pick some and bring Davina with ye."

James tamped down the objection that rose to his lips. He was confident that Davina would refuse Malcolm's offer of marriage—if it was even given—but it wouldn't hurt to be certain.

"If it pleases ye, then I will do as ye bid."

Chapter Eleven

"If ye don't stop yer caterwauling this instant, I'll leave ye here to find yer own way back to the castle," James said forcefully, sending a withering glance at his willful niece.

"James!" Davina cried.

"Ye cannae tell me that her shrill whining doesn't get on yer last nerve?"

"Perhaps it isn't the most pleasant of sounds, but ye have to understand the child is frightened," Davina said.

"My finger hurts," Lileas proclaimed, holding it aloft. "The bush pinched it."

"Frightened and injured," Davina added.

Injured? From a tiny prick on her finger? God's teeth, what evil sounds would emerge if the lass were truly hurt?

"We both told her, more than once, not to reach fer the holly," James retorted. "'Tis her own fault that she was pricked by it."

Davina looked at Lileas sharply, but her voice was gentle and soothing when she spoke. "We've already told ye more than once. Ye mustn't touch any of the greens, Lileas. Do ye understand?"

James watched the child's eyes narrow with displeasure. Aye, she clearly heard, and understood. Yet she just as clearly did not plan to obey.

After spending two more days watching his brother trying to woo Davina, James had reluctantly agreed to his mother's request to take Davina on an outing to collect holiday greenery. It had been an impulsive decision on his part, forged by unexpected frustrations and feelings for Davina that were far too jumbled to understand.

He regretted the invitation nearly the moment he had issued it and when Davina had suggested bringing young Lileas along, it seemed the perfect solution. The child would provide a comfortable buffer between them. Unfortunately, he had woefully failed to consider the added aggravation Lileas so seamlessly wrought on any situation.

"It's darkening," James said, gazing at the sky. "We've ridden much farther from the castle than I had planned. Best we return."

"But I dinnae pick enough ivy," Lileas whined. "Look, there's some over there!"

Quick as a flash, the little girl turned and scampered over a section of jagged rocks toward a climbing cluster of greenery.

"Nay, Lileas, it's too far away," Davina shouted, but the child ignored the command and continued on her way.

Bullocks! Even at this distance, James could tell it wasn't ivy.

The first drop of sleet hit him square in the middle of his forehead. James wiped the moisture from his face and hastily stuffed the remaining greenery into the large leather bag on his saddle. When he was finished, he propped his arm against his stallion and watched Davina chase after Lileas, the skirts of her gown billowing behind her in the breeze.

He felt not a drop of guilt for neglecting to aid her. *'Twas Davina's idea to bring the lass along. Let her manage the unruly brat.*

Another freezing pellet landed on his head just as Davina disappeared from his line of sight.

Suddenly, Lileas let out a high-pitched shriek. "Help! I'm falling!"

Crossing his arms over his chest, James stood, unmoved. No doubt his niece thought this was a game, where she would run and they would chase.

"James, please, come quickly," Davina shouted.

Slowly, James moved away from his horse and began walking. Enough of this nonsense. He was tired and cold and wanted nothing more than to be home, seated in front of a blazing fire, a cup of mulled wine in his hand.

He spied Davina as soon as he crested the rocky hill. Not surprisingly there was no sign of Lileas.

"Careful," Davina warned, as James felt his feet begin to skid. The freezing precipitation had made the rocks slippery and brought him perilously close to the edge of a large crack in a boulder. "Where's the lass?"

Davina's eyes grew wide and he saw her throat move as she swallowed. "I cannae find her. I heard her scream, but then all was silent."

"Och, Davina, dinnae tell me she's hiding?" Patience exhausted, James bellowed, "Lileas, show yerself at once."

A thin wailing sound, with an odd, distant echo reached them. James exchanged a puzzled gaze with Davina. "Did ye hear that?"

"Aye. But it sounded so far away. How could she have gone so far so quickly?"

James rubbed his fingers over the bridge of his nose. "How does she do anything? The lass draws trouble to her like bees to honey."

Davina gave him a sympathetic smile. "She's high-spirited."

"She's spoiled."

"Lileas, where are ye?" Davina shouted.

Silence. James lowered his chin to his chest and prayed for patience.

"Here! I'm down here," a sobbing, shaking voice finally answered.

Astonished, he braced his footing and leaned forward, squinting into the narrow crevice at his feet. "Lileas?"

"Help me, Uncle James. Please!"

The terror in the child's voice changed his prayers to a curse.

"Are ye hurt?" he asked.

Lileas let out another long wail. "I want to get out!"

"She must have slipped when she was running and somehow landed down there," Davina gasped. "My God, she could have been killed falling down through that rock."

James turned a frustrated eye on Davina. "Lower yer voice! The lass is frightened enough without hearing yer words of doom."

"I'm sorry." Davina looked contrite, but then her eyes brightened with hope. "She cannae be too badly injured if she can speak to us."

"And sob," James muttered, then felt guilty for his uncharitable reaction. The child was terrified and rightly so. She was in grave danger. Miraculously, she had survived the fall, yet he needed to ensure she survived the rescue.

James dropped to his knees and then to his belly, straining for a better look. His brow rose in astonishment when he spied Lileas standing precariously on a narrow ledge a good ten feet inside the split.

How the bloody hell had she gotten in there without breaking her neck?

Yet what worried him more was the sight of another ledge a few feet in front of the child. There was no telling how deep it was or how much farther she would drop if she stumbled into it.

"I see some footholds on the side of the rock near her head," Davina said. "Should we encourage her to try and climb out? If she moves up just a few feet, you can grab her."

Startled, James turned to find Davina lying beside him on her stomach as she, too, peered into the opening. She turned her head and they were nose to nose. His heart quickened and a peculiar heat invaded him as memories flashed through his mind of them lying together, locked in a passionate embrace.

'Twas no use. Even under the most trying circumstances, Davina could still make his mind—and his cock—race with wicked images. Shaking away those erotic thoughts, he concentrated on the problem at hand.

"'Tis far too dangerous to tell Lileas to climb up. If she slips, she could be badly injured. Besides, I doubt she has the strength to pull herself very far." James reversed his position and gingerly sat at the edge of the opening, dangling his legs inside.

"Ye willnae fit," Davina said, her face bleak.

Fearing she was right, James nevertheless ignored her. Using the ledge of rock in front of him for leverage, he slowly started lowering himself down the crevice. But as he feared, he stopped dead once he reached his chest. The opening was too narrow to allow him to pass.

Cursing beneath his breath, he pulled himself back.

"Wait! I see yer feet!" Lileas cried. "Come back fer me, Uncle James. Dinnae leave me here! It's dark and cold. I promise I'll be a good lass. I promise."

Her pitiful, terrifying sobs tore at his heart, frustrating him further. An equally agitated Davina paced back and forth in front of him.

"I've no rope with me, but maybe we can fashion one from the vines of ivy we gathered," James suggested.

Davina ceased pacing. Her brow furrowed as she considered the idea. "I fear it willnae be strong enough. She's a wee lass, but a sturdy one." She gulped nervously and held out her arms. "Lower me down."

She had removed her cloak and was shivering. Partly from cold, but also, James suspected, from fear, for he remembered well her aversion to small, dark places.

"Nay, Davina—"

"'Tis the only way, James, and ye know it. I'll lift her onto my shoulders. If she stands tall and holds her arms up, ye should be able to pull her out."

"And how are ye going to get out?"

Davina swallowed hard. "I'll climb up until ye can reach me."

He lifted a skeptical brow. "A lot must have drastically changed these past years. Exactly when did ye become an agile climber?"

Her chin lifted, but she averted her eyes. "When the need became dire."

He glanced uncertainly at Davina. "Nay. 'Tis a foolish plan. If it fails, I'll have two of ye stuck down there, instead of one."

She let out an exasperated sigh. "Aye, I am clumsy and not overly fond of heights. But the sleet is falling and darkness will soon be upon us. I cannae ride alone to get help, nor can ye ride away and leave us here. And we cannae wait until help arrives. It could be hours until someone realizes we haven't yet returned. We must act now."

Her bravery impressed him. As did her argument. Though they were not that far from the castle, they had few choices. Somehow, they must rescue the child themselves.

Davina walked to the lip of the crevice, then turned and held out her hands. "Will ye lower me down?"

James peered into the gap, trying to judge the distance to the ledge where Lileas stood. "I can only put ye so far down. Can ye climb the rest of the way?"

Davina's face whitened. "Perhaps, if I can find a foothold. If not, ye'll have to let go and I'll drop to the bottom."

God's blood! That certainly sounded like a ridiculous plan. But he had none better to suggest.

"Remove yer gloves," he instructed. "Ye'll get a tighter grip with bare hands."

Obediently she did as he commanded. Her lips tightened whitely with nerves, yet her gaze was steady. *Trust.* The expression in her soulful eyes struck him hard. And melted a piece of his frozen heart.

"Ye must stand very still, Lileas," Davina shouted. "I'm coming to get ye."

James gripped Davina's hands tightly and helped guide her into the opening. Slowly, carefully, he lowered her down. "Try to find a foothold."

She nodded, biting her lower lip in concentration. James could feel her body tense as she struggled to comply, but it was clear that she was having difficulty.

"How far am I from the bottom?" she asked, her voice straining with effort.

"Too far," he grunted. "And I fear I cannae let ye down any more."

"I'll be fine," she declared, and before James realized what she was doing, Davina let go of his hands.

"Bloody hell!" he shouted.

Arms flaying, he reached down, but all he felt was air. He heard the sound of tearing cloth and then a loud thud and he realized that Davina had reached the bottom.

"I'm fine," she called out. "Just give me a moment to catch my breath and I'll lift Lileas."

Cursing gruffly beneath his breath, James shifted his position and waited. Davina yelled that she was ready. He could feel his muscles straining as he reached down, stretching as far as he was able without losing his balance. There was a moment of triumph when he touched the tips of Lileas's fingers, but it was fleeting and too quickly gone as she once more moved out of reach.

"Just a few more inches and I'll be able to grab her," he grunted.

He heard Davina take a long, deep breath. "I'm going to hold her feet and lift her over my head."

"Wait!" he shouted. "Do it on my count. One. Two. Three."

Davina let out a yell as she pushed Lileas higher. James nearly shouted with relief when he touched the child's fingers. Quickly, he wrapped his hands firmly around Lileas's wrists, hauled her out, and placed her on the ground beside him.

The lass didn't make a sound. She stood there, utterly still, her eyes round and wide in her pale face. Worried, he ran his hands gingerly over the little girl's shoulders, arms, and legs, searching for injuries, but miraculously there were none. Nary a scrape, bruise, or cut was visible.

"I have to help Davina, now. Dinnae move a muscle, Lileas," he commanded.

The child nodded. She looked limp and dazed. "I promise."

"Good lass." Confident the child would do as she was told, James turned his attention to Davina. "Ye need to climb up several feet before I can help ye."

"I know."

He could see her vigorously rubbing her hands together. Then she stepped forward and ran them along the side of the boulder, searching for something to grip. Her smile broke through when she found what she was looking for.

Letting out a most unladylike grunt, Davina hoisted herself off the ground. James held his breath as he watched her slowly climb, waiting for the moment she was close enough to grab. It seemed to take forever, as Davina was cautious and deliberate with each step.

Finally, her hands were within reach. James yanked hard, pulling her upward until he could catch her firmly around the waist. Davina let out a squeal and clung to him, her feet dangling in the air. He swung around and gently set her down.

They each let out a sigh of relief.

Her breath was warm on his cheek, her hands resting comfortably upon his chest. She was standing much too close and his treacherous body responded. The womanly scent of her hair tantalized his senses. He felt his cock stirring to life, even as his conscience battled with his desire.

Unwittingly, his eyes were drawn to her mouth. More than anything he longed to dip his head down and press his lips to hers, to steal her breath with a bold, uninhibited kiss, releasing the pent-up emotions inside him that had been building since he had first laid eyes upon her.

Her eyes flashed and he knew she read his thoughts. He waited for her reaction of disinterest, or worse, horror, but her expression remained the same—soft and curious. His heart beat faster. He leaned closer, anticipating her retreat. She did not move.

The sound of a single sob broke the spell. He forced himself to look away from Davina and spied Lileas standing in the exact spot he had ordered. Her lower lip quivered. The skirt of her gown was torn and her face was smudged with dirt. He could see the glistening sheen of tears in her eyes and the traces of dried moisture on her cheeks.

"Och, Lileas, ye were a brave lass, to be sure," he said, knowing it must have been terrifying to be trapped in that tight space. "I'm mighty proud of ye."

James opened his arms. Lileas moved with lightning speed, flinging herself into his embrace. He felt her delicate bones, her fragile breath, and wrapped his arms tighter around her as the cold air whipped his cheeks. She buried her face against his chest and hiccupped a small sob.

Without thinking, he let his guard down and kissed the top of the child's head. She snuggled closer. He felt a comforting warmth at her nearness, an odd peacefulness that left him with a lingering feeling of contentment.

It had been so long since he allowed himself to feel tenderness.

"Papa is going to be very mad at me," she sniffled.

"I fear ye are right, lass."

"I dinnae like it when Papa shouts."

"'Tis never pleasant," James agreed.

"He'll shout loud."

"Aye."

"He'll shout until his face gets red." Lileas sniffled again.

"Very red."

"I dinnae want him to shout."

"Well, if ye had listened to me and Davina, there would be no need fer yer Papa to be shouting," James replied, softening his words with another hug.

"I promise I will always listen to ye, Uncle James," Lileas said solemnly. "Davina, too. And Papa and Grandmother and Grandfather. I'll listen to everyone. Truly."

"Good lass."

Lileas released a small sigh and relaxed in his arms. He comforted her for a few moments more and then James saw a mischievous smile lift the corner of her lips. "If I dinnae tell Papa about falling into the rock, he willnae shout at me. Promise ye willnae tell him, Uncle James?"

The little minx! James felt his shoulders tremble with the effort to hold back his laughter. 'Twas an important lesson that the child learn to do as she was told. Fie, it could save her life one day. He gave her a stern look, but she only widened her smile. Her impish charm was nearly impossible to resist. Perhaps the fright of her ordeal was punishment enough, he reasoned.

"Please?" Lileas patted his cheek.

His shoulders shook again as he lost the battle to contain himself. A peal of deep laughter rang out and James was astonished to realize it was the first true bit of mirth he had felt since returning home. All thanks to his niece.

"Secrets are neigh impossible to keep, young Lileas.

But I give ye my word of honor, that yer papa willnae hear of yer adventure from my lips."

Davina stilled, rooted to the spot, her eyes widening in amazement as she listened to something she doubted she would ever hear again—James's delighted laughter. Deep and robust, it wormed its way into her heart and for a moment she retreated into the cherished memories that emerged. Memories of happier times, filled with hope and promise and love.

They washed over her like a healing salve, pushing away the pain, bringing a wistful smile to her lips. She allowed herself a few more comforting moments, then regretfully let the truth seep back into her thoughts.

Those memories were a lifetime ago. Yet the sound of that laughter brought forth the unthinkable idea that mayhap there was hope that those happier times could be recaptured.

Was it truly possible?

"What's wrong?" James asked. "Ye have the most peculiar expression on yer face."

Davina shook her head and lowered her gaze. The need to touch him, to feel the gentleness behind the mirth, almost overwhelmed her, but she resisted. "'Twas only yer laughter. I was pleased to hear it."

Pleased and relieved to have his tight control break in such a manner. It was far better than having his fist smash against a tree, a reaction Davina had fully anticipated as things became more intense during their outing.

James made a croaking sound. A touch of color rose from his throat to his cheeks. Was he embarrassed? The notion amused her, for he took such pride in presenting himself as a hardened warrior. Did at least a glimmer of vulnerability, humanity remain?

Davina's heartbeat quickened at the thought.

A hound bayed in the distance. Lileas straightened, lifting her head curiously. "I hear a dog. Do ye think it's Prince?"

Davina turned to James. "Could someone be searching fer us?"

"We dinnae stray too far from where I told my mother we were going. There's certainly no need to bring the dogs to find us." James narrowed his eyes. "Come, let's return. I've no wish to meet whoever is following those hounds."

The trace of impatience in his tone brought on a ripple of unease. They were on McKenna land, not far from the castle. Yet James clearly felt there could be danger.

Davina scrambled to her horse. James helped her mount, then hoisted Lileas onto his stallion. Instructing the little girl to stay very still, he swung up behind her. The child snuggled into his warmth, giggling with youthful joy, the falling incident apparently forgotten.

The sight had a strange effect on Davina. She felt a pang of envy at seeing Lileas so tenderly nestled in James's embrace, remembering the times when she had been held so lovingly. Remembering the comforting feeling of his arms held securely around her, the gentle, soothing murmur of his voice, the sensation of his warm breath on her cheek.

Oh, how she missed it!

She stole a glance at him. The aura of power and strength that always surrounded him was softened by the child he cradled so protectively. She itched to move closer and squeeze his hand, to somehow become a part of that connection.

Heat scorched Davina's cheeks. Shaking off that witless thought, she reached for the reins of her horse. She had no right to expect anything from him and yearning for the impossible to become a reality was a very dangerous thing.

James shot her a glance over his shoulder and waved her forward. She tensed, then forced herself to relax. There was no risk of him knowing her foolish thoughts.

At his command, Davina rode slightly ahead. She could feel his gaze on her back as they rode. It gave her a sense of security, knowing that James was watching, protecting.

The long, gray curtain wall of McKenna Castle soon came into view. They were quickly recognized by the guards and Davina could hear the heavy gate being raised. The moment they entered the bailey, Malcolm strode over to meet them. 'Twas obvious he had been waiting for them, and none too patiently, judging from his hasty movements.

"Ye were gone far longer than expected," Malcolm said, as he reached up for his daughter and lifted her down from James's horse. "Mother was starting to worry."

Davina could tell from Malcolm's serious, frowning expression that it was not only Lady Aileen who had been concerned.

"Lileas was safe with me," James bristled, apparently also seeing his brother's unease. "There was no need to send the hounds to track us."

"Hounds? I sent none, though I was fully prepared to ride out myself if ye dinnae return within the hour."

An unspoken message of wariness passed between the two men. Davina bit back a sigh. Even an outing as innocent as gathering holiday greenery carried an element of unknown danger. 'Twas a very unsettling thought.

"I'm hungry, Papa."

The concern vanished from Malcolm's face as he turned to his daughter. "I'm not surprised. Searching fer greenery in a stark forest is hard work."

"Aye, I worked very hard today." Lileas leaned against her father's side as he lightly petted her head.

"Then ye shall have yer reward. I'm sure that Cook can spare some honey cakes."

Lileas squealed with delight and Malcolm hoisted the little girl into his arms. She settled easily against him, wrapping her arms around his neck. As they walked away, Davina was struck anew at the care Malcolm paid to his daughter. Most men lavished that sort of attention on their sons, leaving their female progeny as an afterthought.

"The little imp," James muttered as he helped Davina dismount. "She twists her father around her finger as neatly as she twines her arms around his neck."

"She is quite a rascal, with an uncanny talent fer getting herself into all sorts of mischief." Davina watched the pair enter the great hall. "Yet I doubt that Malcolm will feel so benevolent when he learns of Lileas's afternoon adventure."

James whirled to face her. "I gave my word that I wouldn't speak of it. I'm hoping to convince Lileas to tell her father on her own."

"I dinnae foresee that happening."

Davina tucked a stray wisp of hair behind her ear and fought to hide her smile. She was confident that Malcolm was incapable of meting out a harsh punishment to his daughter, making Davina's decision far easier.

Things had turned out well in the end today, but the next time Lileas might not be so fortunate. In order to keep her safe, 'twas important that child learn there would be consequences for disobedience.

"Aye, ye gave yer word." Davina brushed a smudge of dirt off her cloak. "I, however, made no such promise."

Chapter Twelve

James waited until the evening meal was being served before entering the great hall. Though Christmas was two days away, it was already bedecked in holiday greenery. A cheerful buzz could be heard throughout the vast chamber. The mood was festive and for a moment he allowed himself to relax as he tried to enjoy it.

Aye, this was the reason he returned home. To once again experience the security of being surrounded by those you could trust. To witness the joy found in simple pleasures. Plentiful, warm food, a comfortable bed, the companionship of family and friends. Lord knows, there had been far too little of that while living the life of a Crusader.

James's eyes scanned the hall slowly as the sights, sounds, and smells washed over him. Christmas was a time of hope and renewal. He'd be wise to savor this moment, rather than reliving the haunting bitterness and disappointments of the past.

The tables were filled with smiling men and women, feasting on the hot food. A group of lads and lasses ran eagerly through the hall, tying sprigs of evergreens to the legs of the tables. He spied his page, Colin, among their numbers, surprised to see the dour lad with a broad smile upon his face.

Stacks of long, thick logs were positioned near the three fireplaces. The largest would be saved to light on Christmas Eve, a tradition symbolizing the hope that the clan would stay warm throughout the cold winter months ahead.

His late arrival to the meal gave him the opportunity to study Davina without her knowing. She was seated in her usual place at the high table, beside his mother, head bowed, expression intense. The conversation between the two women appeared to be rather one-sided—his mother spoke and Davina listened, every now and again nodding her head.

Davina had changed for the meal into what he assumed was a more fashionable gown. Made of deep blue velvet, it had a tight, fitted bodice and a round neckline embroidered with silver thread. It emphasized the womanly curves of her body in an oddly modest way, yet still managed to heighten her female allure.

God help him, she was lovely. Irresistible, really. Could he find it within himself to stay away? Or was the reward of getting close to her worth the risk?

True, he had seen bonnier women. Flaxen-haired beauties from the north, dark, exotic females from the east. But there was something about Davina that reached deep inside him, took hold, and refused to let go.

She sipped from her goblet, her tongue darting out to lick away a few stray droplets of wine on her lips. They glistened plump and rosy in the candlelight and James's body heated with the memory of nearly kissing her this afternoon. Shifting his feet, he took a deep breath and shook his head.

Two more deep breaths and he had his passion under control. Only then did he approach the dais.

"Where is Lileas?" James asked, as he took the seat beside his brother.

"In bed," Malcolm replied. "I guess yer outing this afternoon tired her out."

"Aye, 'twas an adventure." James concealed a sly grin behind his hand. "Did she tell ye anything about it?"

"Nay, she was nearly asleep on her feet, poor mite. I imagine I'll hear all about it tomorrow."

"No doubt." James's glance darted to Davina. She lifted her brow, then shook her head, letting him know she had not said anything. Yet.

At first the notion of telling Malcolm about Lileas's little adventure—as he now referred to it in his mind— had seemed like a betrayal of Lileas's trust. But the more he thought about it, the more James realized that Davina was right. There was no doubt that Malcolm realized his daughter was a handful, but his brother needed to know exactly how defiant the lass could be, in order to keep her safe.

Nay, he would not try to stop Davina if she spoke with Malcolm, though he would ask her to wait a day or two. 'Twould be a good lesson in responsibility if they could convince Lileas to reveal the incident to her father herself.

"I, fer one, am not at all surprised the lass is sound asleep," the McKenna offered. "James brought back enough greenery to fill a forest. He must have dragged the child through miles of woods to collect it all."

"Aye, but I'm the one that captured the most elusive prize while hunting game this morning," Malcolm said in a swaggering tone. "Mistletoe!"

Their sister, Katherine, recently returned from her religious pilgrimage, let loose a most unladylike snort. "Naturally, Malcolm would make the extra effort to search for mistletoe."

"He's always keen to kiss a pretty lass," the McKenna agreed.

The back of James's neck itched in warning, for he knew precisely which pretty lass Malcolm intended to kiss. He clutched his goblet a bit tighter as he struggled to master his emotions. This wasn't the time or place for a confrontation with his brother.

"Mistletoe is forbidden by the Church, is it not?" Davina asked.

Lady Aileen shrugged. "Many priests willnae allow it to be displayed on the altar, and we respect that decree. But the McKenna hold fast to the traditions of our clan, even though some might refer to them as pagan. We see no reason not to have bunches of festive mistletoe brighten the great hall."

"Is it not dangerous?" Davina frowned in confusion. "I thought the plant was poisonous."

"Aye, it can be, though most who are foolish enough to eat it suffer with sickness, not death," James replied. "When I was six, I swallowed one of the berries."

"On my dare," Malcolm added cheerfully.

James glared at his brother, remembering all too well the sharp pains that had gripped his belly and bowels, even after all these years. "'Twas a cruel prank."

"I dinnae think ye would actually do it," Malcolm exclaimed defensively.

"'Tis no excuse," Aileen interjected, crossing her arms. "I stayed up half the night nursing yer brother, worried sick at the possible outcome. All that kept running through my mind were the rumors that Lady Sutherland disposed of her husband by brewing a potion from the leaves and mixing it with his ale."

"And I hid under my bedcovers and wept, terrified that James was going to die," Katherine recalled.

"Malcolm meant no harm," the McKenna insisted. "He cried like a babe until he knew fer certain James had recovered."

Hearing this for the first time, James turned in surprise toward his brother. Malcolm made a strangled sound of embarrassment and bowed his head. "I dinnae understand how such an innocent plant could cause so much chaos."

"Ye were only a lad yerself." The McKenna shook his head in sympathy. "Fortunately, James recovered without any lasting effects."

Malcolm's eyes grew amused. "Except fer an unnatural fear of mistletoe."

Katherine giggled. James glared at his brother, but refused to give him the satisfaction of rising to the bait.

"'Tis best we forget that childhood incident and remember instead the legend of the plant," the McKenna insisted.

"There's a legend? I've never heard it," Davina admitted. "I suppose it explains why people kiss beneath it?"

"Och, but there's always a legend," James muttered beneath his breath. "This is Scotland."

Dismissing his attitude, Aileen turned to Davina.

"'Twas Frigga, the goddess of love and beauty, who first kissed all those who passed beneath the tree on which the mistletoe grew," Aileen explained. "She then issued a decree that whenever anyone walks beneath the mistletoe, they shall have a token kiss and no harm would befall them."

Davina cocked her head. "'Tis a most friendly decree.

Most of the legends I know have vengeful gods and goddesses doing all sorts of ghastly things."

"Ah, but there's a good reason fer Frigga's largesse," Malcolm added. "The power of the plant saved her son, Balder."

"With a kiss?" Davina questioned.

"Nay. According to the legend, Balder, god of the summer sun, had a terrible dream in which he died. Frigga, his mother, was alarmed when he told her of it and grieved mightily at the thought of losing her child. Even more important, if Balder died, so too would all life on earth," Aileen said.

"Balder was her second son, wasn't he?" James interjected, reaching for another drink. "Killed by his brother, Hadar."

"Who was blind," Aileen insisted. "He dinnae know what he was doing."

James grunted. "Convenient."

The McKenna waved his hand in the air. "Quiet, James. Let yer mother finish the story."

James grunted again, but held his tongue.

"In an attempt to save Balder from the horrible fate of his dream, Frigga went to all the elements, animals, and plants on earth and begged them to spare her son." A sparkle twinkled in Aileen's eyes as she warmed to the telling of the tale. "They all agreed to leave Balder in peace, but his enemy, Loki, the god of evil, found the one plant that Frigga had forgotten to ask not to harm her beloved Balder—mistletoe."

Davina's brows arched knowingly. "I've a feeling this story does not end well."

Aileen's expression grew serious. "The gods attended an assembly where, being male and used to playing ridiculous games, they took turns in shooting arrows at Balder. All were in awe when they saw that nothing could harm him. Then the evil Loki handed Hadar, Balder's blind brother, an arrow with a tip poisoned with mistletoe. He tricked Hadar into shooting the arrow and killing Balder."

"Alas, poor Balder, killed by his brother," James muttered.

"Tricked into killing his brother," Malcolm corrected.

With a pointed stare, Aileen ignored her sons and continued. "For three days, the earth grew dark and the skies poured rain. Every living thing and all the elements tried to bring Balder back to life, but none were successful.

"Finally, he was revived by Frigga and the power of the mistletoe. Legend claims that the tears she shed fer her son during those terrible three days fell on the plant and turned the berries white."

Davina frowned. "What about the kiss?"

Aileen's expression softened. "Overjoyed when her son was resurrected from the dead, Frigga decreed that mistletoe would never again be used as a weapon. She further declared it to be a symbol of love and vowed to kiss all those who passed beneath it."

Davina shared a smile with his mother and sister. "I like a tale that ends well."

"Aye, those are in truth the best kind," Aileen agreed, a trace of laughter in her voice.

"Enough of legends and stories," the McKenna said. "We need music. Someone fetch old Ross."

At the urging of the crowd, old Ross took his place on the dais, fiddle in hand. Two other musicians joined him—one with a drum, another with a flute. The lively music echoed through the great hall, and many started clapping their hands and stomping their feet.

James found it no surprise that his parents were the ones to start the dancing. His mother moved with grace and agility, while his father, well, what the McKenna lacked in skill, he more than compensated for with enthusiasm.

Other couples joined in the merriment and then James saw Malcolm move around the high table and approach Davina. Taking her hand, his brother placed it upon his arm and gently pulled her to her feet. Davina ducked her head shyly, yet allowed herself to be led into the middle of the dancing.

Malcolm stared at Davina like a starving man gazing at a loaf of freshly baked bread. Jealousy burned in James's veins, making him short-tempered and edgy. A serving girl placed a fresh pitcher of ale in front of him and James almost growled at the lass.

James remembered the first time he had spoken with Davina. She had been shy, hesitant, and oh, so young and innocent. Yet after that brief encounter he had believed that his future rested with her—though he could never say why.

The troubadours sang of love striking without warning, often when an unsuspecting lad caught his first sight of a woman. James had never believed there was any truth in the notion, until Davina had come into his life. Yet the emotions he felt for her, the regard he held her in, had ripened over time, until they became a certainty in his heart.

They were meant to be together.

Now he felt the fool for ever believing it—and more the fool for allowing himself to remember it. Yet as he watched his brother tease and flirt with her, a powerful sense of ownership invaded his soul.

Davina belongs with me!

James saw the two of them share a laugh, then realized that Malcolm was trying to steer an unsuspecting Davina beneath the mistletoe. God's teeth! The man was relentless. James felt his temper begin to rise. His eyes bore into his brother, but Malcolm was unaware of the scrutiny. He was concentrating much too hard on creating the chance to steal a kiss from Davina.

James stood. 'Twas his worst fears coming to life— watching his brother openly court his former love. He could feel his self-control slipping as he moved off the dais and approached the crowd of dancers, yet he could no more stop his movements than hold back the sea.

Though he had drunk more ale than usual, James's steps were steady. He slapped his brother on the back, momentarily startling him. But when he moved to place himself in front of Davina, Malcolm balked.

"Ye have to wait yer turn, little brother," Malcolm said pointedly, steering Davina beyond James's reach.

James ground his teeth together, fighting to keep his temper. "The dance has ended and another begun. 'Tis my turn."

"Crusaders like to dance?" Malcolm's face twisted into a comical grin. "I dinnae realize."

"There's much that ye dinnae know," James said through set teeth, bringing his hand down on Davina's shoulder in a possessive gesture.

Malcolm's smile disappeared. Expression tightening, he pushed Davina behind him and moved to stand toe to toe with his brother. James was pleased to note that while Malcolm was slightly taller, his older brother no longer towered over him. The similar height made him feel as though they were on more equal footing.

Both men stared at each other, neither prepared to give an inch. James could see Malcolm's hands open and close at his sides. He leaned forward, daring his brother to take a swing.

But Malcolm refused to take the bait. He refused, also, to relinquish Davina.

As they started arguing again, James saw Davina flinch. He extended his arm in a gesture of contrition, but she backed away from his grasp, placing an obvious distance between them. Her eyes were wary, her discomfort clear.

But even more upsetting was the fact that she hid behind Malcolm. His brother tucked her hand tenderly in his own, causing a fresh wave of irritation to wash over James.

Why is she so damn comfortable in Malcolm's presence and so skittish around me?

"Find another lass to dance with, James," Malcolm commanded. "I'm certain if ye ask politely, there are one or two lasses that would be willing."

Anger and annoyance flared inside him at his brother's mocking words. "I dinnae want another lass. I want Davina."

"So do I." Malcolm's voice was low, but warning.

James ignored Davina's gasp of shock and kept his eyes trained on his brother. *Och, the battle lines are drawn.*

"I see that I shall have to teach you another lesson in humility on the practice field tomorrow morning," James taunted.

Malcolm's expression remained calm, but his body went rigid. "Why wait until tomorrow? Fists work as well as swords. And the victor will have the honor of dancing with the lovely Davina all night."

Davina cringed as a collective gasp went through the crowd standing near enough to hear Malcolm's words. The indomitable will of both men seemed to gather strength and grow as they faced each other. 'Twas a sight to behold, and many eyes in the hall were fixed upon them all.

Well, she would not stand here and subject herself to such a spectacle. Fighting over her? Why the very idea itself was dimwitted. Slowly, she backed away from both men, the heat of embarrassment rising high in her cheeks.

Thankfully, the pair barely seemed to notice her. Nay, they were too intent on their foolish battle of manly pride.

With her as the prize! Honestly. She nearly laughed out loud at the irony, for she was no man's notion of a female conquest. Indeed, virile men like James and Malcolm would be exasperated by her lack of feminine skills.

"There'll be no brawling in my hall," Aileen shouted, coming to stand between her sons.

There were a few cheers—mostly from the women— and many groans of disappointment from the men. Lady Aileen motioned for old Ross to play another tune and the man obligingly picked up his instrument.

Assured that the lady of the castle had her wayward sons well in hand, Davina decided now was the perfect time to make her escape. She wound her way through the dancing couples and quickly exited the hall. But in her haste to leave, she took a wrong turn and found herself in an unfamiliar corridor.

Pausing, Davina placed her thumb and forefinger on the bridge of her nose and pressed hard. 'Twas no wonder that her temples were throbbing. She drew in a deep breath and waited. Luckily, after a few minutes the pounding in her head eased.

She gazed down the empty hallway, debating which way to turn, then admitted the only option was to go back the way she came and pray that neither James nor Malcolm noticed her returning to the great hall.

Her restless strides carried her swiftly through the empty corridor, but then Davina saw a familiar figure approaching from the opposite side. *James!* She paused a moment, looking wildly for a place to hide, yet just as she realized there was nowhere to go, she felt a strong hand close over her wrist.

"Why do I get the feeling that ye're avoiding me?" James asked.

Davina made an exasperated noise and murmured beneath her breath. "Nay, ye are mistaken, James. I'm merely tired. And my head hurts," she added, realizing she had no need to feign an illness, for the pounding had indeed started again.

"Why did ye disappear so suddenly from the hall?"

Davina's mouth twisted. "Ye are an intelligent man, James. Do ye really not know?"

He lowered his chin and for a mere instant looked sheepish. But as quickly as it came, the expression vanished. "I'll not apologize fer my protective nature."

"I was hardly in any danger dancing with yer brother."

"I disagree."

She shook her head and turned to leave, but he took hold of her arm. "We've unfinished business."

She let the exasperation she felt show clearly on her face. "James, I am not returning to the hall to dance with ye."

"I was not referring to a dance." She frowned in puzzlement and he circled her slowly. "Ye were going to kiss me this afternoon, but Lileas interrupted us."

The air in Davina's lungs tightened. "'Tis true that kiss between us might have occurred. But that moment has passed."

"Then we shall share a friendly kiss in the spirit of the season."

"What?"

"A friendly kiss," he repeated.

"There's no mistletoe," she whispered weakly.

James regarded her with amusement. "We dinnae need it."

He carefully guided her until her back was pressed against the wall. He reached for her waist and drew her forward. Their faces were only a few inches apart. James's eyes grew dark with hunger and Davina felt a wave of heat pass over her when she realized the vulnerability of her position.

She was at his mercy. Powerless. She stilled against him, waiting for the fear the nearness of being this close, this intimate, with a man evoked.

"I'll not harm ye," he whispered. "All I want is a wee kiss."

The sound of his deep, sensual voice blazed through her. She remembered the curious feelings that had swamped her when he held her close this afternoon. The notion of being kissed by James then had been more intriguing than fearful, but here, in this darkened, secluded hall, it felt different.

Forbidding.

Davina struggled to hold herself apart from the mindless panic that was sure to come, but it was impossible. She felt her chest flush, her breath shorten, her heart race. The heat of his warm breath brushed her cheek and she whimpered.

Reacting instinctively, Davina turned her head away as his mouth descended, but that did not deter him. Nay, instead of capturing her lips, James nuzzled her neck, then nibbled behind her ear.

She stilled. Shivering sensations invaded her. She

involuntarily clasped his upper arm to keep herself steady.

"James," she pleaded, turning her face, meeting his eyes with a boldness she did not feel.

He bent his head, pressing his cheek to her temple. "A kiss, Davina. One wee kiss."

His voice was a deep growl, yet Davina found herself moistening her lips. There was an air of command about him that should have frightened her witless, but instead she was fascinated.

It had been an age since she had shared a kiss with a man—with James. She had changed so much—and so had he. And yet . . .

What harm could it do? A single kiss—no more, no less.

She slowly lifted her chin. His arms tightened around her, pulling her close to his chest. Davina tensed in anticipation, as he leaned over her. His lips closed over hers, the touch sweet and feather-light. The tip of his tongue slowly explored the fullness of her lips languidly, almost as though he believed she would pull away.

The gentle tenderness caught her off guard. She had expected fierceness from her hardened warrior, but instead his lips teased hers, showing her the gentle young man she had once loved still lived somewhere inside him.

Davina's eyes drifted closed. Warmth and wonder began to flow through her. It was miraculous. She was not senseless with fear at being this close to a man— physically and emotionally. Nay, instead she was awash in delight and freedom.

Overcome with emotion, Davina pressed her hands against his chest, this time capturing his lips with her own. She could feel his startled reaction, but he quickly matched her fervor, groaning as their mouths slipped open, as their tongues met.

The contact sent shafts of excitement shooting through her body, pooling in her nether regions. Davina whimpered, marveling at the unexpected feeling of coming alive again, of waking up after a long dormant sleep.

She lifted her hands from his chest to his shoulders and wrapped her arms around his neck. The heat of him scorched through the thick velvet of her gown. She could feel herself clinging to him, the need to get closer growing inside her with every breath. She'd been numb for so long—distant and fearful and hiding. It felt like a rebirth to kiss him so intimately, to entwine her body with his.

Somehow he sensed her emotions. One hand slid upward to cradle the back of her head, while the other lowered to her waist. Slowly, her body began to quiver with tantalizing sensations. It was so easy to get lost in the feelings he brought forth—the excitement, the anticipation, the passion.

He broke the kiss, yet kept her tightly locked in his arms. Their short, heavy breaths filled the air as each tried to master their passion. Then James reached up and caressed her cheek with his fingertips.

She stared at him, her mind reeling. His eyes seemed to capture her whole being, to hold her under some mysterious power. She swallowed the odd tickle in her throat, searching, and failing, to find the words to express her emotions.

He lifted her hand, turned it over, and kissed the top of her wrist. It felt burning hot; possessive. Her pulse quickened and throbbed.

Their bodies were too close. It was distracting. She struggled not to look into his eyes, and then suddenly

Davina felt something snap inside her. Curling her fingers closed, she pulled her hand free.

Too much, too soon. That she could have kissed him so openly and passionately was a wonder—yet it could be ruined in an instant if things went too far.

"Good night, James."

Before he had a chance to fully comprehend her intentions, Davina escaped. Lifting her skirt so she could move faster, she scurried past him. She heard him shout her name, but she refused to look back.

No matter how much she longed to.

Chapter Thirteen

"How are ye?"

Davina stiffened when she saw James standing a few yards away at the edge of the kitchen winter garden. She had done her best to successfully avoid him all morning, but her luck had just run out.

"I'm fine." She studied him and felt a twinge of annoyance at his apparent ease. She had barely slept last night, her mind filled with the feel and taste of his kisses, her heart puzzled over what they could mean. "And how do ye fare on this cold morning?"

"The same." He stepped over a wide row of herbs to stand at her side. She moved back, her feet wobbling on the uneven ground. His hand shot out to keep her steady. She gasped at the sudden contact and pulled back.

He frowned. "I regret that I frightened ye last night."

"Ye dinnae frighten me, James," she admitted, averting her gaze. "I frightened myself."

"I dinnae understand."

She gazed up at him and immediately wished she had not. There was a trace of wistfulness on his face that tore right through her heart. "Last night was a momentary lapse in judgment," she declared. "It willnae happen again."

James's expression hardened. "Why not?"

"'Tis unseemly."

His body turned rigid. Davina braced herself for his anger, but it never came. "Ye liked my kisses," he insisted in a silky tone.

"Aye." Now it was her turn to sound wistful. "Fer a moment, a single, blissful moment, I was a young lass in love again." She shook away the memory and stared at him with a hard-fought calm. "But the moment passed."

"Ye cannae forgive me," he said bitterly, pushing his hand through his hair.

"Fer the kisses?"

"Fer the past." He turned away, but not before she saw the wild emotions clouding his eyes. "I failed to protect ye, to keep ye safe."

"Against six attackers? 'Twas only because of yer bravery and skill either of us survived."

"I shamed and dishonored myself and my clan."

The sight of his suffering brought on a rush of emotions. "Is that why ye left the Highlands?"

"I needed to atone fer my failings." His voice darkened. "Joining the Crusades was the path I chose."

"Did it help?"

"Fer a time."

She looked away, her gaze resting sightlessly on the horizon. "I wish that I could give ye ease from this unfounded guilt."

"Knowing that ye don't blame me offers me some measure of comfort."

She turned back. She could see his chest rising and

falling with each breath, a clear sign of his agitation. "Neither of us came away from that day unscathed."

His eyes gleamed with speculation. "I've noticed that ye often pull away whenever a man comes near. Though ye seem to overcome this skittish behavior admirably whenever ye are with Malcolm."

"Being away from my home has forced me to face my fears and slowly overcome them. Malcolm has been kind and patient. I'm comfortable around him."

He slanted her a glance as he helped her over a small mound of hard, packed dirt. "What about me?"

"Ye unsettle me far more than he ever could."

James grinned suddenly, and she realized her answer pleased him.

"Ye should be wearing gloves," he admonished, touching her hand. "Yer fingers feel like ice."

"I dinnae plan to be out here very long. I was searching fer some rosemary to add to the sachets I'm making fer yer mother. She's been very kind and I wanted to thank her."

James took her hand and placed it between both of his, warming it. 'Twas a pleasant, comforting sensation, until he began moving his hand. He stroked down her fingertips to her palm with a light, sensual touch. Shivers rippled through her. Gasping, Davina snapped her hand away.

Surprise flashed in his eyes, but he took a deep breath and lowered his arms. "I'm glad to know that my memory dinnae play tricks on me," he said cryptically.

His words made her wonder. She studied him so intently in the tense silence that she took no notice of the small, furry creature than ran across her foot.

She screamed, then jumped, falling into James's arms. Startled, he caught her.

"I believe a rat just ran over my boot," she said breathlessly.

"Och, in my mother's garden?" James looked about the field. "I dinnae see it."

Davina shuddered, the reaction caused not entirely by the varmint or the cold. The intimacy of the situation was affecting her strangely, jumbling her thoughts. She had felt so strongly that avoiding further contact with James was the wisest course and yet she could not deny that she had enjoyed the kisses she shared with him.

Aye, she had enjoyed them far more than she should.

Davina gently pulled herself out of his embrace. "I need to return—"

"Malcolm and I will be sparring on the practice field this morning," he said, cutting her off. "The winner gets the first dance with ye tomorrow on Christmas Day. Will ye come and watch?"

Davina wrinkled her brow, unable to believe she found herself in such a bizarre predicament. James and Malcolm both vying for her affections? The very idea left her breathless.

She folded her arms across her chest. "I'm in no mood to see the two of ye fighting. Can ye not give it a rest for a few days?"

"'Tis only a brotherly rivalry."

"I feel responsible for it. Which is ridiculous, since I've no interest in either of ye."

James smiled ironically. "Yer kisses tell a different story."

She bristled, opening her mouth to deny it and instead letting out a soft chuckle. After a moment, he joined her. The sound warmed her heart and she considered it a good omen that they could laugh together.

But she knew better than to read too much into it.

Cupping her hand to protect the lit candle she carried from the wind, Davina followed Malcolm and Lileas into the bailey. Her breath caught when saw the number of people who had gathered there, each carrying a candle of their own. Night had fallen, and the shimmering glow of these single flames cast a golden light over everything.

"It looks like a fairy land," Lileas exclaimed.

"Aye," James answered as he pushed himself forward to stand beside them. "We all hold a candle to light the way and guide the Holy Family to safety on this Christmas Eve."

"Where's my candle?" Lileas asked.

"Here, take mine," Davina offered.

She blew out the flame and handed it to the little girl. Lileas's brow furrowed as she gazed at the thin plume of smoke that rose from the extinguished wick, but instead of demanding that the candle be lit, she held it close to her heart.

"When will the baby Jesus be here?" Lileas asked.

"He comes at midnight," Katherine explained. "Though we willnae actually see the babe."

Lileas thrust out her lower lip. "Why not?"

"His coming is symbolic," James replied.

Lileas wrinkled her nose. Though most likely not understanding her uncle's explanation, she did grasp that there would be no babe to view.

"I want to see the baby," Lileas declared. "And I want to hold him, too."

"Yer too young to be holding a babe," Malcolm said cheerfully.

"Papa, please," Lileas entreated, her lower lip trembling.

"Is that a snowflake I see?" James asked loudly, holding out his hand as though he were trying to catch it.

"Snow?" Lileas looked skyward. "I like snow."

James pulled Lileas closer and lifted her in his arms. "Then we must watch to see if any more of it falls."

James's ploy worked—Lileas was quickly distracted by the promise of snow. Davina never would have guessed that he could have so much patience. 'Twas good to see him with the lass; she softened his harder edges and had the ability to make him smile.

Lit candles held high, they made their way slowly toward the chapel. It was much too small to hold all those who wished to hear the service, so Father Dominic said the Mass on the front steps at a makeshift altar. There was a cold wind blowing, but everyone was pressed together so tightly, they were warmed by the combined body heat.

Davina stood with the rest of the family at the front, her mouth moving silently in prayer, the familiar words of the Mass a comfort. Lileas fell asleep before the final blessing, though she muttered again about wanting to hold the babe before her father carried her off to bed. Prince followed loyally behind the pair and Davina knew having the hound in her bed would keep the lass contented.

Though the castle went to sleep late that night, all awoke with the dawn. There was an air of excitement as everyone gathered to break their fast and Davina soon realized why—they would spend the entire day in celebration!

The storytelling began before the last of the mince pies were eaten. Men, women, and even a lad or two took turns sitting in the large chair beside a roaring fire, spinning a tale. There were interruptions, along with good-natured corrections and embellishments, which produced a great deal of laughter.

The ale and wine flowed freely and the singing began after the last of the stories were told. Dark clouds were brewing outside and the ominous rumbling of thunder predicted the coming of rain, not snow, though if the temperature dipped lower, it would snow. Yet inside, the fire and fellowship kept everyone warm.

Lileas cuddled in Davina's lap. Davina bounced the little girl in time to the music, feeling breathless after but a few songs, but was having too much fun to care. The rest of the family had disappeared; Davina assumed they were gathering the small gifts to be handed out once the singing ended.

"Come along, sweetheart. Yer grandfather has brought in the piggies." Malcolm scooped his daughter off Davina's lap, then turned and smiled pleasantly at her. "Will ye help us distribute them?"

"Pigs? Ye give swine as gifts?" Davina asked in astonishment.

Malcolm burst out laughing. Embarrassed, Davina followed him to the table where the gifts were assembled. There were bolts of wool, wheels of cheese, casks of ale, and rows of small clay pots with slits on the tops.

"These are the piggies," Malcolm explained, pointing to the clay pots.

Curious, Davina watched as the families lined up to receive their gifts. Wives were given the wool and cheese, husbands the ale, and the youngest child a clay pot. There were giggles of excitement as the families moved to find a private place in the great hall to gather around their pots.

Davina's brow rose in astonishment as she saw pot after pot being smashed to reveal the coins inside.

"I can tell by yer expression that the Armstrongs dinnae partake of this particular Christmas tradition," Aileen remarked.

"Nay. Christmas is a quarter day, so my uncle collects the rents," Davina replied, hardly believing how vastly different the celebrations were from those of her own family.

For the Armstrongs, Christmas was a solemn occasion. They did not indulge in any feasting, singing, or dancing until Hogmanay, the last day of the year. That celebration lasted through the night until the next morning, ending with the traditional *saining*, which offered a protective blessing for the clan and livestock.

Davina had noticed that a substantial pile of juniper branches had been put aside, so she knew the McKennas also held with this custom. Her mind spun at the amount of planning involved and the amount of food and drink that must be prepared to ensure there was enough for all to partake for these many days of feasts.

As if she had conjured it by merely thinking about it, platters piled high with roasted venison, goose, several kinds of fish, onions, peas, beans, and more mince pies were brought from the kitchen, along with jugs of spiced and sweetened wine, ale, and whiskey.

Though it had not been long since breaking the morning fast, the assembled group ate with gusto. Following the feasting, the musicians started to play and the dancing began.

"They are a lively group, milady," Colleen commented

as she sat beside her mistress. "They work hard, yet I've never known a clan that takes to a celebration so fondly."

"'Tis impossible not to feel their joy of life," Davina agreed, glad that she had been able to experience it for herself.

A tall, broad-shouldered man with streaks of gray at his temples approached and executed a clumsy bow. "Would ye do me the great honor of dancing with me?"

For an instant Davina was startled by the request until she realized the man was speaking to her companion. She turned just in time to see the widow blush. Colleen hesitated, but only for a moment. Then she stood and took hold of the man's hand, her blush deepening as he led her away.

Still trying to digest what had just happened, Davina jumped when Malcolm approached her from the side. "Shall we join in?" he asked with a gallant bow.

But before she could take his offered hand, James appeared. "I was the victor in our match on the practice field. Davina is promised to me."

Malcolm's mouth tightened into an even line of disagreement. "The match was a draw."

"I won," James insisted.

"A draw," Malcolm repeated.

Och, not this again!

James's eyes were stark. Hopeful? Or was this merely another opportunity for him to best his brother? Davina was uncertain.

Thankfully, she was rescued from the awkward circumstance by Lady Aileen. "Come and dance with me, James. Yer father claims he's too tired," Aileen said. "It must be all the rich food he's eaten."

James had no choice but to agree, though his scowl let them all know that he was not pleased. Davina and Malcolm joined a circle of dancers, moving gracefully to the lively, bouncing reel. Out of the corner of her eye, Davina could see James and his mother in another group of dancers, but the need to concentrate on her steps made her turn away.

Malcolm led her to the outer circle for the final part of the dance. Just before the music stopped, he caught her hand and pulled her toward one of the long tapestry panels that hung from the rafters.

Too breathless to speak, Davina followed, though she squeaked with protest when he thrust the tapestry hanging aside and pulled her behind it. The small alcove was barely wide enough for them to stand, which forced them very close to each other.

Moonlight poured in through the long, narrow window at the top, casting a romantic glow around them. It was the perfect spot for a lovers' tryst. Or a marriage proposal.

Davina's heart sank with dread. She opened her mouth to object, but Lileas suddenly appeared. She waved at Davina, giggled loudly, handed her father a bouquet, then ran out.

"I wanted a bit of privacy to give ye a small holiday token," Malcolm said, extending his arm. "These are fer ye."

Davina's wariness vanished as she beheld the gift. A dozen perfectly formed white flowers with silvery green foliage were tied with a wide satin ribbon. The flowers resembled a teardrop with the leaves wrapping around each other at the base of the stems.

"Fresh flowers in winter. I'm nearly speechless."

"Do ye like them?"

"Aye, very much. They're so delicate, so beautiful."

"They are called snowdrops. Rare, but not impossible to find, if ye know the right places to search.

Thankfully, there has been just enough sunshine these past few days to bring them to life."

Davina bowed her head to sniff the blooms. They had a faint, sweet smell that bespoke of the promise of spring. More pleased than she could say, Davina lifted her chin. Her words of thanks died on her lips as she saw the smoldering gaze in Malcolm's eyes.

She could feel her heartbeat echoing in her ears. *Saints preserve me, what have I done now?*

"Goodness, I must get my lovely flowers in a vase of water," Davina said hastily. "And I should like to give ye my gift. 'Tis but a small token of embroidery that I hope ye—"

"Davina! Ye know what I want to say." He lifted her hand to his lips, his expression turning serious. "Will ye do me the great honor of becoming my wife?"

"Oh, my, there's no need fer ye to feel obligated to ask! I dinnae believe that yer father was truly serious when he suggested that I marry into the clan," she said, trying to pull her hand away.

"The McKenna never says anything unless he means it." Still holding her hand, Malcolm took a half step closer, all that he could manage in such a tight space. "'Tis the best option fer ye and good for clan McKenna. But there's more. Surely, ye realize that I've a genuine affection fer ye, that can easily lead to something more."

Davina raked her gaze over him, startled to realize that if her heart was free, she might have considered the match. Her fear of men—well, certain men—had diminished that much.

Whether he meant to or not, Malcolm had helped her release some of her fears, had helped her venture forth from her self-induced exile. For that, she would always be grateful.

"I wouldn't be a very good wife," she answered honestly.

"Lileas's mother was a proper wife, a simple, uncomplicated lass. After we married, she decided her only purpose in life was to please me. She consulted me on nearly everything she did and never took any action without first receiving my permission. If I was not here, she reluctantly made her own choices based on what she thought I would do."

"She sounds like a paragon of wifely virtue."

"Some might say that." His eyes flashed with regret. "I treated her with honor and respect and as much patience as I could manage. But the sad truth was that she was more child than wife. Too needy, far too eager to please, lacking an original thought or opinion of her own."

Davina finally succeeded in freeing her hand. She hastily crossed herself. "What a dreadful thing to say about the dead."

He shoved a hand through his hair, looking sheepish. "I mean no disrespect. I merely wanted to be truthful with ye."

"Then I shall return the favor. I would make ye a terrible wife, Malcolm. Truly."

"I want a wife who will challenge me with her own ideas, her own opinions. Ye could be that woman," he coaxed.

"Nay."

"Lileas adores ye. She told me how she fell when ye were gathering Christmas greenery. She said that ye saved her."

"Hardly." Davina blushed. "James was the one who

made sure we were both safe. But I am glad that Lileas told ye what happened. She knew that she was wrong to run off and feared the repercussions if ye were told of her bad behavior."

"Well, I admit that I did yell. Rather loudly, according to Lileas." Malcolm shook his head. "'Tis clear that ye are exactly what my motherless daughter needs."

Davina felt a tug at her heart at the mention of the child. Though the little lass was spoiled and willful, Davina had developed a genuine affection for her. Gaining a husband and a child to mother and love— the combination held strong appeal. But it was the wrong man.

"Shame on ye, Malcolm McKenna, dangling yer daughter as bait to entice me," Davina said.

"Most women would hardly find Lileas a benefit to marrying me." He smiled, his teeth white and even in the scant bit of moonlight. "'Tis but another reason why I know you are the right woman."

"I'm honored. Truly. But I must decline."

"Why?"

"James."

She had whispered his name under her breath, but Malcolm heard. His jaw tightened. "Ye've already accepted his proposal? He's said several times he has no interest in marrying ye."

"There's been no proposal," Davina clarified, reminding herself that Malcolm was unaware of the true nature of her past relationship with James.

"My brother has said that he willnae court ye, yet every time I'm near ye, he interferes. Tell me true, do ye favor him over me?"

"James and I share a past." She swallowed. "A romantic past."

Malcolm's shoulders stiffened. "Has it been rekindled?"

"Not exactly. But it stands firmly in the way of a future fer the two of us."

A shadow touched Malcolm's face. "My brother is more times a fool if he doesn't realize what a treasure he has within his grasp."

"We are a pair of fools, yer brother and I," she said quietly, thankful that Malcolm did not press the matter further.

Malcolm stared at the wall for a long moment. "I would speak with James on yer behalf, but I fear he willnae listen to me. So, instead I will tell ye, Davina. Dinnae be so quick to abandon something so hard to capture and hold."

"It has already been lost," she said, emotion catching in her throat.

"If that were true, then ye would have accepted my proposal." Malcolm turned and peered around the side of the tapestry. "The music is about to start again. Shall we join in on the next dance?"

"I'd like a moment to compose myself," she replied.

He nodded. Relief surged through Davina when he left, followed by a stab of guilt. She held her lovely flowers close to her heart, wondering how her life had gotten so complicated. Wondered, too, how she could set it to rights.

Lost in thought, she was startled by the sound of approaching feet. Fearing that Malcolm had returned, Davina turned, and instead found herself looking into Colleen's disapproving face.

"I assume from the scowl on Sir Malcolm's brow that he proposed and ye rejected him," the widow said.

"I did." Davina sighed. "Ye of all people should know the reason why."

"I know that ye came here to reclaim the life ye lost and ye've done well so far." The widow pointed a finger at her. "But ye have yet to settle the past with Sir James."

Davina lowered her head. "I know."

She had come to McKenna Castle in desperate need of finding an inner strength and somehow, miraculously she had found it. But there was something else she needed and James truly was the only one who could give it to her.

She needed to know, with certainty, that she could be intimate with a man.

Davina scurried down the stairs, one hand skimming the wall for balance, the other trembling so violently that the candle she held cast an eerie, jumping shadow along the corridor.

Saints preserve us, what I am doing?

She had deliberately waited until it was very late and the castle was asleep. Yet as she crept down the hall, the sensible side of her wanted to run back to her own chamber, bar the door, and hide in the bed, with the covers drawn over her head.

Davina's footsteps slowed, but she did not stop, nor turn around. Her decision to be intimate with James seemed such an inspired idea, but the execution of such a plan was proving to be a test of her nerve and determination.

She tugged at the high neckline of her nightgown, feeling suffocated. This might very well be the most witless thing she had ever tried to do, but her desperation had grown to the point where action must be taken.

When she reached his chamber door, her body froze. The candle shook crazily as Davina stood there, searching for her courage.

Her chest felt so tight she was finding it difficult to breathe. Twice she nearly turned away, but then reached deep inside herself, gathered her courage, and flung open the door.

"James, I must speak with ye."

Silence.

"James?"

Eyes pinned to the velvet hangings surrounding the bed, Davina moved forward. Was it possible that he hadn't heard her enter? It seemed unlikely that he could sleep so soundly, but she did notice he had drunk more than his share of ale and whiskey during the long day of holiday celebration.

Walking softly on the balls of her feet, she made her way to the bed, listening for signs of life, yet there were no heavy breaths, no snores or grunts. Her trembling fingers slid down the length of soft bed curtains. Bowing her head, she snapped back the rich fabric.

Empty.

A nervous giggle escaped, followed by a longer laugh. All that irrational fear was for naught—James wasn't even in the room. She slumped against the wall, then thumped her head back against it several times in frustration.

Was it a sign? A reprieve from her mad plan?

Where could he be at this hour of the night? Sharing a bed with some willing lass? The possibility felt like a dirk straight through her heart. Her resolve wavered. Perhaps 'twas time to rethink her plan. If she slipped out of the chamber now, unseen, she could return to her room unscathed.

Yet nothing would be resolved.

She straightened her shoulders. She had come too far to retreat now. Heart pounding, Davina moved closer to the bed to wait for him.

Chapter Fourteen

Tired and out of sorts, James entered his bedchamber, surprised to find it bathed in the soft glow of dim candlelight. 'Twas odd that a servant would waste precious candles when no one occupied the chamber; then again, it seemed as though nearly everything since he returned home was *odd*.

Or mayhap young Colin was responsible? That seemed a more likely explanation, given the lad's lack of training, but James was in no mood to rouse the lad from sleep and scold him. That lecture could wait until morning.

As James waited for his eyes to adjust to the dimness, the hairs on the back of his neck itched with warning. He could feel a presence. Someone was in the chamber, hiding near the bed.

I'm being watched.

Muscles rigid, he slowly reached for the dirk secured in his belt. Light-footed, he moved forward, blinking with shock when he saw a woman leaning over his empty bed.

He took another step and the wooden floorboard

creaked. The female straightened instantly, turning at the sound.

"Jesus, Davina, ye startled me!" Releasing a long breath, he threw the dirk on the table.

Her eyes widened. "Well, that was hardly the reaction that I had hoped to receive."

"I thought ye were an intruder." James willed his alert senses to calm, then narrowed his gaze. "Why are ye here?"

"Is it not obvious what a woman wants when she steals into a man's bedchamber in the middle of the night," she answered, her voice husky and low.

James drew back, feeling as though he'd just been kicked in the gut. Her words brought a violent surge of heat to his manhood. It was then he took full notice of her appearance. Dressed in a linen night rail of white, her braided hair cascading down the middle of her back, she was a vision of beauty and innocence.

A few tendrils of hair had come loose from her braid and were curling on her neck. Her creamy flesh looked so inviting. He knew her skin would feel like silk under his questing hands and lips.

Oh, how he longed to place a kiss in that tender, vulnerable spot at her nape and trail his way downward, kissing and caressing every inch of her! Yet he stoically resisted the temptation, allowing the flame within him to slowly ebb.

"Have ye been drinking?" he asked gently, for he could find no other answer for her uncharacteristic behavior.

"Just one extra glass of wine fer courage," she admitted. "But I'm not drunk. I know exactly what I'm doing."

"Then ye best explain it to me, Davina, 'cause I haven't a clue."

"I want to share yer bed tonight, James."

He snorted ruefully and shook his head. "I fear our past will make marriage between us a hardship."

She withdrew slightly. "I'm not asking fer marriage, James. But I am asking ye to lie with me and help me bury the past once and fer all."

"Ye dinnae mince words, yet it still makes no sense."

He could see that her hands were trembling, yet she fixed an unwavering gaze upon him when she spoke. "The innocent lass who believed that life would treat her well died the afternoon we were attacked. I dinnae remember much of what happened, but the feelings of terror and fear and utter helplessness remain with me.

"Do ye know what it's like to be fearful of yer own shadow? To feel the humiliation of being unable to leave the walls of yer home without shaking so hard yer teeth rattle?"

"God's blood." His voice was raw with tortured emotion.

"I do, James. I know. Ye tried to comfort me after that attack and I turned you away because I couldn't bear to face the truth. Fer the past five years I've locked myself away, hoping to ease the pain, but it only grew worse. Fer so many years, I've prayed fer strength, I've sought solace in strong medicine to ease my pain, to pull me away from the darkness that plagued my mind and heart."

He bit back an oath. "Ye cannae run from the pain, Davina, fer it will always follow. Ye must face it, conquer it."

"As ye did, by running off to the Crusades?"

He turned with a growl and she lowered her head. "Forgive me, James. I've no right to judge. I treated ye cruelly, unfairly. Ye did what ye needed to survive."

"So this is to be my payment? Having ye in my bed fer one night?"

"No, James, this is my way of breaking free from the past and finally escaping the walls of isolation that surround me."

"Ye are no longer fearful of intimacy with a man?"

She swallowed so hard he could see her throat move. "I'm no longer terrified of facing the truth. If I'm not a virgin, then so be it. It almost doesn't matter, fer I will forever feel violated by that horrid outlaw."

James cursed under his breath. "I should have saved ye, Davina."

She reached for his hands and gave them a gentle squeeze. "Oh, James, ye did save me. We are both alive to tell the tale and that's because of ye."

He raised her hands and rubbed them against his cheek. "I dinnae deserve yer forgiveness."

"Ye are being daft!" she cried. "Pigheaded! There's nothing to forgive. Ye did nothing wrong."

James bit the inside of his cheek to prevent an outburst of temper. Arguing would solve little. He would carry this guilt to the grave, yet knowing Davina did not blame him eased a bit of his sorrow. Yet he had no right to expect her to fill the emptiness in his heart.

"I have nightmares too," he confessed quietly.

Her eyes watered and he noticed the trembling of her chin, but she did not let the tears fall. "Let's join together and banish these nightmares forever," she said. "We've both learned 'tis pointless to cry over what's been lost, to spend our days and nights wishing things had been different.

"'Tis a most unusual twist of fate that has brought us together again, James. We should not waste this precious chance. I want the memory of making love with ye to fill my dreams instead of the fear."

Her heartfelt plea rattled him to the core. Emotions he did not want to identify and acknowledge stirred within him. Stalling for time, James added some wood to the small fire burning in the fireplace. The flames rose, dispelling the chill in the chamber. But not the rising fear in his heart.

Once consummated, there would be no graceful way to end the relationship. If he took Davina to his bed, she would become his wife. McKenna honor demanded no less.

Was he ready to take that step?

Just looking at her set off warring feelings inside him. Though he had tried to deny it, his strong desire for her remained, but it was still overshadowed by his need to protect her. He could never atone for the mistakes of the past, could never take away the pain that she suffered. But mayhap he could lessen it by helping her bear it.

Was this the path that would lead her there?

"'Tis a dangerous game that ye are suggesting," he said. "A woman must be very careful when she gives her body to a man."

Even in the dim candlelight, he could see her blushing cheeks. He took a few steps forward, yet maintained a safe distance between them. His jaw tightened as he wondered how in the hell he was going to resist what she offered.

"I've been considering this very carefully. I trust that ye'll be slow and gentle," she said in a quiet, reverent tone. "I trust that if I grow frightened, ye'll stop."

"I'm a man, Davina. Not a saint. If things go too far . . ." He let his voice trail off, fully expecting her to turn tail and run.

She looked at him with imploring eyes. "That's why I'm here, James. I want things to go too far."

James stood in stunned silence for a moment, mulling the choices over in his mind. His pride was soothed, knowing she had come to him instead of his brother. But if he turned her away, would she then seek Malcolm's bed?

The tumult inside him heightened. He knew it had not been easy for her to find the courage to approach him. Whatever demons haunted her still existed in the edges of her mind. Yet she was determined to vanquish them. He could not help but admire her for it.

But her methods flummoxed him utterly. Why were females such confounding creatures? Was this the answer? Sleeping together? His cock certainly thought it a good idea. Yet what if this made things worse?

That thought brought an ironic laugh to his lips. How could the strain between them grow any larger?

He wished he had the magical power to snap his fingers and obliterate her distress. But that was foolish—childish—an answer that Lileas would seek.

Had pure desperation brought this idea to Davina or did it have merit? Would sharing the burden that haunted their past help them heal? Doubt crowded his mind.

"Ye need to know that I can make no promises about the future to ye," he said bluntly, still hoping to frighten her away.

The angry reaction he expected was not forthcoming. She perched on the edge of his mattress, wrapping her arms firmly around her waist, and cast her eyes to the floor.

"I understand."

"It makes no difference to ye?"

"I'm certain this is what I want. Ye are what I want."

"Well, ye hardly look eager, lass."

He infused his comment with a trace of humor, hoping to break through her nerves, and was rewarded with a faint smile.

Aye, now she'll leave. But instead, she licked her lips and rose gracefully to her feet. He was captured by the delicate fragrance drifting toward him. Sweet and floral and uniquely Davina's; it had the power to enrapture him.

She held her arms open and stepped toward him. A timid smile curved her lips as she stared into his eyes. James was certain the searing heat of desire he felt was reflected in his eyes.

It will frighten her and end this madness. And still, she came closer.

"Will ye at least kiss me, James?" she pleaded.

His heart jolted with anticipation, yet he stood still as a stone, his feet slightly apart, his hands clasped behind his back. She wrapped her arms around his neck, whispering his name into the hollow behind his ear. The feel of her warm breath, followed by the gentle pressure of her lips on his neck, aroused him in a way that he never imagined.

He unclenched his hands and splayed his fingers across her back, keeping her close. Her breasts were pressed against his chest and he felt his cock rise and harden with lust. She twisted her body, rubbing against him like a cat, then lifted her chin.

James gazed into her passion-shrouded eyes and suppressed a groan. His need sharpened. Never before had he felt so consumed, so tormented by it. Doubting he would be content with a mere kiss, he nevertheless dipped his head.

She took his face between her hands when he drew near and pressed her soft lips to his. Sensations swamped him. Her lips parted, their breath mingled, and then she welcomed his tongue, thrusting her own boldly forward.

It felt like the sun bursting inside him, splintering

with glorious light. She tasted like heaven. He felt the desire she evoked pumping rapidly through his veins, draining him of any resistance.

She moved her mouth over his jaw, temples, eyes, ears, then back to his mouth. His need swelled to a profound hunger. Damning himself for having such little control, James drank deeply of the sweetness she offered, savoring the moment as though it were his last.

He stroked her back down to the base of her spine, where he slowly traced the graceful indentation. His hands itched to cup the tempting globes of her perfectly rounded buttocks and lift her closer to his desire, but he held back.

This was Davina's seduction. He would follow her lead. No matter how tortuous. No matter how sorely tempted he was to take control, to spread her legs, grasp her hips, and press inside her. To finally claim her as his own.

His body became further inflamed when he heard her whisper his name. So sweetly, breathlessly, and with obvious need. Her untutored hands pulled at his clothing, trying to push it aside and reach his bare flesh.

James held his breath, aching with the need to help her, but he feared his passion would overcome him. Gritting his teeth, he somehow held on to his control as the delicious sensation of her fingertips glided over his partially bare chest.

His loins quickened, his manhood was heavy and aching. His heart caught, knowing this was the time for truth between them. "I've been hurt and angry, but my feelings fer ye have never changed," he whispered.

"I'm humbled to know that ye could still want me,

flawed as I am." A lone tear escaped, trailing down her cheek.

The sight of it made James's chest constrict. "God's blood, dinnae cry, Davina."

"The tears are born of joy, not sorrow," she whispered. "I've waited far too long to belong to ye, James."

He felt himself starting to withdraw, to pull back into the harsh, gruff shell he used to protect himself. Davina's eyes turned sorrowful, as though she knew what he was doing. Then suddenly a helpless feeling sliced through his heart, a fear that if he turned inward again, now, in this moment, he might never be able to escape.

It was madness. And yet . . .

He ran his fingers wearily through his hair, then held up his hands in supplication. Allowing his guard to crumble, James lay down on the bed, folded his hands across his chest, and closed his eyes.

He could feel the mattress dip as Davina scrambled beside him. The air was heavy with the intoxicating scent of her. He took a very deep breath, then opened one eye and peered at her.

"Go on, now. Have yer wicked way with me, wench."

She could not take her eyes from him. Her breath deepened as she looked down at him, seeking to control her uneven pulse. The sight of him lying so still sent a flutter of anticipation through her for beneath the invincibility of his hard body was a sense of vulnerability that she recognized and understood.

She took a deep breath and emptied her mind of everything except James. A twinge of excitement pulsed through her veins and a feeling that could only be described as desire filled her—and gave her hope.

She knew in her heart that no other man was capable of eliciting such a response from her. James. Only James. But it wasn't only passion, there was tenderness, too. The final, small doubt that this was the right path for both of them to take vanished.

Now all she need do was figure out the best way to continue with her seduction. She moistened her lips and stared down at him with helpless exasperation, uncertain where to start. 'Twould be far easier if James were in charge, but that was clearly not his intention.

Nay, if this was going to happen, then she had to be the one to take them on this journey. The realization brought a blush of heat flushing her chest, which crept up her neck and into her cheeks.

The sudden twinkle in James's eyes let her know he'd noticed it. His amusement calmed her nerves and softened the fierceness on his handsome face. Keeping herself raised on one elbow, Davina slowly reclined beside him. Bracing her hand against his chest, she leaned close and pressed her lips to his cheek. It was rough with stubble, but she found it to be a pleasant sensation.

Her mouth shifted, lingering over his lips. She could feel the warmth of his breath, smell the sweetness of the wine he had drunk at dinner. The embers of desire began to glow inside her as she anticipated the feel of his lips and tongue tangling with hers.

"Are ye going to tease me or kiss me, lass?"

"Kiss," she murmured.

She flicked her tongue lightly along the rim of his lips, tempting them both, then embraced him utterly, devouring him with all the pent-up ardor that had been locked inside her for years. He responded with a loud groan. His fingertips dug into her arms as he bit at her bottom lip, taking her mouth with his lips and tongue.

Passion surged through her in a dizzying tide. The kiss woke something deep and hidden within her. Chaotic emotions came to life, making her hot and cold all in the same moment. She suddenly found the cloth of their garments an annoying, frustrating barrier. Longing to feel his skin pressing against her, Davina tugged at his clothing. With impatient hands, she pulled at the edges of his tunic, lifting it off his body. A fine linen shirt followed, the neatly stitched garment flung carelessly on the floor.

Her breath caught, and held, as she reveled in gaining her prize—a beautifully sculpted, naked chest. She momentarily forgot about his brais, concentrating instead on the male splendor set before her.

There was not a spare ounce of flesh anywhere on his body. His chest was lean with corded muscles that bore numerous scars, yet it made him no less attractive. He was beautiful in a raw, rugged way. His flesh was warm and silky. She could feel his muscles knot beneath her touch, but he remained perfectly still as her finger traced the raised white line of an old scar.

He was like a statue sculpted from marble. Well, she must do all that she could to make this statue *feel*.

She leaned down and ran her cheek over his naked chest, then pressed her lips to it, tantalizing his warm flesh with her tongue. She could feel his heart drumming rapidly, could hear his deep, heavy breaths. Encouraged, she continued, allowing her lips and tongue to linger with each caress.

She heard the sharp intake of his breath, followed

by a deep groan. The sound of his pleasure encouraged her. Acting purely on instinct, she bade her hands to move lithely over his flesh, across the flat plane of his stomach and then lower.

Her questing hand roved down the soft wool of his brais, smoothing up and down his legs, feeling the muscles in his thighs and calves. She tugged impatiently at the knot keeping the garment tied to his waist, nearly crowing with triumph when it opened. James let out a breathy moan of laughter as she pulled off the brais, leaving him naked.

Her eyes widened and her lips parted. His penis was bold and hard, jutting proudly skyward. Fascinated, she moved herself closer to his warmth, exploring the contours of his body with frenzied hands, marveling with each new discovery.

Strange, but the more she caressed him, the greater her own excitement grew. She could feel her breasts swelling, her nipples hardening. Her mind tripped wildly with all manner of wicked thoughts. She wanted to feel everything, taste everything.

Did she dare?

Aye! Wildly, she pressed her lips to his inner thigh, just below the triangle of hair that circled his manhood.

His hips jerked upward. Delighted by his reaction, she did it again, this time using her tongue. His hips rose higher, followed by a low moan.

"Does that please ye?" she whispered.

A laugh burst out of his throat that quickly turned to a groan. "Ye're killing me, lass."

"What should I do?"

His chest rose and fell with a deep breath. "Anything ye'd like."

"Can I . . . can I caress ye with my tongue?"

"Aye." His voice was strangled.

She nuzzled him with her nose, curious to see if the gooseflesh covering the flat, muscled plane of his stomach would travel farther. It did. She pulled her head back and held herself motionless, inches from his manhood. Fascinated, she watched his penis thicken and grow larger.

"Are ye doing that deliberately?" she asked.

"What?"

"Making it stand up."

"It has a will of its own," he croaked.

She moistened her lips. "I want to tame the beast," she declared. Her heart racing, Davina did the unthinkable—she placed her lips over the glistening tip and pulled the head of his penis into her mouth.

James's hips shot off the bed as if he had been poked by a hot iron. Contact broken, Davina sat back on her knees. She stared at his back, pondering what could have gone wrong. He seemed to be enjoying her ministrations and then . . .

She could hear him blowing out several deep breaths. He turned back to her and she tried not to let her disappointment show. Yet he must have sensed it. He reached out and slowly traced the outline of her plump lips.

"Ye have the most beautiful mouth," he murmured huskily.

"I want to try it again."

Davina wasn't sure who was more shocked by those words—she or James.

"Ye'll hear no complaints from me," he said hoarsely.

She snuggled close and put her head in the hollow

of his shoulder. He slowly eased back until they were both lying on the bed. She waited a moment, then slid down his chest.

This time she didn't hesitate, stroking and swirling her tongue down the length of one side of his cock, then up the other. He groaned and rocked against her and she took him completely inside her mouth, circling, licking, sucking.

His hands threaded through her hair, clenching tightly with each languid stroke. It was an incredible feeling, knowing that she had the power to bring him such complete pleasure. 'Twas also a tremendous relief, knowing that she could make love to him despite the self-conscious inhibition she had suffered from for so many years.

She tilted her head to observe his reaction. His eyes were closed, his cheeks flushed, his expression was one of pure pleasure. His teeth were biting his lower lip as he tried to contain his groans.

Davina felt a giddy flush of power stain her cheeks. It was so much more difficult than she thought—and yet it was also so simple. If she just allowed it to happen, it took no effort to be pulled into the whirlwind of desire they were creating.

The memories she feared so greatly slowly dimmed. She inhaled deeply, letting the musky, male scent of him flow through her.

"Enough now," he growled suddenly, pulling himself away.

She lifted her head and looked into his eyes. They were dark with pent-up desire, yet when they met hers, they softened. He smiled before reaching out and cupping the side of her face in his palm.

Restless, tingling sensations heated her skin, making

her heart beat faster. That heat moved through her and the wanting surged.

"Dinnae be afraid to touch me," she whispered. "I long to feel yer hands caress me."

"I fear that I'll lose control and hurt ye," he confessed.

"I willnae break," she insisted.

"Ye need to put yerself where I can easily reach ye." Davina frowned. "I'm right beside ye, James."

He pulled her to his chest and kissed her, bending his head to meet her lips. His hand gently caressed her back, moved to her shoulder, and finally her breast. Her body tightened when his thumbs grazed her nipples. She clung to him, burning with the fever of rising passion. He pushed her nightgown off her shoulder and lowered his head.

The feel of his wet mouth on her sensitive nipples made her cry out with pleasure. She bit back another cry and arched against him, offering him more. His teeth roughly grazed the nipple. She cried out yet again, her hands reaching up to touch his hair, to hold him close.

Her body bowed beneath him, straining upward. She could feel his hand reaching between her legs. Her breath caught and held, but then slowly, shyly, she parted her thighs, allowing him an intimacy she believed she would never experience. She sighed with pleasure at his gentle touch, each caress leaving her eager for the next.

"Ye're growing soft and damp fer me, my angel," he murmured. "So sweet, so delicate."

Overwhelming sensations jolted through her body as his fingers skillfully circled, teased, and stroked the sensitive pearl hidden within the folds of her womanhood. Her belly tightened and she twisted restlessly as an odd, anxious ache filled her. She needed something *more*.

"James," she pleaded.

"Aye, love, I know what ye need."

He lowered his head and pulled her nipple into his mouth. Her whole body lifted, stiffened, then began to tremble. His magical hand moved faster, coaxing her. She could feel herself straining toward release. Her legs shook, her breathing grew deep and ragged.

She cried out, a long thin wail of joy and pleasure, riding the wave of unbearable sensations in a haze, her body convulsing mindlessly. It seemed as though her very soul was coming apart, but James was there to catch it, to hold it, to protect it.

As the final bliss claimed her, James growled deep in his throat and suddenly rolled her onto her back. He settled his hard, hot body on top of her, surrounding her with his strength.

Davina let out a soft cry. She could feel all his weight pressing her down against the mattress. Imprisoning her. Her mind clouded, her body rebelled. The edges of terror and memory joined and she panicked, unable to catch her breath as the fear clogged her throat.

"God's bones, Davina, what's wrong?"

"I cannae breathe," she stammered.

"Damn it!"

He pulled his body off, but hovered in place above her, elbows braced on the side of her head. She stared into his face, fighting for calm, struggling to overcome her panic.

"Forgive me," she murmured, wrapping her fingers around his forearms. She could feel the muscles tightly locked in place and it helped, knowing she would be able to pull herself away if she chose.

But I dinnae want to pull away. Tears gathered in her eyes. "I want this," she insisted. "Please, dinnae leave me."

"I'm not going anywhere," he replied with a deep sigh, setting his forehead against hers.

They stayed that way for a minute or two and then he began brushing his nose across hers, back and forth, back and forth. It was a childish action, yet the odd caress eased her panic, helped her regain her trust in herself.

"I'm sorry," she whispered.

"Shh, there's more than one way to accomplish this deed, and I intend fer us both to enjoy finding out which works best." He turned on his back and lifted her above him, reversing their positions. "Straddle my hips."

Nay! It felt strange, unnatural to be positioned in such a way. But she quickly let go of her reservations and did as he commanded, leaning forward until she was lying flat atop him.

"Now kiss me, lass."

It was the perfect angle for kissing and Davina took full advantage of it. The fires of her passion were quickly rekindled. She felt but a small glimmer of trepidation when his hands took hold of her hips, lifted her, and then eased her down onto the tip of his jutting erection.

A fine sheen of sweat broke out on her upper lip as she lowered her hips, trying to take him into her body. Her inner muscles softened and stretched, the wetness from her earlier release making it a bit easier.

Still, it was a tight fit and not an entirely pleasurable feeling. Yet she wanted more. She tried to push his penis farther inside her, but James circled her waist and held her in place.

"What's wrong?" she asked.

"Ye're a virgin."

"What?" She was concentrating so hard, she barely heard him speak.

"Ye are a virgin, Davina. I can feel yer maidenhead."

"Oh."

"Do ye want to stop?"

"No!"

She punctuated her response with a downward thrust. The pain was sharp and swift, but it faded the moment she met James's eyes.

"Did I do it right?" she asked.

He groaned and lifted his hips. She reached frantically for his shoulders to steady herself, then drove down, burying him to the hilt. His chest heaved and he groaned again. Davina rocked her hips slowly, delighting in the sound.

She set the pace, pushing downward harder and faster, but they moved together, in a primitive rhythm as old as time itself. James ran one hand down her hip and reached between her legs. Lightning raced through her body. Davina cried out as his thumb rotated over the most sensitive part of her womanhood. She could feel the heat and wetness emanating from her body and it heightened her excitement.

"More," she whimpered.

His hips bucked upward and he thrust deeply, quickening the rhythm. Heart thundering, she answered, pushing her hips against him again and again. It was exhilarating. She closed her eyes and allowed her body to feel everything, allowed these glorious sensations to sweep away her haunted memories.

The desperate sense of need and tension she now recognized started building inside her. Whimpering,

Davina struggled to reach it, pressing her slick flesh more firmly against his stroking thumb.

"Ye're almost there, Davina," he whispered.

Her inner muscles tightened, pulsed. Her eyes popped open in astonishment. Again? How was that possible?

Beneath her, James looked to be in agony. His jaw clenched, his shoulders arched, his breathing loud and harsh. Had she breath to speak, Davina would have asked if aught were amiss, but all she could do was hang on as they raced together to the peak.

Suddenly, James stiffened and shouted her name and Davina felt the hot flood of his seed deep inside her. She stroked his hair, uttering sweet words of nonsense, then clung to him, seeking the comfort only he could bring to her wounded heart.

Tears were running down her cheeks. She quickly wiped them from her face with the back of her hand, fearing that if James saw them he would misunderstand. 'Twas not sorrow that brought them, but intense relief.

She felt a lightness in her heart, a wholeness in her spirit. It was as though the shattered pieces of her life that she had struggled so long to repair were finally mended.

She resisted the urge to burst into giggles, thinking the moment too meaningful for such levity.

She could love again, and equally as important, she could accept the love and affections of a man. Completely and without reservation.

James rolled her to his side and drew her into his arms. She rubbed her cheek back and forth over his shoulder and curled closer. Her body tingled with sated pleasure, but it was the realization that for the first time in five years she felt whole again that gave her the greatest ease.

"Are ye tired?" he asked.

"Hmm."

She could feel his body tense against hers. "Davina, love, we need to talk."

Davina answered with a loud yawn. "Just let me rest my eyes fer a few minutes first, James," she muttered as her voice trailed off and sleep claimed her.

Chapter Fifteen

James stared down at the meal laid out before him. The oatcakes were nicely browned and warm, the small pot of honey sitting beside the platter a rare luxury. Taking full advantage of the bounty, he tore a cake in half, drizzled it liberally with the sticky nectar, and put it in his mouth. The sweetness burst upon his tongue and he allowed himself a brief moment to savor the ambrosia before once again training his eye upon the archway leading into the great hall.

Where was she?

At this late hour of the morning only a few lingered at the trestle tables breaking their fast. Thankfully, none were members of his family. Facing their curious scrutiny while he was feeling so unsettled would have been pure torture.

He had fallen into an exhausted sleep holding Davina tightly against his chest, his spirits lifted, his heart hopeful. But when he woke with the dawn, she was gone, leaving his bed the same way she had arrived—quietly, stealthy, without his knowledge.

A part of him didn't understand why he felt so outraged. More than once he had slipped from a woman's bed as the dawn approached while on Crusade. Except for the fact that he was the one left behind, was this any different?

Aye, it was. Making love with Davina had awakened feelings within him he long believed dead and gone. Even now, hours later, the emotions continued thrumming through his mind and heart. She had yielded her body to him, satiating his physical desire as no other had ever done. But in doing so had somehow reached the very core of his being, touching his soul.

He had always known he had lingering feelings for her, yet he had not expected to care so much.

Then, if by some mystical conjuring, Davina suddenly appeared in the great hall. His control slipped for a moment and he jumped to his feet, demonstrating all the eagerness of a green lad. Irritated at the reaction, James turned his head away, yet the heated feeling continued to consume him.

He heard her approach and breathed in deeply, trying to dispel the sharp stab of longing that tore through him. Yet manners prevailed. He drew out the chair beside him for her and she sat, her hands folded in her lap.

"Good morning, James."

He glanced down at his clenched fist. Jesus, just the sound of her voice had the power to tie him in knots.

"Davina." He nodded his head and slowly unclenched his fist. "Ye look lovely."

Her eyebrows rose and she cocked her head. "Ye look . . . out of sorts."

He gazed back at her. "I dinnae like waking up alone in my bed. Especially after it has been filled with such a sensual, willing, bonny lass."

Guilt touched her eyes. "My behavior last night was exceedingly improper. I had to leave yer bedchamber before the household awoke. I couldn't insult the generous hospitality of yer parents by being discovered somewhere that I should not have been."

Her words pierced him sharply. If they had been found together they would have had no choice but to marry. Did this mean she did not want to be his wife? "Ye regret what happened between us last night?"

Her cheeks bloomed with color. "James, please, just leave it be."

He clenched his hand and the oatcake he held crumbled. The ease and comfort they had gained last night was now gone. "Come with me. Now!"

Her head lowered slightly. "Please, calm yerself."

He drew in a deep breath, making an effort to conceal the anger that continued to rise. "I need to speak with ye and I prefer to do so somewhere private. Unless ye wish all to know what passed between us last night?"

She sent him a dark look, then managed a forced smile. "Yer mother is expecting me in her solar this morning. I'm helping her embroider the new tunics that were made fer the squires."

She was being deliberately evasive. Why? "I'll send Colin with a message, letting her know that ye are with me. She willnae mind."

Davina's mouth set in a rebellious line, but he knew that he had won when she exhaled a soft sigh of resignation and pocketed two oatcakes. "I'll have Colleen fetch my cloak."

Impatient to be alone with her, James left his half-eaten breakfast on the table. His foot tapped impatiently as they waited for Colleen to arrive. Finally, she appeared.

She draped the heavy cloak on Davina's shoulders and helped her fasten the garment. After casting a speculative eye at James, Colleen respectfully withdrew, though her behavior made him wonder if her companion knew—or merely suspected—that Davina had spent most of the night in his bed.

Electing to leave their horses behind, they walked through the castle gates into the sunshine. There was a distinct chill in the air, but the sun had burned away the early morning mist and dampness. James chose a path that went up a hill, through a thick growth of trees.

To the left, the water that fed into the loch danced over the rocks and boulders, creating small falls and mossy green coverings. The rushing sound required the need to shout at each other in order to converse, so instead they stayed silent.

James welcomed the quiet. He had much to say, much to ask, and the words were crowding his head. He needed this time to gather his thoughts, to gain command of his tongue.

Out of the corner of his eye he could see her casting him sideways glances, but her eyes would quickly dart away if he caught her. They reached the summit and stood side by side, gazing at the landscape below; the bare treetops, bushy green pines, shimmering water of the loch.

"This rugged beauty reminds me of ye," he murmured. "Stark and dormant in the cold, but when the weather warms and the spring rains come, it softens. The earth turns green with promise, the fields are alive with heather blooms."

"Goodness! The cool air has brought out the troubadour in ye, James." She laughed nervously, then offered him a small smile.

He did not return it. Instead, he inhaled his frustration, then came directly to the heart of the matter. "I want the truth from ye, Davina. Why did ye come to my bed last night, only to leave it before the dawn broke?"

* * *

Davina swallowed against the emotion crowding her throat. It was horrible seeing the hurt in James's face, but worse knowing she was the cause of his misery.

"What in heaven's name . . ."

"What?" Davina turned her head sharply, squinting to see what had so suddenly captured James's full attention.

"There's something moving in the trees," he declared.

Davina stepped forward and squinted harder. "I dinnae see anything." She had no sooner spoken the words when her eye caught a glint of sunlight reflecting off the blade of a drawn sword. For an instant she was mesmerized, but then a flash of a second, third, and more blades broke the spell.

"Damn it! We shouldn't have walked so far from the castle without a guard." James drew his lips together grimly. "There are too many of them fer us to fight."

Davina shuddered. "Perhaps they dinnae mean us any harm?" The look of disbelief he sent her way made her throat go dry. "Mayhap we can bargain with them?" she croaked.

"They dinnae appear to be in a bargaining mood."

The men were climbing steadily, spreading out in a formation that covered all avenues of escape. "We're trapped," she whispered bleakly.

"Not if we can find a way down where we won't meet them coming up," James muttered.

"'Tis impossible. They have fanned out to cover all the pathways. We willnae be able to slip by them."

James shifted his stance and looked down at the gray waters of the loch. His brow furrowed for a moment, then suddenly his expression brightened.

"Ye have a plan?" she asked hopefully.

"Aye." He stared again at the rippling water and Davina gasped in sudden panic. "James, ye cannae mean fer us to jump into the loch?"

"It's not that far. Malcolm and I did it often as lads."

"In the middle of winter? We'll freeze to death."

He flashed a smile so wicked her heart leaped. "Better to risk a watery grave than to be taken by an unknown foe."

Davina stared down at the murky surface of the water. They were so high! Her eyes widened as she turned back to him. "Is there no other way?"

He shook his head and her heart sank further. "I'm not a very strong swimmer," she admitted.

"Neither am I."

Davina's head whipped around at the quip. She nearly screeched when she saw his eyes dancing with amusement, but then her fear calmed. If James was able to tease her, he must have complete confidence in their chances of escape.

"We probably need not worry about the swimming," she said quietly. "Most likely the fall will kill us."

"That's the spirit." James's lips tightened into a cheeky grin. "Will ye trust me to keep ye safe?"

"Aye." Her lower lip trembled and she caught it between her teeth. She did not want James to think her fear was born out of a lack of confidence in him.

"Hold on to me tightly," he whispered.

"Always." Heart pounding, Davina pressed herself against his chest. His strong arms encircled her and she sighed, reveling in the warmth and power of his body. She had every faith in his ability to protect her; yet she knew the odds were not in their favor.

"I love ye, Davina Armstrong."

His words startled her so completely, for an instant

she forgot to be afraid. Her eyes were level with his and in them she saw the truth of those magical words. Her heart soared.

"I love ye, James McKenna."

His bright smile gave her a burst of pure joy. She placed a hasty kiss on his cheek, then buried her head into his neck. He tightened his grip on her. Davina could feel his powerful muscles tense as he crouched, then leaped forward. She tried—and failed—to prevent the scream that tore from her throat as she felt herself falling.

Frantically, she clung to James's strength, though it was hardly necessary. He held her so tightly, there was no chance that she would slip away from him.

They hit the water with unspeakable force. The wet, biting cold immediately wrapped around Davina's lungs, stealing her breath. Another scream lodged in her throat as she felt them sinking deeper and deeper into the frigid loch. Branches, twigs, and slick vegetation scraped against her body as they fell deeper and deeper.

I love ye, Davina Armstrong.

The words echoed in her heart and mind, giving her strength to face the cold, black darkness that surrounded them. She let her body go limp, allowing the water to claim her as she fell. But then suddenly they were no longer sinking. Davina could feel James kicking and pulling their bodies upward, toward the surface.

She tried to help, but had difficulty making her frozen limbs cooperate. Still, she did the best that she could, copying James's movements. Her lungs were near to bursting when they finally broke through the surface. Gasping and sputtering, Davina held tightly to James as he treaded water, keeping them both afloat.

The band of men appeared on the mountain ridge. Davina could hear their shouts of anger, but could not decipher the words, as they pointed down at her and James.

"Let's pray they have no bows and arrows," James said, as he towed her through the icy water.

Davina marveled at how he had somehow managed to keep her head above the water as he moved. Her limbs felt leaden; she could barely make them move and the wet material of her cloak and gown were like stones, pulling her down. Yet James appeared to have no difficulty pulling them toward the shore.

When they reached the muddy bank, she struggled out of the water, crawling on her knees, her breath bursting in short pants.

"Are ye all right, Davina?"

She lifted her head at the absurd question, squinting at James through the wet, tangled strands of her hair. Her braid had come loose and the sodden mass was now covering her face.

"I'm frozen to the bone, half-drowned, and scared of out my wits," she chattered through her teeth.

"Och, it does my heart good to hear the indignity in yer voice," James said, as he swept her into his arms and settled her over his shoulder.

Upended, Davina felt the bile rise in her throat. "I can walk," she insisted. "Just give me a minute to catch my breath."

"We dinnae have a minute to waste," James grunted. "Those men will be down the mountain soon. Our only chance to prevent them from taking ye is to hide in the forest."

"Why do ye assume it's me that they are after?" Davina huffed, rising up on his shoulder. "Have ye never made an enemy?"

"Never one that's so persistent," he answered grimly.

Her teeth chattered and she tried to clamp them shut. She slumped over his shoulder and wrapped her arms around him, grateful that the heat of his body provided some warmth.

"How far are we from the castle?" she asked.

"Far enough," he grunted. "We'd have to run through open fields to reach the gates, making us an easy target. I know somewhere that we can hide that is closer."

"Put me down, James. We'll move faster if I run with ye."

He didn't answer, nor did he set her down. Instead, he began running through the forest, hurling over large rocks, ducking to avoid the branches from slapping their faces. Davina could feel thorns catching on the fabric of her wet cloak and she worried about the scratches James was most likely getting on various parts of his body.

He stopped for a moment to get his bearings in the dense woods and Davina slowly wiggled herself down off his shoulder. When he allowed it, she realized that he must be tiring.

"It's not much farther," he said. "But it's best to keep moving quickly, so they cannae find our trail."

Davina nodded and took the outstretched hand he offered. They resumed their mad dash through the woods. Even though she heard no one in pursuit, James set a grueling pace.

After but a few minutes, Davina felt an ache in her side. Her lungs were bursting with the pain of each labored breath, her limbs ached from carrying the weight of her wet clothing, yet she stubbornly refused to complain, refused to ask him to stop or slow down, because she knew he would merely nod his head, pick her up, and carry her.

Nay, she would not be a burden and drain his strength. She would persevere. Suddenly, James came to a halt. Davina stumbled forward, knocking into his back. With a startled cry, she fought for balance.

Strong arms captured her. Lifting her chin, she gave James a wan smile of thanks, trying to hide the exhaustion from her face.

Why have we stopped? She would have asked the question, if she could have found the breath to speak.

"Come," he said. "We are here."

Truly? Davina heaved a sigh. They had stopped in a copse of trees that looked no different from any others they had just run through. How could he be so certain?

Motioning for Davina to follow, James tramped through the dense bushes. She dutifully dogged his footsteps, growing more confused as they drew deeper into thick brush.

Then James dropped to his knees and began to crawl. Clamping her chattering teeth firmly together, Davina did the same. He started poking at a thorny bramble bush and she realized it hid the entrance to a low cave.

"We have to crawl on our bellies to get inside," James said, speaking to her over his shoulder.

Davina instinctively reared back. "Good Lord."

"I know ye dinnae like tight spaces, yet ye found the courage to rescue Lileas from the crater. This will be easier. The space is not so closed once we are inside."

Trusting that he was being truthful, Davina ignored the discomfort that assailed her. She imitated his movements, crawling on her belly. Sharp rocks dug into her tender flesh, but she kept moving.

There was nothing but darkness and the rustling sound of James's body as he pulled himself forward. At one point she could barely lift her head without hitting it on the cave ceiling. Panic swept through her, but she kept going.

Finally, they were able to stand upright. Davina swayed with momentary dizziness, but she willed away the queasiness. It took a few minutes for her eyes to adjust to the darkness, to realize that the ominous shadows were really only harmless bits of logs and rock formations.

"We must wait to build a fire to dry out our garments or else the smoke will draw those men to us," James said.

Davina crossed her arms over her chest and nodded. As much as she longed for the warmth of the flames, she knew James was right. At least they were out of the wind.

Her gaze went around the cave, taking in the gloomy darkness. "Is that water I hear?"

"Aye. Just up ahead."

James took her hand and guided her farther into the cave. Davina kept her eyes on her feet, carefully picking her way over the stones. After a few moments, they entered a second chamber, far larger than the first.

She lifted her chin when they stopped, gasping in astonishment. The area in which they stood was massive in size. Soaring columns of twisted rocks that appeared to be floating in midair were scattered around them, making her feel small and insignificant.

The top of the cave was shaped like a beehive, with shafts of light streaming in from an opening at the peak. Davina craned her neck so she could better see the distinct color variations in the layers of rock that made up the walls and ceiling. Some were dark in color, but others shimmered like silver and gold. It was an enchanting, magical place; a place one imagined to be inhabited by fairies and other mystical creatures.

But the most incredible part was the circular-shaped hole in the ground filled with water. It was fed by a narrow stream trickling down the side of the cave. Vapors of steam rose from the pool's surface, beckoning with its inviting warmth.

"I've heard tales of hidden water pools, but have never seen one," she said.

"Malcolm and I accidentally discovered it when we were lads. Our father insisted we stay away, but that proved impossible once we took our first swim."

"Why would anyone want to keep such a magnificent place like this a secret?" she asked.

James shrugged. "We were told not to reveal where it was hidden, nor were we ever to return because the cave was cursed."

Her mouth fell open. "Nay! How can something this magical be cursed?"

His gaze swept her face. "It's the perfect spot fer a lovers' tryst."

She swallowed. "Aye."

"But a hundred years ago the serenity of the cave was marred by death and violence. According to my father, two lovers met a most gruesome death at the hands of the woman's husband after being discovered here by him. Mad with grief and remorseful over the deed, the husband slit his own throat. Months later, the three bodies were found in here together."

"How awful."

"My father insisted that their restless spirits would

haunt the cave fer all eternity. But I think he conjured the tale in order to keep us away."

"Well, it probably wasn't safe fer two mischievous lads to be here on their own," Davina concluded.

"A fair point. However, I also believe he enjoyed taking my mother here and wanted to make certain he had privacy."

As Davina looked again at the pool, she could not help but agree that it was the ideal spot for lovers to frolic. "Haunted or not, I'm glad that ye remembered where to find the cave. I was near frozen being outside in the cold wind."

"Never fear, I know precisely how to get ye warm."

"James," she scolded.

His brow lifted mockingly. "Ye have a most wicked mind, Lady Davina."

"Hmmm."

"I, on the other hand, am a most practical man. A few minutes in this water is all ye need to be warm again. Now, come here and I'll help ye undress."

The promise of warmth overcame any trepidation she had about removing her clothing. Teeth chattering, she followed his command. He flung her wet cloak over a large boulder, then knelt before her. She put her hands upon his shoulders and braced herself against him as he tugged her leather boots off her feet, then removed the wet woolen stockings. Wiggling her aching toes, Davina began rubbing her feet together.

Next off was her gold circlet and short veil. The thin fabric was already dry in some places, most likely because of the speed at which they had run through the forest. Gazing longingly at the warm water, she presented her back to James, but the wet laces of her gown were neigh impossible to untie.

"Cut them," she said wearily.

"Nay, I can loosen them if ye just stand still," James insisted stubbornly.

Davina stood quietly, feeling his fingers fumbling with the wet knots. She was about to repeat her request that he simply cut them, when she felt the fabric give way.

"Leave my chemise," she requested, suddenly feeling an unexpected shyness at standing naked before him.

He ignored her, stripping her of her final garment. He tossed it toward a flat rock. From the corner of her eye, Davina saw it glance off the top and slide to the ground. In an effort to keep her modesty, she crossed her arms and clutched her breasts as she approached the pool, but James seemed unaffected by the sight of her unclothed body.

She sat at the edge, dangling her legs in the water. It was hot! Davina was contemplating the best way to get immersed in this glorious warmth when she felt James standing behind her.

"Let me help ye," he said briskly.

His hands spanned her waist and he gently lowered her into the pool. She kicked anxiously, feeling for the bottom as the water rose higher and higher, then sighed with relief when her feet touched solid rock.

The water lapped over her shoulders and her flesh tingled at the heat, prickling back to life. She turned and looked up at James, kneeling at the edge. Their eyes met. He dipped his hand into the water, swirling it through his fingers.

His hand touched her shoulder and she tensed. But it felt so tender, she allowed herself to relax and enjoy the sensual stroke of his strong fingers.

"Are ye going to join me?" she asked.

He leaned forward. A tremor moved through her and awareness sprang to life. Davina knew that she must be blushing fiercely. To hide her embarrassment, she flicked her fingers and splashed him playfully. Water droplets ran down his cheek, though a few clung stubbornly to his lashes. He looked young and boyish.

"I'll wait fer my turn until ye're finished," he replied.

He stood and walked away. She watched him scour the cave, collecting a few small branches and what appeared to be a fur blanket. As he stacked the wood in a small pile, she realized he was going to try to light a fire.

"Is it safe?" she asked.

"Aye. I'd forgotten how high it is in here. If I keep the blaze small, by the time the smoke escapes through the top of the cave, it will be too weak to be seen."

Trusting his word, Davina pushed herself off the edge of the pool. She stretched out on her back and floated, letting the warmth surround her, wishing she had some soap. It felt wonderful to rinse the muck from the loch off her body and out of her hair. But the pool water in which she now swam had a decidedly mineral odor, reminiscent of rotten eggs.

Davina drifted to the center of the pool, then cautiously swam back to the edge. She could see that James had been most successful in his endeavors—a small fire was burning directly under the opening in the cave ceiling.

It would provide a bit of warmth in the vast space, but more importantly aid in drying their clothes. Now that she was delightfully warm, the idea of putting on her cold, wet garments was most distasteful.

"Come and soak yer cold bones, James. Though I confess I could stay in here fer hours,'tis past time that ye took yer ease."

He moved into the shaft of light near the pool and for a moment all Davina could do was stare. Hands on his hips, James stood dressed only in his brais, which were molded to his legs like a second skin. Glistening with moisture, his naked chest was all hard muscle and sinew strength. A sight of pure perfection, in spite of the scars that marred his side and shoulder.

"Are ye getting out?" he asked.

She swallowed hard. Then nodded, not trusting her voice.

"Here. It's not much, but it will keep ye covered until yer clothes dry."

She pulled herself out of the water and took the molted fur he offered with a nod of thanks, wrapping it around her shoulders. It was not very clean and smelled of the earth, but Davina didn't care. "Come, snuggle inside with me, James."

His brow rose. "Are ye trying to seduce me, lass?"

A small, nervous laugh bubbled from her chest. "I'm certain I look a fright. Ye would be a desperate man indeed to find me attractive in this state."

"I'm confident we are hidden from our mysterious foes, but 'tis best not to be distracted."

She nodded in agreement. Yet unable to stop herself, Davina put her fingers on his chest, needing to feel his solid strength. It calmed her, yet also intrigued. Of their own volition, her fingers glided sensually over his chest, swirling through the crisp hairs, glancing over the firm nipples.

He gasped, touching her hair, smoothing it behind her ear, then brushed his lips against her earlobe. She squirmed at the sensation, lifting herself toward him.

"There is a tempest that rules me whenever I'm near ye, Davina. The need to hold ye, to kiss and caress ye drives me wild."

Davina licked her lips. "I dinnae mean to be the cause of so much turmoil, good sir."

"Ye relish it." Though his tone was light and mocking, his eyes were solemn. "Before we jumped into the loch, ye said that ye loved me. If that's true, why did ye leave my bed?"

"I'm sorry," she said, placing her hand upon his cheek. "I left because I dinnae want ye to feel obligated toward me."

To her relief, the tightness in his jaw eased. He framed her face with his hands, brushing his lips softly against her. "Best be warned, the only woman I'll be taking to my bed from this day forward is my wife. So if ye want me, ye'll have to marry me."

She curled against his chest, hearing his heart thumping wildly. "Ye said last night that ye couldn't promise me marriage."

"I lied."

"Did ye lie about anything else?"

"I dinnae recall much of what I said. My mind—and body—were too overcome to remember more than the sensations we shared. The pleasure, of course, but it was so much more. It was *right*, Davina, the joy of it all, taking possession of ye, filling ye with my seed. 'Tis what I want fer the rest of my life and I can only hope and pray that ye feel the same."

She felt the tears sting her eyes and she hugged him tightly. "I do, James. I do feel the same."

He threaded his fingers through her damp hair and held her closer to his heart. "'Tis decided. The first thing we'll do after we get out of this cave is find a priest!"

Chapter Sixteen

The sound of a single scream woke him. A piercing, painful cry so filled with anguish that it chilled his very soul. Heart racing, James reached for his sword and sprang to his feet. His eyes searched the dim light that surrounded them, but found no one. Rising, he moved toward the opening of the cave, but saw no movement in the second, smaller chamber.

James swung back around at the sound of another moan of pain and saw Davina sitting upright, her body rigid, her face staring into the darkness. Her breath came in short, bursting pants, mingled with soft, muted moans of fear and distress.

"Davina!" He rushed to her side to offer comfort, but when he drew near, she struck out, flaying wildly at his chest, nearly striking him on the jaw.

"Dinnae touch me!" she cried, fighting harder.

He reached for her hands and she again pulled away. Her eyes were wide open, but James realized that she did not see him. Nay, she was trapped in the grip of a nightmare, unaware of him, unaware of anything.

He caught her wrists. "'Tis a dream, Davina. A wicked nightmare. Ye are in no danger. Open yer eyes."

She shuddered, shaking her head. He continued speaking to her in a low tone and she finally blinked, her eyes focusing on him. "James?"

"Aye, lass, I have ye. Ye're safe here with me."

She went limp in his arms. "It was horrible."

"Ah, love."

"Real, so real," she muttered. Her voice was a hoarse whisper and he had to strain to hear it. "There were scores of men. Giant, faceless men, brandishing swords. They were chasing me through the forest. I could hear them trampling behind me as I ran, getting closer and closer. My lungs were bursting, but I couldn't get away. No matter which way I turned, they found me, they followed me. I tripped and fell and suddenly they were standing there in a circle, glaring down at me.

"They sneered and laughed amongst themselves and encouraged their leader to take me. He threw himself on top of me while the others held me down. I could feel the fear clutching at my throat. I tried to scream fer help, but there was no sound when I opened my mouth.

"I bucked and twisted and somehow freed one of my hands. I beat the brute against his shoulders, even pulled his hair so hard his head fell back, but nothing could move him off me. He tore at my gown, ripping away the fabric."

James smoothed his hand tenderly over her damp hair, trying to stop her trembling. "Shh, 'twas only a bad dream."

"Aye, a dream. An evil, wretched nightmare." She shuddered and gripped the edges of the fur blanket so tightly the tips of her fingers turned white. "I dinnae like being afraid. Awake or asleep."

Her vulnerability struck a chord inside him. He wondered at the demons that plagued her, that disturbed her rest. Though the attack had happened years ago, she still suffered the effects.

As did he.

"The fear is real, but only in yer mind." Cradling her in his arms, James continued stroking her hair. He wished he could do something more to ease her fright, but knew this was a battle she must wage on her own.

Davina's hands slipped around his waist. James felt her sigh of relief and gradually her trembling ceased and her breathing slowed. He pulled his sword within easy reach, resting his back against the hard rock. The small fire he had built still burned low, the flames casting shadows that flickered and danced across the wall.

She stayed burrowed against him for the longest time. It seemed such a simple thing, but the act brought them both a strong measure of contentment. Maybe because the intimacy of the moment had nothing to do with sex, but everything to do with love and trust.

"Do ye think anyone at the castle has noticed that we are missing?" Davina asked, breaking the silence.

"I'm uncertain, though I imagine they'll realize that ye aren't there long before they know I'm away."

She turned her head up and frowned at him. "What?"

"It's not unusual fer me to be off on my own fer hours at a time," James explained. "But my mother will be wondering what has happened to her favorite holiday guest when she doesn't see ye all morning."

The confusion in Davina's eyes faded, replaced by a curious light. "How do ye think she'll react when she learns we wish to be married? Will she approve?"

James brightened. "She'll be very happy, though I suspect not one bit surprised when we tell her. The McKenna, too. After all, it was his idea that ye wed one of his sons."

Davina groaned. "I have a feeling that yer father is

going to take great pleasure in reminding us of that in the years to come."

"Aye, he'll not let it go unsaid."

"Well, ye did tell him that ye had no interest in me," Davina said.

"And ye said that ye'd never wed," James countered, his lip quirking in amusement.

"Och, yer mother will have to protect us from the worst of yer father's gloating," Davina joked.

"We can count upon her to aid us," James agreed with a smile. It was good to see the color returning to Davina's cheeks and the sparkle of wit in her eyes, proof that the terrors of her nightmare had faded.

"I willnae mind a bit of teasing if it means I am yer wife. 'Tis a price I am more than willing to pay," she said.

"Shall we move to a keep far away, so we only need face my father once or twice every few years?" James teased, kissing her temple softly.

"Nay! We shall live at Torridon Keep, which is a journey of only a fortnight from McKenna Castle. Far enough to give us the privacy we need, yet close enough to allow fer visits with yer family."

"Occasional visits," James amended with a laugh.

Relief swept over him. This fanciful talk of their future was a welcome respite from their sobering situation. It made him cherish life all the more, made him more determined that they would not only survive, they would flourish.

"We will be happy together, James," Davina said, her voice firm, her eyes filled with hope.

"I already am happy, sweetheart," he declared, dropping a kiss on the top of her nose.

"How much longer should we stay here?" she asked.

"It would be safest to wait until nightfall to leave, to make our way back to the castle under cover of darkness."

Davina nodded. She shifted, placing her hand over her belly. "Goodness, I'm hungry. Ye might remember that I missed breaking my fast this morning."

Aye, he'd been so anxious to be alone with her, he hadn't allowed her any time to eat before whisking her away from the great hall. "Dinnae ye nibble on those oatcakes ye took from the table?"

"Nay, I put them in my pocket."

"Shall I check if they are still there?"

She burst out laughing. "If they survived our swim in the loch, then I'm going to sit here and watch ye eat every soggy crumb."

"I should do it, just to make amends."

He lowered his head and kissed her bare shoulder. "Yer clothes should be dry soon. Why don't ye try and rest until then? Unless ye fear the return of yer nightmares?"

"Knowing ye are close should hold them at bay." Smiling, she traced her finger along his arm. "Sleeping will take my mind off my grumbling stomach."

"I shall order a haunch of venison to be roasted the moment we return home," he replied. "'Twill be a celebration of our impending nuptials."

Davina adjusted her position and placed her head in his lap. His manhood stirred with interest at the feel of her breath so near. She let out a wicked little laugh. "Like my promised meal, this too must wait until we return to the castle. 'Tis only fair."

He groaned, low and deep. "Cease yer teasing, wench."

"Aye, good sir."

She wiggled about, then settled herself. James waited until her breathing slowed and deepened before taking the hilt of his sword in his hand. Eyes trained on the cave entrance, he sat, watched, and waited.

A while later, James heard the distinct sound of footsteps crunching on stones. An uneasy sensation gripped his gut, but he forced himself to remain calm, logical. It had been hours since they escaped their would-be attackers; 'twas impossible for them to have been followed here.

The cave was well hidden, which made the likelihood of their pursuers happening upon it a very small possibility. Nay, if someone were coming, it had to be someone who knew about the cave.

And there were very few people who fit that description.

Or so he believed.

Davina lifted her head off his lap and turned to him with questioning eyes. He nodded. She rolled off him, hastily donning her clothes. He quickly pulled on his brais and still-damp tunic, then picked up his sword. Reaching into his boot, he pulled out one of his dirks.

"Here." James turned and handed the blade to Davina. "I hope and pray it's a McKenna warrior making all that noise. But if not . . ."

Her eyes grew wide, but she took the weapon with a nod of thanks. James glimpsed the raw determination in Davina's face and found a small measure of comfort. Pray God it did not happen, but if it came to it, she would not go down without a fight.

"How long before they find us?" she whispered.

James cocked his head and listened, straining to hear.

"Not long. Crouch down behind that large rock and stay hidden until I tell ye to come out," he commanded.

When Davina had done as he asked, James moved to the other side of the cave. He wanted to make certain to draw the attention of whoever stepped inside toward him and away from Davina. Fitting himself between a narrow crack in the rock wall, he watched from the shadows.

He didn't have long to wait. A man, his sword drawn, walked through the natural archway of stone into their section of the cave. He held a torch aloft in one hand and his sword in the other, the long, sharp blade glistening in the light.

For an instant James was blinded, but then he saw the distinct colors of the McKenna plaid. Yet he didn't relax his grip on his sword until he recognized the warrior's features.

"Malcolm!"

"James! At last!" Malcolm brandished his sword in the air. "We've been searching these woods fer hours. Is Davina with ye?"

"I'm here, Malcolm," she answered, emerging from her hiding spot.

"Thank the good Lord! Mother would have had my hide if I dinnae return with at least one of ye."

"As I am so very pleased to see ye, brother, I willnae ask which one of us ye preferred to find," James grumbled, though he smiled when he said it.

Malcolm drew closer. He surprised James utterly by pulling him into a manly hug and slapping him on the back.

"Ye seem unharmed," Malcolm observed. "Both of ye."

"We are well," Davina answered. "How did ye know where to find us?"

"Luck. I wish I had thought to look here first. I recognized the area the moment we crested the ridge and remembered our secret cave." Malcolm turned to James. "We always had a grand time here, even after father forbade us to come. I decided that if I were being chased, this would be a fine place to hide."

"How did ye know we were in trouble?" James asked.

"The watch spotted what he thought was a beggar tramping through the woods. But when he noticed the man was well armed, he called fer the guard. 'Twas only after they started tracking him that the others were spotted.

"By then we realized both ye and Davina were gone, so we assumed ye were their target. We gave chase, but they eluded us. I'm so relieved they dinnae catch ye."

"They were after Davina."

Malcolm grimaced. "Just as Father feared."

"Are ye alone?" Davina asked.

"Nay, I've got twenty men outside as escort and nearly one hundred combing these woods looking fer ye and those knaves trespassing on McKenna land. But I fear they are long gone."

James blew out his breath. "Ye weren't able to capture at least one of them?"

Malcolm shook his head in disgust. "They scattered to the winds once we rode from the castle gates. They seem to know these woods well; I suspect they have been hiding in them fer several days, if not weeks."

"I'll put out the fire. Gather the rest of yer clothes, Davina." James turned to his brother. "Did ye bring any extra mounts fer us to ride?"

A strange look flashed in Malcolm's eyes as he slowly

took in their disheveled, half-dressed appearance. "How long have ye been in here?"

James shrugged. "I'm not certain. Several hours at least."

James could see a muscle ticking in his brother's jaw, as though he suddenly became aware of something very important.

"I fear that yer honor might be compromised, Davina," Malcolm said, his gaze sharpening as he studied their faces.

"No matter. Let the gossips say what they will." James took Davina's hand in his. "We are to be married."

Malcolm's gaze shot to Davina. "Truly?"

"Aye." Davina smiled, then blushed and lowered her chin. "We decided today."

The announcement did little to mollify his brother's sour expression. And perversely, that brought James a wicked jolt of pleasure.

The fog and cold rolled in at the same time, making the ride miserable for all. Freezing rain and wind blew against them, but the brigand saw it as the first good sign since the McKenna soldiers had thundered through the castle gates and given chase.

The cold would slow the McKenna warriors down and the fog would aid the brigand and his men in their escape, for it obscured all but the closest objects. He pushed the men hard, knowing it would take a full day until they had ridden off McKenna land—and even then, there was no assurance that the clan warriors wouldn't follow.

"I grow weary of this game of cat and mouse," one of the men complained through chattering teeth. "My mount is ready to drop from exhaustion."

Several of the others echoed the same sentiment and the brigand's stomach tightened. The men had lost confidence in his abilities to lead them and there was little he could say in his defense. This last ambush—this final chance to capture or kill Lady Davina—had failed. There was nothing left to do but scatter and pray they weren't caught, for it was doubtful the McKenna would show them any mercy.

Despite the need to keep moving, the brigand held up his arm. "We'll take shelter in those trees and give the horses an hour to rest. Any more time than that is far too dangerous."

They stopped, dismounted, and huddled in a circle, sharing what little food they had among themselves. No one offered the brigand any. Several of the men spoke to each other in low tones, casting him open looks of displeasure. The brigand rubbed his hand across his brow. 'Twas obvious they trusted each other far more than they trusted him.

The brigand was starting to get a bad feeling in his gut. The Highlands were filled with desperate rogues willing to do just about anything to earn a bit of coin. Since he needed to act quickly, he took whomever he could find. Consequently, he didn't know very well the men he had recruited for this job.

"I'll shoulder some of the blame for our failures, but not all," the brigand admitted.

"Aye, the best chance we had to snatch the wench was when she was outside the castle walls with the lass and only a single knight to protect her," one of the men replied. "We could have easily caught her, if only Liam had kept his eyes open."

"I dinnae fall asleep!" Liam shouted. "I've told ye again and again, my horse came up lame."

"Then ye should have stolen another one," the man cried.

Liam shot him a hostile glare. "And brought the entire McKenna guard to our camp? I dinnae think ye would be too pleased if that happened."

"What difference does it make now?" the brigand asked. "The chance was lost and here we stand with nothing to show for our weeks of hiding and waiting."

There was a heavy silence. The men shifted on their feet; none would look at him directly. Fists clenched against his forehead, the brigand threw back his head and shouted in frustration. The horses shied at the sudden noise; the men did not.

"Who's going to pay us?" one of them asked.

"We dinnae do what was required," the brigand insisted. "They'll be no money."

"There has to be some!" another yelled, his hands clenched into fists.

"I'll share what I've got, but I warn ye, it isn't much."

The brigand pulled out the leather purse, knowing he would have to give them something if he wanted to avoid a rebellion. He had failed as a leader and his security of being the one to make contact with their mysterious employer was gone. The possibility of having his throat slit loomed frighteningly large.

He had already taken the precaution of hiding two coins in his boot. They rubbed painfully against the ball of his foot, creating a blister, but it was a pain well worth enduring if he could walk away from this with some money and his life.

"Liam gets nothing," one of the men decided, a sly look on his face.

Liam sputtered in outrage, his face clouding with anger. "I risked my neck, the same as any man. I deserve my share."

He turned to the brigand for support. The brigand looked away. Two against ten were not odds he'd consider; not when he was one of the two. Nay, he'd let the rabble have the money and hoped they would be content with it.

"We've tarried long enough," the brigand warned. "Best get on our horses and be on our way."

"We'll scatter," one of the men decided. "'Tis safer fer all of us."

The brigand held back as the others mounted, keeping a close eye on Liam, worried the lad would do something foolish. Though he knew he was defeated, Liam lifted his head high and watched the others ride away.

"I'll confess I'm not sorry to see the last of them," Liam said. "Now we can make plans to collect and keep the final payment fer ourselves."

The brigand gave Liam a long, hard look, then walked to his horse. "Ye're speaking nonsense, lad. Two men cannae possibly accomplish what twelve couldn't do."

"Ye're wrong. Having too many men was our downfall. But two clever fellows can accomplish the deed." Liam puffed out his chest. "Will ye join me?"

The question took the brigand aback. "If ye think it was hard before, it will be impossible now. We've tipped our hand. The McKennas will double, even triple the guard. Ye'll never even get close to her."

Liam shook his head. "McKenna Castle is a vast holding. People come and go through those open gates all day. I saw it with my own eyes. They cannae all be known by the guard. We can disguise ourselves as merchants. Or beggars. Once we've slipped inside, we'll find the lady and steal her away."

The brigand smiled. "Och, and she'll come easily, willingly?"

"We'll gag her. Tie her hands and feet."

"And ye dinnae think anyone in the entire castle will notice us carrying her about like a sack of grain?"

Liam's eyes darkened. "Then we'll kill her. Ye said we could earn double if she died."

"Ye'll have to get very close to kill her. Ye haven't got the stomach, or the stones, fer it, lad."

"I'll do it! I swear."

The brigand wiped his hand over his face and shook his head. He had enough of treachery. And failure. "Have ye ever killed a defenseless woman?"

Liam's body stiffened. "I've killed before and not only with my sword, but with a dirk. Close enough to see their eyes, close enough to smell their fear."

"A woman?"

"Nay."

The brigand gave the lad a compassionate look. "'Tis far more difficult than ye think. And it's not just the deed, it's living with the deed after it's done. Go home, Liam, and find some other line of work."

"I have no home. My da was a traitor to our clan. He was caught and killed. My mother and I were lucky to escape with our lives."

The brigand felt an unexpected jolt of sympathy for the lad's plight. "I'll say again, this path is madness, but I've no right to stop ye."

Liam threw back his shoulders in a defiant gesture. "Well, that's more coin fer me. How do I collect my payment once the deed is done?"

The brigand's mouth quirked. "Ye'll need to leave a signal, then wait until she arrives."

Liam's eyes widened. "She?"

"Aye, but dinnae be fooled and let yer guard down. Ye'll find no mercy or compassion in her," the brigand warned.

He gave Liam the final details, then swung up on his

horse. Liam remained on his feet, challenging him with an unflinching gaze. The brigand tried to ignore it, but as he led his mount away, a sharp prickle of unease prevailed.

The lad had made his choice, but the brigand hoped he would change his mind. The McKenna were not men to trifle with and he had a strong feeling that all would not bode well for young Liam if he challenged them.

Chapter Seventeen

The church bells rang out, letting everyone know a wedding was about to take place. The sound brought on a flutter of butterflies in Davina's stomach. Taking a deep breath, she somehow managed to sit quietly as Lady Aileen placed a gold circlet studded with gems on her head to hold her blue silk veil in place.

"Stand up so we can make certain the headpiece is secured," Lady Aileen commanded.

Davina obeyed, walking the entire length of the chamber. When she was done, James's sister, Katherine, approached and tied a matching gold link girdle around her waist. "Ye look a vision of beauty," she whispered. "James will be speechless when he sees ye."

Davina smiled inwardly. She wanted to look beautiful for James, wanted his jaw to drop when he caught his first glimpse of her.

The bells continued ringing. Davina anxiously looked at Lady Aileen. "We need to hurry."

"In a minute," Aileen replied, fussing with the hem of Davina's gown. "The ceremony cannae start without the bride."

"Wait, milady. I have a length of Armstrong plaid,"

Colleen said, holding out the folded tartan. "I thought ye'd like to wear our clan colors one last time."

Davina gave the widow a watery smile. "It's perfect. Can ye help me find a brooch to pin it?"

"I've just the thing fer ye," Katherine said. "'Tis a gift from James. He wanted me to surprise ye with it in hopes that ye'd wear it fer the ceremony."

Katherine handed Davina a delicate gold brooch. The center design was a thistle flower, surrounded by intricate leaves and interlaced vines. Davina immediately saw it was a unique, expensive piece of jewelry, the finest she had ever been gifted. Yet far more important than its value was the fact that James had chosen it for her. Her trembling fingers fumbled with the lovely piece as she tried to secure the tartan over one shoulder.

"Nervous?" Aileen asked sympathetically, as she took the broach and pinned it into place.

"Excited," Davina clarified. "Though I confess to feeling sad that none of my kin are here to celebrate this joyful occasion with me."

"Travel always takes much longer in this winter weather. My son couldn't wait another day to claim ye as his bride. Are ye very disappointed?"

"A bit. Though truthfully, I couldn't wait either," Davina admitted with a blush.

"Then let's get ye married." Aileen smiled and held out her hand. Davina took it, glad for the support. Aileen led her through the great hall and into the courtyard.

The moment she stepped into the bailey, all eyes turned toward her. Aileen let go of her hand. Davina took a deep breath and walked through the parting crowd. In keeping with Highland tradition, the ceremony would be held outside the chapel. This way all could bear witness to their union and it seemed as though every clan member was in attendance.

Thanks to his height, she could see the top of James's head as he stood on the chapel's steps, his back to the open doorway. She straightened her shoulders and held her head proudly as she approached her groom.

Their eyes locked. James stared at her with the love she had dreamed of seeing for the last five years. A soft winter wind blew around her face, but Davina didn't feel the cold. Her heart was beating rapidly, filled with more joy than she could ever imagine.

James looked magnificent in his wedding finery, his muscles taut under his snug, richly embroidered tunic, the heavy sword gleaming at his side. Bathed in the fading rays of the evening sun, he looked like a Highland warrior of old. A length of McKenna plaid with its bold colors was pinned over his left shoulder. As she drew near, Davina could see the brooch he wore to hold the tartan in place matched hers.

Unable to wait until she reached him, James stepped forward to greet her. "Ye look like an angel come down from the heavens," he whispered as he took her hand.

"I've already agreed to marry ye," she answered. "There's no need fer such flowery compliments."

Her teasing response had the desired effect of calming her nerves—and those of her groom.

"Do ye take these vows of yer own free will?" the priest asked.

"Aye!"

The crowd laughed at James's eager response. Davina smiled, too, and answered with equal enthusiasm, though not as loudly as her groom.

"Is there any man here who can give just reason why this marriage should not proceed?" the priest asked.

Breath held, Davina watched the priest carefully as the clergyman scanned the crowd gathered around them. She could hear a low rustling behind her and envisioned the crowd turning and glancing at each other, making certain no one would respond.

Tilting her chin, Davina accidentally caught Malcolm's eye. For a fleeting moment there was an expression of sad longing shadowing his face, but then it vanished like a puff of smoke. He nodded his head regally, mouthing the words *be happy* to her.

Davina's mouth twisted in relief. Malcolm's endorsement was yet another piece of joy adding to this special day. The reconciliation between the brothers was fragile and new. It was her fervent wish that James and his brother would grow closer. 'Twas a relief knowing that her marriage to James would not impede that possibility.

Davina swallowed, inexplicably near tears.

Vows exchanged, they walked into the chapel and knelt to receive the priest's blessing. Before he gave it, Father Dominic spoke solemnly of the duties between wife and husband. Davina tried to absorb every word, for above all she wanted to be a good wife to James. But her groom was determined to take advantage of her nearness, his fingertips swirling in a sensual pattern over her wrist and palm.

Concentration fled as her flesh prickled with awareness. Her blood raced as an intoxicating heat rolled through her. She felt James squirming beside her and guessed that his desire was also rising. Father Dominic kept talking—lecturing, really—either unaware or untroubled by their actions.

The good priest paused to take a deep breath and James seized the moment. "Are ye finished?" he asked.

"Aye, Sir James,'tis done," the priest answered as he smiled. "Ye're married."

That was all it took. Without warning, James leapt to his feet, pulling Davina with him. His arms encircled her waist and he lifted her against his chest. She barely had time to catch her breath before his lips descended.

It was a seductive caress, a promise of the pleasures they would soon share. He let the kiss linger, far longer than was appropriate, until the shouts and hoots and whistles from the crowd grew longer and louder.

"Mark my words, we'll be blessed with another grandchild before the year is out," the McKenna declared.

The crowd cheered. James finally lifted his head. Davina met his bemused gaze and smiled. Her knees felt weak, she was breathless and disheveled. And happier than words could express.

She glanced down at the gold band on her finger, the solid weight a reminder of her vows. Her new life had begun and she could hardly wait to see what happened.

The great hall was near to bursting when all the clan members joined in to partake of the wedding feast. The tables were laden with delicious food and the wine, ale, and whiskey flowed freely.

Toast after toast were made to the good health, happiness, and fertility of the bride and groom. Davina lost count of the number of times goblets were raised, but she smiled with genuine delight at each one.

"I'm sorry the weather prevented us from hosting a tournament or a melee in celebration of yer marriage," the McKenna said, as he patted Davina's hand affectionately. "There's nothing more thrilling than watching a fine group of Highland warriors, some mounted, some on foot, in mock combat."

Truthfully, Davina couldn't imagine anything less romantic than seeing men stage a battle, but she was not about to argue with the laird. Only the richest and most prestigious clans held elaborate, expensive weddings, with days of feasting, hunting, and tournaments. That the McKenna even suggested such a thing was a sure sign of the regard he held for her and James, and that warmed Davina's heart.

"'Tis a fine wedding celebration, fit fer a princess," she said sincerely. "I could ask fer nothing more. I am honored by all that has been done to make me welcome and am very proud to be part of the clan. Thank ye." Davina leaned forward and kissed the McKenna's cheek.

Lileas came skipping over and climbed into Davina's lap. "Grandpa says that ye're a McKenna now."

Davina smiled and cuddled the little girl. "Aye, I've wed yer uncle James, so that means I'm yer aunt Davina."

Lileas sighed deeply. "I dinnae want an aunt. I wanted ye to marry Papa and be my new mama."

Davina hid her smile. Naturally, Lileas would still be harping on her quest to gain a mother. The child possessed the McKenna trait of stubborn determination tenfold.

"Someday yer Papa will find a lady to love and he'll marry her and then she'll be yer new mama," Davina answered.

Clearly displeased with the reply, Lileas wrinkled her nose. She appeared on the verge of a tantrum, but thankfully didn't throw one. Instead, she gave Davina a tight hug, slipped off her lap, and muttered something about going to find her papa so he could start looking for her new mama *right now.*

The musicians began playing a lively tune. Trestle tables were shoved away from the center of the hall to make room for the dancing. A group of men and women joined hands to form a large circle.

"Time to start the dancing," Aileen said, pulling Davina and James away from their seats.

The bride and groom were plunged into the center of the circle. Trying not to stumble, Davina held tightly to James's hands and struggled to match his footwork, but her feet could not move as nimbly as her husband's. Giggling, she felt herself starting to lose her balance, but just as she began to fall, James caught her. She came to a breathless halt against him, her palms braced on his chest.

"Kiss her, Sir James!" someone shouted.

Davina eagerly lifted her chin and swayed into her husband, her lips brushing against his. She felt his hand slip to her nape and he deepened the contact, sweeping his tongue across her lips. She opened her mouth, sinking into him with a pleasurable sigh.

The sound of hoots and whistles, mixed with stamping feet, thundered up to the rafters. James gave her one final kiss, then pulled away. His gaze smoldered with seduction and she felt herself blushing. Others noticed her hot color and that brought on even more cheering.

Throughout it all the musicians continued to play, the merry sound of the pipes, fiddle strings, and drum ringing out a lively tune. After a few more shouts, the dancing resumed.

The hour was well past midnight before the clan was ready to let the newlyweds retire to the bridal chamber. Of all the feasting that had been done these past few days, the nuptial celebration was by far the most exuberant and no one wanted to see it come to an end.

As was the custom, Davina left first, escorted to the

bridal chamber by a group of giggling, whispering women. Since none of her female relations was in attendance, Lady Aileen directed Davina's disrobing, hurrying the process in deference to the cold and her daughter-in-law's modesty.

Lacking fresh flowers at this time of year, Lady Aileen and the women of the castle had used holiday greenery to make the room sparkle and shine. Swags of freshly cut pine were hung on the walls, its fragrant scent mingling with the holiday aromas of cinnamon and spice. Ribbons of red and gold were wrapped around the pine bowers.

Bouquets of holly and ivy were placed on the table and a large cluster of mistletoe shaped into a ball hung from the bedpost. Candles lit the chamber, the flames dancing merrily.

A naked Davina managed to slip between the sheets just as the men arrived, pounding on the closed bedchamber door, demanding entrance. At Aileen's signal, Colleen opened the door and the men stumbled inside. Shouting and laughing, they carried an unsmiling, half-dressed James upon their shoulders.

James allowed his shirt and brais to be removed by his rowdy companions, who delighted in yelling bawdy advice on the best way to please the bride. James endured the bedding ceremony with as much good will as he could muster, but he refused to be placed in the bed beside her and Davina could tell by the tight set of his jaw that her new husband was not pleased.

Fortunately, his mother was also attuned to her son's feelings, and she managed to hustle the drunken revelers out of the bedchamber before James pulled his sword on them. The moment they left, James swiftly bolted the door, then turned and pressed his ear against it.

"Are they gone?" Davina asked.

"At last. I paid the musicians a goodly amount to ensure they wouldn't participate in the shivaree. Thank God it's too cold fer the McKenna knights to stand below our window and beat their swords on their shields or else we would never find any peace this night."

"Aye, it seems as though it willnae take much to get this crowd riled," she agreed.

James walked to a small table and poured two goblets of wine. "Drink?"

Davina shook her head. She'd already had far more than usual. Any more and she might pass out and that would completely ruin what had so far been a perfect day.

The chamber fell silent as James finished his wine, then lifted the goblet he had filled for her and drank.

Davina aimed a teasing grin at her husband. "Highland lore says a marriage will be happy if the bride is merry. Is the same not true fer the groom?"

James cocked his head. "Ye think I'm unhappy?"

"I think ye spent far too much of our bridal banquet scowling."

He furrowed his brow. "The men find it amusing when I gaze at ye like a besotted half-wit, so I tried to temper my enthusiasm."

"Should I be insulted that ye dinnae want everyone to know how ye truly feel about me?"

James downed his drink. He came to the bed, but did not climb under the covers with her. Instead, he lounged casually on the mattress, his elbow propped on the pillow, eyeing her.

God above, he was a handsome devil. Her pulse became a rapid pounding in her ear, while a steady stream of warmth filled her heart until it was almost too full to hold it inside.

"'Tis no secret that I adore ye. But I prefer privacy when I pour my heart out to my wife."

He pressed a soft kiss on her lips and she leaned forward, wanting more, but he pulled back.

"What's wrong?"

He ran his hand through his hair. "I want this night to be filled with memories that ye will always cherish."

She tipped her head at a flirtatious angle. "I'm the one who is supposed to be filled with bridal nerves, not ye."

James rubbed his freshly shaved jaw. "'Tis our wedding night," he said, as though that explained everything.

The sheet that the women had carefully tucked around her naked form to preserve her modesty began to slide away. She could feel the cool night air on her exposed flesh, but the desire that flashed in James's eyes heated her blood.

"Tell me, husband, will ye be able to summon up some sweet words fer yer bride or will this be a long, cold night?"

"My brother is the one blessed with a silver tongue."

"But I dinnae want yer brother," she whispered throatily. "I wanted ye."

The words had barely left her mouth when James pounced. Cupping the back of her head, he claimed her lips in a kiss so heady that she felt dizzy.

He kissed his way down her throat to her breast and captured her nipple between his lips. She gasped in delight and he suckled until she was panting and squirming. Then he dipped his head lower, down to her soft belly and beyond, touching the heart of her womanhood with the tip of his tongue. Davina screamed in surprise, pulling away, but he held her hips tightly.

"Ye need to trust me, Davina. I promise ye willnae be disappointed."

Well, he had promised her a memorable wedding night. Trapped between desire and mortification, Davina allowed him to nudge her legs wider apart. She bit her lower lip nervously when he sank between her thighs, but all thoughts of modesty and embarrassment fled when his tongue returned to that sweet spot and swept over it again.

"James." She gripped his shoulders. "Are ye certain?"

"Aye. It gives me such pleasure to know ye in this way. Ye're so pretty. So pink, so lush."

His searching tongue laved her gently, swirling, circling, then suckling. She cried out again, arching herself against his greedy mouth, the mindless joy intensifying. Desire and need blazed inside her. She tried to speak, but the tension was too overwhelming.

The throbbing was almost painful and she struggled to end it, moaning and thrashing. Her breathing was rough and ragged, she could hear it echoing through the chamber. It felt as though every inch of her flesh had come to life; the wetness between her legs, the aching of her breasts, the throbbing of her womanhood.

Then suddenly it all crested. Her body began shuddering, trembling uncontrollably. Her capacity to think vanished. Aye, all she could do was *feel* and it truly was as glorious as James had promised.

She went limp when it ended. James moved up to hold her. He stroked her hair, whispered in her ear, nuzzled her neck. Her eyes closed and a feeling of utter exhaustion, mingled with delighted contentment, came over her.

Davina felt herself drifting off to sleep. *Nay, I want my wedding night!*

Shaking her head vigorously, she opened her eyes. James held himself above her, one arm resting on the mattress. She cast him a wicked smile, then a slight shift of her hips brought his body precisely where she wanted it, pressing tightly against his straining penis.

"Ye promised me a memorable wedding night, husband."

He flexed his hips and let out a half groan, half laugh. "A Highlander is true to his word. Never more so than when he is speaking to his woman."

His woman. Hearing those words fall from his lips sent a new thrill through Davina's body. She felt his hands slide under her buttocks, lifting her, and she felt a renewed sense of tingling excitement.

"Open fer me, sweetheart." His voice was raspy, tortured, and she was glad to know his need was as great as hers.

She obeyed his command, spreading her legs apart. He trembled as he arched over her. She felt his hard length probing for entrance and for a moment she tensed, digging her nails into his arms. He groaned loudly, but ceased moving.

"Go slowly," she pleaded.

A low growl filled her ears. "I'll try."

Davina took a deep breath. She felt the tip of him pressing inside her and she did as he instructed, relaxing her inner muscles. Her arms went around his back and she hugged him. He thrust deeper. Another low growl filled her ears and she moaned as the pleasure grew.

She found the rhythm effortlessly, lifting herself to meet his every stroke. The urgency started again, sending a flush of heat washing over her. She felt herself driving the cadence faster and harder. Her moans grew louder and she heard herself gasping with an almost desperate longing.

"Open yer eyes, Davina. Look at me!"

Startled, she did as he bade, staring into his eyes. The hunger and yearning she expected, but the naked love was a gift, the most precious of all.

The pleasure rose again quickly and suddenly she felt herself straining and shuddering. With a soft cry Davina buried her face in the hollow of his shoulder and surrendered to the explosive ecstasy.

Her release hastened his. James thrust harder, faster, his breath harsh against her ear. Then he went still and she could feel the pulse of him deep inside her as he spilled his seed.

He collapsed on top of her, pinning her with his weight, but this time there was no rush of fear or panic. The sensuous daze of their lovemaking still held her enthralled.

"I'm too heavy," James muttered, making a lackluster effort to move himself off her.

"Nay, stay," she whispered. Lifting her legs, she wrapped them around his thighs, holding him in place. "I like having ye this close to me."

She ran her hand lightly over his back, brushing kisses over his shoulder and neck. Her heart ached with love, and the smile on her lips would not fade.

Never had she felt such joy. Such deep contentment. Such total exhaustion.

"I love ye, Davina."

A smile touched her lips. If she lived to be a hundred,

she would never grow tired of hearing those words from him.

"I love ye, James. Ye and no other man."

He emitted a masculine growl of gratification, then rolled over, taking her with him. She settled comfortably beside him and he kissed her temple. Her eyes drifted shut and she fell in a deep, dreamless sleep.

James watched Davina while she slept, staring at her profile, committing each delicate feature to memory. She was so lovely, he ached, his chest heaving with emotion. What he felt for Davina went beyond desire, beyond passion, beyond love.

They had connected on a level higher than the physical, a humbling realization. Being with Davina filled the holes in James's heart, somehow melting away the thoughts of reckoning that had consumed him. Erasing the desperate years of loneliness when he had yearned so intently for what he had lost, becoming angry and despondent.

Observing her now he wanted to lean over and gently kiss her plump lips, but her slow breaths told him that she was in a deep sleep, and he didn't have the heart to wake her. She had more than earned her rest after their spirited lovemaking. He would not be an inconsiderate, demanding husband.

He hoped he hadn't been too rough in their coupling this night. A mere glimpse of her lovely, white flesh had been enough to fuel his ardor and his passion had been difficult to control.

Carefully, he brushed a tendril of damp hair from her face. He felt a searing burst of possession, followed by a dark yearning so strong it pierced his heart like a knife.

God grant me another chance.

He muttered the words beneath his breath like a prayer. James knew he had her love, but equally important was her trust, for without it their marriage had no chance of lasting happiness.

She reached for him in her slumber and he promptly forgot his resolve to let her sleep. She was simply too much of a temptation to resist. He kissed her neck, her shoulder, then swirled his tongue over her nipple. He heard hear gasp as her eyelids opened.

An impish spark lit her eyes. She curled her fingers around his erection and began fondling him. "Ye must think me a bold and brazen lass to wake me from a peaceful slumber like that, James McKenna."

He felt his heart catch tight in his chest. "Ye are a passionate woman, Davina McKenna. I'm proud to be the man to awaken yer womanly desires."

She scrunched her nose. "My womanly desires? Och, ye sound like a troubadour spinning a fancy tale and bad one, too. Ye best not be letting anyone else hear ye spout such flowery nonsense."

"I told ye that I lack a silver tongue," he said, raising his hand to trace a finger along the slope of her cheek.

"Ye have a magical tongue, sir knight, as my well-sated body can attest." She shifted to her side and they lay face-to-face. "I cannae fathom sharing these intimacies with any other man but ye, James. Not only because ye are my husband, but because I love ye."

"And trust me?"

"With my life and my heart."

"I'm a fortunate man."

"That ye are, dear husband."

She accompanied her words with a saucy wink. James burst into laughter. He had expected her to shower him with exaggerated flattery, hoping she would turn a phrase he could tease her about, but once again she had surprised him. And he liked it, for deep in his heart he knew she spoke the truth.

He was, indeed, a most fortunate man.

Chapter Eighteen

The next weeks were peaceful for James and Davina. His family gave them the privacy they craved, for the most part, and they spent their days enjoying each other's company and their nights in passion and pleasure. They spoke of the future, of the life they would build at Torridon Keep, with excitement and anticipation, yet secretly James fretted over Davina's safety, worrying that once they left the thick walls of McKenna Castle, her life would be in peril.

Consequently, he spent hours training with the McKenna soldiers, honing his own skills and assessing theirs. His father had given James leave to choose a contingent of McKenna warriors as an escort and offer positions as his men-at-arms. As his funds to pay these men were limited, James wanted to make certain he selected the best.

The McKenna sent a message to Davina's uncle, informing him of their marriage. Davina included a short missive of her own, proclaiming her love for her husband and her great happiness over their union. Her uncle's reply fell short of outright objection, but was brief and terse enough to relay the message of disapproval.

Davina claimed it mattered little to her, but after being reunited with his family, James felt it was important to mend the breach with the Armstrong clan. Once he and Davina were properly settled,'twas one of the first things he planned to fix.

Malcolm seemed to accept their marriage with good grace, though every now and again James would catch his brother staring at Davina with a curious mix of puzzlement and longing.

Though tired and hungry, James's mood was light-hearted as he left the practice field. The weather had been milder, yet the breeze cool enough to keep the sweat from dripping into his eyes as he parlayed with the McKenna soldiers. Two additional men had accepted his invitation to join him and he felt confident in their skills and loyalty.

He spied Colin the moment he entered the great hall and instructed the lad to have bathwater brought to his chamber. Best to enjoy the luxuries of McKenna Castle while he was able, James decided, suspecting in his new home there would be few opportunities to indulge in a hot bath before the evening meal.

Davina looked up in surprise when he entered their chamber. She was standing over two large trunks that were stacked high with goods. Around her feet were bolts of fabric, sewing notions, piles of furs, and mountains of clothing.

"I can see that ye've been busy," he remarked, placing a gentle kiss on her cheek.

She wrinkled her nose at his pungent odor, yet kissed his lips tenderly anyway. "Ye need a bath, husband."

"Colin is seeing to it." James shrugged off his tunic, then sat to unlace his boots.

"I spent the afternoon with yer mother and Katherine, packing supplies fer the journey and fer our household." Davina flopped on the bed. "'Twas exhausting. I felt like a soldier preparing to lay siege to a town."

James laughed. "Mother does tend to overprepare for things."

"I appreciated her generosity, though I confess at times it made me feel like a beggar."

"We dinnae know what we will find when we arrive at the keep," James argued. "'Tis most likely understocked, possibly in disrepair. That's why I want to go ahead of ye."

"Nay. I'll not be left behind, James. The keep was my childhood home and now it is our home, the place where we will raise our family. 'Tis only right and proper that we arrive together." Davina rolled to her side, facing him. "As fer food, ye need not worry. Yer mother is sending enough to feed an army—fer a year!"

"Ye'll be glad to have it when yer belly grumbles."

"Aye, that's true enough."

Hearing a commotion outside the door, James bade the servants carrying the wooden tub to enter. They were soon followed by a line of pages, with Colin in the lead, bringing buckets of hot water. It took three trips before the tub was filled. With a nod of thanks, James dismissed them.

"Has Colleen made a decision about her future?" he asked, wondering what Davina's companion would do now that her charge was married and no longer in need of a chaperone.

"We spoke of it this morning. She would like to accompany us and make the keep her new home."

"Splendid. We can always find a place fer an honest, hardworking woman." James pulled off his shirt and brais. Naked, he moved toward the tub.

"Colleen did mention how much she loves children and regrets she was never able to have any of her own. She thinks that she would make a fine nursemaid." Davina blushed, then bent forward so her hair fell over her profile, hiding her expression.

The world tilted. James nearly fell into the steaming water as he whirled around. "Oh, God, Davina, what are ye saying? Are ye with child?"

She tossed her hair aside and regarded him with a faint, mysterious smile. "Perhaps. 'Tis too soon to know fer certain."

He opened his mouth, shut it, opened it again. "When will ye know?"

"Not fer another week at least." She cleared her throat. "I shouldn't have said anything, but I was too excited. Would it please ye to have a child?"

"Aye, but . . ." He had difficulty speaking. "We are only just married."

She blinked at him. "Aye, and we have spent nearly all of that time in bed together. What did ye think would happen?"

Feeling a bit dizzy, James put a finger to his temple and rubbed. Davina was right. Children were the natural result of all their lovemaking and he was pleased at the idea of having them. He just thought he'd have a bit more time before they arrived, before he would have to share her.

Her expression turned anxious and he felt like a brute for causing her worry. James squared his shoulders and favored her with his most charming grin. "I'll be happy if ye promise me that our child willnae be as willful and spoiled as Lileas."

The tension around her eyes eased. "If the babe inherits the McKenna temperament, I cannae do much about the willfulness. But I firmly believe that no one can spoil a child as much as yer brother. Ours will be an angel in comparison."

James settled himself in the bath. The warm water aided in lessening his shock, helped to clear his head. "Unless it's a boy. Then I want him to be a real hellion."

"Saints preserve us!" Davina approached the tub. She picked up a cloth, dipped it in the water, and lathered it with soap. "There is, however, one child that I would like to bring with us. Colin."

"My page?"

"Aye. I've spoken with yer mother and she agrees it's a good idea."

James rubbed the stubble on his jaw. "That lad is frightened of his own shadow. I dinnae think he will manage a journey to a strange keep very well."

"Then we must assure him that he will enjoy this grand adventure."

James raised a dubious brow. "Won't his family be insulted that we've taken him away from McKenna Castle? They sent him here so that he could be trained by my father."

Davina ran the soapy cloth over his shoulders and back. "Yer father trained ye as a page and a full year as a squire before he sent ye away. Ye'll teach the lad as yer father taught ye."

"Most Highlanders wouldn't think it's the same."

"Colin is a third son. I dinnae think his parents care where he is fostered."

Davina squeezed the water from the cloth over James's head, then began washing his hair. Her nimble fingers dug into his skull, massaging his scalp. He closed his eyes and relaxed.

"Are ye certain ye want to take on the responsibility of looking after the lad?" he asked.

"Aye." Davina lifted a fresh bucket of water and

poured it over James's head. "Yer mother worries about him. The other lads tease him. Colin might do best with us, away from them."

"Ye've a soft heart, Davina McKenna," he whispered, casting her an approving gaze.

"Aye, well, 'tis better than a soft head."

She laughed and held out a towel. James rose from the tub, dribbling water on the stone floor. He rubbed himself dry, then fastened the towel low on his hips.

Grinning, he approached his wife. Her hands slipped around his waist and she held fast to him. He lowered his mouth to hers. They kissed, sweetly, lovingly.

James's towel fell to the floor. Yet despite the chill in their bedchamber, he found a most delightful way to chase away the cold, though in truth it made his wife shiver.

A few days later, James and Davina left McKenna Castle. The journey took nearly a fortnight. They traveled with a large contingent of soldiers, wagons overloaded with food, wine, ale, and various household items. The weather remained unpredictable, mild one day, cold and blustery the next.

They were prepared for the chill, erecting sturdy tents each night to ward off the cold. But Davina was shivering when James entered their tent one evening and he hurried to her side. "What's wrong? Are ye ill?"

"Nay." Though she tried to prevent it, emotions made her hands shake. "I started my monthly flow this evening."

It took James a moment to realize what she was saying. "Ah, love, there's plenty of time fer us to have a babe."

She fell into his arms. They were strong and warm, soothing her tattered emotions. "I know 'twas foolish of me to even think it. But I had hoped."

"If I remember correctly, it takes more than hope to create a child." The teasing humor and love in James's eyes softened the blow.

"There will be sons one day, with yer wicked grin and warrior's skills," she said with yearning.

He grinned, then whispered in her ear. "I'd also like a few daughters, please, with yer bright eyes, kind heart, and sense of honor."

"I'll try my best—if ye'll do the same."

He laughed and kissed her gently. The sorrow that had been trapped inside her leaked away, like water breaking through a dam. There would be children, she reassured herself, as many as God saw fit to give them. Spirits calmed, Davina ate a light meal, but slept well that night, cradled in James's embrace.

On the afternoon they reached Torridon Keep, the biting wind howled, the sky darkened, and thunder rumbled in the distance. The animals were skittish and restless as they stopped on a slight rise; the humans, too. Davina felt the knot of anticipation in her belly tighten as she gazed into the valley below.

In front, the dense woods thinned, then gently sloped down. The keep was visible in the fading light, a tall, thin stone structure surrounded by a single low curtain wall. Despite the clouds, the golden stone glowed, a stark contrast to the gray of the winter sky.

There were no pennants snapping in the wind, and only a few wisps of smoke curling from the thatched cottages clustered in the meager village outside the fortress walls.

"It looks much smaller than I remember," Davina said, reining in her horse.

"Ye were a lass when ye left," James replied, studying the keep with interest. "Ye've never returned since yer parents died?"

"Nay. I asked often at first, but my uncle always said no. I suppose I simply got tired of being denied, so I ceased asking." She sighed with poignant regret. "I wish now that I had not so easily given up the quest to return, if only to assure the villagers that I remembered and cared about them."

"They will have no doubt of it once we greet them and they see that we mean to stay," James said cheerfully.

Davina smiled wanly, not as confident of their reception as her husband. They spurred their horses, riding ahead of the clumsy caravan. Davina puzzled over the silence as they drew near. There were no shepherds tending the sheep, no children playing on the hills, no women gathered by the stream doing wash.

James raised his arm and a group of soldiers behind them broke ranks and came forward. A whisper of foreboding tightened her scalp.

"Do ye suspect a trap?" Davina asked nervously.

"We sent no word of our arrival, but yer uncle knows of our marriage and should have informed them to expect us at some point."

They continued forward, riding through the silent village. She could see that James's eyes were trained on the top of the wall. Davina raised her eyes, too, counting the soldiers. They were still too far away to clearly see features, though she knew it was unlikely that she would recognize any of them.

A sturdy wooden bridge spanned a dry moat that was mined with sharpened sticks. This defense butted against the stone curtain wall and encircled the entire keep. Davina remembered her father speaking of the need for a drawbridge, but he never found the time or coin to have one built.

Instead, he had spent his money on tall, broad oak gates, bound with iron and set with metal studs designed to split a battering ram. He had also widened the top of the walls, so his guards could stand two deep.

"I count a dozen men on the wall," she said, when they brought their horses to a halt at the start of the bridge.

"Are any of them known to ye?" James asked, his hand resting on his sword hilt.

"Nay."

"Then ye had best announce yerself," James said with an encouraging smile.

She sat taller in the saddle, cloaking herself in commanding dignity. "I am Lady Davina Armstrong McKenna, daughter of Lachlan Armstrong and mistress of this keep. I come with my husband and his guard to take up residence in our home. I command ye to lower the gates and grant us entrance before the rains come and we are soaked to the skin."

As though to emphasize her point, the sky rumbled ominously. But if she had hoped the threat of impending rain would hasten their entrance, she was sadly mistaken.

"We had no word to expect ye," one of the soldiers called down from the wall.

"Aye, I dinnae send word. But I'm here now." Davina peered up at the wall, noticing several of the men shifting on their feet. "Open the gate."

"Who did ye say wants entrance?" the soldier asked.

"Lady Davina Armstrong McKenna!" James shouted.

"Who are ye?" the soldier wanted to know.

"Her husband, Sir James McKenna." James patted the neck of his restless horse and glared at the man.

"I cannae open the gate unless the steward commands it," the soldier insisted.

"Then call the steward, so that Lady Davina can speak to him directly. And be quick about it! I'll be very displeased if my wife catches a chill in the rain."

Davina felt her face heat with annoyance. While she appreciated the soldier's efforts to protect the keep, their manner was overly cautious.

After a few minutes, the steward appeared. He carried a chicken leg in his right hand, proof they had interrupted his dinner. He exchanged some words with the soldiers, paused, looked down at them, then resumed the conversation with the men on the wall.

"My man informs me that ye wish to gain entry to the keep," the steward said.

"Aye," James replied curtly.

"Ye claim that Lady Davina Armstrong rides among yer party?"

"I dinnae claim it, I know it. Now open the damn gate!"

James shouted so loudly, the precious few panes of glass on the keep windows shook.

The steward's face whitened. He tossed his chicken bone aside and wiped his greasy fingers on the front of his tunic. "Forgive my confusion on this matter, Sir James, but Lady Davina is already here. She's resting in her private chambers."

Davina was so stunned by the announcement that for an instant all she could do was stare. She turned toward James and saw the shock she felt reflected in her husband's eyes. "Did he just say that I was already in residence?"

"Aye." The astonishment on James's face gave way to puzzlement, then anger. He shifted in the saddle. "Bring her here immediately."

"But she is resting," the steward exclaimed.

James swung his shield around, drew his sword, and began beating the sword against the shield. The McKenna men surrounding them took up the chant, imitating their leader. The fierce sound reverberated through the valley, a chilling, violent warning. Davina could almost see their fear as the men on the wall exchanged nervous glances.

James raised his sword, and the pounding ceased. "Ye have been lied to, my good man, by a clever, deceitful female. Bring her to the wall this instant, and I shall consider sparing yer life once we are inside."

The steward's jowls quivered. He spoke to the soldier on his left and the man scurried away. Just as Davina felt the first fat raindrop on her arm, the soldier reappeared. There was another person with him, smaller in stature and obviously a female.

The imposter.

"Who dares to claim my identity?" Davina shouted.

The imposter stepped forward. Her head was bent so low that Davina could see nothing of her face—yet there was something about her manner that was familiar. Gooseflesh pricked down Davina's arms and an uneasy feeling settled in her stomach.

"Joan?" Davina gasped.

The imposter let out a high, keening cry and stumbled forward. The steward reached out, catching her in his arms as she fell to the ground.

"Well, that's one mystery solved." James smirked.

* * *

Less than an hour later, Davina and James sat across from a defiant Joan in the great hall. Her golden hair hung around her shoulders like a veil, making her appear far younger than her years. She wore a blue silk gown, with long tight sleeves and an equally snug bodice that clung to her slender figure.

Her expression was calm, her manner haughty. One would think that she was the offended party in this sham, not the other way around.

"What sort of game are ye playing, Joan?" James asked, anger lurking in his gaze.

"'Tis no game. I was traveling home after visiting my parents and stopped here to spend the night. The gates were barred, much as they were today. It simply seemed easier to gain entrance by telling them that I was ye." Joan had the grace to flinch, though her chin remained proudly raised. "'Twas only a small fib. I planned to leave within a few days."

James turned to the steward, who was hovering in the shadows. "How long has Lady Joan been here?"

The steward blinked rapidly, clearly terrified to have been asked. "Neigh on three weeks, Sir James."

Joan's expression hardened to stone. "I caught a chill, which necessitated a longer stay."

"Ye seem perfectly healthy to me." James scowled. "Why haven't ye gone? And where, may I ask, is yer husband?"

The smoldering flame of resentment in Joan's eyes didn't surprise Davina. Joan had always objected to answering questions about what she said and did. Apparently, that hadn't changed. "Archibald had Fraser business that needed his attention."

"Where?" James wanted to know.

"At court."

Davina shot a disbelieving look at her cousin. Her husband was at court and Joan elected to be here, instead of with him? The tale did not ring true. Joan thrived on the intrigue and gossip of court life, speaking often of how she hated being stuck so far from anything of interest, wasting away in the Highlands.

James offered Joan a sad, suspicious smile and Davina knew he also doubted her words. He opened his mouth to question her cousin further, when Davina's belly rumbled with hunger.

"Milady, forgive me," the steward exclaimed. "I'll have food and drink brought to ye immediately."

Davina took a deep breath to stay her fraying nerves. James had been ready to string the poor steward up by his thumbs for refusing them entrance, but Davina had convinced him that the man was just trying to do his duty. He, too, had been duped by Joan; they must give the steward a chance to redeem himself.

Unfortunately, the food they were served was cold, tough, sour, and smelled faintly of mold. Even though he had taken a small mouthful, James seemed unable to swallow it. Instead, he spit it out on the rushes that covered the floor.

Joan lifted her brows, then smirked. "Apparently, one loses all sense of manners and civility when they become a Crusader."

"Please bring us something we can eat without becoming ill," Davina commanded, embarrassed by the poor showing.

She had wanted James to feel a connection, a commitment to their home, to be proud of it. Instead, this homecoming had been nothing short of disastrous.

The steward returned with a thin broth with bits of stringy chicken floating in it. Davina took one look at the grease congealed on the top and pushed her bowl away.

"I'm not very hungry," she lied.

"Ye need to eat," James insisted. "I'll get something from the stores we brought."

He stormed out, calling for his men, the steward doggedly following on his heels. Davina could hear the man apologizing profusely, insisting that the larder was poorly stocked, but he was certain with fresh food he would be able to set a table worthy of them.

"My, my, isn't James the solicitous husband," Joan clucked, reaching for a goblet of wine.

When she moved, her sleeve rode up, revealing her forearm. Davina gasped when she saw the line of yellow and blue bruises marring the flesh. Joan, feeling her cousin's eyes upon her, hastily pulled her arm back so the fabric would conceal the discolored flesh.

Joan's eyes met hers. "The floors in this keep are an abomination. 'Tis very easy to lose yer footing and tumble down on the hard stone."

"That doesn't look anything like a bruise from a fall," Davina said quietly. "Let me see the rest of yer arm."

Joan hesitated. Then averting her gaze, she slowly lifted first one sleeve, then the other. Davina winced. Joan's arms were grossly streaked with yellow and purple bruises that Davina was certain went even farther up her body. Even after three weeks of healing they were still vivid and looked painful.

Joan's eyes flashed and she raised her chin. "I dinnae want yer pity or yer judgment. Ye have no notion of what it's like to live with a man like Archibald Fraser."

"Have ye run away from him? Is that the real reason ye are here, pretending to be me?"

Joan let out a hollow burst of laughter. "Ye cannae hide from the Frasers."

"There must be something ye can do," Davina insisted.

The mirthless smile remained on her cousin's lips. "Archibald is my lawful husband. No one has the right to censure his behavior."

"Ye deserve to be treated with dignity and respect," Davina said, reaching forward to place her hand upon Joan's. "Not beaten like an animal."

Joan's head tilted. "Ye've changed, Davina. Ye used to run from yer own shadow and now ye're ready to challenge a man as powerful and ruthless as Archibald." Joan's voice turned bitter. "I thank ye fer yer efforts, but there's naught to be done."

Stiffly, Joan rose to her feet. Her face was flushed as she struggled to maintain her dignity. *How lowly the mighty have fallen.* Ashamed of her unkind thoughts, Davina lowered her gaze, realizing that she was unable to control the stab of pity she felt as she watched her proud cousin stride away.

James entered the great hall, his eyes flickering across the chamber as he searched for Davina. "Where's Joan?"

"She's left to rest in her chamber." Davina turned troubled eyes toward James. "I believe I've discovered the real reason she's here. She's run away from her husband."

James scoffed. "Is she sulking? Angry over not getting her way?"

"Nay, James. 'Tis serious. He beats her, often I think, and very violently. I'll admit she's not the most biddable woman, but that doesn't give him the right to beat her." A dozen warring emotions flared inside Davina. "I'm angry with her and yet I couldn't help but feel sorry fer her. She spoke only a few words about her plight, but paled whenever Archibald's name was spoken."

"No man of honor or valor strikes a woman, no matter how angry. Especially if she is his lady wife." James sighed. "Yet even ye must admit, yer cousin can try the patience of a saint."

"She cannae help it. She's been spoiled and pampered all her life, her every wish granted. Naturally she has grown to be a difficult, demanding woman."

"I cannae believe that ye're defending her. She'd not do the same fer ye."

Emotions sparked in Davina's heart. "Joan's fear makes her haughty, cold. I look at her life and then at mine, and I feel a twinge of guilt. I have a good, loving husband and a life of happiness in front of me. Joan has naught but heartache."

"What of her child?"

"She dinnae speak of her son."

James stroked his chin thoughtfully. "She's obviously had to leave him behind. If yer suspicions are correct and she has run away, she wouldn't dare take Fraser's son and heir. If she did, she'd have no chance of escape."

"Can we give her sanctuary, James?"

His lips parted in obvious surprise. "The Frasers are a powerful clan. 'Twould be most unwise to make an enemy of them."

"I doubt they will think to look fer her here. Can she stay fer at least a few weeks more?" Davina pleaded.

"I'll consider it. Now, come and eat some of the food I brought fer ye," he cajoled.

"I've no appetite," she answered truthfully, disappointed at his answer. But she wasn't worried. Beneath his warrior's muscled form was a heart filled with compassion. As long as she pleaded her cousin's case, Joan would not be abandoned.

"We best decide where we will sleep tonight before it gets too late," James said, signaling for the steward to attend them.

"The master's chambers are at the top of the keep's north turret," Davina replied. "We shall occupy those rooms."

The steward blanched. "It hasn't been used fer decades, milady. Though I'm sure with a thorough cleaning it can be set to rights."

"We shall inspect them now," Davina decided.

Hand in hand, Davina and James climbed the wooden staircase. It was dimly lit by narrow slits in the thick stone walls, but Davina's memories were strong enough to find the way even if they were plunged into complete darkness.

The musty smell became staggering as they reached the landing, but they pressed on, slowly opening the door. As the steward had warned her, the chamber was in a disgraceful state. James pulled back the furs covering the windows and dust motes flew into the air.

Davina's nose twitched at the unpleasant smell of dampness mixing with the dust. She closed her mouth and covered her nose with her hand, but the thick odor settled in the back of her throat. A huge curtained bed stood against one wall; on the opposite wall was a table and chair. One of the wooden chair legs was shorter than the other three; it listed drunkenly to one side.

Davina approached the bed, dismayed to see the mattress had been chewed. She feared the dark shadows in the corner were the carcasses of the vermin who had done the deed. Behind her, James circled the chamber slowly.

Davina looked up to meet his sober gaze. No words were needed to know he felt the same as she did—utterly disappointed. Aside from the dirt and decay, melancholy seemed to linger here and that bothered Davina more than anything.

"I have such fond memories of this chamber," she said. "'Twas never lavishly appointed, but it was warm and comfortable, safe and happy. There were tapestries adorning the stone walls and bed curtains of red velvet. My mother was so proud of those curtains. She sewed them herself with her mother and sisters and brought them here as part of her dowry."

"We will sleep here tonight," James declared.

Davina rubbed her forehead. "Och, James, it will take an army a month to get this place cleaned."

"Then we shall rouse an army."

James bellowed for the steward and the man came running. His expression grew increasingly horrified as James gave him instructions, but the steward didn't dare protest.

Once they were alone again, James pulled Davina into his strong embrace and she went willingly, in need of his comfort. "'Tis only a minor problem, easily solved," he insisted.

"Aye, James." She sighed wearily. "As long as we have each other, nothing can defeat us."

"That's my lass," he whispered, kissing her brow.

Yet the following morning James sent a message to McKenna Castle asking for reinforcements.

Chapter Nineteen

"Are ye awake, Davina?"

James's voice rumbled, deep and sensual, in the silence of the night. Davina turned on her side, punched the pillow beneath her head, and sighed.

"Sorry," she answered. "Did I wake ye?"

"Aye, from a sound sleep. Clearly, I have not done my duty as a husband if ye aren't fully exhausted from our earlier coupling."

The feel of his fingers against her naked breast startled her. Stiffening, she pushed his hand away.

"James, making love is not the answer to every problem," Davina exclaimed, glad that in the darkness he could not see the flush spreading across her cheeks.

Nearly six weeks married and she still suffered bouts of modesty when he acted so boldly. Worse, he found her blushes vastly amusing and greatly enjoyed teasing her about them, a situation she normally didn't mind.

But tonight she was too upset.

"I was trying to distract ye," he said softly, easing her into his arms. "Ye haven't slept a peaceful night since we arrived."

"I know and I feel foolish because of it."

"It's not an uncommon problem," James said sympathetically.

"Well, judging by the volume of yer snoring, I can safely say that ye dinnae have any trouble sleeping here," Davina retorted.

"When ye live the life of a Crusader, ye quickly learn to sleep anywhere. My brothers-in-arms liked to joke that I could easily sleep standing up, like a horse." He kissed the top of her head. "Ye merely need time to adjust."

"McKenna Castle was unfamiliar to me, yet I dinnae have nearly this much difficulty drifting off to sleep."

Davina's heart twisted. It had been the realization of a dream having James as her husband and the chance to return to her childhood home as its mistress. The sorry state of the keep had been an unexpected letdown, but she had never shied away from hard work.

Laboring all day and making love with James each night should have left her exhausted and contented. Yet instead, she felt oddly unsettled and that feeling of unease grew with each passing day.

Though he denied it, James felt it too. Why else would he have sent for aid from his family? Malcolm's arrival had been a surprise to both of them; obviously James had not expected his brother to answer his plea for help.

"Is it Joan? I know it cannae be easy having yer cousin here," James asked.

Davina sucked in a sigh. "Joan was a most unexpected, unwelcome surprise, but I cannae blame this unsettled feeling on her."

James's arms tightened around her. It was a great comfort, though the sense of calmness she sought still eluded her. She twined herself around his body, needing to get closer. James groaned. His hand rested near her bottom and seemed unable to resist a sensual caress across her curves, but he stopped after one languid stroke.

Davina shivered and moved her legs restlessly. "Why did ye stop?"

"God's bones, Davina, ye just told me that everything cannae be solved by coupling."

She shook his shoulders. "Honestly, James McKenna, do ye always listen to yer daft wife?"

He chuckled, as she knew he would, and claimed her lips in a sweet kiss. It took but a few kisses until she felt the fullness of his erect penis pressing against her belly. Davina rolled onto her back, letting her body soften beneath his and a deep, sensual sound rumbled from James's chest.

He raised himself on his elbows and looked down at her. Davina slipped her hand between their bodies. Her fingers glided over his chest, across his abdomen, and finally down to his penis. Curling her fingers around him, she stroked his thick, hard length.

He hissed in a breath. The sound brought forth even more wetness between her legs. She lifted her hips. Her body was moist and ready. He brushed a kiss over her lips as he slid inside her. Davina closed her eyes and sighed with contentment.

There was no rush to climax for either of them. James pulled back slowly, thrusting in a languid tempo. It was a gentle loving, exciting in a different way. Her arms tightened around him, keeping him as close as possible, as her breathing grew ragged and hoarse.

They reached their pleasure together, bodies shuddering and shaking and then going still. Davina could feel his seed spill within her. The promise of a child brought tears to her eyes; having a family with James would truly make her life complete.

The heat of his breath on her neck helped her relax. It felt familiar, safe. She ran her hand lightly over his muscled back. When he rolled to his side, she followed.

Finally drowsy, Davina looked to the fireplace, taking note of the small pile of glowing embers. Her eyelids grew heavy, but then her nose started to twitch.

"James, do ye smell smoke?"

"Hmm?"

"Smoke. I smell smoke."

He shifted and drew in a deep breath. "Hell! Ye're right. Put on yer nightgown. We need to sound the alarm and get out of here."

Heart pounding, Davina raced to her trunk, haphazardly pulling out garments, grabbing the first item she could easily slip over her head. It was a rather revealing nightgown, part of the trousseau that Lady Aileen had insisted be made for Davina and appropriate only for her husband's eyes.

In deference to sheer fabric, Davina threw her cloak over her shoulders. James grabbed her hand and she saw that he too had hastily thrown on a pair of brais and a tunic. Barefooted, they raced to the chamber door.

James yanked it open. A rush of heat enveloped them and the smell of burning wood brought on fits of coughing. At the end of the corridor they could see flames shooting into the air, producing billows of black smoke, could hear the crackle of burning wood.

"The stairs are on fire!" she shouted, covering her mouth and nose to prevent breathing in the worst of the smoke. She pivoted on her heel, scanning the other side of the hall, even though she knew there was no other exit. "We're trapped."

James turned and ran back into their bedchamber, emerging with a tapestry in his hands. Holding one end firmly, he began beating the flames. Following his lead, Davina snatched the pillows from their bed and returned to help.

"Watch yer hair," James cried.

Wasting precious time, Davina quickly braided her hair and tossed it over her shoulder. Working together, they managed to smother one section, but the flames quickly spread to another. The heat was unbearable. Davina's eyes watered, her throat stung, her arms grew heavy. But she matched her husband stroke for stroke as they fought for their lives and home.

"Sir James!" a voice called from the other side of the fire. "Help is on the way. The villagers are gathering buckets and water."

"Colin?" Davina shouted.

"Aye, milady."

"Be careful. Dinnae get too close."

"I saw the flames from my pallet and roused the household," Colin called excitedly.

"Are we under attack?" James asked.

"I'm not sure," the lad answered. "Sir Malcolm is on the wall with the guard, but they've not sounded a battle alarm."

"That's good, isn't it?" Davina rasped, turning to her husband.

James coughed long and loud. A deep frown of concern lined his forehead. "If necessary, Malcolm will defend the keep. But we must contain the blaze here. If any sparks hit the thatched roofs in the village, every cottage could be lost."

It seemed to take an eternity, but in truth was no more than a few minutes before the sound of water being hurled at the flames filled the hall. Female cries could be heard mixed with the male voices shouting commands and Davina was heartened to realize the women had also joined the bucket line.

Eventually, she started seeing puddles of water on the charred wooden landing. Hope claimed her heart as they continued to battle the blaze and appeared to be winning.

The fire was nearly out when suddenly there was a burst of motion behind them and a man leaped from the shadows. Davina screamed in shock. The man charged James and launched himself forward, hitting James squarely in the chest. James caught his attacker by the arms, attempting to hold him off. The pair pushed and shoved their way down the hall, toward the blaze.

Eyes wild, teeth bared, the attacker fought like a madman. James cursed loudly, drew back his fist, and landed a sharp blow on the man's jaw. It knocked his opponent off balance, but the man clutched James's tunic and they fell down together.

Behind them Davina could see the flames of the fire still burning, even as the buckets of water were being thrown on them. James and his attacker rolled away from the fire, a snarling jumble of legs and arms and fists. Another scream lodged in Davina's throat when she saw the attacker pull out a knife, the long blade flashing in the firelight, sharp and lethal.

Davina stood frozen and terrified, wanting to help, but knowing she would only be in the way. A chill slipped down her spine when she heard the attacker's shout of triumph, but as the pair regained their feet, it was James who held the knife.

She saw a vivid red blood smear across her husband's arm. Her knees began to shake and she fought to compose herself. She shifted out of the attacker's line of sight, not wanting to give him any ideas.

If he caught her, the intruder would have a powerful weapon to use against James. For she knew with certainty her husband would not hesitate to sacrifice his own life to save hers.

Suddenly, the man charged, bellowing like someone possessed by a demon. James met him full on, then at the last instant pivoted to his left. James struck hard, burying the dirk deep in his attacker's unguarded middle. As the man clutched his stomach, his mouth opened and closed and he staggered a few steps, then dropped to his knees.

Eyes glazed, he toppled forward, hitting the floor with a resounding thump. The deep wound began to bleed immediately, draining away his life's blood. Davina's own stomach turned as a rush of bright red stained the man's chest and tunic, pulsing onto the floor.

"Are there any others?" James cried.

Davina's anxious gaze darted about the hallway. "I dinnae see any."

"The fire?"

"It's out."

James cursed vehemently under his breath and hauled Davina into his arms. He held her for a long moment and then Davina felt his embrace tighten. "James, love, ye are holding me so tight I can barely catch my breath."

"If I had failed ye again . . ."

"James, ye never failed me."

"James! Davina!"

"Malcolm?" James called. "Are we under attack?"

"Nay," Malcolm answered. "We're getting boards to lay across the charred beams so you can climb down. Are either of ye injured?"

"James was assaulted," Davina cried.

She heard the sound of a sword being drawn, a loud

thump, and amazingly Malcolm stood in front of her. She blinked, realizing he must have vaulted over the ruined section of the landing to reach them.

"Careful or ye'll fall through," James shouted.

Malcolm gingerly took a few steps forward. Deep concern touched his face as he glanced from her to James and then back to his brother. "Are ye hurt?"

"A scratch." James shrugged, glancing down at his bleeding arm.

Streaks of bright crimson belied James's assessment of his injury. With a soft cry of distress, Davina lifted his arm, then realized she had nothing to bind his wound. Malcolm solved the problem neatly by passing a clean strip of cloth to her. Davina was so relieved she didn't even question how he came to be carrying it.

Ever the difficult patient, James tapped his foot impatiently while she bound his arm. She knew it would need to be properly washed and dressed with salves, but for now was content to stop the bleeding.

Malcolm's lips thinned into a grim line as he gazed down at the body. "Do ye think he set the fire?"

"It seems highly likely, yet he waited at the other end of the hallway once it flared to life," James replied. "Why? Surely he realized he would be trapped."

"Perhaps he meant to draw ye from the chamber, but the blaze grew too quickly," Malcolm suggested.

"Well, we certainly cannae ask him about it now," James cried, throwing down the dirk in frustration. "I was hoping he would live long enough to tell us why he did it."

"Or more importantly, who paid him." Malcolm moved closer to the body. The attacker lay facedown, a pool of dark blood surrounding him. Using the tip of his boot, Malcolm rolled the body over. The man's head lolled awkwardly to one side, his eyes glassy in death. "Do ye recognize him?"

Davina gasped. "My God, he's just a lad, no more than fifteen or sixteen. Why would he do such a thing?"

"Most likely he was paid," Malcolm speculated.

Davina wrapped her arms around James's waist and leaned her cheek against his strong shoulder. The smell of smoke and blood clogged her nostrils. Tears rose. She'd almost lost him. First to fire and then to an assassin's dirk. It didn't bear thinking.

"Is this keep cursed?" she asked, daring to voice yet another fear.

"Not by ghostly spirits," James said.

"Aye," Malcolm said grimly. "I found a pool of melted wax on the charred staircase. This was no accident. Whoever set the fire, meant to kill ye both."

The acrid smell of smoke tinged James's nostrils, bringing back memories of the sieges he had endured while on Crusades. Thankfully, the nauseating smell of burnt flesh was not present; according to Malcolm no one was injured, except for the knife wound James had sustained.

Holding Davina's hand, he navigated over the thick wooden planks that Malcolm had placed over the charred stairs and landing. Once safely down, they gathered in the great hall.

James's throat was dry and parched, his lungs sore from inhaling the smoke. He walked rapidly, felt the ground begin to spin, and abruptly sat, not wanting to draw any additional attention to himself.

He downed a tankard of ale and a second tankard of water. The liquids helped to invigorate him and his mind soon began tripping over itself with questions.

Why would someone want them dead?

He turned his head, glancing suspiciously at the soot-lined faces of the people gathered in the great hall. They had worked hard to save him and Davina. Was one, or more, of them a traitor?

"Sit down, James, and let me tend to yer arm," Davina pleaded. "Colleen has brought medicine from the stillroom."

Davina lifted a basket and he saw clean linen strips of bandages and a poultice filled with pungent herbs. He sincerely hoped that she did not intend to put that on his arm, as the smell was turning his stomach.

He fidgeted while Davina fussed, holding on to his patience with effort. He could see that she was still shaken and realized tending to him helped keep her calm. His arm stung and throbbed, but he stayed silent, even when she sewed his torn flesh with her needle. 'Twas no question that he would do anything to give solace to his wife, even suffer her medical care.

"There, all done." She smiled, but he could see a furrow in her brow. "'Tis a nasty gash, though not as brutal as it might have been. I've put in a few stitches, which will help stop the bleeding. We must keep it dry and clean to make certain it heals without bringing on a fever."

Davina's furrowed brow deepened when she mentioned the possibility of an infection, as if the thought had just occurred to her. Anxiously, she pressed her hand to his cheek and temple.

"I'm fine, Davina. Truly."

"I'll prepare a dram, to ward off the fever."

Heads pressed together, Davina and Colleen started rummaging through her basket. His arm was on fire, but the love and concern he saw in his wife's face eased his physical pain.

"Where is Lady Joan?" Malcolm asked.

"She couldn't possibly have slept through all this mayhem," James commented. "Have someone fetch her."

It took Joan nearly an hour to answer his summons. By then, James had drunk Davina's medicinal dram and several tankards of ale. The pain in his arm had finally dulled, but his wits remained sharp.

Joan entered the great hall and strolled regally toward them, her maid trailing dutifully behind her. She waited while the servant cleaned the bench of soot, then perched on the edge of it, crossed her ankles, and arranged the skirt of her gown artfully over her legs.

She was dressed in a formal silk gown that matched the color of her eyes. The neck and sleeves were intricately embroidered with gold threads. There was a long, white silk veil and a jewel-encrusted gold circlet upon her head. Her hair was neatly plaited and pinned atop her head. She was, in truth, the very picture of a wealthy noblewoman.

She was dressed in feminine splendor more suited to a social gathering. No wonder it had taken her so long to make an appearance!

She made no inquiries as to their welfare, nor asked to know what had occurred. Her composure was practiced to the extent that it almost seemed false.

James felt an almost overwhelming urge to grab her by the arm and pull her to her feet, but he refrained. He glanced over at his brother, noting by Malcolm's annoyed expression that his brother held with a similar notion.

Yet neither would act upon it. They had been raised to respect and revere women. No matter their character.

James took a sip of his ale and regarded Joan steadily for a long moment. "'Tis good of ye to finally join us,

Joan. I assume that ye suffered no ill effects from the fire?"

"I am fine." She let out a dramatic sigh and pressed the back of her hand to her forehead. "Badly shaken, of course, but unharmed."

"Truly?" Malcolm drawled. "Ye appear quite calm. Aye, calm and dressed as though ye're attending court."

Joan bristled and sat straighter. "Would ye have preferred that I come in my nightclothes, Sir Malcolm?"

Malcolm glared, but Joan seemed unaffected by the taunt. She met his gaze unflinchingly.

"No one recognizes the man who attacked James," Malcolm said. "We want ye to also view the body to see if he is known to ye."

Joan shuddered with maidenly distress. "I'd prefer not to do something so gruesome."

Malcolm's expression narrowed. "It's not a request, milady."

Joan's lips firmed. "If ye command it, then I will gaze upon the corpse, though if others cannae identify him, there is no earthly reason why I would know him."

"Ye've been here longer than we have, and therefore have had more exposure to the locals," James said.

Annoyance tightened Joan's delicate features. "I take little notice of the underlings and servants. If pressed, I doubt I could identify more than one or two of them."

"The body is over here," Malcolm said.

Joan swayed slightly as she stood. Malcolm's hand reached out to steady her, but she shrugged it off and took her maid's arm. The maid licked her bottom lip and watched Joan nervously as they stood over the body.

"I've never seen the poor sod before," Joan declared, making the sign of the cross.

"And yer maid?" Malcolm asked sharply.

The servant turned so pale she looked ready to drop to the floor. "I dinnae know the lad," she warbled.

The pair made their way back to the table. Joan sank gracefully onto the bench and cast a regal eye upon them all.

"Ye dinnae seem overly concerned about the fire or the attack," Malcolm observed.

"Nonsense!" Joan looked between them with astonishment. "I am deeply distressed. Forgive me, Sir Malcolm, if I do not display the hysterical, female anguish ye expect, but I believed such behavior would be unwanted as well as unhelpful."

"Can ye think of any reason someone would want to hurt James and Davina?" Malcolm asked.

"We all have enemies, do we not? My survival depends on knowing those who wish me harm. I have neither the time nor the inclination to concern myself with people who might have reason to harm my cousin." Joan's impassive expression shifted. "No matter how much the very idea of it distresses me."

James looked at Joan's eyes, searching for signs of treachery or deceit. But he saw nothing. She hid her true feelings well.

"Well, someone sent the lad," Malcolm said dryly.

"Unfortunately, the only person who could answer yer questions is dead. Perhaps next time, James, ye'll not be so quick to kill," Joan commented, her tone shrewish.

James went very still. "Is that a warning, Joan?"

"Dinnae be ridiculous." She flushed and turned away, the first break in her facial armor. "I'm only reminding ye that it would be sensible to remain on guard."

"I thank ye fer yer concern," James said sarcastically.

"Now, if ye have no further need of me, I will return to my bed."

"Nay. Davina and I will be using it fer what is left of the night," James said.

Joan's face scrunched in horror. "Where will I sleep if ye take my chamber?"

"Ye can have the east corner of the great hall," James decided. "I'll have Colin string a line of rope and hang some blankets fer privacy."

"Blankets? 'Tis unthinkable." In full fury, Joan straightened like a queen and turned to Davina. "How can ye treat me so unkindly?"

Davina's lips tightened. "James needs to rest in a proper bed. Our chamber reeks of smoke. We cannae stay there fer the night."

"Then take Malcolm's bed," Joan said, her voice rising another octave.

"Malcolm sleeps in the barracks," Davina replied. "I cannae go there and I must stay at James's side to make certain his wound does not fester and bring on a fever."

"Those are my linens on the mattress!"

Davina's lips grew tighter. "I'll make certain they are washed."

Annoyance flickered across Joan's features and she did little to hide it. "Clearly, I am to be given no choice in the matter," she said tartly.

"None at all," James responded cheerfully, the effects of the ale finally catching up to him. "Of course, if ye are displeased with the accommodations, I can provide an escort to yer husband's castle."

James did not imagine the sudden fear that shone in Joan's eyes. Davina must have seen it also. She came to her cousin's side and placed a comforting arm on her shoulder.

"Ye must forgive James. We are all tired and out of sorts," she said, shooting him a reprimanding look.

"No matter. I am well used to the cruelty of men," Joan hissed. "I must gather some things from my chamber. Am I free to leave?"

"Good night," James said dismissively.

Lips thin with displeasure, Joan cast him a final glance of disdain as she made her way out of the hall.

Davina sighed. "I fear she will spend the next few days sulking."

"Mayhap that will prompt her to leave," James grumbled.

Malcolm's mouth drew into a conspiratorial line. "Ye could always send a message to her husband."

"Nay!" Davina's eyes widened in distress. "I agree that Joan is difficult and occasionally unpleasant. But I've seen the bruises she tries to hide. Her husband's brutality cannae be excused, no matter what her behavior. I wouldn't be able to live with myself if I deliberately placed her in harm's way."

"Dinnae worry, love. We'll not be putting Joan out." James stretched out his wounded arm and let out an exaggerated groan. "My arm is starting to pain me. Do ye have any more of that dram ye and Colleen concocted?"

"I'll get some." With a worried look, Davina hurried from the great hall.

James turned to his brother the moment they were alone. "If we died, who would inherit Torridon Keep?" James asked.

Malcolm shrugged. "I dinnae know the legalities. When ye married Davina, ye gained an equal claim on the property. If she died before birthing an heir, it would be harder fer ye to keep the land, but not impossible."

"But if we both perished?"

Malcolm shook his head. "I suppose the land would revert to the Armstrongs."

"That has to be at the root of all this," James insisted.

"A part of me agrees with ye, but then I look around." Malcolm lifted his arm, swinging it in a wide, encompassing circle. "This keep has been neglected fer decades. It will take far more coin to put it to rights than can ever be earned back from working this land or raising sheep."

Frustration swirled in James's gut. Malcolm was right—there was nothing of obvious value here. Yet someone was prepared to kill for it.

He needed to find out why before they succeeded.

Chapter Twenty

As he stood alone in his bedchamber dressing for a morning ride on the southern borders, James pondered all that had happened in the two weeks since the fire. Or rather, all that hadn't happened. There had been no further mishaps; all had been quiet—almost too quiet.

Then again, he and Malcolm had been constantly vigilant, shoring up the keep's defenses, riding the borders daily, training with the McKenna guard. Davina went nowhere without an escort, even inside the keep, though it was usually Colleen or Colin who trailed her steps while she was within the walls of the keep.

James belted his tunic, added two dirks, picked up his sword, and left the bedchamber. The smell of burnt wood lingered in his nostrils as he hurried down the newly built wooden staircase, knowing his plans to replace it with stone would have to wait until he could scrape together the coin to pay a stonemason.

There was so much that needed his attention; 'twas daunting at times to think of how long and how costly it would be to set the keep to rights. It was also yet another reason why he could not understand how anyone would be eager to possess this dwelling and these lands.

The one bright spot—aside from having Davina at his side day and night—was the people. He had expected resistance, suspicion, possibly outright defiance to his rule, but they had bowed to his command with good humor and hard work. He believed a large part of that was due to their affection for Davina, yet also surmised they were astute enough to realize that the improvements being made would benefit them all.

The handful of soldiers at the keep were eager to prove their worth and earn a place among his guard. James was even more cautious with them, making certain his own men outnumbered them three to one whenever they were on the practice field.

"Sir James!" Colin called to him the moment he entered the great hall. "I'll tell Cook that ye are ready to break yer fast."

James peered around the hall at the few inhabitants enjoying their morning meal. Davina was not among them.

"Where's my wife?" James asked when Colin returned with a tray of food.

"Lady Davina is in the bailey. Shall I summon her?"

"Nay. I'm leaving to patrol the southern borders."

"May I ride with ye today?" Colin asked hopefully. "I promise not to be a bother."

The lad had blossomed in the weeks since their arrival. No longer timid and sullen, he had proven himself to be an eager, hardworking lad. James fully intended to reward his diligence by making him a squire, but he was waiting until he had the time to devote to training the lad.

"Not today, Colin. But soon," James promised, ruffling

the lad's hair affectionately. "I shall rely upon ye to watch over my lady while I am gone."

Still standing, James quickly gulped his oatcakes and washed it down with a tankard of ale. The ale tasted sour and he made a mental note to speak to the brewer later today. Wiping his mouth with his sleeve, James quit the great hall.

Just as Colin had told him, James found Davina in the bailey with several of the other women. He puzzled at the piles of ashes, sieves, rags, and large iron pots of boiling liquid, then realized they were making soap. Instead of shouting instructions from a respectable distance as most ladies were wont to do, Davina was in the thick of it, toiling alongside the other women.

Her face was red and glowing from her exertions, yet the sight of her always brought a skip of excitement to James's heart. *I must be completely daft if watching a woman standing over a steaming cauldron of boiling lye leaves me weak-kneed*, he thought, shaking his head ruefully.

"I'll be gone most of the morning," he called out to Davina.

She turned toward him and lifted her arm, shading her eyes from the sun. "Ye'll be taking an escort?" Davina asked, lines of worry etched in her brow.

"Aye, four of our best men."

She nodded with approval and returned to her work. His step was light when he walked to the stables. His horse was saddled and the men he had chosen were mounted and ready. As they rode through the gates, Malcolm waved from the practice field. James saluted his brother, acknowledging the reason he felt confident leaving the keep was because Malcolm would be there to protect it. To protect Davina.

The morning stretched out before him, beckoning

James with the promise of sunshine. He rode hard, the four guardsmen at his back. All around him he could see the signs of spring, bursting forth in buds of green. The air was fresh, the sun warm. For the first time since the fire, the scowl on his brow relaxed.

All was quiet, with no signs of trouble. When they reached the jagged outcropping of rocks that marked the southern borders, James reined in his horse. "We'll give the mounts a cool drink and a bit of a rest before turning back," he told the guard.

Dismounting, James walked to a small grove of trees, nestled in the valley between two hills. A stream flowed through the middle, the winking rays of the sun reflected through the young, delicate leaves. Pungent heather dotted the hillside. All was peaceful, except for the sound of the rushing water. 'Twas one of the rare spots of the estate that could claim real beauty and James took a moment to savor it.

Throat parched, he knelt at the edge of the stream and scooped up a handful of the cold, clear liquid. He reached for another, but stilled when a glittering flash caught his eye.

My God!

James leaned closer, almost losing his balance and tumbling headfirst into the stream. Heart pounding, he pushed his hand deep into the rocks and stones, clutching as much as he could hold. He raised his hand, letting the water slip through his fingers, then stared in amazement at what remained behind, nestled in his palm.

Have I gone daft? Taken too many blows to the head that my eyes are imaging things?

The shock of his discovery hit him so hard James staggered to his feet. His mind rapidly turned over the events of the past five years. The attack that had broken his relationship with Davina, the isolation her family encouraged her to embrace, the fear of men and taking a husband they had fostered, the subsequent attacks on her—and him—since she left Armstrong Castle and the bosom of her family.

Someone had not wanted her to return to this small estate and her inheritance. It had made little sense—until now. James drew a ragged breath and closed his fist firmly over the evidence he held in his palm.

He finally knew why someone wanted Torridon Keep badly enough to kill for it.

Davina entered the keep with a strong feeling of satisfaction. Her hands were chafed by the cold and hard work, but their hours of toil had produced enough soap to last through the spring. All she need do now was to decide where in the storeroom to keep it.

She moved through the great hall, down to the kitchen. A small fire was banked in the hearth, but the room was empty. Cook was obviously attending to other duties, but would likely return soon.

Davina easily found her way into the storeroom, pleased to note the shelves were stocked with a wide variety of food. In addition to several barrels of salted fish and meat, a fresh haunch of venison hung from a large beam in the coldest part of the cellar, the remaining bounty from yesterday's hunt.

As Davina looked about the room, a glimmer of memory invaded. Back to a time when she'd been a little girl, probably no older than Lileas. It had been a dreary, rainy day and she and several other children were playing a favorite game of hide and seek.

Davina had been daring that day, going into the forbidden storeroom to hide, when her father suddenly appeared. Worried that she would be scolded for disobeying, she sunk behind a barrel of oats. Holding her breath, she waited for what seemed like a very long time. Fearing she was missing all the fun, she had timidly poked her head around the barrel and witnessed an amazing sight.

Spurred by this long forgotten memory, Davina lit a candle and moved to the spot where her father had stood. She reached behind the various jugs and baskets on the shelf, running her fingers slowly over the wall, just as her father had done.

Suddenly, her hand caught on a piece of metal jutting out of the stone. She lifted the candle higher for a closer look.

"'Tis a lever," she whispered in surprise.

She tugged on the mechanism; it didn't move. Determined, she pulled harder. Once, twice. On the third try there was a click and a narrow section of the wall separated. Amazed, Davina pushed and it slowly creaked open. She took a half step forward, her flickering candle creating eerie shadows against the stone.

Expecting to see a hidden chamber, she instead found herself looking down a narrow spiral of stone steps. Unable to resist, she went down a few. The air was damp and musty, the walls glistening with moisture. She only intended to go down a few more, but each step pulled at her curiosity and she'd descend deeper.

At last she reached the bottom. She looked up, trying to judge how far she had come down, but saw only darkness. Excited at what she might discover, Davina held her candle high. The chamber in which she stood was oblong in shape, narrowing at the far end to complete darkness.

She batted away the cobwebs that clung to her face and proceeded through the chamber, this time finding what she expected—a tunnel!

Her excitement grew. Was this an escape tunnel? Or perhaps a secret passageway into the keep? Anxious to tell James of her discovery, Davina turned to make her way back.

Suddenly, a sharp, staggering pain cut across her temple and then she was falling, crumbling helplessly onto the damp, stone floor. She hit the floor hard, wincing at the pain in her hips and shoulder. Miraculously, she kept a grip on the candle, holding it upright. Hot wax dripped onto her hand, but she didn't let go.

By the Saints, someone struck me!

Terror speared through her. She looked frantically over her shoulder, but no one was there. Blinking, she turned to search all four corners of the chamber. Thinking she heard a noise, she lifted the candle higher, illuminating the shadows.

Nothing. She was alone. Whoever hit her must have been hiding in the tunnels and escaped back through them. Pray God they didn't decide to return.

A chilling breeze blew through the gaps in the stone wall. Nervously, Davina cupped her hand over the candle flame, groaning at the pain in her shoulder. But she was not quick enough. The light flickered, wavered, then went out, plunging her into total darkness. Trembling, she lifted her hand in front of her face, gasping when she realized she couldn't see it. She couldn't see anything.

Breathing hard, Davina lay on the floor for a long minute, listening to the noises above her. It sounded like the stomping of feet or perhaps the movement of tables and benches and she realized she must be directly beneath the great hall.

Fear crept through her, but she pushed it far back in her mind. Panic would do naught but make things worse. Her thoughts turned to James and she knew he would tear the keep apart stone by stone when he discovered that she was missing.

Yet she could not simply lie here and wait to be rescued. Her body shook, but she forced herself to think clearly. Without light, it would be madness to move forward through the tunnel. Nay, she needed to find her way back to the staircase and return the same way she came down.

Crawling slowly on her hands and knees Davina moved forward until she found the wall. She swayed dizzily when she stood, leaning heavily against the stone. Her knees were shaking. She wrapped her arms around herself and shivered, trying to get her bearings in the darkness.

Her eyes gradually adjusted, yet she could still see almost nothing. She reached behind her, pressing her hand against the damp stone wall. Hand over hand, she carefully guided herself along the wall, searching for the opening to the stairwell.

Found it! A nervous giggle of relief escaped her lips. Using the same method, she placed her hand on the wall. Gingerly, Davina stepped up, slowly ascending the slippery steps. They were rough and uneven; difficult to negotiate in the dark, but she continued to climb.

A scurrying noise caught Davina's ears. Rats? Mice? Or some other foul creature that lived in this damp, darkness?

No matter. They were more afraid of her than she of them—or so she told herself. Davina inhaled slowly and then exhaled, calming her nerves. Squinting hard, she peered into the darkness, but still saw nothing.

Tentatively, she took another step, clinging to the stairwell wall for guidance. She managed to rise three more steps before feeling something brush over her hand as it raced over the wall. Shrieking, she yanked her hand away and in the process lost her balance.

Crying out, Davina struggled to keep herself from tumbling, but she felt herself slipping. She went backward, somehow managing to land on her arse when she reached the bottom. The fall knocked the breath from her lungs and she gulped, struggling to pull in air.

Chest heaving, Davina folded her arms and buried her head on them, fighting to stay calm. Fear blurred her pain, but desperation drove her to act. She tried to rise, but a searing, stabbing jolt shot through her leg. Tears of agony filled her eyes.

Visions of being trapped down here for hours, even days, haunted her thoughts. Fear made her mouth go dry and her entire body tremble. She swallowed hard and closed her eyes.

Rest. I'll rest fer just a few minutes to gain some strength and then I'll try again.

"Where have ye been, James?" Malcolm asked, his eyes dark and troubled. "I expected ye back two hours ago."

James tossed his reins to one of the stable lads and vaulted off his horse. "Ye'll not believe what I've found, Malcolm." James reached into his pocket, but his hand stilled when he saw his brother's expression.

"What's wrong?"

"'Tis Davina. We cannae find her."

* * *

The air was very still. Davina grimaced. Her leg throbbed, the pain sharp and intense whenever she tried to move. She prayed that it wasn't broken.

Her eyes had gradually adjusted to the darkness, yet she could see little. She couldn't stand, but if she dragged herself to the staircase, she might be able to pull herself high enough to scream for help. Cook must have returned to the kitchens by now. Surely, someone would hear her.

A shadow of movement caught her eye. "Hello? Is anyone there?"

Suddenly, a voice sounded in the distance. "Davina?"

Disoriented, Davina looked up. "Aye! I'm here!"

"Davina?"

The voice sounded much closer. More importantly, it sounded familiar. Relief burgeoned in Davina's breast. *I'm saved!*

A cloaked figure emerged, illuminated by the glow of a single lit candle it carried. "Are ye injured?"

"'Tis my leg."

"Oh, dear. We'll need help getting ye out of here."

The figure raised the candle, momentarily blinding Davina. She blinked repeatedly. Her rescuer slowly came into focus, and Davina pulled in a breath of surprise. "Aunt Isobel?"

James stormed into the great hall, Malcolm hot on his heels. He was met with an empty silence. "Davina! Davina!"

Colin came running, his face streaked with tears.

"Forgive me, Sir James. Ye bade me to watch over Lady Davina and I failed ye."

Colleen soon joined them, her eyes filled with alarm. "We've searched everywhere. Inside and out." The older woman's voice quivered as she spoke. "I just dinnae know what could have happened to her."

"The soldiers on the ramparts saw nothing?" James questioned his brother.

"No one has entered or exited through the gates," Malcolm replied. "Davina must be inside the keep."

"Where?" Fretful and restless, James anxiously paced in front of the cold hearth. He felt a sickness in his stomach and drove his clenched fist into the palm of his other hand at the thought of Davina in danger.

"We'll find her," Malcolm insisted, as Joan entered the chamber.

James immediately noticed her dabbing at the sweat on her brow, then shifting uneasily on her feet. He pinned her with a withering stare. "What are ye hiding, Joan?"

Joan took a step away from him. "I might know where to find Davina," she admitted.

"What?" A muscle jumped in James's cheek. "Tell me!"

"There's a hidden passageway under the keep. She might be down there."

Malcolm frowned. "How do ye know about it?"

"I discovered it soon after I arrived. We have several at Armstrong Castle. My kin are partial to building them, so I assumed Davina's father would have at least one here."

"Why would ye search fer such a thing?" James wanted to know.

"I feared I might have to use it to make a fast escape." Joan's voice shivered with the words, but she kept her chin high and her back straight.

"If Fraser came fer ye?" James guessed.

She raised a haughty brow at him. "Aye."

"Show me," James demanded, pushing on Joan's back.

She scurried from the great hall and they all followed. After what seemed like an eternity they entered the storeroom. Confused, James turned menacingly toward Joan. "If this is some sort of trickery . . ."

"It's not," Joan stated flatly. She ran her hands deliberately over the wall, and then suddenly, amazingly, a section opened, revealing a set of stairs.

"It's black as pitch in there," James said, squeezing his shoulders through the opening.

"Here." Malcolm handed him a torch. James drew his sword; Malcolm did the same. With James leading the way, they began climbing down the winding stairs. The sight that greeted James when they finally reached the bottom froze his heart. Davina was on the floor, her head bowed low. A cloaked figure was crouched beside her.

"Mother?" Joan cried out in astonishment.

James rushed forward. Davina lifted her head, her eyes widening in alarm. "Careful!" she shouted. "She has a dirk."

"Aye, and it's pressed at Davina's throat," Isobel proclaimed smugly.

James stopped dead in his tracks. He lifted his torch higher, dismayed to see the frantic madness in Lady Isobel's eyes.

"It was ye, wasn't it, Lady Isobel?" James regarded the older woman cautiously. "Ye hired those men to harm Davina, to kill us both."

"I wasted good coin on those half-wits! They failed at every turn. I needed Davina to remain unwed, to stay under my watchful eye. But she left to be with the

McKennas fer Christmas and then she married ye. I thought I was well rid of ye five years ago, James McKenna!" Isobel's face reddened. "Once Davina married, I knew she'd want to claim her inheritance, to make a home fer herself and her family here. I couldn't let that happen."

"But why?" Davina cried with dismay.

"I know." Reaching inside his pocket, James held out the nugget he had found in the river. "Is this what ye sought?"

Isobel's head tilted. "Och, so ye've finally discovered the secret of Torridon Keep."

"Aye." Hoping to distract her, James inched forward. "How long have ye known about the gold, Lady Isobel?"

"Since Davina's parents died. I came to help nurse them through their illness and discovered her father's secret."

"Did ye . . ." Davina's voice choked with emotion.

"Kill them? Nay. The fever took them, though perhaps I was not quite as diligent in my healing duties as I should have been." Isobel cackled with delight. "Davina's father never told us about the riches on this land, never offered to share it with his only brother." Isobel's eyes narrowed with bitterness. "Fergus is the laird. 'Twas his right to have this treasure."

"Is that what Laird Armstrong told ye?" Malcolm asked.

"Bah, Fergus knows nothing of this matter," Isobel retorted. "He wouldn't listen to me. Called me a daft fool when I told him about the gold. Well, look who's the fool now!"

James's mind was churning, but he knew he needed to keep Lady Isobel talking. The older woman's left hand was twined in Davina's hair, pulling her head back far enough to expose her neck. The dirk was pressed firmly against Davina's throat.

"No doubt Laird Armstrong will change his mind when he sees the gold," James said in an amiable voice as he took another small step.

Lady Isobel smiled briefly, then narrowed her eyes suspiciously. "Dinnae come any closer," she threatened, pressing the dirk tighter against Davina's neck. Davina cried out as a thin trickle of blood ran down her throat.

"Mother, please. Let her go!"

Isobel turned her eyes toward Joan and James seized the advantage. He leaped, knocking Davina away from the deadly blade. Then he lunged for Isobel, wresting the dirk from her hand. She spun away and ran toward the tunnel. Malcolm and Joan gave chase, but Isobel reached the tunnel first, disappearing into the darkness.

Suddenly, there was a tremendous crash, followed by a loud scream. A large cloud of dust billowed out of the tunnel. James could feel the ground beneath them shift as pieces of stone dropped from the ceiling. He huddled over Davina, sheltering her with his body, wincing as the rocks rained on his back and shoulders.

"The tunnel is collapsing," Davina exclaimed.

"Malcolm!" James shouted frantically.

A heartbeat later, a coughing Malcolm appeared, pulling a whimpering Joan behind him. They were covered in dirt and debris.

"Where's Isobel?" James asked.

"Buried beneath the rubble," Malcolm replied. "The tunnel is braced with timbers. One of them cracked and the earth above it fell in. Joan and I pulled back, but Isobel kept running. A large beam struck her head and within moments she was buried."

"I'm certain she's dead," Joan added tonelessly.

James looked to his brother and Malcolm nodded in agreement.

"Nevertheless, we need to get some men down here to dig her body out," James decided.

"I'll see to it," Malcolm volunteered. "Ye attend to yer wife."

There was a hard lump of emotion lodged in James's throat as he approached their bed. It tore at his soul to see Davina's face so pale, her features so wan and crestfallen. Her aunt's betrayal cut deep, and when she suffered, so did he.

He hadn't left Davina's side since he carried her from the passageway. He had tried not to jostle her leg, which was thankfully not broken, but badly sprained. Colin had run to fetch the healer from the village, but Davina had insisted she needed rest and quiet far more than potions.

James soaked a clean cloth in cool water, then pressed it to her brow. With gentle hands, he examined her head. Davina hissed with pain when he found the swelling bruise at the base of her skull.

"This should heal in a few days," he said gently. "Shall I ask Colleen to brew ye something fer the pain?"

"Nay. My head feels fuzzy enough."

James sat on the edge of the bed and took Davina's hand. The possibility of losing her hit him hard. "I've never been so scared in my life. How did ye come to be down in that passageway?"

"I was in the storeroom and remembered seeing my father go through the hidden door when I was a child. I found the lever to open it and started to explore. Aunt Isobel must have been coming into the keep through the tunnel. She struck me on the head and left me. I dinnae know why she returned." Davina let out a long, shuddering breath. "I still dinnae understand what she wanted."

"Gold," James said quietly.

Davina took the nugget he held out to her and ran her thumb over it. "Where did ye find it?"

"In the riverbed on our southern border."

Davina shook her head. "I find this all very difficult to believe. My parents led a simple life. If there was gold running through the streams, they would have mined it. We could have had a life of ease and wealth."

James nodded. "I think Isobel exaggerated in her mind the amount of gold she believed was here. Something that extraordinary would not be kept secret fer long. Every man, woman, and child within a hundred miles would be mining the riverbed searching fer it."

Davina held the nugget up to the light. "Yet ye easily found this prize."

James smiled. "'Twas fate. It owed us a turn of good luck after all that we've endured."

Davina squeezed his hand, tears glistening in her eyes. "All this time wasted. If Aunt Isobel had not interfered, we'd be married five years already."

"Aye, and most likely bored and restless with each other," he teased.

"James McKenna!" She poked his arm, then managed a grin. "Ye are an incorrigible man."

He looked deep into her eyes. "I love ye, Davina. With all my heart and soul. 'Tis time to finally put the past to rest and start the future we both desire."

Her eyes softened. She lifted her hand and cradled his face. "Incorrigible, yet wise beyond yer years. I love ye, James."

Their lips met in a passionate kiss. Though edged with desire, their kiss conveyed the deep feelings they had for each other. James knew their love was something that couldn't ever be found with another.

They belonged together—in this life and the next. They had from the beginning. It might have taken them longer than most to reach for a life of happiness, but now that it was firmly within their grasp, James knew he would never let it go.

Epilogue

One year later

Davina opened her eyes and gave a lazy yawn, then snuggled closer to the warmth. Her palm lay flat over James's heart, the steady beating a comforting lull, his familiar scent teasing her nostrils. Cocooned with her husband, Davina could momentarily forget the demands and responsibilities of the outside world and simply enjoy the bliss of a peaceful slumber.

But not for long.

A cock crowed, loud and shrill, and the bleating of sheep filled the air. Reluctantly, she pulled herself away from the delicious warmth and rose from the bed, heading straight for the window. A spring chill hung in the air, but the clear morning promised sunshine for the day.

She smiled. 'Twas a good sign. Today the shearing would start and old Mangus had told her it would be easier for all, including the sheep, if the weather was fair.

She heard the mournful call of a bullfinch and glanced down at the cluster of cottages that surrounded the keep.

All looked in fine condition, with many boasting newly thatched roofs and neat rows of freshly planted home gardens. The variety of seeds Lady Aileen had gifted to her had been put to good use and she was glad there had been enough to give each family a share.

Her eye drifted to the bailey. Smoke from the forge billowed and twisted into the sky and the sound of cattle and chickens cut through the quiet. Stones lay at the ready to complete the fortifications on the south side of the curtain wall and, next to the newly built weaver's hut, the area where the chapel would be built was outlined with stakes and rope.

The sight filled her with pride and hope. They had managed so many improvements in such a short time, though there was still much work to be done. 'Twas not easy, ensuring that all at the keep had warm shelter and enough food, but it was a task she and James had embraced with determination and optimism.

The people of the village had been suspicious at first, but eventually realized that she had returned to make a home. Their moist, boggy land would never grow enough food, but it could produce goods that would supplement what they needed to ensure that none went hungry.

Davina understood that many of the villagers were doubtful that a knight Crusader would choose to become a steward of the land. But James surprised everyone with his natural affinity for running a keep. 'Twas an even greater comfort knowing his sword and ability to lead and train men would protect them all.

Bits of gold were found in the stream at the southern border, but it took a considerable amount of time and effort. As James had suspected, they could not rely on the gold for a steady source of income to maintain the estate.

Uncle Fergus had made a half-hearted effort to repay them for his dead wife's crimes, but Davina had wanted something more precious than coin—her independence. Her uncle had reluctantly agreed with her demand that the keep no longer be considered part of clan Armstrong. Instead, they were aligned with clan McKenna, though she and James were free to make any decisions regarding their property without first consulting his father, the laird. It was an arrangement that suited them best.

Word of Isobel's deeds and madness proved to be great fodder for gossip, but her death was an unexpected boon for Joan. Archibald Fraser was appalled by his mother-in-law's actions. Fearing to pass her madness on to his offspring, he set Joan aside, declaring his intentions to divorce her. He disowned their son, allowing Joan to take the lad to Armstrong Castle, where she now lived and ruled as mistress.

"Why have ye left our bed, wife?" called a husky voice.

The familiar voice rumbled through her and Davina turned. James was sprawled on his stomach, his head resting on a pillow, staring at her from the bed. The covers rode low on his hips and she could see a tantalizing view of the muscles in his arms, back, and shoulders.

Her stomach did a little flip. Even from this angle, he was a fine specimen of a Highland warrior, everything that she had ever wanted. And he was all hers.

She returned to his side and cuddled beside him. He nuzzled her temple, then kissed her brow. His arms tightened and she smiled at the sweetness of his embrace. His fingers moved down her arm in a lazy stroke, a hypnotic caress that left her feeling safe and secure.

"How is my son on this fine morning?" he asked, placing his hand gently on her rounded stomach.

"Yer son—or daughter—is sleeping quietly inside me."

She grinned as a wave of contentment washed through her. The love she felt for James seemed to grow more and more each day and there were times she struggled to find the words to tell him how much.

Thinking of it now brought an inner glow to her heart. She turned her head to look up at him and he kissed her, long and deep, his hands moving down to her thighs. Those sensual, wandering fingers were starting to distract her. She allowed it for a few moments, then stopped him with a quick kiss, pulling away.

James let out an exaggerated groan. He rolled onto his back and put his arms behind his head. "Ye look tired, love. Come back to bed."

She gave him a wry smile. "If I return to that bed, I doubt I'll be doing much sleeping."

"How is that wrong?"

"We've much to do."

"Och, ye're a cruel woman, Davina. Leaving our bed after giving me one miserly kiss."

She laughed at the petulance in his voice. He sounded so aggrieved. "I cannae laze the day away in bed with ye, husband. Have ye forgotten we start the shearing today?"

James sat up quickly. "Ye're not going to be helping."

"I'm with child, James. Not infirmed. I feel wonderful. The nausea and weakness are completely gone, just as the midwife said."

"Ye fainted."

"Once, James. I fainted once, nearly two months ago."

"I worry fer ye and our babe."

"And I love ye for it." Oddly enough, the ferocity of his voice made her feel cherished. She returned to his side, sitting on the edge of the bed.

James wrapped her in his arms, pulling her back so

she leaned into him. "My mother told me that I must make certain to treat ye tenderly and with great care."

"Ye do, James, even when I'm not carrying our child." She framed his face in her hands and kissed him lovingly, reverently. "But ye must not smother me with so much constant kindness or else I'll go mad."

"There's no need fer ye to be at the shearing. The shepherds know their duties and I trust they will work hard, if only to please ye," James said.

"I want to make certain every bit of wool is shaved and collected," Davina said as she pulled an old gown from the trunk and began to dress. "The fleece will be spun into wool, then weaved into cloth. We paid an exorbitant price for good wool last year; this year I intend to be the one selling, not buying."

James studied her from the bed while she dressed, but made no further attempts to lure her back. By the time Davina had finishing dressing, James had also risen. On her way down to the great hall she met a sleepy-looking Colin going up, carrying a pitcher of hot water James required each morning to wash.

By the time she arrived, the hall was already bustling with hungry workers eating their fill. After checking with the cook that all was in order, Davina joined them. She ate quickly, enjoying each bite of her oatcakes, smothered in honey, then gulped a goblet of tangy buttermilk, pleased that she was able to keep down her meal, unlike the early months of her pregnancy when just the smell of food would make her stomach churn.

The bailey was filled with a restless excitement as the sheep were herded into pens to be shorn. For the most part, she and James observed, offering an opinion when asked. By the late afternoon impressive piles of wool dotted an entire section of the bailey.

As old Mangus had warned, the ewes were visibly

anxious, having gone from a full thick winter wool coat to almost nothing. A sheep without her fleece looked naked, but the lambs would have an easier time finding the udder on a shorn ewe. And there would be many lambs in a few weeks, Davina was pleased to see, as so many of the sheep were pregnant.

Though she would never admit it to James, the day's activities had left her feeling tired. Deciding that a short nap before the evening meal would be most welcome, Davina began making her way inside.

But a sudden commotion at the gate caught her attention. She shielded her eyes, tensing when she saw an unknown group of knights on horseback crowding the open portcullis.

James was instantly at her side, placing a soothing hand on her shoulder. His touch brought her an instant sense of calm. There was no need to be fearful—James would protect them.

One man broke from the group and entered the bailey. He came within a few yards of them before reining in his horse and dismounting. Then he removed his helmet and shook out his dark hair, which hung in waves down to his shoulders.

Her fear momentarily forgotten, Davina stared at his extraordinarily handsome face with its proud chin and angular jaw. As her gaze roamed his sculpted features, she realized that while she could appreciate his good looks, they did not call to her the way James's did.

The stranger approached and when he was near enough, James astonished her by taking his hand off his sword hilt and reaching out his arm. The man grasped it and they locked arms, their muscles bulging as they held tightly to each other.

"My God, Gideon, is it really ye?" James asked.

"Aye, James. I thought the Scottish soil had opened

and swallowed you whole, but then heard you were living out here," Gideon answered.

The two men laughed.

"Come, meet my lady wife." James's chest and shoulders puffed out with pride as he brought her forward. "Davina, this ugly cur is Sir Gideon Croft, a brother Crusader."

Sir Gideon executed a faultless, courtly bow. "I can see that you have made a conquest of this rogue. Well done, milady."

Davina smiled, deciding that she liked the affable Sir Gideon. "I assure ye, 'tis a mutual affection."

"James always did have the best damn luck when it came to the ladies."

"Oh, really?" Davina looked between the two men with great interest. "Do tell me more."

"Pay no heed to this glib-tongued rouge. Have ye come looking fer a position?" James asked, hastily changing the subject. "I've a solid contingent of warriors, but would gladly make room fer a knight with yer skills."

Looking pensive, Sir Gideon surveyed the desolate landscape, but when he turned back, Davina caught a fleeting furrow in his brow.

"There are some advantages to living in such a remote area," she said.

A blush of red covered Sir Gideon's cheeks. "I mean no disrespect, milady. 'Tis a fine holding."

"No need to make a decision right now," James said cheerfully. "Once given, the offer remains, if and when ye ever decide it would suit ye."

Sir Gideon seemed relieved. "I'm on my way to a tournament in the south. The purse is enough to tempt any knight, though I see it will take more than coin to pry you away from your lady."

"I've more riches than I can count right here," James said, pulling Davina into his arms and kissing her soundly.

His open, uninhibited affection made Davina's heart race almost as much as his sensual kiss. Still, she wanted to maintain some dignity and decorum in front of their guest, so she reluctantly pulled away from her amorous husband. Though she continued to tightly hold his hand.

"I've other news to share with you, James," Sir Gideon said as they entered the great hall. "It concerns your family, specifically your brother, Malcolm."

James stilled. "Is he in danger?"

"Possibly." Sir Gideon glanced pointedly at her, clearly reluctant to say more.

"Ye can speak freely in front of Davina. It will save me the trouble of recalling all the details of this conversation later."

Though he said it with a grin, Davina could feel the tension grip James's shoulders as they leaned in to listen.

"We took shelter with the MacPhearsons on our journey here. The laird was in a fit of temper, as he had just discovered his daughter had given birth to a bastard son. He claims that Malcolm McKenna fathered the babe and has vowed vengeance upon Malcolm for daring to dishonor his kin."

"'Tis a lie," James said vehemently.

"Malcolm would never treat a lass so cruelly," Davina interjected, her voice rising with indignity. "And he most certainly wouldn't abandon his child."

"There's more." Compassion filled Sir Gideon's eyes. "Laird MacPhearson has put a price upon Malcolm's head, promising a tidy sum to any man who captures him and brings him before the MacPhearson council to face justice."

"God's teeth, every scoundrel in the Highlands who hears of this will be hunting my brother," James said.

"True." Sir Gideon nodded. "You need to warn Malcolm to be on guard."

"Malcolm needs to do more than that," James declared. "He needs to confront the MacPhearsons and clear his name. I'll write a missive with this news tonight. Will ye deliver it fer me, Gideon?"

"Nay, James," Davina said, her mouth forming a tight line. "This news is too important to trust to a letter. Ye must ride to McKenna Castle yerself and tell Malcolm what ye've learned."

James shook his head, lowering his hand protectively over her burgeoning belly. "I cannae leave ye, Davina."

In spite of the tension swirling in the air, Davina managed a soft laugh. "Fie, James, our babe is not due fer several months. The journey there and back from McKenna Castle will take less than a month's time."

A slight frown formed between his brows. "Are ye trying to get rid of me?"

"Aye. I need some peace from having ye pestering me day and night to rest and eat well. Last week I sneezed three times and ye insisted that I stay in bed all afternoon."

Sir Gideon laughed. "I always believed that when James gave his love to a woman, it would be with his whole being."

"He's done that and more. I am truly blessed. But a lass needs to breathe every now and again."

James trailed his callused fingertips lightly over her face. "I dinnae wish to leave ye."

She rested her forehead against his and sighed. "If I promise to miss ye every minute of every day, will ye go?"

"Reluctantly," he agreed.

The heat of his body touched her skin and she sighed, savoring the joy of having him near. Her heart felt full, overflowing with both the love she felt for him and the love he gave so completely to her. Though teasing him, she knew that she would miss him dreadfully while he was gone. But thanks to him, she possessed the strength to endure it.

A smile twitched at her lips. She leaned close and whispered in his ear. "I love ye, James McKenna, and if ye behave yerself fer the rest of the day, I'll be more than willing to show ye how much when we're in our bed tonight."

"Ye think to sweeten our separation with the promise of a wild bed romp?"

"I do."

"Och, love, ye know me too well."

Aye, she did, and she was more than glad of it.

GREAT BOOKS,
GREAT SAVINGS!

When You Visit Our Website:
www.kensingtonbooks.com
You Can Save Money Off The Retail Price
Of Any Book You Purchase!

- All Your Favorite Kensington Authors
- New Releases & Timeless Classics
- Overnight Shipping Available
- eBooks Available For Many Titles
- All Major Credit Cards Accepted

Visit Us Today To Start Saving!
www.kensingtonbooks.com

All Orders Are Subject To Availability.
Shipping and Handling Charges Apply.
Offers and Prices Subject To Change Without Notice.

More by Bestselling Author
Hannah Howell

__Highland Angel	978-1-4201-0864-4	$6.99US/$8.99CAN
__If He's Sinful	978-1-4201-0461-5	$6.99US/$8.99CAN
__Wild Conquest	978-1-4201-0464-6	$6.99US/$8.99CAN
__If He's Wicked	978-1-4201-0460-8	$6.99US/$8.49CAN
__My Lady Captor	978-0-8217-7430-4	$6.99US/$8.49CAN
__Highland Sinner	978-0-8217-8001-5	$6.99US/$8.49CAN
__Highland Captive	978-0-8217-8003-9	$6.99US/$8.49CAN
__Nature of the Beast	978-1-4201-0435-6	$6.99US/$8.49CAN
__Highland Fire	978-0-8217-7429-8	$6.99US/$8.49CAN
__Silver Flame	978-1-4201-0107-2	$6.99US/$8.49CAN
__Highland Wolf	978-0-8217-8000-8	$6.99US/$9.99CAN
__Highland Wedding	978-0-8217-8002-2	$4.99US/$6.99CAN
__Highland Destiny	978-1-4201-0259-8	$4.99US/$6.99CAN
__Only for You	978-0-8217-8151-7	$6.99US/$8.99CAN
__Highland Promise	978-1-4201-0261-1	$4.99US/$6.99CAN
__Highland Vow	978-1-4201-0260-4	$4.99US/$6.99CAN
__Highland Savage	978-0-8217-7999-6	$6.99US/$9.99CAN
__Beauty and the Beast	978-0-8217-8004-6	$4.99US/$6.99CAN
__Unconquered	978-0-8217-8088-6	$4.99US/$6.99CAN
__Highland Barbarian	978-0-8217-7998-9	$6.99US/$9.99CAN
__Highland Conqueror	978-0-8217-8148-7	$6.99US/$9.99CAN
__Conqueror's Kiss	978-0-8217-8005-3	$4.99US/$6.99CAN
__A Stockingful of Joy	978-1-4201-0018-1	$4.99US/$6.99CAN
__Highland Bride	978-0-8217-7995-8	$4.99US/$6.99CAN
__Highland Lover	978-0-8217-7759-6	$6.99US/$9.99CAN

Available Wherever Books Are Sold!

Check out our website at
http://www.kensingtonbooks.com